The Phoebe Trilogy

Phoebe

Douse

Secret Society

for

Special Abilities and Artefacts

Book One

The Phoebe Douse Trilogy

PHOEBE DOUSE: S3A2

Written and Illustrated by L. Samuels

Valued Educational Services, LLC

Published first in 2019 by Valued Educational Services, LLC
5520 Lyndon B. Johnson Freeway, Suite 365
Dallas, Texas 75240
www.globalves.com

Phoebe Douse: Secret Society for Special Abilities and Artefacts /
L. Samuels

Issued in print formats:
ISBN 978-1-7322846-6-1 (PB)
ISBN 978-1-7322846-7-8 (HC)

Library of Congress Control Number: 2019907245

10 9 8 7 6 5 4 3 2 1

Cover design and book illustrations © L. Samuels

Printed in the U.S.A.

Quantity sales: Special discounts are available on quantity purchases by corporations, associations, and others. For more details, contact the publisher at the address above.

TO MY MOTHER: AFTER
DECADES OF YOUR
ENCOURAGEMENT TO FINISH
ONE OF MY STORIES,
I FINALLY DID

AND

TO MY GRANDMOTHER AND
GREAT-GRANDMOTHERS,
WHO HELPED TO INSPIRE THIS
STORY

Contents

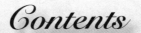

Contents

Author's Message

Phoebe Douse: Secret Society for Special Abilities and Artefacts (S3A2) is book #1 in a trilogy and also the first complete novel I've written. Throughout the process, I really enjoyed creating and developing each character, scene, and chapter.

It's my hope that as you read, you'll connect with the characters (their virtues and flaws) and enjoy the mystery and intrigue. Of equal importance, please welcome the messages about self-belief, trust, individuality, and friendship.

Phoebe Douse: S3A2 is fiction; however, some of the scenes you are about to read have been inspired by events, people, and places throughout my life. What and how much is inspiration versus imagination I'll leave as a mystery.

Prologue

Can you run?

Good, good. Can you run fast? You'll need strong legs.

This way. It's better. Hopefully we won't be seen.

You're bleeding! Are you sure you can run?

Here, let me help. Put your arm around my neck. That's it.

Not much farther, I promise. Our little friend should signal to us soon.

I know, such a helpful little boy. How will we ever thank him with more than just toffees?

Be careful. Watch your step. Those are thorns. Some are more than just a sting—some are poisonous.

Ah, thank goodness! He's giving us the signal that the coast is clear.

Don't worry, don't worry. I'll be fine. I'll return in time before anyone suspects a thing. Besides, I have to remain, at least for now. I have my reasons.

Please don't cry. It'll be okay. I see you in my future but not anytime soon. Take care and stay alive.

Look, the light! He's signaling again. Go now! He'll lead the way. Run as fast as you can! Even if your legs burn and your stomach aches, don't stop until you get to the cliffs!

"Run!" I cried out, looking up at fluorescent lights.

"No, *dummy*! We're playing dodgeball, and you're making us lose!"

Just then a wicked red ball flew at me and whacked my arm.

The blow was so powerful that it felt like a rock had just struck my skin.

1

"He*he! Out!* You're o-*uuut!*" My sixth grade attacker laughed and danced on the gym floor, shoes squeaking with a mocking sound.

I couldn't blame him.

At the same age and almost the same height, we were practically equals in this match. Plus, he was just doing what we had been told to do—pummel each other with balls after the whistle blows.

"Good," I mumbled, gripping my throbbing arm and relieved to sit on the bleachers. "It's this game that's dumb, not me."

But I cursed my vivid, random imagination. This time, it was just a voice and no images, which all seemed to happen in seconds.

Another uninvited daydream that I would soon forget.

Chapter One

AN END IS ANOTHER BEGINNING

I had heard these stories before.

They were just tales. Children's fables. Superstitious foolishness. Ghost stories told between friends to entertain or scare each other on stormy, lightning-filled nights when the power has gone out too long.

When my grandmother called me over with only a nod, I hid a sigh, knowing *exactly* what she wanted to do. My first impulse was to tell her I was too old to believe in such things.

I'm almost thirteen! I thought as I sat at her feet.

But Naan would probably always see me as the chubby, moon-faced four-year-old, even though I'd grown out of my swollen cheeks phase. I could also say it was a story she'd told before. Instead, I stopped myself.

Reclining on her cream settee with her feet up on the smooth cushion, she began to speak as if she were an oracle on her throne. "It's all a choice, Phoebe darling. You being here with me, me telling you this—a series of choices…. Are you *listening?*"

"Uhm, yes?"

"I want to be certain," she said as her amber-colored eyes fixed on me. "I *need* you to understand."

"I'm listening, Naan," I insisted, hugging my knees to my chest. "And I understand."

She studied me, and it was obvious she wasn't convinced. "There's more. *So* much more…. When I wasn't much older than you, I chose one of the grandest adventures of my life. In fact, it was beyond an adventure. It became a legacy."

I sat up just a little. What Naan was saying could *actually* be believable (if I ignored the exaggerated parts).

"It was dangerous and risky, but it was necessary," she continued. "I couldn't refuse and didn't want to, because I was a much-needed person in the entire plan."

Then, in an instant, Naan became very still, as if suspended in space. Her breathing looked like it had stopped while her face and body reminded me of sculpted, polished marble. Even the long folds of her white flowing dress didn't budge. Naan always knew how to do that—be right in front of someone and, at the same time, seem to be somewhere else.

Eventually she returned from that distant place. "Back home I was called a See-an'-Know woman. My town knew I was one from a very early age." Her eyes narrowed at me. "I know how our destinies are shaped, Phoebe darling. See-an'-Knows are people who can *see* the *unseen* and …"

Shaping destinies? See-an'-Knows? Here we go.

If you'd heard my Naan that day, you probably would've gotten spooked or at least thought she was odd. Maybe you would've wanted to hear more, out of interest or sheer curiosity. But I was used to these kinds of stories—*too* used to them.

I stared down at the thick carpet, jabbing my fingers into it and making holes. Frankly, I became too preoccupied with my own unsolvable problem—trying to get out of Crockett Middle School for good.

My latest plan was to fake a letter from Principal Westergren; I pictured it would say something like:

Dear Mr. and Mrs. Douse,

Phoebe is a hardworking and smart student, but she's not doing great here. This is why we absolutely know she would be better at another school.

That was all I had so far, because I didn't know the perfect school, but I was convinced anywhere else would be better. If I could finish the letter, I knew I had to use official school paper. I'd also seen Principal Westergren's signature enough times on my report cards and take-home forms. His name had lots of letters, and his handwriting was crooked, but it was worth a try to copy it.

I glanced up and noticed that Naan's mouth had stopped moving. She took her time adjusting the turquoise-and-red earrings that dangled above her collarbone. When she did, her dress brushed the carpet, right in front of my impatient fingers.

This is way out of my league. It'll look fake, and Mom and Dad would never believe. I paused and tilted my head. *Maybe ... instead of a letter ... I could get ... kicked out.* I smirked.

Suddenly, a pressure tightened around my wrist. I tried to pull back, but the unforgiving force squeezed me even tighter. It was Naan. She had stretched down and was holding onto me like a vise.

5

Her powerful grip pulled me out of my thoughts as her eyes became so clear and focused on mine. "*Remember* what I've told you. And remember that you *must* find them both," she urged.

Naan stunned me. In fact, she scared me. "Wh-what do you mean, 'I must find them'? Find *who*?"

"It *needs* to be made right. Do what's right and be good." Her grip slowly loosened.

"Please … I don't know … I …"

Immediately, I tried to remember but couldn't come up with anything to piece together. What I'd heard were just some words and phrases here and there: "… wedding … broke the code … separated." An odd combination, I know. They were scrambled and jumbled with no sense about them.

I opened my mouth to ask again, but Naan began to shut down as her eyelids drooped and she tiredly sank back into the cushion.

Mom rushed in. "You're upsetting her. Let her be for now," she scolded.

Is she talking to me or Naan? I wasn't sure.

I *should've* listened to my grandmother.

I *should've* remembered her words.

At twelve, I thought days lasted forever and that she would live forever. But only a few days later, my parents sat with my older brother, Graham, and me during one of our family talks—usually for serious matters.

"There's something important we need to share," Mom began with a grim expression.

Graham's mouth tightened and his gaze darted between Mom and Dad. "Share *what*? *I* didn't do anything wrong this time."

"You shouldn't always think we're here to lecture you," Mom said.

"Isn't that what usually happens?" Graham challenged with a slight smile.

She let out an exasperated sigh as I turned my head away and rolled my eyes. *Time to shut up, Graham.*

"Don't speak to your mother like that," Dad warned, taking over in a tone that we all knew would get louder if Graham pushed it. "Today is about your grandmother. She's sick. She has dementia."

"What's dementia?" I asked right away.

"It's something that happens to the brain that affects someone's thinking and memory," Mom explained.

My parents even had a small medical pamphlet that helped to describe Naan's condition. Their voices droned on and eventually faded as I remembered the times Naan would stutter when she tried to find her words or when she'd forgotten important facts and became silent.

"Does this mean she won't remember us?" Graham asked.

"Yes and no," Dad replied. "There will be times she will and maybe other times she won't. Dementia impacts each person differently. You understand?"

Graham nodded. Then he asked another question, but I stopped listening again. I felt numb about the fact that Naan would never be the same.

"Phoebe," Mom said. "Do you have any more questions? You've barely said a word."

"Nope, no more," I whispered.

"Your Aunt Josephine and I have agreed," she continued, "that Naan should spend her last days in her childhood home."

Naan came to America to help take care of Graham and me. While living with us, she loved speaking about her island home and missed seeing the emerald-colored hills outside her windows, feeling the soothing salt-filled breeze, and spending time with friends and family. Mom and Aunt Josephine were probably hoping that if Naan returned in time, it would bring her some comfort.

"And we've made plans for her to leave next week," Mom finished.

My head shot up.

"So *soon!*" Graham exclaimed.

"Can't she stay a little *longer?*" I pleaded.

Mom's neck tensed, and she swallowed as if a boulder were going down her throat. "I know it's sudden," she said finally. "But her condition is progressing fast."

I noticed the way Dad's hands kept folding and unfolding the pamphlet. I'd never seen him look so nervous before. "The best we can do is appreciate the time we have with her," he said, and stood up abruptly. "Continue to make good memories, all right?"

And for the entire week, that's exactly what I did. I tried to spend all my time with Naan.

The morning Naan was leaving, she was happy. In fact, she was *elated*. It was like she was going on one of those grand vacations or cruises that last for several months.

Naan even wore a large-brimmed straw hat and stylish sunglasses, looking forward to the tropical sun. If we'd gotten caught up in her excitement, we could've easily fooled ourselves into feeling just as thrilled.

But we didn't, because we knew better.

As Naan sat in her wheelchair, she took off her sunglasses and looked at me. "You have *great* abilities, Phoebe darling, and you need to use them for good. *Promise* me you will."

She always said this, and I just assumed it was her way of telling me that I was special and needed to be a good girl—something most grandmothers liked to say.

"I promise. Love you," I said as I looked down at her beaming face.

Her story. Does she even remember telling it to me?

Naan turned and focused on Graham. "Listen more to your parents." She wagged her glasses at his chest. "You're smart. But not when you think you know everything. Because you don't. *Pay* more attention and *mind* your sister."

Instantly, Graham's back straightened, and he shuffled his feet. "Yes, Naan. Love you too," he said after getting over his embarrassment.

I snickered softly behind his back. My brother could be such a pain, and Naan's warning was sweet justice.

After our hugs, Dad stayed with us while Mom went to the airport with Naan and Aunt Josephine. We stood and waved until the car's taillights were no longer visible down our small lane. Then, without saying a word, Dad, Graham, and I turned to reenter our home.

It felt empty inside. After living with us for so many years … ever since I was born … Naan was gone.

Dealing with loss. I still don't think I know the best way. *If* there's even a best way.

At that time, I tried to cope by putting Naan in a place hidden in the back of my mind. But three months later, she passed away, and all the thoughts of her that I'd tried to push away came rushing forward like a huge tsunami.

During her last days, Naan was surrounded by most of her family. We couldn't travel to go see her, and I was told it had to do with money. But I often wondered if there were other reasons I didn't know about.

Mom constantly talked on the phone with Aunt Josephine, hearing and sharing stories and updates. She told Graham and me that the *entire* town celebrated Nine-Night for Naan.

Nine-Night, she explained, was a West African funerary tradition brought to the Caribbean and a special time when family and friends celebrate the life of a loved one who has died. Although it came to the islands from Africa, everyone of all ancestries celebrated it.

It seemed like a huge neighborhood party—people singing, bringing food, or playing music for all those days and nights.

At Naan's Nine-Night, groups large and small talked about how she cured sick people with ointments and mixtures. They even said she could foretell the future, interpret dreams, and know everything about a person with just a single glance.

They made her mythical, spinning legends that couldn't stand up to reality.

And I got annoyed about all of it.

"Foolishness," I grumbled, after overhearing Mom talking on the phone one morning. I stomped away, headed straight to Naan's settee, and curled up on it.

The problem was: every time I lay on Naan's cushion, regret seeped inside of me, because I didn't pay close attention to all of her stories—especially her last one.

"You want to talk about it?" Graham asked, walking up to me with his soccer cleats in his hand.

"Not with you," I muttered grumpily, and rolled over.

"I'm just trying to help."

"Mm-hmm. And what's the catch?"

"Why would there be a catch?" he asked to my back.

Good question. Can't answer that. So I switched the subject. "Aren't you going somewhere?"

"She was *my* grandmother too. *I* miss her—it's not just you."

Then I heard the back door shut.

What Graham said made me antsy. I'd been irritated with him, and he didn't deserve it this time. I tossed and turned, still hearing Mom's voice on the phone. And when I got tired of tossing and turning, I got up and went over to a cabinet on the opposite side of the living room. Knowing what I needed in that moment, I opened a drawer and glided my hand over a bumpy and scratched leather cover.

When you're in a thoughtful, uneasy, or even sad mood, try looking through photo albums, especially old ones. The types where the corners are worn and discolored and the pages are filled with pictures that are faded or stuck to the paper. It can be very comforting.

I picked up the oldest album I could find and shut myself in my room. While turning the stiff pages, I found a sepia-colored photo that I'd *never* seen before—like it had decided to appear right before my eyes.

A young woman, a few years older than me, stared out from a

mango tree. Barefoot, she sat, balancing on a branch with her legs crossed. Her glossy dark hair flowed in large, loose waves down to her shoulders and over her summer romper. And she had on a bracelet and a necklace with a cross pendant. Although youthful, she had a deep, serious expression that you would see on someone four times her age.

And I knew exactly who this teenager was.

Jumping up to show my new discovery, I found Mom in the kitchen, preparing our weekend brunch. She held the photo between flour-covered fingers and smiled as her gaze moved across the image.

"I had *no idea* this is how Naan used to look," I said.

"Oh?" Mom raised an eyebrow.

"I mean, I only saw her when she was, you know …" My voice trailed off.

A soft, wind chime-sounding laugh leapt out of her mouth. Mom had a beautiful voice. Even when she got angry, it sounded like a nice song. "Don't forget we were all young once," she said, and then nodded. "It's understandable you didn't know. It's the only picture we have of her from back then."

"Why's that?"

The thick dough made a slapping sound as it landed inside the bowl. Mom's forehead wrinkled. "Maybe there are more from those days, but I've never seen them."

"I was thinking we kind of look alike. Not totally, just the eyes, maybe."

"You remind me a lot of her," she observed. "And it's not only because of what you look like."

I sat on the stool and stared at the picture to let that sink in. "But

Naan was so pretty," I replied, dumbfounded. "She always seemed to know so much. *And* she had an answer for *everything*. I'm just *me*."

"Of *course* you remind me of her," Mom repeated, and moved on to seasoning the chicken with habañeros, allspice, and other tasty spices. Then, her voice took on a strange, flat tone. "You're more like her than you can imagine."

Seeing Mom stare into the bowl with the corners of her mouth looking defeated, I reached over and hugged her. She wiped her hands in a dishcloth and held me. I relaxed against her body when I felt her warmth, and I breathed in the scent of spices and her favorite lavender lotion.

"Go find a nice new home for your photo," she said, and rubbed my back. "And go outside and get some fresh air!" She laughed again, finally.

I went straight to my room to put Naan's picture in my wallet—in the place where there's a plastic covering for pictures or business cards.

Admiring her through the shiny plastic, I smiled. She had returned to me! My memories of her were just as real as if she were alive. I realized this when I thought about the times we spoke about her.

Naan stared at me, as if she were sending silent messages that I needed to understand in order to solve something very important.

When your thoughts are more than just words... They're messages.

Chapter Two

THOUGHTS THAT SPEAK

$\mathscr{I}$n my hometown of Crockett, Texas—a tiny dot on the map—Ava Dougherty was my best friend during childhood and most of middle school. In fact, she'd been my only real friend.

We began our friendship in kindergarten, and it started through the convenient habit of our teachers. They found it was easy to remember us by alphabetizing their seating charts. As Phoebe Douse (said like *Zeus*, but with a *D*), I sat next to Ava Dougherty throughout elementary school. And it just seemed natural to spark a friendship with the person who always sat beside me. The first words spoken between us had something to do with food during our first week of kindergarten.

"*Woot! Woot!*" Ava whooped, lifting her arms straight up and jigging on the cafeteria stool. Her sloppy blond bob with blunt bangs whipped around her elvish face.

"Ava, is that you again?" Ms. Roland, our kindergarten teacher, chided.

After only a week of school, Ava had already gained a reputation.

As Ms. Roland hurried over to our table, her blinding floral tent dress smacked kids left and right. "What has gotten into you? Keep your voice down," she warned through pursed lips that reminded me of a prune.

Ava's eyes widened, and she blinked like an innocent fawn. "Please forgive me," she said in such a sweet voice that Ms. Roland's prune lips transformed into a grin as big as a slice of watermelon. She patted Ava's head and walked away.

"She loves me now," Ava boasted, and her excitement came back as she pointed with fingernails decorated with tiny stickers of spiders and flowers. "Look what I got. My favorite—Goldfish and Fruit Roll-Ups."

I peeked into her pink plastic lunch box.

"Want some?"

Before I could answer, she poured the cheesy, salty snack onto a napkin and slid them over to me. I put some fish in my mouth and thanked her.

Ava leaned over, wrapped her arm around my waist, and squeezed. "Phoebe, remember, I came here to be your friend. For *your* sake. And I'm keeping the offer open. It'll be rugged, but I'll keep it open."

I knitted my eyebrows as I tilted my head. "Huh?" I asked in between chews.

She let go of my waist, sat up proudly, and flashed a smile that sported a few missing teeth and silver caps over some of her molars. "It's Eloise in Mogambo!"

My head tilted further. "Magoo? What's that?"

She giggled and crumbs flew out of her mouth. "*No*," she insisted. "Mo … gam … *bo*. Eloise is played by Ava Gardner, *silly*."

"Oh, okay," I said, still confused but also amused.

"Mama named me after her cuz I'm a star too." She held the red Fruit Roll-Up in front of her face and peered at me through two holes she'd bitten out of it. "See how my eyes twinkle?"

Ms. Roland came back to our table. I thought that after her warning, this was it. Now, we were in real trouble. But instead, she handed Ava something square, wrapped in plastic. Ava hurriedly opened it, and I realized it was a plain baloney sandwich dripping with mayonnaise.

Ms. Roland noticed something I'd failed to see at the time, which was that inside Ava's lunch box, there wasn't anything else but the snacks and a box of juice.

From Ava's first offering of food, we were inseparable in elementary school. For years, we wrote stories in shared journals and took turns keeping them. Ava had it one week and I the next.

Our stories were outrageous and had no reasonable end. Sometimes we drew sketches or wrote kooky poems.

And when we finished one journal, we started another, and another, *and* another until between us, there were piles of spirals filled with our thoughts, drawings, and jokes.

"Save me!" Ava exclaimed over the phone. She let out a deafening groan. "If we don't come up with something interesting to talk about, I'm hanging up right now and doing somethin' *risky*!"

It was a few days before the start of seventh grade, and the August sun blazed mercilessly over Crockett. This forced us to stay indoors and made Ava hyper.

"Wait," I stopped her, watching the hospital scene with sappy violin music playing in the background. "Don't you want to see if Julia wakes up from her coma?"

"Don't care," she said flatly. "Julia's too annoying and not even believable. Look! *Look!*" She hooted with laughter. "She's moving around too much in the bed. So *fake!*"

I looked, and Ava was right.

"*I* could do that ten times better. Besides, I want *real-life* juiciness." And Ava didn't waste a second to share. "My dad's in prison!"

Lounging on the floor, I immediately sat up straighter. "*What?!*"

I'd never known anyone in prison or anyone who knew anyone in prison…. Well, at least not until that moment.

"Luanne came over the other night. She and Mama were drinking out on the porch, and Mama thought I was sleeping. But I heard most of it." She giggled. "I don't know why he's there, but it must be something serious cuz Mama was sayin' she's glad she doesn't *ever* have to see his busted, *worthless* face again."

Deep down, I knew it was a serious matter, but the way Ava told her secret confused me—ending each sentence with a hyper giggle. So I didn't know what to say.

"*Well*, what do you think?"

"I promise not to tell anyone," I said finally.

"*Your* turn."

"I didn't know that's how this would go," I said, trying to argue out of it.

"Can't back out now," she demanded. "You already know my secret. You're in too deep."

I sighed, paused, and thought.

"Hello, I'm still here … *waiting*." Ava let out an impatient sigh. "If it helps," she added, "close your eyes and say it first in your head. Then just say it. I heard that's what actors do, not to get nervous before the camera starts rolling."

I chuckled. "Closing my eyes doesn't make any sense. I'm not even seeing you."

"Whatever! Are you gonna *tell me* or not?" she pleaded.

We tell each other most things anyway. I shrugged and gave in.

I took a deep, audible breath, and then another one for courage. "My Naan told me I have … abilities like her. She said she knew this even before I was born." Wanting to fill any odd silence that might follow, I said, "I don't really believe her. She's very superstitious."

"Ooh, tell me *more!*" The excitement and curiosity rose in Ava's voice.

"I think she means I can see things other people can't see."

As I shared with Ava, I had to think about how to put my words in a way that would make sense without sounding strange. I didn't know how to explain something I didn't even understand myself. I also felt guilty for telling something that was important and serious to Naan.

"That's *awe*some!" she exclaimed. "So can you read minds?"

"No," I said, but wasn't sure.

"See ghosts?"

"Uh-uh … at least, I don't remember it happening."

"So, what exactly *can* you do?"

"Uhm … I think I can … maybe know something before it happens." With no proof, I realized my secret was sounding phony and made-up. I quickly added, "Like I said, it was my Naan who told me. I don't even think it's true."

"Do you miss her?"

"What?"

Her sudden serious tone had caught me off guard. And since my grandmother's death, I hadn't spoken to her about it.

"Your grandma?" she said. "Do … you … miss … her?" She stressed each word as if I didn't understand English.

"Well, I—"

"Are you talkin' to *that* girl again?!" a voice boomed.

I jumped as my hand squeezed the phone. *That girl?* It was Ava's mother. I'd never met her and only seen her in the carpool lane. She always seemed tense, smoking a cigarette and looking more at herself in the rearview mirror than around her.

"Get your lazy butt over *here*! And *stop* runnin' out my minutes. *You* don't pay my bills!"

"Hold on. I'll be right back," Ava whispered.

Their voices got louder and louder, but I couldn't hear their words. It felt strange being a faraway witness to Ava and her mom screaming at each other.

"*Yikes*," I winced when it sounded as if a sack of bricks had clattered to the ground. Then, everything went silent.

When Ava eventually came back, she was wheezing. "I've gotta … go … do some chores."

I bit my lip. She didn't seem okay. "You all right, Ava? There was a sound."

"*Yep* … sure.… Talk with ya later!"

The phone clicked before I could even open my mouth.

She's lying. I'd remembered Ava telling me she hated doing chores, and her mom didn't force her. Ava didn't even have to put her own dirty clothes in the hamper.

I never brought up Ava's secret, not even to her. But sometimes she would ask me about mine—questions like if I'd been haunted by any ghosts following me home after school. My answer was, of course, no. Or, she would ask for some numbers that her mother could play in the lottery, but there was no help I could give.

At times, I wasn't sure if she was serious or joking.

We rarely saw each other during our last two years of middle school, especially after Ava was placed into remedial classes. When that happened, she announced, "I'm not going to college anyway."

I told her that there were Hollywood stars who cared about school and even went to college. But she just shrugged it off as if I were making it up.

So, imagine my surprise when, one afternoon, Ava invited me to celebrate her getting the lead role in Crockett Middle School's fall musical, *South Pacific*. Ava spent weeks reciting her lines when we occasionally spoke and even belted out the songs.

"You *must* join us as the The Square next weekend," she declared in the hallway between classes.

I fidgeted with the latch of my locker. "Who's 'us'?" I stalled.

Compared to most kids in my town, I was … how should I put it? The polar opposite. I was too different—the girl whose family wasn't from Crockett and had family rules that didn't make sense. The girl who brought funny-looking homemade food for lunch. And to top it all off, the girl who had the strange grandmother.

"You still there?" She snapped her fingers in front of my face.

I blinked a couple of times. "Of course," I insisted.

"As I *said*, it'll be me, Jason, Becca, Nate, and maybe there will be others." Ava clasped her hands and started bending her knees. "Please, *please*," she pleaded, as if she were going to beg right there on the scuffed-up linoleum floor. "I feel like I haven't talked to my *best* friend this entire year."

I grinned and shook my head. "Where's it at?"

"Wilma's Diner. 12:30."

The bell rang as Ava said her last words and practically skipped away. I shut my locker and headed to class in the opposite direction.

The Square, short for Davy Crockett Memorial Square, was one of our town's one-stop areas. It was said that the buildings stood on what was once an important outpost for the Texas militia to gather and hatch strategies to fight the Mexican army.

In fact, Mayor Cooper liked to boast to passersby on road trips that in the very parking lot was where our Texas hero, Davy Crockett, decided to fight in the battle for independence at the Alamo.

In present day, The Square couldn't live up to its once impressive reputation. Lined with tired-looking trees, it had a grand total of two eateries, a post office, one clothing shop, and a grocery store at the end of the complex.

And I arrived there late that Saturday afternoon, thanks to Mom. Rushing into Wilma's, I saw that the diner was packed with its usual guests and noisy with conversation and the local radio station piping through the speakers.

Ava saw me first and waved me over to their booth by a window.

21

"Hey," Becca said, glancing over at me as I joined them.

"Hey," Nate echoed, sticking his finger in his ear.

"How's it…?" My voice faded, and I cringed when Nate's finger popped out and a large gob of ear wax sat on top of it. He examined it, grinned, and then wiped it off on his jeans.

I didn't know Nate and Becca that well, except that they were one of Crockett Middle School's prized couples. Jason, on the other hand, I knew. He was laid back and in my art class. At already six feet tall and very athletic, Jason was a triple threat—a football, baseball, *and* basketball player.

He also tried to show me how to draw cartoons and comic art a few times, but my attempts always ended up looking like ridiculous, bloated monsters.

"I saw the project you did in class the other day," Jason started. "I really liked the—"

"Let's not talk about school," Ava cut in, rolling her eyes. "So *boring*, isn't it? No offense, I know art is y'all's thing, but let's talk about the *play*!"

"But Ava, the play *is* about school," I said.

"Phoebe's right," Jason added. "We already started set design."

Ava's mouth clamped shut as her eyes widened. "Whatever," she said with a dismissive wave of her hand. She leaned closer to Jason and giggled in his ear, causing her hair to cover part of his face.

Just then, I realized that Ava's signature short bob and blunt bangs had grown several inches. I stared in disbelief and wondered why I hadn't seen something so obvious on my best friend.

Isn't it funny when you don't notice something about someone until it's extremely different? And then you're left wondering, *If this person is so important to me, why didn't I notice this change before?*

22

Thinking that, I began to feel more and more out of place, especially after the waiter took our orders and when Ava got up, demanding for Becca and me to have "girl time" in the restroom.

Standing up to let Becca out, I decided to pass on gossiping and putting on makeup around eavesdroppers in toilet stalls.

"Works for us," Becca grumbled out of the corner of her mouth, and they walked off.

Like a caveman, Nate lumbered out of the booth, grunting about trying to win a bet. "Wanna come?" he asked Jason, and pointed at the video game area. Jason shook his head, and Nate went to what seemed like his usual spot and got right into action—slapping the buttons and making noises with his mouth as if grenades were exploding.

"Check this out," Jason said to me as he took out his pocket-size sketchbook and a pencil. He looked up at me a few times while his pencil hurriedly moved across the paper.

When he finished, he began to spin the pencil between his fingers and triumphantly handed me the finished product. It was of me as a cartoon, sitting in the booth but in a futuristic spaceship.

"You know what?" I said, admiring his creation. "I think you'll be a professional artist one day. Like the ones who draw for movies."

"A graphic artist," Jason beamed, but then shrugged as his face dropped. "I wish … maybe … but my dad wants me to go pro. He said that way I can make lots of money."

"Well, he's wrong," I asserted.

Jason's eyes widened, as if nobody had ever said his dad was wrong. "You say interesting things."

"I hope interesting things that make sense."

"Perfect sense." Rubbing his hand over his buzzed cut, Jason was quiet and then added, "You're not like Ava, and you're *definitely* not like Becca."

I wondered if that was his way of saying the same thing I'd been asking myself, which was: *What am I doing here?*

"It's nothing bad or anything like that. It's just—" He stopped and looked up past my face.

"*Ooh!* What's this?" Ava said, standing over me. With a coy smile, she snatched the sketchpad from my hands. But soon after, her bright, coral lips fell and her face flushed. Ava narrowed her eyes at Jason and then glared at me.

Becca leaned over, whispering something into Ava's ear. The freshly applied purple eyeshadow looked like two large stains on her face.

"What's the problem?" I mouthed to Jason.

"No idea," he mouthed back.

Out of nowhere, papers flew wildly past my face.

Jason's quick reflexes stopped the sketchpad from smacking into the window. His pale eyebrows furrowed. "What was *that* for?"

"You should've drawn her on a broomstick and some *warts* on her face," Ava sneered.

Becca glanced at me in disgust. "And you didn't draw her hair right. It's a lot curlier. And it bunches up."

My face burned. Jason shook his head, looking just as stunned as I felt.

"*Dang!*" Nate bellowed and burst into the thick cloud of tension as he returned. "How long do we have to wait for our food?" Somehow he was smart enough to realize something was going on and stood back.

"Tell them, Phoebe," Ava taunted as she eased into the booth next to Jason, and Becca followed. "Tell them about your magic powers." She wriggled her fingers. "Phoebe thinks she's a *witch*. Her *nanny* granny told her so."

My heart jumped. *Why would you tell my secret? And lie about it?* The questions flooded my mind, but I just sat, staring.

"Is she doing some mumbo jumbo hex right now?" Becca taunted, looking at Nate and Ava. "Is that why she's staring at us like that?"

Nate backed up some more and pointed his thumb to his chest. "Nuh-uh, I'm *not* answering that. You're not getting me into this mess."

Our waiter came to our table. "If there's a problem," he said through tight lips, and set down our food, "just let me know." Then, he hurried off with nervous steps.

It had sounded like code for: *Please* don't make a scene.

"Why?" I finally said to Ava.

She avoided my stare, and I noticed that a heavy sadness had covered her face like a dark, drooping veil.

"The witch speaks!" Becca mocked, shoving some fries into her mouth and slurping her soda. She laughed so big that the gloppy food jumped around on her tongue. But then her mouth snapped shut, and her eyes bulged. "*Aagh! Hagh! Aargh!...*" Like a blowfish, Becca's cheeks puffed as she coughed and gagged.

Ava groaned and half-heartedly slapped Becca's back. In that moment, I wished Becca had choked on her greasy meal, but she soon recovered.

"Don't be so sensitive, Phoebe," Ava said, now looking at me. "We're all friends here."

The veil of sadness had vanished, and her wide-set eyes revealed an emotion I couldn't totally understand. I swallowed slowly, staring at a someone who was now foreign to me.

25

Ava continued with a grimace. "You and Jason already seem to be *really* good friends."

"Y'all don't have to be so mean," Jason whispered, staring at the table.

"And you know so much, Phoebe. You always did," Ava taunted. "We just want to learn more about what you can do."

"And what I'm learning is *so much* fun," Becca added.

"Let's just eat," Nate chimed in.

Ava smiled. It reminded me of how a spider probably appeared to a fly that has been caught in its web. "It's fun, Nate," she said. "That's all it is. Friends having fun. Don't you want to see what she can do?"

Speechless, Nate scratched his head and exchanged glances with everyone, except me.

Basking in the attention as if she'd just won an Oscar for Lead Actress, Ava wasn't the carefree, fast-talking free spirit I grew up with anymore. I fumed at her cruelty and selfishness. I fumed until I thought my chest would explode. And I literally thought it would until I suddenly began to hear clear words forming.

My chest relaxed as the words seeped into my brain slowly but forcefully. *You think it's fun now.... You think you're so sure about things, Ava Dougherty. But you don't even know what's around the corner for you.*

The thoughts didn't ramble, and they weren't my opinions or feelings. They were different. These words were like strong messages that enveloped me and took over. They were deliberate and sure, and they were *very* persistent.

"I called my grandmother *Naan*. *Not* nanny granny," I seethed.

Ava rolled her eyes and opened her mouth.

"And before you say, whatever," I said, shutting her up, "you should know this. He's going to come back. And when it happens, you'll remember this moment. Wait and see."

"What the …?" Nate whispered.

My body stiffened as Ava's stunned eyes locked with mine.

"That doesn't even make sense," Becca scoffed. "Don't listen t—" But Becca couldn't finish. Looking at Ava, she realized I'd said something important—something powerful.

Ava's lips trembled. "Wh-what's that s-s-supposed to mean?"

Silence.

"T-tell me! What are you *saying*?!" she demanded, violently slapping her palm down on the table.

Jason jumped in his seat.

"What the *heck* are you talking about?" she shrieked.

My mouth refused to open. I'd said enough and too much.

A baby nearby started crying as customers began to stare.

"Ava, it's okay," Jason said, reaching for her shoulder. "She didn't mean anything by it."

She pushed his hand away. "You *would* defend her, wouldn't you." Then, like a cobra ready to strike, Ava stood and leaned over the table toward me. "You tell me right *now. This second!*"

Suddenly, I felt exposed and regretful. I couldn't be in that diner anymore. I had to get out. Before Ava could lunge at me or scream at the desperate waiter who had rushed over, I jumped up and pushed Nate out of the way.

"I should've *never* invited you, you ugly *witch*?!" Ava yelled and then sobbed loudly as I darted out the diner.

I headed to the closest place of refuge—the grocery store at the other end. As soon as I entered my safe haven, I slowed my steps and paced the aisles, one after the other, trying to calm my nerves. Counting down the minutes until Mom arrived, I continued pacing and every now and then stopped in front of a shelf, pretending I was looking at something to buy—rolls of paper towels, a bottle of tomato sauce, a bag of chips.

While looking at another random item, I shook my head, feeling powerless that I couldn't undo the past. The damage had already been done. And I realized I never really knew Ava.

When Mom drove into the parking lot, I jogged from the corner of the store and waved her down. The silver sedan jolted to a stop.

"What are you doing all the way over *here*?" she asked as soon as I got in. She watched me slouch low in my seat when we passed the diner. "And what happened?"

Mom could see through lies, especially when I was in front of her. It was pointless to tell her anything but the truth. So I told her what had happened at Wilma's, minus the final minutes about what I said to Ava about her father.

Mom's forehead did a trademark wrinkle as she listened. "Ava is a troubled girl," she said at last. "If you can understand this, then you'll see why she was hurtful to you."

"What does Ava being troubled have *anything* to do with how she treated me? You should've seen her. It was complete *sabotage*."

"Phoebe, sometimes a person can act awfully toward others who aren't the cause of their problems," she tried to explain.

I shook my head. "I know you're trying, but it's still not helpful."

We slowed to a stop at a traffic light.

"Phoebe, look at me."

I did, reluctantly. The red traffic light beamed through the windshield and brightened the crimson highlights she'd recently put in her curly hair.

Her fingers nervously tapped the steering wheel. "I've always known that Ava's friends and her mother, like many people in our town, don't like ... er ..." She shifted in her seat. "Let me just say, some people can be close-minded about who to accept. And I think Ava feels pressured to be this way because she wants to be accepted."

"So, what you're saying is that it boiled down to a choice she had to make, and she decided to toss the loyal friend." I shook my head and leaned back. "That's a harsh reality to swallow," I mumbled.

The light changed, and Mom had to look ahead to drive on. "Unfortunately, that's the choice many people make. They're not strong enough. Or they're scared. Fitting into a group, *especially* one that doesn't suit someone or has bad intentions ... has its consequences."

A part of me understood. And in that moment, I felt like I could share more. "Mom ... there's something else ...," I whispered slowly.

"What's that?"

I paused too long.

"What *else*?" Her voice dropped as she glanced over at me.

"Never mind," I lied. "It's nothing."

One of Mom's eyebrows arched, and I knew she didn't believe me. But then her face relaxed.

We drove on in silence, and I took out Naan's picture. If she'd been alive, I believed and hoped she would've told me something that would make me feel victorious about the situation and understand why I said something to Ava that hadn't happened. I also wondered if I really had lost my nerve at Wilma's, because when I spoke to Ava, I actually felt *completely* in control.

Ava and I never spoke to each other again. In fact, she avoided me. I was either feared or her worst enemy, and neither felt good. It was also awkward during art class. Jason still smiled at me, but we no longer chatted or looked over each other's drawings. Other students would stare at me strangely or say hateful things, and I acted like I didn't hear them.

If I had tried to defend myself, they probably would've thought I was even more strange or guilty for overreacting. The rumors were too potent and the interest too deep.

Chapter Three

THE GIRLS WHO LEFT

In fact, the rumors and whispers didn't budge, even during high school. I managed to prevent many confrontations—physical and verbal—by using the age-old tactic of avoidance. And I wished for something miraculous to happen, an earth-bending shift to occur in my timeline of life that would change my destiny forever.

Ninth grade wasn't entirely torturous, and that was thanks to Mr. Franklin's English class. Mr. Franklin was new to Crockett, from Boston. We'd heard he went to fancy schools, and depending on who you spoke with, the town was either fortunate to have him or it didn't need a newcomer telling their children what to learn.

We'd been studying *Macbeth* in Mr. Franklin's class. And on the last day of the unit, Mr. Franklin somberly entered the classroom, attired in a period costume, and turned off the lights. Staring at him and each other, we sat in our seats, uncertain about what would happen next.

That was until Mr. Franklin pierced the quizzical silence with his baritone voice. Looking down at his cupped hands, as if holding something, he began, "Tomorrow, and tomorrow, and tomorrow, creeps in this petty pace from day to day."

We realized he was reenacting the scene where Macbeth holds his dead wife, and his ambitions to become king are tragically falling apart. Mr. Franklin paced and knelt in front of us. "To the last syllable of recorded time. And all our yesterdays have lighted fools …"

The broad daylight filtered through the closed blinds, as if actual medieval candles lit the room. Mr. Franklin didn't break character for the entire class, not even to give instructions. We somehow knew how to follow along. His performance set us in eleventh-century Scotland as we took turns reciting the play aloud with our best efforts.

In those short, artfully crafted lines of Shakespeare's soliloquy, I felt Macbeth's regret, emptiness, and hopelessness all at the same time. I wondered if Mr. Franklin felt this way about his own life and that was why he could so vividly bring those words to life.

Later that week, I worked on my art project after school. I stayed so late that the custodian practically swept me out of the side door with his wide dust mop.

I decided to take a shortcut through the pasture to avoid any students on the street. More importantly, the pasture reminded me of Naan. She used to take walks by it, sometimes with me.

Pushing through the unkept grass, I sidestepped puddles and enormous anthills.

And that was when I got the feeling that I was being followed.

At first, I thought I heard a voice in the air. The sound blended in with the grazing cows and chirping crickets. Then, the grass behind me crunched and snapped in a rhythm that sounded like steps.

I quickened my pace as I glanced over my shoulder. My breath caught in my throat when I saw, in the distance, a thin blurred figure moving toward me. I faced forward and began to run.

Was that my name? I couldn't be sure.

My heart thudded. Wearing my Doc Martens boots, I felt my feet strike the thick rubber soles with each pounding step I took. The thoughts in my mind raced between the dark blur being a creep or a bully, and then rested on something stupid: a ghost following me home, like the one Ava would always ask about.

Still running, I hopped over pesky cow patties as if they were land mines, and I searched the ground for something useful. *That rock? No, too small. Some dirt? Wouldn't do the trick if I threw it at someone.* The steps stomped behind me and the blades of grass popped as the noises only got louder.

It must've been my name that I'd heard, because I heard it again. The deep voice sounded like a teenage boy or a man. But my ears started ringing with fear, drowning out any chance of hearing clearly.

Seeing a small branch, I ran to it. It was thin, crooked, and had a few limbs. Even if it were a ghost, I would still try and fight back.

"Phoebe." The voice was now clear and close behind me.

Too close for me to avoid it, and I had no choice. I jumped down and picked up my natural weapon. "*Aaah!*" I yelled a battle cry as I stood up and spun around with the branch in my hand, brandishing it like a pitchfork to stab the figure.

"*Aaah!*" the voice cried out.

My eyes widened so large that my face hurt. I released my grasp around the stick. "Mr. *Franklin*?" My chest heaved as I gulped the warm, early evening air to catch my breath.

"Apologies, I didn't mean to startle you," he wheezed, leaning over. "*Goodness!* You're quite a runner." His hollow cheeks seemed even more sunken from his own quick breaths.

The sun cast an orange glow over Mr. Franklin's raven black hair and pale skin, and he stood again. "I was calling you."

Mr. Franklin sounded different, not like himself. His vowels were rounded, like he was still playing his Shakespearean role in class.

"I thought it was …" My words faded when I decided I didn't want to admit to my favorite teacher that I had mistaken him for a phantom, a psycho, or a high school tormentor.

He stared at me through his deep brown eyes, as if pondering a question. "Crockett's Witch," he said at last with a saddened expression and a tilted head. "Is that what they're calling you these days?"

Avoiding his eyes, I dragged the heel of my boot in the dirt and made a Tic-tac-toe grid. "Er … Among other things, not rated PG," I said as I used my heel again to draw a big *X* in the middle.

"Kids can be nasty," he said soberly, still saying his vowels like a proper English gent.

"I guess." I stopped my little game to look up at him. "But I *never* said I was a witch," I protested. "And it's not just that. They don't get me or my family."

Mr. Franklin nodded. It seemed like he understood being on the outside, beyond the fact that he wasn't from Crockett.

He looked down at his dark jeans, which were blotched with specks of mud. "The three witches in Macbeth," he said. "There's such power in prophecy." His thick, long lashes raised like wings when he looked up at me again. "You've been on point in how you interpret my lessons."

"Uhm, thanks?"

Did he stop me just to continue our lesson? Well, he did have a flair for the dramatic.

Mr. Franklin must've noticed my confusion and started to explain, "I came to present you with this." His hand moved and that was when I noticed there had been a brown envelope in it. "It seems you didn't receive my note from the office, requesting to see you after school." Without stepping forward, he extended his arm, and I took the envelope. "I recommended you," he said.

"For what?" I asked immediately.

"To a good school." He shook his head. "No, not a good school. A superb school."

An automatic smile spread across my face. It sounded like Mr. Franklin may have just helped to shift my world.

"You're a very talented student," he went on, standing with his hands behind his back. "Don't waste your gifts here."

Although pleasantly surprised, I was still curious why he needed to track me down after school and in the middle of a pasture.

He leaned in a bit and lowered his voice. "It's time sensitive, and I will be on travel, starting tomorrow."

"Oh," I said, looking down at the envelope and then at him.

As I studied Mr. Franklin outside of his classroom, I realized that he was probably younger than mid-thirties. And although he wore jeans and a navy blue Polo shirt, there was a timeless sophistication about him. Like he was the tragic hero in an old English novel. He already seemed to have the accent down pat.

"Well, I won't keep you any longer and a good evening to you." He smiled, but his eyes were still pensive. "Remember your upcoming assignment."

"Yes, chapter two with discussion questions. Safe travels, Mr. Franklin," I finished.

He gave a small bow, and then I watched his slender frame turn away, step around some puddles, and eventually disappear behind tall blades of grass. I glanced down at the envelope again and jogged home.

The Murray School, Scotland the envelope read when I studied it in my room. There was also a coat of arms with a unicorn and a wolf on either side of a shield. Words or symbols that looked like another language were at the bottom.

When I opened it, a piece of paper and glossy magazine fell onto my lap. I picked up the paper and turned it over:

Dear Ms. Phoebe Douse,

It is with great pleasure that we congratulate you on your admittance to The Murray School. You have been selected amongst a pool of highly qualified candidates. Should you decide to be a part of our renowned institution, please confirm your decision within two weeks.

With kindest regards,

Taggart Duff

Professor Taggart Duff, 15th Earl of Murrayshire
The Murray School Headmaster

Scotland? Within two weeks? When Mr. Franklin had said it was a superb school and that it was time sensitive, I hadn't expected *this*.

I picked up the magazine. Front and center on the cover was a massive brownish-gray stone building that looked like a castle. In fact, I was convinced it *had* to be a castle, with its green domed towers, large windows on the lower floors, and small windows at the top. There were also pictures of students and classrooms. The students wore uniforms, and I figured that the school colors were red and green, because of the plaid skirts and ties that they wore.

Everyone either had large grins with their arms around each other, or looked extremely studious, hunched over desks. It all seemed too staged and fake, and I didn't trust anything that seemed so perfect.

My initial curiosity was replaced with skepticism. I dropped the paper and magazine, and they tumbled into a heap on the floor. I didn't think one more second about the package....

Until later that night, however, curiosity and interest crept in, and this time, they stayed. I showed my parents the letter and magazine after dinner and told them about Mr. Franklin's recommendation.

"Such a thoughtful teacher," Mom said.

"He's smart. That's what he is," Dad said proudly. "He appreciates our daughter's intelligence."

Mom's face brightened. "Don't you *see*? Your wish has been granted!"

Dad, and I looked at each other with blank expressions. "That sounds like something Naan would've said," I said sarcastically. *Maybe Naan's my fairy godmother*, I joked to myself.

"Okay, Doubting Douses," Mom said after we sat in silence for a bit. "Maybe you can be on board with *this* idea. How about we look more into this school? At the end of the week, we can discuss things, before any decision is made."

"I'm with you on that," I said, and Dad nodded.

It was practical advice we could all take seriously.

I used a computer in my school library to look into The Murray School. It maintained a limited profile, which was unusual. There wasn't much information about it, other than what I'd already read and saw in the magazine.

And I was right. The Murray School was *actually* a castle. Built in the 1600s. It was later founded as a boarding school in 1953. School grades were First Year through Sixth Year. I figured out it was like the equivalent of American middle school and high school rolled into one.

When we came together to share what we'd found out, on my parents' end, Mom went straight to the source. She had called and spoken with the head of administration, Mrs. Vyda.

"The headmaster has been recruiting American students," Mom explained. "And Mr. Franklin provided a glowing recommendation."

"How did Mr. Franklin know about this school? And why *Scotland*?" I wondered aloud.

"He went to top-notch schools, didn't he?" Dad asserted. "He's probably very connected." He paused, and then continued, "At any rate, I think it's a legitimate offer."

Graham had been passing the kitchen and stepped in. "And why not Scotland?" he said matter-of-factly. "It's well known for its schools. Actually, Scotland has had a history of intellectual enlightenment—in the sciences, philosophy, economics, and more."

Mom smiled. "I'm so pleased you have an interest in your sister's future."

His square shoulders dipped to block her hand, which was aiming for his cheek to rub it. "Mo-om, *stop*," he insisted as she giggled.

Graham didn't like it when Mom seemed to ignore that he was seventeen, but she couldn't help herself. He would always be her baby boy who used to throw his toys and bawl if he didn't have her in his sight. I always thought he must've been a demanding brat, but Mom thought it was endearing. Go figure.

"It's something I'd already known about," Graham said with a shrug. "But yeah, I also do care."

"Phoebe, an offer like this only happens once in a blue moon," Mom advised as we ended our discussion. "I'm sure you know that it'll never come again. Consider that."

On my way to my room, Graham tapped me on the shoulder. I thought he was going to say something annoying, but he surprised me. "What are you waiting for? You can't even stand it here. I thought you wouldn't need to think another second about this."

"Be encouraging!" Dad called out from the living room.

"I *am*," Graham insisted. "I'm speaking truth."

Graham's blunt comment, I had to admit, *was* true.

Have you ever believed your circumstances to be really terrible, and when you're finally faced with a decision to change them, you start seeing all the good that had always been around you? That was my dilemma.

I weighed my options and possibilities for days. I could go and explore a new place, maybe answer questions about myself, and discover new people.

Or, I could stay and ignore the invitation—stay with the familiar and what I'd always known. It was then that I began to truly acknowledge the positive and comfortable aspects of the life that surrounded me.

I knew my town. Crockett was a small, slow-growing, rural community with a main road of only two lanes where cars shared space with people on horseback. Summers were long and sweltering, with glowing fireflies and noisy cicadas. And on the Fourth of July, while eating ice cream, you could watch fireworks from miles away just by sitting on the roof of your truck or car.

If someone drove me home from The Square, I could guess where I was going nine times out of ten when I closed my eyes and felt each turn and bend in the road. I knew when the streetlamps would come on to illuminate our darkened lane. And the local pharmacist, Mr. Palmers, always recommended the best cough syrup for my seasonal allergies—not the bitter-tasting one; I liked the cherry flavor.

I knew my home. It was a three-bedroom bungalow made with sandy-brown bricks and had gardens in the front and back. And there was so much more character and stories it told on the inside. My room faced the street, where I could hear children's voices as they walked to school or the clank of our metal mailbox when the mailman filled it with envelopes and shut it. And the settee that Naan adored remained in the living room, exactly where she had left it. It faced me whenever I walked through the front door.

I knew my family. My parents were caring and hardworking, and they spoke with such humor and knowledge. They could seamlessly switch between their patois dialect and the most formal-sounding

English I'd ever heard. Graham loved anything and everything about science—outer space, electricity, tornadoes.... You name it. Even though I couldn't stand him most of the time, he also wanted to teach me things. And Naan *always* remained present.

These tiny pieces, when glued together, created the colorful mosaic of my life.

I tried convincing myself that I could finish high school in Crockett. Plus, I had a seemingly successful method of avoiding people. But deep down, I knew that it was my fear and hesitation making these excuses. My parents and Graham were right. And as much as my town, home, and family were my life, I'd shut most people out.

I was still mulling over the decision when I headed to Biology class the next day. Turning the corner, Bethanny, a sophomore, all of a sudden came up to me. "You were friends with Ava, right?" she asked, pointing at my face and chewing on a wad of bright purple gum. It didn't help that Bethanny was inches taller than me, so her finger came right between my eyes.

Annoyed, I stepped back. "Once upon a time," I said dryly.

"Did you hear what happened?" Bethanny's stale grape breath blew over my entire face.

"No, what ha—?"

Her lips flapped before I could finish. "She had to leave town with her mom. Something about her dad showing up at their house. Luckily, Ava was at school and her mom was at work. A neighbor called the police about a man acting strange and lurking around. But before the police showed up, he left." She gulped in some air and jabbered on.

"Ava and her mom heard what happened, got creeped out, and packed what they could when they got home."

Finally, she stopped to take a needed breath and stared, smacking and popping her gum.

I was silent. I mean, what could be said? This was sudden news, and it was about Ava Dougherty. The person I thought would be my best friend for the rest of my life.

Bethanny tapped her foot. I figured she was expecting at least some reaction on my part. She forcefully rubbed her large, fleshy nose. "Just thought you'd want to know," she said, and turned on her heel. "Freak," she muttered over her shoulder at me.

Suddenly, my diner memory resurfaced, and I immediately felt responsible. Whatever the circumstance, I was somehow a part of it. I felt foreign in my own body, and my throat tightened as my vision blurred.

Pulling out Naan's picture, I looked at her to focus my eyes. I remembered when she told me to be good, and I half expected her to jump out of the tree and into the hallway to scold me. *Am I actually thinking this?* I crammed her photo back into my wallet. Not taking the usual care of it, I even bent an edge.

It was then I decided I needed to leave Crockett. I was tired of the gossip and bad attitudes. I didn't want to be constantly reminded of a lost friendship, and I needed something more than a place that only had one grocery store and too many judgmental people.

Somewhere I could be someone who no one knew. I could mold myself into the person I was meant to be—a person who didn't feel strange and judged.

That night, I filled out the forms and signed the acceptance letter.

"I think it'll be a good experience to try out a new place," I said to my parents. "Plus it'll be great preparation for college."

I tried to sound convincing and very confident. Did it work? Well, they just stood there, not saying anything.

So I went on. "Everything's already filled out. All that's left is for you to sign. See?" I handed Mom the papers.

"What do you think, hon?" Mom asked Dad.

"Well," he said, crossing his arms, "when Phoebe is determined and sets her mind to something, she's already thought about it forward and backward."

"Also, I could make plans to go with her. To see what it's like," Mom added.

They seemed convinced enough, because Dad uncrossed his arms and Mom simply said, "Okay."

Counting down the final days at school, I acted like nothing had changed in my world. It was all routine in my classes, in the hallways, and so on. The only person I would've told was Mr. Franklin, but he was still away.

I would miss some parts of my life in Crockett. But, I was ready to move on.

In a town where nothing ever changed, Ava and I, who were once best friends, both departed within the same month. We'd be known as the girls who left Crockett and to places that would remain a mystery to each other.

Chapter Four

IT'S IN THE AIR

*C*abin crew, ten minutes to landing, ten minutes to landing," the pilot announced over the intercom.

It was less than two weeks after I received my fateful letter, and I was now flying over a new country. Our journey up to this point had taken twelve hours and two flights.

Pushing up the window shield, mounds of green and brown—mossy, emerald, tan, and olive shades—were seen far below in patchworks that rolled and settled along the hills and flatter landscape. And jagged hills, like sharp claws and mangled teeth, were formed by boulders and rocks that jutted out at odd angles.

Small villages dotted the land, while glistening lakes were so crystal clear that I could see the entire shadow of the plane as it flew above the water. The closer we got to the ground, the more I could make sense of the tiny people, cars, and animals as they became more visible and alive.

And then I spotted a home on a small island—alone with tall spires. It had a small boat at its dock, which seemed to be the only way of getting to and from the island. I stared at the home until the plane turned. Although it was out of sight, I imagined that whoever lived in that solitary space was alone and wanted to hide, away from the world.

After we landed, the crisp fall air stunned me as I stepped out of the plane and onto the metal stairs that the airport crew had rolled out.

"Be careful on the stairs. They can be slippery," the smiling flight attendant told each passenger as we exited.

"And be sure to hold tight to the railin' if ye can!" a man below in a neon yellow windbreaker, holding a walkie-talkie, yelled up to us.

As bright as the sky was while the plane was landing, it quickly switched to an eerie gray tone with thick, heavy clouds as we walked into the airport to retrieve our suitcases.

The Murray School was far from any city or large town. And that meant we still had another one-hour train ride. Being outside again to find the nearby train station, I felt the invigorating air. I filled my lungs with two deep breaths while clumsily pushing the trolley with one hand and trying to close my jacket with the other.

The wind whipped my face, howled, and burned my ears and nose. With a sudden stronger gust, I almost lifted completely off my feet and momentarily choked. It was as if the wind had long, forceful arms that reached deep inside me with a killer grip on my lungs.

Before I could panic, the arms let go, and I started breathing again and regained my footing. The sky changed yet again to a mix of sun and grayish-blue clouds.

"First time in Sco'land?" the cabdriver asked cheerfully after he helped us with our luggage and Mom and I settled into the back seat.

We had just finished our train journey. Exhausted, we looked at each other through bloodshot eyes. "Yes," Mom said.

"It should rain today. They say Sco'land has two types of weather—rain an' more rain." He chuckled.

Mom and I looked at each other again and politely chuckled.

"Where ye off to?" He turned around to look at us. A large nose protruded at a sharp angle from his profile, and his close-set eyes were rimmed with wrinkles. They squinted into small slits as he waited.

"The Murray School. It's …," I said as I started digging for a folded piece of paper deep inside my duffel bag.

"Aye, no need to look. Know exactly where it is."

He put the cab's gearshift into drive and left the tiny village station. While he drove on the winding road, he spoke profusely. "That over there's Elderon Rock. It's said to be a sleepin' giant. That's his head and nose bulgin' from the ground. Ye see?" He pointed, trying to trace the make-believe outline of large humps that were covered in moss. The taxi swerved a bit off the road, and he quickly turned the steering wheel to avoid the ditch.

I slid sideways and bumped into Mom.

Her body stiffened. "I wish he'd keep *both* hands on the wheel and eyes on the road," she whispered.

"Like fish?" And before we could answer, he went on, "If ye lookin' for the best fish an' chips in this area, ye only need to go to Crails Pub. It's a wee bit away. Only ten minutes' drive in that direction." Once again, he pointed and stretched across the passenger seat to make sure we saw. "Ask for Fiona. Tell her James sent ye. She'll take care of ye."

James had turned into our very own tour guide, and it was oftentimes difficult to understand his accent. So we would get fragments of words and sounds that we tried to piece together.

Outside my window, the view opened out to rolling hills that stretched until they merged with the blue horizon of sky, water, and bays. The road eventually became a small lane when James veered right. He drove onward and then began to slow down.

Seeing the decorative iron bars through the front window of our taxi, I knew we were approaching the school grounds at the main gate. James only had to pause for a millisecond before the gate groaned and the wheels and pulleys engaged. The large brass coat of arms separated.

"Beautiful!" Mom exclaimed.

The campus was incredible—a straight, broad boulevard lined with enormous trees. The road was so long that when I looked behind me, the massive gate was just a blurred outline in the distance. The students, who walked about or stopped and chatted, were like polka dots among the gardens and vast fields.

"Could you drop us off at the side entrance, please?" Mom asked.

All of a sudden speechless and in awe, James could only nod as we drove on.

My new school, the castle, commanded me to look up at it. I wanted to touch its stone; it looked so alive. And the windows and doors seemed like they were for giants, not humans.

James parked the taxi and hopped out to open the doors for us. "I'll help with that," he said, managing to find his voice again. He reached for our suitcases, and we followed him as he pulled them effortlessly up the ramp to the side door.

Mom gave him the fare and then pulled out some extra coins. "To say thank you," she said.

He shrugged and shook his head. "It's no worries, ma'am. It's what I do. Being helpful is who *I am.*"

"Please, you've also been so welcoming. I *insist.*"

And with her soft persistence, James accepted the tip, dropping the coins into the wallet he'd retrieved from his back pocket.

I realized, in that short exchange, that kindness for James was natural—it was unassuming, and it was expected. It was as refreshing as the air.

The wind almost smashed my nose as it slammed the massive office door shut in my face when I tried to enter the building. With Mom's help the second time, we were successful.

As we stepped inside, Mom quickly shook her head, forcing her hair to fall into place. This season, she had electric blue highlights in her bob.

It was an ordinary space where administrators sat, clicking away at their computers with expressions that appeared as wooden as the furniture. No one spoke.

Then, a woman, with short mousy-brown hair that had gray patches, got up from one of the desks, took off her reading glasses, and approached us with heavy, wide steps. The clicking stopped as pairs of eyes examined us over the computer monitors.

"Welcome to The Murray School. I'm Mrs. Vyda." Her husky voice perfectly matched her stocky frame. Mrs. Vyda smoothed the front of her blouse and her black slacks, which seemed too small—the material stretched and twisted at odd angles.

After our brief introductions, Mrs. Vyda handed me a small canvas bag. I peeked inside and found pieces of my new life—a handbook, keys, schedule, and a map. Still examining the items, I heard Mrs. Vyda and Mom agree that Mom could stay in the office to review and sign some forms while Mrs. Vyda would take me to my boarding house.

Mrs. Vyda easily opened the heavy door, and I followed her out of the office. As we walked on a sidewalk and passed several gardens with wild flowers, I pulled my suitcases in a tired, trancelike state, and the bursts of wind partially deafened me.

Meanwhile, Mrs. Vyda, with not even a sweater on, seemed unfazed by the weather as she pointed out buildings on the campus. Her wide frame and stone-like face looked like she could withstand any force of nature. She was adapted to the place.

From what I could gather while trying to stay awake and on my feet, the sprawling campus had the castle for most classes and smaller buildings for other classes. On either side of the castle were the boarding houses. Boys were housed on one side and girls on the other.

Tennis courts, rugby and soccer fields, and large quads occupied the grounds as well. Students were walking along the manicured lawns, talking around tables, or leisurely kicking a ball around on different fields. Their uniforms were just as I'd seen in the magazine.

"Here we are," Mrs. Vyda announced in front of a large house.

Clairmount House was engraved on a *very* visible, shiny metal sign nailed above the doorway. The sign was so obvious that if I ever got lost trying to find the house, it would be my own careless, dumb fault.

"Oh, *come on*, now," Mrs. Vyda muttered, struggling to pull something out from the tight space inside her pants pocket. She eventually managed to take out an old-fashioned key and opened the door.

I rolled my suitcases inside and turned in a complete circle. Clairmount House looked like one of those mansions I'd seen on the internet or on TV, with wooden floors, decorative rugs, and expensive furniture and paintings. There was a huge fireplace in the living room area and the ceilings had chandeliers.

I was looking around so much that I almost missed everything Mrs. Vyda was saying, but caught the last part.

"… Ms. Daniels, your house mother, should be in her office." She pointed past my head toward a room with tons of pictures and posters taped all over the walls. "She'll greet you and show you to your room. And I'll tell your mum where to find you."

"Much appreciated, Mrs. Vyda." I gave her a big, thankful smile.

The corners of her stiff lips barely moved as her rigid face refused to budge. Mrs. Vyda didn't seem like the type to spare smiles. She turned and took powerful steps toward the castle, this time in the direction of the gusts of wind.

I'd been unpacking after Ms. Daniels showed me to my room. She was welcoming but couldn't stay long because she had a meeting on the other side of campus.

"Hiya! My new roommate, fantastic! It has been *so* quiet since Cara left." My new roommate stepped up to me and stuck out her hand. "Zoe Houlihan."

Her name sounded fun to say, and she had a powerful grip as we shook hands. "Phoebe Douse. Nice to meet you."

Zoe was of average height, like me, but she appeared taller because her body was slender like a ruler while mine was a bit curvy. Zoe's long chestnut-colored hair flowed down her back. She had a narrow nose, and her green eyes had bursts of brighter green, like exploding firecrackers. And if you looked even deeper, there was also a defiance that jumped around inside of them.

While Zoe spoke, I noticed she didn't sound Scottish.

"I'm Irish," she declared. "I don't know why foreigners mix-up our accents." Still holding my hand, she gave it a firm squeeze before letting it go. "But you heard the difference."

I nodded. "I just wasn't sure from where." I said, and then continued to unpack.

"It's exciting to have a new roommate. I've been without one for almost *two* months."

"Yep, exciting," I said flatly, examining the old wardrobe that stood against the wall beside my bed. We each had one, and I caught my reflection in one of its long mirrors on the doors. My thick, dark hair, which was usually in a ponytail, was poking out in odd directions, and my eyes were red from a lack of decent sleep.

I noticed again how my eyes were large like Naan's—except hers were amber and mine were dark brown. I tried to smooth my hair, but it was no use, so I continued my more successful task of hanging and folding clothes.

"Once you get some sleep, you'll feel much better."

Is she watching me? Not really. She was now rummaging through her desk drawers looking for something. Socks, papers, pens, candy wrappers, and other objects began to fly and tumble out.

"Aha, *finally*!" she announced, lifting a notepad from the messy pile.

"Been looking for this for some time." She turned to me. "If you need any help finding your way around or figuring out the teachers, I'm here."

"Appreciate it," I mumbled.

I wasn't sure how to let Zoe down nicely. Making friends at The Murray School wasn't on my agenda. I was there to escape Crockett, finish high school, and find out more about myself.

Zoe crammed the junk back where it came from and rammed her thigh against the drawers. But when she stepped back, the drawers popped open like an overstuffed taco.

She tried again, but then shrugged when the drawers didn't obey. With an outstretched hand, she walked over to my desk. "What's your schedule look like?"

I stepped in front of her. "I'm fine." Hearing the annoyance in my voice, I added softly, "Thanks for wanting to help."

But Zoe didn't seem bothered. She smiled slyly out of one side of her mouth as she stepped away from my desk with both hands up in surrender. "Like I said. If you need any help, just ask."

"Okay." *Good, now I can be left alone.*

But she kept on. "A few of my friends and I are going to the atrium in the courtyard. If you'd like, you can meet us there when you're done."

"Uhm … I need to rest. Plus, I'm going to spend some time with my mom before she leaves."

"Right," she nodded, causing her hair to fall over half of her face. "I'm sure you're exhausted from traveling all the way from Texas."

How does she know I'm from Texas? I quickly looked at her. She was still smiling slyly, but I shrugged it off after realizing my entire itinerary and ticket stubs were in full view on my table.

"Welcome again," she said, and turned to leave.

After Zoe left, I heard her speaking outside with Mom. Through the thick wooden door and solid stone walls, it was difficult to hear much of anything.

"Zoe seems like a nice young woman," Mom said, walking in. "Messy," she added as her eyes scanned the space, "but nice."

Mom couldn't stand mess.

"Yeah, I guess," I said with a shrug.

I didn't realize Mom was watching me until I finished emptying my suitcases. "Why are you looking at me like that?" I asked, rubbing my tired face.

"Like what?"

"All googly-eyed, like a sad puppy."

She smiled as she folded and put the last of my clothes in a drawer and closed the wardrobe door. "I'll miss you, that's all. And now that we're actually here, I'm just wondering ... how do you feel?" She paused. "You can tell me the truth. Remember what your father and I promised. If it's not what you expected or if you don't think it's best for you, we can make a nice trip out of this and return home together."

I sat on the edge of my bed and bounced on it, testing out the mattress. It felt a little stiff, but it would do. Then I looked at Mom again. "I'm good. Believe me. Actually, I think it'll be interesting."

Personally, I needed to see what this experience could do for me. It was this particular school that found me, and for some reason, I felt like Naan wanted me here.

We spent the next few days together—Mom and me.

She had looked into staying at a small inn that was located in a nearby village; however, Headmaster Duff, who was out of the country, had made arrangements for Mom to be on campus in quarters where some of the administrators, who didn't have homes in town, lived.

We enjoyed our time together on campus, purchased books and my uniforms, and she was even able to meet some of my teachers.

The days, of course, flew by. And when it was time for her to leave very early Sunday morning, it was still dark outside.

"It's not goodbye," she began.

"It's until next time," I finished.

We hugged, and before our embrace ended, she leaned in for an extra squeeze and said into my ear, "You're brave and strong. And I know you'll be your best here."

Once she said those words, I felt tears forming. I forced them back, hoping she wouldn't see.

Mom got into the cab as we waved. She was on her way back to Crockett while I stayed behind in Scotland.

During the hours that followed, I spent them entirely in my room. It had sunk in that I was thousands of miles away from home. My first time outside of Texas, and my first time being away from my family. I didn't even leave to eat or explore. Signs of life passed by outside my window—talking and laughing, bike bells clanging, and, of course, the wind.

I replayed my journey to Scotland and envisioned my tomorrow. I did this over and over, like pushing rewind, fast-forward, and replay on a movie. Each time, I would insert more memories or scenes to develop the story.

Pulling out Naan's picture, I decided she needed a better home than my purse. After all, we were both in a new place. So I carefully placed her in a journal for safekeeping.

I would give myself little notes of advice and encouragement for the next day. *Remember to set your alarm to give yourself at least thirty minutes to get ready.* Or, I would laugh softly at a funny scene with my family that replayed in my mind.

My mom's words also gave me strength … and so did the faces of my dad and even Graham.

Whenever I heard Zoe entering to get or drop off something, I jumped in bed and pulled my sheets over my head, pretending to sleep. She left me alone, and I had a feeling she was being considerate.

By late afternoon, the room was so stuffy that I had to open the windows and take several deep, reviving breaths. And when I looked out above the school's green-domed rooftops and into the distance, I was surprised to see something I'd *never* seen before.

I rubbed my eyes to steady my focus. I even blinked a few times to sharpen my vision. In the sky, there were not one, not two, but *three* perfectly arched rainbows, one on top of the other. I stared at the magnificent display. For me, it was a message—a promise. Something about the air and the place was already speaking to me.

When I began to fall asleep in the dusky, early evening light, I was hopeful that in the morning I would look less scraggly and be ready to face my first day of classes.

Chapter Five

DR. BRAITHWAITE'S TOWER OF IMPOSSIBILITIES

*B*onk! Blee! Blee! Bonk! Bonk! Bonk! My alarm blared and honked with the loudest, most cacophonous sound. I'd chosen it so it would be impossible to oversleep. The downside was waking up.

Jumping up, I yanked off my headphones and looked around, confused. I almost tumbled out of bed, but my sheets caught me in a tangled web, saving my knees from hitting the floor. My memory jolted—I wasn't home, waking up in Crockett. Instead, I was in a room … at Clairmount House … at The Murray School … in *Scotland*!

Zoe's bed was already empty, and I could hear water running.

"Here goes," I said as I gathered my things and entered the bathroom.

"Morning. Sleep well?" Zoe sang. She looked almost completely ready and was standing in front of a basin with a toothbrush dangling from her mouth.

"Like I slept into next year," I said, truly feeling revived. "But waking up to my alarm was *horrid*." I laid out my items to start my morning routine.

"I'm an early riser," Zoe said through a sudsy mouth. "Actually, I can stay up pretty late too." She spat into the basin and turned on the faucet.

"I'm not sure what I am. I just know if I'm extremely tired, a cranky little gremlin comes out."

She laughed. "I can't stand those things."

"Gremlins?"

"No, alarms. I don't even use them. Instead, I use my mind." Zoe tapped her temple.

"Huh?"

"I just tell myself when I want to wake up before I go to sleep, and then I wake up at the *exact* time, not even a second off. It always works."

Yeah, sure. Pushing aside what I really thought, I asked, "Can anyone do that?"

Zoe shook her head. "It's only for those who have real steady mind control." She looked at me through the foggy mirror with a serious expression. "Believe me, it's so."

Another housemate entered. I looked away from Zoe's intense stare and noticed the smell of floral shampoo wafting in the humid space. The girl smiled and went into a small dressing area.

Zoe changed the subject and packed up her items. "Are you having breakfast here at the house or in the dining hall?"

"Here, I think. I hope the food is good downstairs."

She shrugged. "Depends. But for the most part, you can't really go wrong with breakfast, right?"

I had to agree. "It takes a lot of effort to ruin it."

"Maybe I'll see you then," she said, walking out.

When I was dressed, I examined myself in the wardrobe mirror. *Eyes rested and alert? Check. Hair brushed and in its usual ponytail? Check.* And the uniform fit okay. I liked the plaid skirt, but the black tights would take some getting used to. I tugged at them again, trying to straighten the thick, stretchy material around my legs. *Brain ready?… I think so.*

In the end it didn't matter if the kitchen had good food, because I only ate a banana. My nerves wouldn't allow for anything more as I anticipated my first day, starting with the morning assembly.

Students streamed in from either side of the quad, boys from one side and girls from the other. There was a mixture of early morning chatter and sleepy silence in the dewy morning air, which smelled like flowers and freshly cut grass.

To get to Edwards Hall, we had to walk to the east quad and behind the castle. The huge, solid stone structure loomed over me as I looked up; it was telling me that I better be ready.

The chatter ceased, and it all seemed so formal as we filed into the hall. Stately chandeliers lit the dark, wood-paneled space. The vaulted ceiling rose to the highest point of the building, and cathedral windows welcomed the morning as the sun's rays bounced onto our bodies and illuminated the space. And on the stage, only a few chairs were filled with administrators and teachers.

"Where's everyone?" I whispered to Zoe, who had found me.

"They don't always attend. Unless it's an important meeting, like end-of-year ceremony." She added, "What's your first class?"

"Chemistry with Dr. Braithwaite."

Her sly smile reappeared. "That's mine too. If you need help getting there, we can leave together."

"Thanks, but I think I'll manage."

Zoe just nodded, because the administrators scanned our movements, keeping a watchful eye. We sat together, and another girl joined us. I had met her earlier at the house. But I couldn't remember her name—Enid? Ingrid? Irene?

What I did remember from my first impression of her was that she radiated an energy. An energy that was so stunning and ethereal that if I had believed in tales, she would've been a fairy.

Sitting beside Zoe, she leaned forward and her cherub lips formed a sweet smile as she looked at me through dark almond-shaped eyes. I smiled back, also admiring her glossy black hair, styled in a short pageboy cut. While gazing at her, I felt calm and at ease.

Mrs. Vyda's steps thundered ahead of us. When the real-life fairy quickly looked up at the stage, the spell was broken, and my nerves crept back up inside of me.

Mrs. Vyda stood, center stage, behind the podium. "Good Monday morning," she announced.

She commanded the utmost attention. So much so that she didn't need the microphone.

"Good morning, Mrs. Vyda," we answered in unison.

Just then, her mouth clamped shut as she stiffened and stared out above our heads. Three students hurried in, tucking their shirts into their pants and combing their hair with their fingers. Snickers rang out as we watched them teeter to get to empty chairs among the clusters of legs and backpacks.

The snickers transformed into mumbles and then to outright talking.

Mrs. Vyda pressed her lips right onto the microphone and a terrible noise erupted from her mouth. It sounded like the time I accidentally dropped a fork into the garbage disposal after I'd turned it on.

We jumped and winced, covering our ears.

"Students *must* arrive at our assemblies *on time*," she commanded. "Assemblies are only held once per month. There's *no excuse* for being late." Her face became even more rigid and looked like it would crack into a thousand pieces if she moved a tiny muscle.

Mrs. Vyda proceeded to talk about some administrative procedures, upcoming games, and so on. After her, two teachers stood to speak. They taught the First Years, so I didn't pay much attention. Then, Mrs. Vyda closed the assembly, and we were given twenty minutes to regroup and get to our first class of the day.

While students began to rise and shuffle out of the hall, I pretended to search through my bag for an object. I'd seen adults do that trick all the time to avoid conversation, and it always worked.

"*Mind* the grass!" growled the shed on a corner of the manicured garden. A tall, blocklike man in brown trousers, boots, and an incredibly clean white shirt emerged with a rake in hand. On his belt loop jangled numerous keys.

A small group of younger students had been wrestling and tumbled into his sacred territory. They steadied themselves on the rightful path of the paved walkway.

"Very sorry," one said, absolutely terrified, and they ran off.

"Spoiled little vagabonds," he grumbled and then scowled. His furrowed face looked like piles of soggy driftwood. When he turned his back to rake some leaves, his balding head shined as it reflected the morning light. "Keep to *your* business. And be on your way!" he snapped over his shoulder at me.

I took quick backward steps in the opposite direction.

Mr. MacLeod, I later learned, was The Murray School's main groundskeeper. His family had been connected to the estate and land for centuries. He was an expert recluse. Students, as a result, barely saw him and only witnessed evidence of his work—Mr. MacLeod wasn't one to mess with.

Looking down at my map again, I tried to figure out where my Chemistry class was located. It should've been nearby, but I felt like I was walking in a maze and was probably moving even farther away with each step I took.

"Should've taken Zoe up on her offer," I said to myself, turning the map upside down. I changed my mind and rotated the paper again. "No, you can figure this out," I muttered, and bit my tongue.

"Talking to yourself already?" a guy said with a laugh. "I know classes can be maddening, but they haven't even started yet."

My head popped up, and playful blue-green eyes greeted me.

"Can't seem to find my Chemistry class," I said, shaking my head.

"Is it with Dr. Braithwaite, by chance? I'm guessing since you're close *and* lost." I nodded. "I have him too," he continued, and glanced down at my hands. A lighthearted smile appeared on his face. "You're better off chucking that map. It doesn't help."

"One of my welcome gifts from Mrs. Vyda," I said, shoving the paper in my bag.

He chuckled, and we naturally started walking together. "My

name's Colin Stevens," he added, pointing to his chest. Colin's athletic build had a carefree stride beside me. And it would've been impossible to ignore that he was the perfect combination of handsome and cute, with bright eyes, a prominent nose, and faint freckles.

"Phoebe. Phoebe Douse. I'm a transfer student," I said, trying not to stare at his face, which didn't have an angle out of place.

Colin gave me a slight wink. "I figured already. I've never seen you in class before."

Of course, Phoebe! That's very obvious.

"So … since you're in Dr. B.'s class … you're one of the special students then?" Colin looked at me expectantly.

Before I could think of an answer, a student called out from a distance, "Prince C!"

We stopped and spotted him across the lawn. He was sitting on a table with two other guys. And you could easily pick him out from a crowd, because he had a large afro that made him look several inches taller.

"Yeah, yeah, I hear ye!" Colin yelled back, lifting his arm and pointing at them. He laughed quietly and shook his head. "I don't know why they keep calling me that," he said to me.

Short for Prince Charming, I'm gonna guess, I thought.

"We need to get more practice in," another guy from the group said. His tie was loose and his shirt was barely tucked in, but he seemed to get away with it.

They finished their short chat, and Colin glanced behind us as we continued to walk. "I'm in a band with them."

"I can tell," I blurted out. In fact, I would've even bet my entire year's tuition that he was the lead.

"Oh, really? How so?" he asked, stepping closer to me.

I examined his shaggy brunette hair that tumbled carelessly around his face and his blazer with a popped collar and sleeves that were rolled up.

"You just seem like the type," I said. Also, for some reason, I just had a hunch.

Colin nodded and seemed pleased. "Next week we're playing in a concert for the upperclassmen. Some other schools in the region also attend. It's a big deal." He glided his hand over his jawline and flashed a brilliant smile.

Yeah, definitely Prince Charming.

While talking, I didn't notice we had approached a detached structure enveloped in a thickly wooded area until Colin stopped walking, forcing me to look ahead. Like the castle, it was stone and had a domed roof, but that was where the similarities stopped.

This building was a circular tower, and a notable feature was its glass roof, which looked more like crystal because of the way it reflected and emitted streaks of multicolored light into the misty atmosphere. Vines grew alongside the stone masonry, and the ground was damp with moss, clovers, and grass. It was wild and unruly in this part of campus, and I didn't think Mr. MacLeod had any reign over the area.

Colin opened the heavy wooden door for us.

"I would've *never* found this place," I said over my shoulder.

"It's difficult to find the first time," he replied, sauntering in behind me. "But once you do, you'll never forget."

Inside was literally one room with no corners. However, the space was large, because a metal spiral staircase led upward to a gallery with a circular balcony. From what I could see, there were several types of plants and flowers upstairs—some spindly and crooked, some with broad fuzzy leaves, and others with thick branches that had talon-like thorns.

Along the back wall downstairs, numerous cabinets and shelves were filled with oddly shaped glass bottles that contained various colored liquids and solids. Other shelves had recognizable equipment for Chemistry.

Labeled containers had combinations of letters and numbers that looked like chemical compounds and substances. I was sure I'd never heard of or seen them on the periodic table. From where I stood, three tables were each perfectly surrounded by three stools, in equal distance to each other. An even larger circular table was located at the center of the room. Overall, there was a concise order and harmony.

An empty stool was at the table where Colin joined Zoe. I chose a table with the ethereal Clairmount girl. There was also a boy who was mumbling something while his head was slumped forward. His shirt was so tight, it caused two of his buttons to pop open, revealing a fleshy, protruding belly. I wasn't sure if I should tell him. After opening my mouth to say something, I closed it. He didn't seem inviting.

A few seconds passed and the boy stopped mumbling, wrote something down, and then repeated this odd pattern. Suddenly, one of his eyelids lifted, revealing a glazed-over blue eye, like a dead fish.

I waved, trying to hide the fact that I'd been staring. But he just examined me, and then his eyelid closed slowly.

"He's meditating and chooses not to talk," the real-life fairy whispered to me. "He likes to summon and write things down. Not the best at it, yet."

"Summon?" I asked.

First, Zoe's mind trick and now a meditating boy ... hmm ...

He must've overheard us, because now both eyes opened, and he frowned at us.

She patted his shoulder. "No need to be *so* sensitive about it, Atwila. You'll get better. Just keep trying."

Her encouragement only made Atwila more annoyed. He frowned again and spun away from us on his stool. All we could see was his thick back and messy brown hair.

She shrugged, and her eyes twinkled. "What did you think about your first assembly?"

"I liked how it was ceremonial," I said. Then I remembered assemblies at Crockett. "What I'm used to were just in the gym, and we'd sit on cold bleachers that scratched our legs." Seeing that she wanted to hear more, I added, "We would go for pep rallies or have to listen to our counselor lecture us about stealing, cheating, and a bunch of other stuff."

I was certain she would think that my Crockett assemblies were too down-to-earth and couldn't measure up. But to my surprise, her face brightened. "I would *love* to go to an American pep rally," she marveled and then asked, "Phoebe, you're Zoe's new roommate, right?"

"The one and only," I said.

"Ingrid, don't tell anything scandalous about me," Zoe joked across the tables.

Ah, yes—Ingrid. Zoe had saved me from asking the uncomfortable question of: Sorry, what's your name again?

Before their playful spar could begin, a cool air suddenly blasted us in our faces. Dr. Braithwaite had entered from the back door, bringing a gust of wind with him. And as he stood at the doorway to assess his space, I assessed him.

Dr. Braithwaite's frame was straight and adorned with monochromatic tones of gray—a long, starched, and tailored blazer, pants with a perfect crease down the middle of each leg, and shoes so polished they were like glossy mirrors. His round-lensed glasses fit firmly on his face, and behind them were focused gray eyes, like a hawk. The most unexpected feature, which was a welcome shock of color, was his fiery orange hair, cropped close on his head. In the tower's space of detail and organization, Dr. Braithwaite's appearance didn't disrupt or disappoint, for he was refined, defined, and confined.

He pulled out his shiny golden pocket watch with swift precision, glanced at it, and cleared his throat to demand our attention.

Class began in this fashion. Three minutes past the hour—at 9:03:03 to be precise—Dr. Braithwaite took roll while I noticed the empty stool remained empty. Calling us by our last names, he did it with the succinctness of a military roll call. "Bertrand."

"Present," a tall student answered.

When Dr. Braithwaite got to my name, he looked over his glasses at me. I thought he was going to ask me a probing question that I would have to stand up and answer. Something like, why I believed that I deserved to be in his class.

But, he just said my name, pronouncing the vowels like "house"—a mistake people often, and understandably, make.

"Here," I said. "It's actually said like the Greek god Zeus, but with a *D*."

Dr. Braithwaite raised his eyebrow so high I thought it would fly right off of his face.

"D*ouse*," he said correctly, emphasizing the vowels, and then added in a low voice, "You may very well be a beneficial addition."

An awkward smile plastered itself on my face. I had no idea what he meant, and his expression didn't look like he was going to explain.

Dr. Braithwaite moved on. "Hogg."

Atwila raised his hand.

"Houlihan."

"Present."

"Lee."

"Present," Ingrid answered.

"Robinson."

"Alive, up, and ready, sir," a guy, with a raspy voice, piped in. Another guy beside him, with an identical face and voice, laughed and said, "Here."

Twins, I assumed.

Meanwhile, Dr. Braithwaite's face didn't crack a smile. "Stevens."

Silence.

"*Stevens*," he insisted, clearly impatient.

Colin jumped and folded some papers that had music notes and scribbles on it. "Present. Sorry." He pushed the papers into his backpack.

At exactly 9:06:06, Dr. Braithwaite began his lesson. "Last week and for the rest of this term, we will be discussing the transformative properties of matter."

He stopped and looked straight at me. My heart fluttered. "Ms. Phoebe, as you're new, you more than likely will need extra time or instruction. I would suggest you set up tutoring sessions with me or Mr. Renaud, who is an excellent pupil."

His head motioned to the tall, lanky student who was sitting at the table with the twins. "Actually, Ms. Ingrid, please switch places with Mr. Renaud."

They dutifully followed his instruction, and when Renaud sat beside me, he was even taller than I'd imagined.

He had a serious expression on his long face but kind hazel eyes behind his glasses. And his neatly cut light-brown hair still had evidence of loose waves. He bowed his head at me. I nodded back in salutation.

Dr. Braithwaite continued, "What I will be teaching you for the remainder of the term is that under certain conditions you can actually *manipulate* matter to create a system that ultimately *reverses* disorder."

Everyone was nodding and taking notes as if they understood what he was saying. But I was convinced that Dr. Braithwaite didn't make any sense, and I dared to speak as I raised my hand.

Like a camera lens, his gaze zoomed in on my face. "Ms. Phoebe."

I cleared my throat. "Uhm … I'm not understanding. I've never heard this before—reversing disorder. Not even in my science class back home in Crockett." Atwila grunted beside me, and I glanced at him just in time to see him rolling his eyes. My face burned, but I managed to finish. "I thought we'd be doing experiments like osmosis, filtration … or something like that."

"Ms. Phoebe," he said right away. "I realize you're new, and so I'll excuse your failure to fully comprehend. In this class, you will hopefully realize that things you thought were impossible or unreal are *indeed* possible *and* real."

His answer wasn't really an answer, and Dr. Braithwaite promptly returned to his lesson. "Today, we are going to test this theory. We'll start slowly with a basic experiment."

The students were eager as he handed out worksheets. Meanwhile, I tried to bury my embarrassment.

Our table agreed that Atwila would be the one to record our observations, since he obviously couldn't stop himself from writing.

While I was retrieving supplies from the back cupboard, Zoe came up to me. "He takes some time to understand."

"Only *some* time?"

"He's a good teacher. You'll see. I've had him since I started here, and what he teaches us is *brilliant*."

"No dawdling back there, ladies." Without even raising his voice, Dr. Braithwaite's commanding words lanced from the front of the classroom straight to the back and right into our conversation. "Time does *not* wait for us."

"*Sheesh*," Zoe whispered, and grinned as we went back to our tables.

Throughout our experiment, Renaud was very helpful, and I wondered why he was taking the class; he seemed to know everything already. He didn't speak much, but when he did, his voice sounded literally like when I played the audio voice on my computer. As Renaud led our group, with some input from Atwila, *I* was still trying to make sense of the letters and symbols.

It was frustrating, and I needed to relax. So, being mischievous, I tried to get Atwila to speak. "I'm not sure what you wrote. It's hard to read. What does it say?" I pointed at the paper.

Atwila drew back from my hand as if it were laced with poison. And Renaud looked on in silent amusement, like he was watching someone who had poked a bear and should've known better.

Sure enough, the bear pounced. Atwila's thick lips twitched and his eyes hardened. He knew exactly what game I was up to, and he wasn't going to play. Instead, he furiously erased his letters and stabbed at the paper to rewrite the symbols. He pressed down so hard that the tip of his pencil snapped off. The sharp lead launched in my direction and hit my cheek, just below my goggles.

When I winced and rubbed my skin, a satisfied smile spread across Atwila's plump face.

"You're bleeding a little," Renaud observed, and bent over to open a drawer.

Looking at my fingertip, I saw a tiny red smear. The little beast drew blood and was happy about it!

"Here," Renaud said, handing me a wet wipe.

"Thanks," I muttered, and took the toilette.

Near the end of class, while I was placing our group's flask on the designated shelf, I couldn't help myself. I went over to a bottle filled with a bright, golden liquid and looked closely into it. The liquid was moving on its own—like there was something alive rolling around inside the bottle. I felt my hand rising.

"Do *not* touch." Dr. Braithwaite's warning was only inches away.

My hand dropped as if a three-hundred-pound weight had just been strapped to it, and I spun around.

He was right behind me, studying me with his slate-gray eyes. "Permission is earned, Ms. Phoebe," he advised.

Speechless, I ducked my head and scooted past him.

At 10:03:03 on the dot, Dr. Braithwaite closed the session with no further instructions.

A science class where we didn't know what the result would be—that was dubious.

After Chemistry was English in the main building, and it wasn't *any-thing* like Mr. Franklin's class. Mr. Franklin would always be my favorite. Well, unless someone was stellar and bumped him out of first place.

The other classes I had were also in the main building, and there were more students in each of them. I was formally introduced in one class, while in the others, I was given a casual welcome by the teachers and students. Then it was business as usual.

At the end of the day, Zoe entered our room. "You'll see that Dr. Braithwaite will be *very* helpful for you to advance," she advised.

"I hope so," I said, organizing some papers around me. "Because so far I don't see how *any* of this will be useful for college," she advised.

Zoe looked confused but didn't respond. Then she left for the dining hall while I stayed at the house to eat.

"You see the *wonder* of it all," Dr. Braithwaite proclaimed.

It was Wednesday in Dr. Braithwaite's tower, and we'd returned to our incubating experiments. Sitting with them, we uncorked the flasks and immediately started coughing and making gagging noises.

Our solutions smelled *repulsive*! Even Renaud, who seemed reserved and collected, couldn't hide his displeasure with a clenched jaw. Dr. Braithwaite, however, looked like we'd just discovered precious crude oil after months of drilling.

"It's wonderfully *rank*!" William belted out.

Wallace laughed. "Rank like *sh*—"

Ingrid pinched his arm.

"*Oww*," he whined, and rubbed his skin. A "serves you right" laugh jumped out of his brother's mouth.

Dr. Braithwaite gave Wallace a stern look. "Mr. Wallace, that's a warning for you. Are we going to have any more issues today?"

"No, sir. Sorry, sir." Wallace dipped his head in shame.

"You *think* this utterly repugnant smell is unbearable," Dr. Braithwaite commanded. "You may even think it should be rejected and thrown aside because of its odor. But don't be fooled. What you're in the process of attempting to make is a *highly* important and useful compound. But, the experiment is not complete. Now, you must add Syncabydle."

The green powdery substance was already at our tables in a bottle.

"Is this stuff for *real?*" I asked Renaud as I spun the bottle like a top.

"Very much so," Renaud replied.

Just then, Atwila reached over the table and snatched the bottle.

"*Hey,*" I said, glaring him.

"He's right," Renaud said. "You shouldn't shake the Syncabydle before it's been added to the solution."

Atwila grinned at Renaud's approval and couldn't stop grinning when he stared at the aftermath of his lead missile—a tiny scab on my cheek.

I did my best to ignore his smug face and stuck my nose underneath the collar of my lab coat while he poured the Syncabydle.

Stirring only awakened the smell even more and the foul odor still wafted into my nostrils. Luckily, after a minute or so the odor went away, and Atwila began to write observations.

"You need to correct this," Renaud said to Atwila, and started to explain more.

Automatically, Atwila put down his pencil, and he began to nod like a bobblehead toy while he latched onto everything Renaud was saying. Even rude, crabby Atwila respected Renaud—*miraculous!*

Soon after, it was time to test our experiments. Our completion grade for the week depended on its success. So the grand finale for our disgusting concoction was when Dr. Braithwaite brought a plant to each table. There wasn't anything special about the plants. As a matter of fact, they were *dead*—dry, pathetic twigs poking out of cracked dirt.

"Pour your substance onto the plant," Dr. Braithwaite said.

We followed his instruction and waited … *and* waited. We looked at one another through our goggles with blank expressions.

"*Now* what?" Wallace mumbled from his table.

And finally, the suspense was answered.

Well, *not really*.

"It's not the end of the week, now is it?" Dr. Braithwaite declared. "Return Friday to see what your experiment has yielded."

There was a collective groan of disappointment from the students, except Renaud, who probably knew what was going to happen. I also didn't groan, thinking it was all foolishness. I could hear my dad saying that too. He liked using the word *foolishness*. I personally liked how the word rolled off my tongue and got straight to the point.

"What's it supposed to do?" Colin asked.

"Yeah, can you give us a hint?" William chimed in.

"Time is at the nucleus of our existence. And so now …" Dr. Braithwaite paused to look at his pocket watch, "… we must end." He promptly exited to his office.

And just like that, class was over.

Zoe and Ingrid talked on and on about the mystery substance as we left.

Ingrid thought that we would return to a tower that smelled as fragrant as a chic perfumery. Zoe imagined that the plants would—

poof—be gone. And all the while they sounded like they still believed in Santa Claus and the Easter Bunny.

"What do you think, Phoebe?" Ingrid asked.

"I dunno," I said. "But doesn't it all seem *weird*?"

"Weird how?"

"I mean, we're doing an experiment I've *never* heard of. To make something I've *never* seen before. It stinks and then we pour it on a dead plant. Seems pointless to me."

"There's *always* a purpose to what Dr. Braithwaite teaches. Once we created a metal. It was called—"

"*Ingrid*," Zoe interrupted. "I'm not sure Phoebe would understand."

Ingrid's eyes widened, then relaxed. "You're right."

Deep inside, whether I wanted to admit it or not, Dr. Braithwaite's first-week experiment had captured some of my interest. That night, and even the next day, I thought about it.

Somehow I had a feeling the plant would come back to life.

When Friday came, the students were filled with anticipation. Reaching for our plants couldn't come soon enough. Entering class with a gust of wind and checking his pocket watch, Dr. Braithwaite instructed us to sit and not retrieve them. We tried craning our necks toward the back of the room, but they were out of our range of sight.

As he stood before us in the center of his domain, Dr. Braithwaite examined us one by one. "There are those who, time and time again, reject the truth. They refuse to believe what is so, dismissing it as what they call myth or magic. This is done to diminish or negate the significance and breadth of our world.

"*You* should *not* do as such. There's so much that exists beyond what most can comprehend."

Our fidgety impatience vanished. We were hooked on every word Dr. Braithwaite was saying.

"I'm here to teach you that you *must* endeavor to remain open to the myriads of possibilities that exist around us each day—what we see *and* cannot see with the naked eye." Dr. Braithwaite paused, looking at each of us again with a deep stare.

When he focused on me, it felt like he was scrutinizing one of those skeptics he was talking about. I wriggled on my stool, trying to avoid his eyes.

He proceeded, "Only those who are truly gifted and knowing will learn this and know how to not only manipulate but also alter and improve upon the status quo of science. *Always* be open to the truth. Now you may retrieve your experiments."

We didn't move or speak right away. We *couldn't*. Dr. Braithwaite's speech astounded us. Only after what seemed like minutes of thoughtful silence, we finally got to work.

"Would you like to do the honors?" Renaud asked me.

I shrugged. "Nah, it's okay."

I was acting like I didn't care. Not mature or honest of me, I know.

Atwila pushed his face close to Renaud, looked up, and smiled. Renaud nodded, and Atwila giddily hopped off his stool and headed to the back of the room. Gasps came from William's and Zoe's mouths. And when Atwila approached us with his round jaw hanging and practically drooling, what I saw was—

"Amazing," Renaud said under his breath.

Sprouting almost fully grown leaves, the plant's once grayish, dried stems had transformed into a muddy green color. I gulped, not knowing if I should feel satisfied or uneasy. But my surprise faded.

It wasn't even dead before. Maybe it just needed some fertilizer and that's what we made. There isn't anything spectacular about this experiment.

This was how I explained it away in my mind as the class proceeded with a discussion about the idea that we'd made a regenerative solution supposedly called $Re_1Gen_{14}So_4$.

"Therefore, we have reversed the disorder of decay and death by bringing the plant back to life," William said. And he wasn't kidding.

All the students added feedback. Even Atwila wrote something for Dr. Braithwaite to read aloud.

Inwardly rolling my eyes, I wasn't going to be hoodwinked. And yet, a little part of me wondered if there was any truth to it (just a little part, though).

"I've received input from all the students except you, Ms. Phoebe."

My shoulders tensed. I needed to come up with something, *pronto*. Breaking the awkward silence, I managed to say, "It'd be interesting to see what would happen if, uhm … we made something stronger and tested it on … a dead animal."

Dr. Braithwaite seemed satisfied enough, because he nodded and said, "I'll accept that," then concluded our class.

Walking out of the tower, Zoe turned to me. "You didn't believe what you said, did you?"

"What do you mean?" I tried to act unassuming.

"C'mon, *I* know," she insisted.

It was like Zoe had a radar for detecting hogwash.

So I caved. "How?"

"Call it … instincts." She added, "It was a good cover, though."

I glanced behind us. There the tower was, with its vines, unruly shrubs, and twisted trees. My skepticism *had been* challenged (even if it was just a little). Or maybe, it was the opposite that had happened. Maybe the beliefs I'd tried to discredit and ignore for years were slowly coming back.

Despite its hidden location, the tower stood out with all its uniqueness. The round stone building with its crystal dome was like a cylindrical sanctuary filled with never-before-seen chemicals, peculiar plants, and questionable compounds and concoctions.

Maybe, *just maybe,* Dr. Braithwaite's class would be an important learning experience for me.

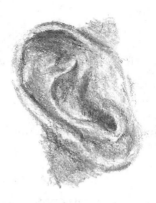

Chapter Six

LISTEN

I overheard Colin talking to the brothers about the upcoming concert at the end of another class we had together—History with Ms. Belzeebar.

In fact, the other students who were in Dr. Braithwaite's class were also in this class.

The brothers weren't twins. William was older by one year. But, they could've fooled anyone, with the same height and toffee-brown hair in similar crew cuts. If you looked close enough, you could see the slight differences. William had blue eyes while Wallace had brown. And William's nose had a bump on the bridge—an injury he proudly sported from a tackle he'd made during a rugby match the year before.

I turned to Renaud. "Are you going?"

"Probably not," he said. "I work this evening at the library." He pushed all the books he could into his bag and still had extra, so he squeezed the rest under his arm.

Sneaking a peek at them, I saw an entire range of subjects—from philosophy and chemistry to economics and trade. I wondered how his lanky frame supported so much weight as we told each other "bye."

"I agree, it's too many for one person to carry," Zoe said, walking up beside me.

She was in my head *again*.

"Ingrid and I are going. We could meet up after dinner at the house, get ready, and go together."

I hesitated.

Ingrid grinned beside Zoe. "It'll be like a *fun*, official welcome for you. You'll get a chance to be off campus and not wear your uniform."

"And we can see if our rival schools are even worthy to be called competition," Zoe added.

My eyes shifted back and forth between Zoe's insistent ones and Ingrid's hopeful ones.

Give it a try. Life is lived through the chances we take and the opportunities we make is what my dad would say.

"Why not," I said at last.

Ingrid's room was on the top floor of Clairmount House. Actually, it was the *entire* top floor. Her parents were successful businesspeople from Hong Kong, in international trade and shipping, and they gave nothing but the best to their only daughter. Ingrid also had two younger brothers. A family picture was beautifully and happily framed and sitting on her dresser.

Before Scotland, Ingrid lived in Hong Kong and England. And she traveled—*lots* of traveling. Wherever her family went on business trips or vacation, Ingrid would go, if possible—Singapore, Australia, New York, Toronto, Miami, Paris, London, and the list went on.

"I was invited here when I finished primary school in England, which was also a boarding school," she told me. She pulled on a cream-colored sweater and looked in a full-length mirror.

"Don't you miss your family?" I asked while sitting at her desk.

Ingrid turned to examine the buttons on her sweater. "When I was younger I did, but now I've gotten used to it. Also, they try their best to see me whenever possible," she said thoughtfully.

Ingrid loved her parents' attention, but they didn't understand her. They wanted her to focus on math and finance and eventually help run the family business. Ingrid, however, loved fashion. Her room was like being in a magazine or backstage at a fashion show.

There were racks of clothes, trays of makeup and nail polish, boxes of accessories, and mirrors of all sizes. There was a wall mirror, a standing mirror, hand mirrors, and even a mirror on her vanity table that could magnify your face five times larger than its original size.

"They just don't get it," she said. "I have *so many* ideas in my head. The only problem is, I can't draw. Isn't it funny? Having ideas in your head of the most wonderful designs but can't draw them? No wonder they don't take me seriously!"

"Phoebe's a good drawer. Maybe you could work with her," Zoe offered, probably remembering my drawings tacked to our walls.

"*Really?!*" Ingrid's eyes got big with excitement as she spun around.

"I've never drawn clothes before but …," I started to answer.

"If you saw what she could do, Ingrid, you'd know she'd be great at drawing your ideas," Zoe encouraged.

It would be awkward to draw someone else's ideas, but maybe

it would be fun at the same time. Besides, I couldn't refuse Ingrid's enchanting eyes. "We can see how it goes, I guess," I said.

"Fantastic!" Ingrid threw another sweater in a "reject pile" on her bed. "I'm looking for something that expresses my mood. And right now I feel *ecstatic!*" She finally settled on a vivid magenta sweater and charcoal gray shorts with decorative tights underneath.

At the moment, Ingrid's room looked like a tornado had blown through, which would've made anyone think she was a slob. On the contrary, Ingrid loved order and neatness. Just as soon as she found the outfit she wanted to wear, she took the time to tidy her room. Mom would've loved her meticulous habits.

We made it to the bus in time. There was a bus for each boarding house, and they were all parked along the main boulevard. So Clairmount girls, all thirty of us, packed into ours, very chatty and giggly. I felt a bit out of place, still not used to being around so many girls at once.

As we left the campus, the shadowy forms of trees and hills jutted and rolled on as they joined us on our journey. I looked up at the moon. The sleek curves of the glowing crescent stamped the dark sky. I liked all shapes of the moon—crescent, half, full. Naan had told me the moon was special, like me. Maybe that was why I loved it so much.

Staring out the window, I caught glimpses of my reflection in it as it blended with the glass and scenery—not what I looked like but how I felt. My face looked content. No, it was *more* than content; it was happy.

The concert actually turned out to be a battle of the bands combined with a school dance, but there wasn't much dancing. Murray students mixed in with Strathcliffe Prep, Andrews, and Albion School. Most of them seemed to know one another. They formed clusters of small groups and cliques, which is something that never changes, no matter where you go.

Electronic dance music was blaring, and teachers surrounded us on the periphery of the auditorium and near the restrooms. They even guarded areas that were roped off with red chords. It was like Secret Service for the president.

Ingrid had found William when we arrived, and Zoe and I stood together. I spotted Colin near the stage setting up with his friends. If this was a competition, he didn't seem nervous.

"Everyone likes him, that one," Zoe said loudly into my ear while the thumps of heavy percussions filled the air.

"I can see why," I answered, feeling a little uneasy that she noticed me staring.

"I've known Colin for years. And that's the way it's always been for him. He's the center of attention, even when he's not seeking it."

From the few times I'd observed Colin, I already saw how he had all the opportunity to fit in, to be part of any group, but he chose to be himself and stand out among the crowd. Colin had a relaxing and fun personality that everyone wanted to be around. And because of that, he seemed to be admired by most students.

"You're *not* his type, Zoe. Too intense."

Startled, we turned to see a Clairmount girl—Joy. She towered over us, wearing a tight black dress and heels so high that she reminded me of a clown on stilts.

"And you," Joy continued, scornfully looking me up and down, "He wouldn't fancy an American from a small, dusty town—not worldly enough."

Zoe narrowed her eyes. "It's creepy to lurk about, listening in on other people's conversations."

Joy frowned but then snickered, covering her mouth with freshly manicured fingers. "There wasn't anything I heard. It was all rubbish." She pivoted away in her shoes with surprising skill, and, I had to also admit, a natural grace too.

"*Ugh!* The cheek of her!" Zoe huffed. "She's always been that way, thinking she can carry on as she wants." A slanted smile curled from the corner of her mouth. "She's afflicted with self-entitlement syndrome."

"The princess of her own make-believe kingdom," I added jokingly.

"You're not that far off. She *is* a lady."

"*That's* obvious. Although it's a real fancy way of calling her a girl."

Zoe shook her head and smiled again, this time bigger. "*No,* I meant, she's a *Lady*. Her family is aristocracy with a castle, lots of land, and hundreds of years of influence."

"*Oh,*" I said with raised eyebrows.

"She goes by Joy. And her full name is Lady Jocelyn Elizabeth Diana something, something. Can't remember the rest. But I've come up with a better nickname—*Killjoy*."

"That works," I said with a small laugh.

Zoe became serious again and even squeezed my shoulder to get my full attention. "Colin's fun, nice, and very attractive, but he has some serious stuff to figure out."

Zoe obviously knew something more about him. Something he was dealing with that maybe had to do with his past. I understood wanting to figure stuff out. I was trying to do that for myself.

"He's trying to make sense of certain things," I said.

Her eyes narrowed. "You're very perceptive," she whispered.

When Colin got on stage with the others in his group (simply called, The Rebels), the students cheered even louder than before, especially The Murray School students. It seemed like The Rebels was known across the region. They took their time to prepare, and I recognized the guys from my first day of school, plus one other member.

The bandmate with the large afro slung his guitar on over his leather jacket, and Colin was behind the turntable. Colin pushed back his hair to put on his large headphones, and raised his hand to his mates to let them know he was ready.

They started with an intense, hypnotic beat, and as the tune developed, I wasn't disappointed. It was like listening to a professional group. The Rebels easily transitioned between different music styles. The more they played, the more we wanted to hear.

And when they finished, we hollered, whistled, and cheered for minutes. I felt sorry for the act that had to follow. And sadly for them, the lead singer fumbled and almost dropped the microphone. It wasn't a good start, and to make matters worse, she began to croon dramatically.

"*Boooo*," some students mumbled.

"Get off!" one rudely yelled, but he was hidden in the crowd.

"That's harsh," I said to Zoe.

Zoe nodded, feeling sorry for the singer too. "Rude *coward*!" she hollered and waved her fist in the air.

The tone-deaf music played on, and I had to get some fresh air. I left the auditorium soon after Zoe went over to some other students. Walking beyond the front steps of the school, I decided to go farther out onto the campus grounds until there was no one around.

I became an explorer, putting one foot in front of the other and did this for a while until the lawn turned into a big green pasture of tall grass.

And then the time passed. *Too* much time.

Suddenly, I was among dense trees and shrubs that engulfed me in a thick shroud. My eyes darted around, trying to see something familiar, but everything seemed to multiply and annoyingly all looked the same. *Nothing* was recognizable. My heart hammered in my chest when it sunk in—I was lost.

I should stay put, right? Right. Someone will find out I'm missing and look for me, right? Right.

But, my thoughts soon soured.

Oh, they'll find you. But by then, it'll be too late. You'll trip on some rotten stump in this creepy place and break your leg. Then you'll have to try to crawl your way out. But it'll be too late as you slowly freeze to death. A stiff body is what someone will find.

I shook my head, trying to get rid of those morbid thoughts, but I was lost inside my head, much like I was lost outside.

"Don't be foolish and *listen*," I said instinctively. Stunned, I stood still, not knowing what next to expect. "Go left. Keep left. And *don't* stop."

I shivered at the force of my own words.

If anyone else could've seen me that night—alone and turning around in rapid circles—they would've thought I was talking to myself, probably even hallucinating. But it was real, and it strangely reminded me of when I last spoke to Ava.

Go left. Keep left. And don't stop. The thoughts became more persistent. Instead of pushing them aside, I focused on them and decided to obey the commands.

Taking small, hesitant steps, I began to go left. After I took a few more steps, the moon suddenly burst through the trees like a strobe light. Its beams flashed and bounced around me and then sprayed over me like a cool shower.

Believe me, at any other time, I would've been *absolutely* cynical, but being in survival mode, I didn't ignore the guiding light as it extended farther ahead, brightening a way for me. I followed the path with quick, desperate steps.

And when I saw the clearing I'd previously passed, my legs pumped into a sprint. I glanced up at the moon. Was the crescent actually a smile? I smiled back at it, thankful to be out of those woods and ran through the field until I finally saw the red-stone surface of the darkened school ahead.

The buses were now in front of me, rumbling with their engines on. I slowed my pace, not wanting to look like a wild child surging through the grass. Taking deep breaths, I finally stepped onto my bus. Above my lip was slick with sweat, and I quickly wiped it off, trying to look normal. A seat near the back was empty, and I welcomed the moment I planted myself on the cool leather.

Ingrid stretched around in her seat. "Where were you?"

Steadying my breath, I managed to say with the most collected voice, "Just enjoying outside." Then, filled with sudden confidence, I added, "The place is nice, but it's *no* match for our school."

"And that's why Colin's band *won!*" Maisie, a Fourth Year, said loudly.

They all cheered, and I looked around at their excited faces—clapping and talking. School pride was definitely strong.

Then, my gaze stopped on Zoe. She wasn't clapping or cheering like the others. Instead, she examined me curiously. It was as if she somehow knew that what I'd just experienced didn't go as smoothly as I'd shared.

Chapter Seven

THE MURRAY SCHOOL, STARRING …

*B*y late October, the colder air felt like winter and the early darkness played tricks on me. The last class of the day ended at its usual time, but it seemed like night as the days became shorter and shorter. Often, it would rain for hours on end, and the winds whipped so violently that an umbrella couldn't survive. Some mornings, the sun was so bright it stung our eyes.

I thought about my family and my home, but less about Crockett. And in those moments, when I felt something more, I would think about Naan, remembering bits of her last story.

Gradually, the campus became my new town. I knew, for instance, the atrium was a popular hangout for Fourth Years on Wednesdays and Fridays. It was a five-minute walk from the main building and overlooked the distant sea. I figured out the best time to eat at the dining hall to get the best portions of food for dinner—anytime between 5:30 and 6:00 was when the kitchen staff was overly generous. And I found that Zoe and Ingrid were good company.

During one of my afternoon walks, I was passing the sports field where the soccer team was practicing. I took out Naan's picture. "What's going on?" I whispered to her as I thought about what had happened in the woods.

But, of course, the girl in the tree didn't answer. I put Naan away in my journal and zipped up my bag.

"Could ya throw the ball back in?!" a team member in a red-and-black jersey called out to me.

Trying to test my technique, I kicked the ball with my best attempt. It had an awkward spin and almost hit his shoulder, but he moved just in time. I cringed. "Sorry!"

"No worries!" he yelled back. Then he skillfully lifted the ball onto his thigh and up onto his chest before he headbutted it to the rest of the team.

"Not bad, Phoebe! Just need to practice the angle of your foot!" Colin yelled out.

I didn't even notice Colin was among them. But I wasn't surprised. *Is there anything he can't do?*

"I'll give it a try next time." I gave him a thumbs-up and walked on.

"Wait!… Hold on!"

I stopped and waited for him. When he was close enough, I could smell his sweat and faint cologne. Colin lifted up the bottom of his jersey to wipe off the sweat that was dripping from his face. "The Robinson brothers and I are going to Crails tomorrow. Also, Zoe and Ingrid are going. Maybe even Renaud too. You should come."

"Colin! You comin' back?! Stop holdin' up practice."

"Yeah, man, you can talk to girls *any* other time!"

We both turned to see his fidgety, impatient team members.

"Prince C! Prince C!" another sang out as he did a hip-hop dance move.

"Ignore them," Colin said to me. I wasn't sure if his red, flushed face suddenly appeared from the practice or from being embarrassed. "They lack propa' trainin'!" Colin yelled in jest over to them.

"*Aww!* Naw, he's *lyin'*!" one said with a laugh.

And then they kicked around the ball without him. They would just have to be patient.

"So …," he said, looking at me again and waiting.

"Sure, I think that'd be nice." My face hurt from smiling. "I'll get the details from Zoe."

"Yes, n-i-i-ce." He heard my slight Texas drawl and tried to mimic it.

It rained the morning we went to Crails. We woke to misty, steady showers and clouds so swollen and heavy they looked as if they were tumbling to the ground and swallowing the trees. But rain didn't stop any Scotlander, and it wouldn't stop me.

Ms. Daniels took a small group of us—Zoe, Ingrid, me, Alexa, Nicky, Kathryn, and Maisie. Oh, and then there was Joy, who ran to the van late, but just in time.

She entered triumphantly, said a quick hello to everyone, and began chatting with Alexa and Nicky. As Joy spoke, she reapplied some sweet-smelling lip gloss and readjusted her French braid. She wasn't going to let rushing and some rain ruin her presentation, and I admired her determination.

Joy was beautiful, with a cute nose, plump lips, and large light-brown eyes draped with long eyelashes. She could be on any runway for sure. I didn't think Joy needed to do much with her appearance to look great. As for her personality, she needed a lot of work *and* a makeover.

After my encounter with her at the concert, and every now and then when she would ignore Zoe, Ingrid, and me or give us lethal stares, I got the message about what type of person she was. But Joy couldn't ruin my first outing. It would've been stupid of me to give her that power.

As we left the school grounds, I felt like I was going on a field trip. The night before, I'd read that Crails was a small fishing town that attracted tourists, mainly during the summers, because of its food, beautiful scenery, and a traditional festival.

The pictures of the town looked like a postcard, with hilly streets, colorful fishing boats, and stone masonry buildings. I was even prepared to look like a tourist and take pictures.

"So, here's the deal," Ingrid said, turning to us with a surprising amount of morning energy. "When we get into town, we can walk around and go to Finsbury to get some supplies. Then we'll have something to eat before we leave."

The van bounced and jostled us as we went along the grassy bends and up and down around winding hills, and all the while Zoe quietly held her stomach—motion sickness.

"Never like riding on these roads into town," she declared. "*Hate* it."

Joy spun around with melodrama storming in her eyes. "Just don't make a mess," she snapped.

"And if I do, I'll know *exactly* where to put it!" Zoe snapped back.

"She'll be *fine*, Joy," Ingrid said quickly.

Joy turned back to her friends, laughing and joking, as if nothing was said.

"The split personalities of *Killjoy*," Zoe mumbled before her face wrenched.

"Just take deep breaths," I said to her, and Ingrid opened the window.

Zoe managed not throw up by sticking her face out of the window and holding firmly to the seat or her stomach.

When we arrived in Crails, our van stopped in a small parking lot next to the town's only church, which had a cemetery at the side.

"We meet here at two o'clock, ladies," Ms. Daniels said. Looking just as young as a Murray student, Ms. Daniels hopped out of the van and slid open the heavy door for us to step down.

Zoe was a bit wobbly, so I held her arm as we alighted. "Thanks much," she said, deeply inhaling to steady herself.

Ms. Daniels slammed the van door shut. "Have a *wonderful* time, ladies." She waved to us and excitedly walked in the opposite direction of the town square.

I took out my phone. Turning right, I lifted it to my face and watched the scene unfold through the rectangular screen. The view of the town in that *very* spot, at that *very* angle was perfect, with the sea close by, glistening between the narrow cobbled pathways and stone buildings with single-peaked roofs.

The people of Crails had already woken up. Shopkeepers unlocked their doors and had them propped open with wooden signs that displayed daily sales written in chalk. Townspeople and some tourists had bought the weekend edition of newspapers and were walking with them in hand or sitting on damp benches to read.

Men in windbreakers and water boots lit cigarettes and talked among themselves as they marched toward the harbor. And parents strolled with playful dogs and energetic children; their voices rang out in the humid air.

If I could just get this all in one frame. Get it to focus and include that building. The one with the dark orange roof in the dist—

"Make way, miss!" A bell noisily clinked, and I jumped aside just as a townsman, in a flapping navy blue raincoat, whizzed past me. The bike kicked up some water and muddy bits into the air, but I was fast enough to avoid it.

"*Aaah!*" Ingrid cried after I'd stepped back *directly* into her, and we tumbled onto the wet cobblestone.

"So sorry, Ingrid," I said, feeling really clumsy and dumb.

We helped each other up. Luckily, with waterproof jackets on, we didn't get soaked.

"*Haha! Haw! Haw! Haw! Ha!*" a surprisingly boisterous laugh belted out of her mouth.

For such a small girl, Ingrid had a booming and infectious laugh— imagine a hyena and a donkey blended together. It was fun and it made me laugh to hear her.

"*Phoebe!* Your face when the man … *Haha! Haw!* He … *Haw! Haw!* … you …" Ingrid bent over, holding her sides.

I was relieved she wasn't mad *and* that my phone didn't smash into pieces. While still laughing, I picked it up and wiped off the screen with my fingers—determined to take that picture.

"Did we miss something?" Renaud asked, walking up to us.

He was with William and Wallace. Their van must've arrived minutes later, and it was now parked behind ours. I hadn't expected Renaud. He seemed to be all about books, classes, and the library. And speaking of books, he had a canvas satchel slung over his shoulder.

"I didn't realize that bikes had their own lanes. But, I guess if horses can, bikes can too," I said.

"There are horse lanes in Crockett?" Zoe asked as she joined us.

"Well … sort of. In a way, yes." I blushed a little.

"That's class!" she exclaimed.

"Like a *real* western movie," William added.

Ingrid recovered from her fit of laughter and was back to business. "So, Zoe and I are going to show Phoebe around," she said to the boys. "We meet up for lunch around noon, okay?"

They all seemed to know the jig.

When we parted ways with the boys, I silently looked around for Colin as Ingrid, Zoe, and I walked in the direction of the square.

"He's over there with Joy," Zoe said as she pointed ahead.

And sure enough, there they were, ambling down a narrow decline. Joy's braid swished from side to side as she took long strides to keep up with Colin's gait. Alexa and Nicky were with a few guys behind them.

"Just curious where he was since he told me about the outing and said that he'd be coming," I said, trying to act disinterested.

"Mm-hmm," Zoe replied as we walked on.

We made a day of it in the on-and-off rain. Zoe and Ingrid showed me where the first settlers of Crails arrived. There was a large anchor marking the spot. They also showed me the council buildings on our way to Finsbury. Finsbury was the local grocery store. When we exited, they pointed out a spot just beyond the dock in the distance.

"Do you see it? The pier just beyond that blue boat?" Zoe asked me. "Where some seagulls are flying over?"

"You got it."

"That's where William and Wallace took a dare to jump into the bay," Ingrid bubbled. "They almost got expelled."

"That jump looks *wild*!" I exclaimed. "Did they hit the rocks?" I was surprised . . . but then again, after thinking about William and Wallace, I shouldn't have been.

"Nope, they only got some bruises," Zoe replied. "They probably would've wanted something broken. It would've given them more to boast about."

As we continued meandering through the townspeople and small walkways to the eatery, I thought about how Zoe, Ingrid, Renaud, Colin, William, Wallace, and Atwila weren't like the other students at The Murray School. Or, should I say *we* weren't like the other students.

How were we different? you might ask. Well, we were the only students in our Chemistry and History classes, while in Algebra and English, for example, there were different combinations of students. Also, we weren't the same ages—Renaud was sixteen while Atwila was thirteen. But then again, I figured, private schools had the freedom to structure classes the way they wanted.

Another interesting detail was that the other students seemed to have no clue what we were learning in Chemistry and History. It all seemed to be cloaked in mystery. I'd asked some classmates if they ever had Dr. Braithwaite as a teacher, but they just shook their heads. And a few of them didn't seem to know of him.

I quickly got the feeling that what we were learning was *only* for us eight students.

"Why don't the other students know about our lessons in History and Chemistry?" I asked while we were walking to the restaurant.

Ingrid and Zoe glanced at each other with the same expression—a raised eyebrow.

"We're just different," Ingrid answered matter-of-factly.

"Different how?"

"When you're here longer, you'll begin to understand."

"Think of it like we're in advanced classes," Zoe said.

I just stared, waiting to hear more.

Ingrid stopped and faced me with brown eyes and pursed lips. "You're new here, and I understand your confusion. But hopefully you'll realize that we're special. And that's why." She was suddenly intense.

I stared at her eyes darkening to black. Then, in an instant, they were a light, warm amber color again. Her eyes were changing as fast as the skin of one of those lizards Graham had really wanted as a pet—a chameleon.

"Let's not talk about that right now. I'm ready to eat!" And just like that, Ingrid's mood switched as we entered the small restaurant.

The small restaurant was tucked away at the edge of town. It was a place with no name, and the only sign at the door was a coat of arms covered with vines. The small windows were spotted with pink and yellow stained glass panes, and inside, the air was heavy and damp.

It felt medieval, like at any moment I would see men in armor and a mean-looking innkeeper serving ale.

Visitors must've spilled juice or beer on the ground, which had dried up, because the rubber soles of my sneakers stuck to the wood with each step I took.

The place with no name served the usual lunch foods—sandwiches, soups, and desserts—as well as traditional Scottish and English dishes like bangers and mash, mince and tatties, and haggis.

Just inside the doorway, we saw the others—Renaud, Colin, William, and Wallace.

A man in an apron, behind the bar, saw us. "I see it's your day in town."

"And it's good to be out!" William said as he and Wallace led the way to a long wooden table in the back.

Another man, holding a heavy iron pan above the stove-top, asked over his shoulder, "Want the usual lads?"

Wallace gave a fist pump. "Aye, you know the one."

When we were all seated, Colin turned to me. "Would you like to try something traditionally Scottish?"

"I'll just have a tuna sandwich and some fries … uhm, I mean, chips."

He smiled and gave me a playful nudge with his shoulder. "It's okay, I know what you meant."

When our food was ready, the man in the apron came over to serve us. He balanced our plates on his muscular arms, which were covered with colorful tattoos. "Ye ha'e a new friend?" he observed as he handed me my plate.

"Yeah," Zoe answered, and the others nodded.

Friend. They said I was their friend. It felt welcoming and odd at the same time.

"Enjoy," he said, placing the last glass on the table.

Right away, the brothers and Colin began digging and shoveling into their food. Bangers and mash, which William and Wallace ordered, I found out was a huge plate of mashed potatoes topped with big, thick beef sausages drowned in gravy. They were fondly given an extra sausage each, along with a large glass of soda.

Besides two other customers, it was just us. For such a small town, I was surprised that not even one or two other Murray students had stumbled in from the rain.

While we ate, my classmates shared more stories about their time at The Murray School. My eyes darted between their faces as they spoke and finished one another's sentences. They asked me questions about life in Crockett and my interests, and they seemed fascinated.

I learned that the brothers were from Edinburgh. Renaud was from Geneva. And Ingrid hated ketchup and frequently burst out with her infectious laugh, which we *all* thought was hilarious.

There were other revelations through even the silent moments. Like, when we spoke about our families, Renaud, Colin, and Zoe got really quiet. And Colin wasn't the only one with a charming smile. Not seen nearly as often, Renaud's was endearingly lopsided with a dimple on his left cheek that seemed to come out of nowhere. If Colin's smile was brilliant like the sun, Renaud's was deep like the ocean.

And then there were moments when we would look at each other in silence, as if there was an unspoken understanding among us.

Once the brothers were satisfied that they had eaten enough, we left the place with no name and found our way back to the buses. I promised myself that the next time I returned to Crails, I would go to the place that James, the cabdriver, had recommended. I would even remember to ask for Fiona. I stood at the same spot where I almost got ran over, determined to take the picture. And I did.

I felt like I could be more myself at The Murray School. There were students who were like me, not because we acted, talked, or dressed the same, but because they were each unique and wonderfully different and peculiar. Still, I wasn't ready to call them friends. *Maybe later … maybe one day*, I thought as I opened my journal and began to write:

THE MURRAY SCHOOL, STARRING …

The Mysterious Monk

Brooding Atwila never speaks to anyone, only grunts or writes down what he wants to say. A vow of silence is his method of perfecting the art of meditation. He's intense. Friend or foe? No one really knows.

The Secret Agent Spy

Clever Zoe seems to know how to finish people's sentences, and she's always in our heads. She's a brilliant sleuth. Very challenging if you want privacy but also helpful when you need someone to solve problems.

The Fairy

Whimsical Ingrid is beautiful and bold. Her eyes seem to change colors with her moods. Not shades of the same color but literally different colors. She seems to understand our feelings and cares about everyone and everything. Can she also become overly sensitive?

The Brainy Professor

Robotic Renaud is eternally attached to books. If his face is not planted in between its pages, then he's holding a book. If he's not holding a book, he's surrounded by books. He seems to generate new books just by breathing! He's first to know the answers and outsmarts us all. A computer is no match for him. But like a computer, what happens if he has a glitch?

The Dynamic Duo
Inseparable William and Wallace (aka Willy and Wally) are brothers a year apart but look exactly alike. There is no mistaking the power they have when they unite. There is no stopping them ... Unless, probably, if they are separated.

Then there was me:

The Maverick
Phantom Rider Phoebe is the new girl in town. She rode in from the west, a small country place. She's a fast-thinking straight shooter with a knack for seeing and guessing unknown things and events just around the corner. She's a mystery, even to herself. Will she figure out what she needs to learn in time?

And Colin? No, I hadn't forgotten him. It was just that the jury was still out. But there *had* to be something. He wasn't in our classes for no reason. So this is what I wrote about him:

The Leading Man
Prince Charming is everybody's friend. The quintessential popular boy in school. Always seen chatting and joking with all the students. Girls are obsessed. But who can blame them? He's smooth-talking, talented, and outgoing. Is there more than what meets the eye? We'll just have to wait and see ...

Our History and Chemistry teachers were so eccentric that I could've included them in my cast of characters.

For instance, Dr. Braithwaite rarely used a textbook and claimed that everyday scientists didn't have the ability to create or comprehend the solutions we were learning. We would spend our classes mixing concoctions with weird names like, Bobalgong, Patuoxyde, or Totosol.

I still wasn't convinced. And I believed Dr. Braithwaite knew of my skepticism, because his hawkish eyes would examine my reactions, and he would say, "The process of science is the element of surprise and believing."

It was an interesting choice of words. I always thought science was about logic and planning. We actually did do some regular experiments, like the ones you find in textbooks. Dr. Braithwaite would also say, "The basics are also fundamentally important to learn and appreciate."

I could agree with him on that.

Whenever an odd experiment was completed, I tried to have a practical explanation. But sometimes I didn't have one. I couldn't create one for the orange gas that dissolved a thick, solid block of wood into salt! Any explanation I tried to make up would've made even less sense than the experiment itself.

When I told my parents about my Chemistry class, without sharing all the details, Dad said, "Sounds like foolishness. Make sure you're learning what you need to know. Do I need to call the school?"

I assured him that it wasn't necessary.

Mom was more open-minded. "Your teacher sounds unconventional. Maybe he's just teaching a different method."

"Unconventional"—yes. "A different method"—absolutely not.

Ms. Belzeebar, our History teacher, had a very interesting perspective, and I remained curious. She taught us about objects from all over the world. She told us, for example, about a staff from ancient Greece that wrote the future and a tablet from the Persian Empire that translated *all* spoken languages. When she explained them, she would show slides. I was convinced it was local legend or folklore, but the way she described them sounded so real.

Ms. Belzeebar seemed to know everything she taught—I mean

everything. There was no question she couldn't answer at length. So lengthy that she would lose track of her own lesson. Colin, William, and Wallace enjoyed asking her distracting questions, because they knew she would spend the entire class answering them, which meant they didn't have to pay attention.

And did I mention that Ms. Belzeebar had an uncanny knack for languages? Well, she did. Imagine *any* language. She could read, speak, and write it with complete fluency. Being in Ms. Belzeebar's class was like learning several subjects at once—history, art, and any language you could think of.

While I was sitting in one of my "regular" classes one gray afternoon and listening to Ms. Fife explain another algebraic proof, a First Year or Second Year student knocked on the door and entered. His jittery glances scanned the classroom. It reminded me of a terrified squirrel staring into the headlights of my mom's car, wanting to flee but scared stiff. When the student saw Ms. Fife, he timidly went up to her and whispered.

"Phoebe, the headmaster would like to see you," Ms. Fife announced. "Take your belongings with you, and I'll send you the homework assignment."

Afraid it might be bad news from home, I packed up my things slowly. "Sure thing, Ms. Fife."

This would be the first time I would meet the headmaster. I saw him once at a morning assembly but only from a distance. He sat sternly on the stage—front and center. And he didn't speak, just listened.

Headmaster Duff looked like he was maybe in his seventies. I wasn't sure, but I just knew he looked old enough to be a grandfather. He had sleek silvery hair, was tall, and used a cane for support. The black suit he wore was impeccable. And I could even swear he was peering at me curiously during that assembly.

"I don't think you're in trouble. He seems to be in an okay mood," the student said, walking with me to the headmaster's office.

"That's good to know," I said.

He must've been the hall monitor or office aide. A toothy grin on his freckled face revealed shiny braces; I could even see he had chosen green rubber bands to help align his bite.

Our shoes squeaked on the tiled surface and then up the wooden stairs as we walked to the third floor.

"You from America?"

I'd been expecting that. "Yep. You from Scotland?"

"Aberdeen. So where exactly? New York? California?"

And that was usually the follow-up question, with *precisely* those two states (probably because they were always in the movies).

"Texas."

"Oh, you don't sound like you're from there."

I was about to ask him how I was supposed to sound, but by then we had reached the office door.

"Bye," he said, giving me another toothy grin, and he turned in the direction of where we'd come from.

I knocked, still feeling nervous.

"Enter," a deep voice from the other side instructed.

And when I did, there was Headmaster Duff, deeply immersed in reading with his elbows on the table and hands under his chin. His long fingers were pressed together like he was praying. Headmaster

Duff folded the paper and looked up at me. When his icy, translucent blue eyes met mine, my neck involuntarily stiffened. It was like a light had been shined into my face after being in a dark tunnel.

"*Ah* yes, Ms. Phoebe Douse. How are you today?"

"I'm fine, thank you. And you?" I managed to say.

"Much better now that I've been able to procure an important object during my last trip. But enough about that. Please have a seat." He gestured to a wooden chair that faced his desk. "Care for any tea or water?"

"No thank you, Headmaster Duff," I declined politely as I took a seat. "I'll be having lunch soon. So I'm fine for now."

He seems welcoming enough, I thought. *Serious, but welcoming.* I wouldn't judge a person for being serious.

I stole a few glances to examine his office. Aside from his desk and leather chair, there were two wooden chairs (one of which I was sitting in) and a grandfather clock behind me—nothing else. The windows behind him looked down onto the main quad, and they offered him a view that told everyone he was in control.

There were no pictures on his desk or on the walls, which seemed peculiar. For a man of his age, I would've thought maybe he had a family—a wife, children, grandchildren—or maybe even a dog or two. He did, however, have many stacks of newspapers, periodicals, and books that were neatly arranged in a built-in bookcase and on his desk.

"I called you into my office today simply to introduce myself and see how you are getting on at The Murray School."

My attention snapped back to his face, and I eased a bit into the chair. *No bad news*, I thought in relief.

"You have been here about five or six weeks?"

"Yes, about that amount of time."

"Tell me about your experience thus far."

I thought for a moment to make sure I was going to say the best thing—to make a good impression. "Well, I first want to say thank you for this opportunity to come to this school. I really appreciate it. So far, it's been a great experience for me." I paused. Headmaster Duff, still with those piercing eyes, was quiet. I realized he was waiting for me to say more. So, I nervously continued, "I'm really enjoying Ms. Belzeebar's class."

"And what about the students in her class? How are they? How do you find them?" He leaned in a bit to hear what I had to say.

"They're fine.... *Great,* actually. For the most part, they've been welcoming, and I've gotten to know my roommate, Zoe. She's been nice. Overall, all the students at this school have been better than I'd expected. I mean, there's always good and bad, right?... I also no—"

Suddenly, I stopped myself; I was saying too much. I was going to tell him that I'd noticed in certain classes things were taught differently, and I was curious to know why but instantly felt like it was best to leave that out.

Instead, I said something you could put on the cover of a school brochure with my smiling face beside it—something a school could use to boost recruitment. "I also know that it's a great place to learn and meet people. It has been very eye-opening and positive for me."

As I spoke, he didn't move, and I wasn't sure if he was convinced, if he expected me to say more, if he was hearing more than what I'd said, *or even* if he was seeing more than me sitting there. He was an intense man, and his presence scrambled my thoughts.

I fidgeted and acted like I was picking lint off my tights.

If Dr. Braithwaite was an eight on the scale of intensity, Headmaster Duff was *definitely* over a ten. Although Dr. Braithwaite was intense, his passion and commitment for science shined through, and there was an excitement in that. Headmaster Duff was stoic—more a head man and probably no heart. But overall, Headmaster Duff was accommodating. And, like I said, I didn't judge people for being serious.

Interrupting the silence, the hallway bell rang and simultaneously his grandfather clock chimed. Class was over.

"I do not want to keep you from your meal." He stood with the aid of his cane to walk me out. "It was a pleasure meeting and talking with you."

Relieved, I also stood and gripped the handle of my backpack. "Thanks again, Headmaster Duff and nice meeting you too."

The door closed slowly behind me.

It was a brief and strange meeting, and it was memorable.

Chapter Eight

THEY HAPPEN IN THREES

*T*hree events forced me to believe. Three events told me I couldn't deny the truth anymore. Only three. And they were significant and necessary. Why the number three? I can't be sure.

But what I do know is that there's a saying Naan used to tell me over and over again. That is, when something odd or unfortunate happens, it usually occurs in a series of three. "Learn from what has happened, and you can try to wish the third one away," she would add.

As I got older, I stopped believing her words because bad and unfortunate things still happened, even after I'd tried to wish them away.

In my doubtfulness, I'd overlooked an important part of Naan's message. It wasn't only about wishing away the bad. It was mainly about being aware of what is happening to you and around you and determining what you need to learn from the experience.

Not long after my meeting with Headmaster Duff, I found myself on a fast track to understanding this lesson. And it all started with a celestial event.

First Incident—Wednesday: The Solar Eclipse

"Don't forget that tomorrow afternoon there will be a solar eclipse. So mark your calendars and set your clocks!" Ms. Belzeebar chirped. "We'll have absolute totality, which means the sun will be one hundred percent covered by the moon!" Bouncing in her seat, she added, "This will be the *first* one seen in this region in *over* two hundred years. Anyone recall another special feature of this eclipse?"

Renaud answered, "The sun and moon will appear two times larger, because the eclipse will happen while the sun is setting."

Wallace added, "And totality will be about two minutes, which is rare." He was slouching back in his chair, like at any moment he would tune out and fall asleep.

Ms. Belzeebar was so pleased and surprised that she jumped up and scurried over to him. "Yes, *yes*! Exactly!" she exclaimed and clapped right over his head.

Startled, Wallace scrambled to sit up, knocking his book to the floor.

Ms. Belzeebar's amazement, however, was short lived.

"Does this mean no class?" William blurted out.

"A-a-a*ooooooo*!" Wallace howled.

She sucked in air through her teeth and shook her head in dismay.

When the bell rang, the brothers dashed out, excited to be somewhere else.

On the Wednesday afternoon of the solar eclipse, the entire campus gathered to watch. The school stopped classes, and we were given special glasses to protect our eyes. It was an Event—with a capital *E*. All the students, administrators, and staff stood outside, *even* on the manicured lawns. Looking up at the sky, we awaited the phenomenon, not to be seen again for another two-hundred-plus years.

When the moon began to pass over the sun, everything and everyone was still, except the sea tide. It became even more alive, roaring and raging as the waves crashed against the docks and cliff edges. The sky darkened and deepened, and I shuddered as the air became colder. The moon boldly shrouded the sun.

Oddly, the more the moon covered the bright light, the more my head felt like a balloon, bobbing and floating. My legs wobbled as I swayed, and my glasses dropped to the grass. Bending down to pick them up, my skull and brain suddenly transformed into a heavy slab of concrete.

Splash … Splash … Splash, Splash, Splash. Dark red drops spattered to the ground, and a copper taste filled my mouth. My body jolted with an intense energy that caused my heart to race.

"Don't look strai … the su …" were the last muffled sounds I remembered hearing.

My body crumpled, and I hit the ground.

"*Where* am I? *Why* am I here?" I asked a lady standing over me as something was tightening around my upper arm.

"My name's Ms. Clarke. I'm the school nurse," she said, squeezing the bulb of a blood pressure monitor. "You fainted." Nurse Clarke's gray hair was pulled back in a tight bun, except two long tendrils tickled my forehead when she leaned forward. The pressure released around my arm, letting out a loud hiss.

"How long have I been here?"

"About five minutes," she said as she handed me a Kleenex and gestured toward my nose. My nose had bled, and I quickly wiped it.

She checked my pulse, asked me a series of questions, and handed me some water with something fizzy inside. Thirsty, I drank hurriedly, ignoring its bitter flavor.

I heard Ingrid's and Zoe's voices on the other side of the door when Nurse Clarke stepped out of the room. When she returned, my parents were called. Can you imagine the panic Mom had over the phone?

"Return first thing in the morning. I don't think it's anything serious. But just in case," Nurse Clarke instructed after hanging up the phone.

Zoe and Ingrid came in as she left the room. They were genuinely concerned, and it felt awkward getting this kind of attention from my schoolmates.

"I'm fine," I assured them, slowly getting up. "By the way, how did I get here?"

"Two guys on the rugby team had to carry you," Zoe replied.

I covered my face and shook my head. I imagined myself passed out with a bloody nose and flailing arms as two guys had to carry me.

"Don't worry, you still looked great," Ingrid said, and I managed a weak smile.

We left the infirmary together. Outside, students were walking around like normal. The only thing extraordinary that had happened for them was the eclipse. Some were still talking about it, sharing photos from their phones.

The next day, I felt fine, but Ingrid wasn't convinced, and she insisted on walking with me to the infirmary. When Nurse Clarke looked at my vitals again, with the on-call doctor over the phone, I heard the best news ever. There was definitely no problem! I updated my parents. And with the end of our conversation, I closed the chapter on my little fainting episode.

If I'd thought about what Naan taught me, I would've been more aware. I would've noticed the significance of fainting on the same day a solar eclipse happened.

Second Incident—Saturday: 3:32 a.m.

"Three thirty-two!" I heard myself cry out. It felt like electricity was pulsating through my body. But the funny thing was—I didn't move.

"Wake up," a voice demanded.

"Huh?" I opened my eyes and looked around the dark room.

Zoe sat over me in my desk chair. "What's going on, Phoebe?" Her hands were on my shoulders, and her eyes narrowed with concern. "You were talking in your sleep, and then you yelled out the time."

"I just called out some numbers," I whispered, trying to calm my racing heart. "How could I know the time? You just woke me up."

"Well you *did*. I was sitting right here and heard."

I dared to look at my clock—3:33 a.m.—and shuddered. "What else was I saying?"

"That an honored code was broken and caused separation. Two people are missing. I'm not sure of the rest." Zoe's voice trailed off, trying to come up with more, but she shook her head.

Naan's story! I sat up straighter. "You didn't hear anything else? Anything *more*?" I pleaded. The look on Zoe's face made me uneasy. "What is it? Just *say* it."

"You've had experiences that most people wouldn't understand. Things that people would call you a liar or crazy for saying."

In the darkness, with a hint of moonlight, her eyes glowed like a deep lagoon that flickered with turquoise neon light. I quickly looked away from her intense stare.

I'd learned my lesson about telling secrets and wouldn't make that mistake again. "Nope," I said.

"Haven't you wondered why you're here? Why you're learning those experiments in Dr. Braithwaite's class? Why Ms. Belzeebar knows so much about what she teaches? I know you've wondered because I *can* know."

"*Stop.* Stop right there," I demanded, holding up my hand. It was too much for me to hear.

"But you *do* know," Zoe insisted.

"Look, I appreciate your kindness. You're a good roommate. Really, you are. I'm here because a teacher in Crockett recommended me. If there's anything else going on with me, it's *my* business." I regretted my words the moment they tumbled out of my mouth. But I still added, "I've *only* known you for a few weeks out of my *entire* life."

For the first time since I'd known her, Zoe looked dejected, and she silently scooted out of my desk chair.

But, in true Zoe fashion, she scolded me. "You're being a ripe idiot, if you ask me," she said, getting under her covers. "You can't explain away everything with so-called logic and facts. It's *foolishness*."

My mouth dropped open. "That's my ..."

Zoe had used my word. A word I thought of all the time but *never* said aloud. She turned her back to me in her bed, and I fell asleep feeling extremely guilty. My stupid pride had stopped me from apologizing.

Zoe's bed was empty when I woke up the next morning, and my

guilt was still there. Deep in my gut, it felt sour and it churned. My computer interrupted my thoughts. It was Mom checking up on me.

"How are you, dear?"

"Great. I'm great," I said, sounding short and irritated. "The only thing is I'm tired, so I can't talk long."

"Hmm, maybe you should see the nurse again," she mused.

"I'm o-*KAY*. I'm just trying to make sense of some things."

"What things?" Mom sounded curious.

"Fainting and then …"

"And then what?" she prompted.

"I talked in my sleep this morning—called out three thirty-two."

In an instant, the mood changed when Mom gasped. "Phoebe, that was when you were born," she whispered.

My stomach churned again. "Are you … sure?"

"Of *course*. A mother wouldn't forget that. For weeks, your Naan insisted that you would be born during a full moon."

As I listened, I could hear my uneasy breaths echoing through the airwaves.

"Sure enough, you did. Three thirty-two in the morning. And your grandmother was there for your birth. She named you. Remember I told you that?"

"Yep," I lied.

She laughed a beautiful sound. "Since you *don't* remember, I'll also tell you *again* that Phoebe is associated with the moon."

"A mighty Greek Titaness. It means, bright and shining," I added, trying to impress her as I looked up more information on the internet.

"The moon and you. A lovely connection, don't you think?" Mom admired.

Lovely wasn't the word that had come to mind. For me, I felt strange. The solar eclipse and the moon that led the way the night I got lost in the woods were connected to me.

"Me fainting and waking up at this time—of *all* times. What do you think Naan would say?" I was actually looking at her picture when I asked that.

"Very often," Mom said with a sigh. "I didn't understand my mother."

"*Really?*" I said, sitting back. "I thought you were both close."

"We cared for each other, but often times, she was very distant. *But,* I always believed there was something about her. Something that allowed her to … How do I say? … See?"

"A See-an'-Know."

"What was that, dear?"

"She was a See-an'-Know. She told me."

"*Oh,*" she said, sounding stunned. "She never told me that."

We were silent as I realized that Naan would probably always remain an enigma.

"Whatever this is," Mom said, breaking the silence, "don't ignore its significance. And maybe it's a good message. Your birth was a happy occasion, and your grandmother loved you specially."

After Mom and I hung up, Zoe walked in soon after, and I tried to sound extra cheerful. "Morning!"

"Mornin'," she grumbled, barely looking at me and went straight to the bathroom.

I ran downstairs to the kitchen and made the shake she enjoyed drinking, then made one for myself. I wrote a short note on her napkin:

Sorry about ~~last night~~ early this morning :-)

Zoe was at her desk when I entered. It didn't seem like she even noticed my existence. I couldn't blame her as I handed my offering to her.

Would she forgive me? Throw it in my face? Ignore me?

Taking the cool glass, Zoe stared down into it. Then she finally spoke. "I don't have the kind of support I would've ..." Her voice became shaky, and she quickly clasped her throat as if she were annoyed for sounding vulnerable. Zoe let go of her neck, but her slouching posture showed her discomfort. "Ingrid, Colin, Renaud, William, Wallace, and Atwila ... well sometimes Atwila," she smiled and glanced up at me, "are like family. I don't have anyone else, really. So sometimes, I can be a bit clingy."

It made sense why Zoe never really spoke about home, didn't have weekend phone conversations, and didn't receive packages like the other students or I did.

"*Ugh,*" Zoe muttered, and quickly rubbed her eyes.

Zoe, like me, didn't like to show tears.

And seeing her like this, I decided to open up as my tense shoulders relaxed and I sat on my bed. "Zoe, I've never really asked about your life or your home and that's been selfish of me. But since I've been here, I've been realizing again what real friendship could be like."

Zoe's sly smile returned. "And you could be a part of it, *with* us ... if you want." Taking a drink, she accepted my offer.

A truce was made.

Third Incident—Sunday: The Figure in the Tree

Sunday, I managed to sleep without waking up too early. *Success!* I went on my morning walk to organize my thoughts. I knew there was something odd happening, which had always been happening to me. I would've been dumb and clueless if I didn't accept that. Even a logical and rational person *had* to admit there was *something* going on.

There's a winding path behind the castle that has the best view of the sea and bluffs in the distance.

And as I strolled along it this particular Sunday, I opened my journal and began to jot down phrases: **Born at 3:32 a.m. on a full moon. Naan named me Phoebe = moon. Solar eclipse and fainted. "Find them both." An honored code was broken.**

Then I wrote down things that I began admitting to myself: **I can sometimes know when things will happen. And even see past events. I can know details about people I barely know. Naan said she was a See-an'-Know. Am I?**

As I stared at the question I'd just written, a soft scratching sound came from a darkened place where the trees grew thicker. The scratching grew more persistent, which forced me to stare between the branches.

Whatever it was began to *move*. The space around me darkened as its wingspan covered every patch of light. Feeling like an Olympic track athlete jumping off the blocks, I bolted in the opposite direction.

"I don't know why you bother," Zoe said to Ingrid. "Those brothers don't take anything seriously. You're wasting your time with him."

"But somehow William and I get each other," Ingrid said.

Ingrid's and Zoe's chatter sounded faraway, as I stared at my shoes, watching shadows leap around them.

During dinner at the dining hall, and now walking back to our house, I'd been thinking about when the moon guided me out of the woods, Ingrid's mood-switching eyes, Zoe's ability to know what I was thinking, and whatever it was that I had run from that very morning.

Just then, my hands felt empty. "I left my wallet," I announced.

"Want us to come?" Ingrid asked.

"No worries," I said, shaking my head. "You can go on without me." We parted ways in the main quad.

I was positive there would've been at least one thief in the hall that night, but my wallet was exactly where I'd left it. Pleased and surprised, I headed back to Clairmount. While passing a few trees and empty benches, I suddenly stopped. At that moment, I felt the same shocking electric pulse. It started at my feet and rushed all the way up to the crown of my head.

Out of the corner of my eye, a presence emerged, and I slowly turned to face it. There the figure was again—perched in a darkened tree. Shock took over, but instead of running like I did that morning, I allowed it to run its course through my veins until fright took its place. But then fright quickly disappeared and interest seeped in.

It was an owl, with a wizened and hypnotic look in its feathered face and large amber eyes. I peered at it, and it peered at me. I ducked my body behind another tree to hide, and it dipped and swiveled its head to find me.

That was when I realized … the owl *knew* me.

Immediately, a memory surged forward in my mind. One night, while my family and I were watching comedies, Naan stopped our laughter by just raising her hand.

She gathered Graham and me under each arm, guided us to the window, and pointed. "You see the owl?" she asked.

117

"Yes, Naan," Graham and I answered as we glanced at each other confused.

"It's wanting to share something important. It wants to share that someone will pass and will no longer be on this earth."

I shrunk back under her arm.

"You're scaring them," Mom urged under her breath. "It's not the best way to share this information, don't you agree?"

Naan shook her head. "Nonsense." Her amber eyes softened when she looked down at me and rubbed the top of my head. "Phoebe darling, we all pass this way. It's part of our journey. We're living beings connected to an earth that takes care of us."

Naan always had a way of reassuring me. Her words could soothe me like a cup of hot chocolate.

"The owl is there to tell us that, yes, there's death. But also whoever it is, the person is special and thinks we're special. A message of comfort is being sent to us."

I sighed with relief, and she hugged me.

Two nights after we saw the owl on our roof in Crockett, my father got a call. His childhood friend had passed away from a long battle with cancer.

While remembering Naan's message in the main quad of The Murray School, I understood why the owl knew me—the way it perched in the tree and those amber-colored eyes. When the bird knew I recognized its purpose, it gracefully expanded its wings, hovered above my head, and then flew away toward the sea.

The three events weren't random and unfortunate. Yes, they were odd, but in a good way. I finally decided I needed to know and truly find out more about who I am.

Chapter Nine

THE PATH TO DISCOVERY IS RARELY STRAIGHT

*M*r. Onslow, my seventh grade History teacher, skimmed over the lesson about Christopher Columbus's voyage. Leaning back in his chair with legs stretched and mud-caked cowboy boots propped on top of his desk, he stared blankly at the pages of the textbook he was holding. "Columbus set out for India to get spices for the Spanish monarchy," he drawled. "Instead, Columbus unknowingly found the Caribbean and … er … uhm …" He frowned and snapped the book shut. "That's why the Caribbean is also named the West Indies."

I inwardly laughed at Columbus's mistake. Why didn't he know he was in the wrong place when other explorers had already been to India and described what it was like?

Mr. Onslow took a swig of coffee from his overused mug and groaned through gritted teeth—the hot liquid must've burned his throat. Then, he looked up as if he finally cared to notice a classroom filled with impressionable twelve- and thirteen-year-olds.

"Look, you get the gist," he went on, tapping the textbook against his thigh. "Frankly, I don't know why I've gotta tell y'all all of this. *None* of this matters. Believe me, by the time you're my age, you'll realize this. If you're smart enough, you'll realize much sooner." He gulped down the last of his coffee and groaned again. "All y'all need to know for the upcoming test is the year 1492 and that Columbus is known for discovering the new world."

And that was that.

I don't think you'd be surprised to hear that Mr. Onslow was fired soon after that lesson. But it wasn't even for his "don't care" attitude; he was arrested for disorderly conduct outside of town—a drunken brawl. After the school caught wind of it, he was fired.

When I told my parents about the lesson, Dad was obviously annoyed. "Is this what my tax dollars are paying for? Is that all he taught you?" He shook his head. "Christopher Columbus is not the be-all and end-all," he added. Determined to set things straight, he said, "Let me share with you the *real* history of the West Indies, particularly Jamaica. It's one filled with intrigue, power, and pirates."

And what he said to me went like this: Yes, Christopher Columbus did mistakenly find the Caribbean, but there was so much more that followed. Columbus's arrival opened the Caribbean to exploration from Europeans, and the sea became a battleground for global domination. Warring Spanish conquistadors and English Royal Navy ships constantly fought for control of the region.

With the promise of wealth and hunger for power, there came greed and mayhem. Violent, adventure-seeking pirates and buccaneers stole from wealthy ships and stashed their booty in caves and hidden places throughout the islands.

England swiftly took control of Jamaica from Spain, and by then, the native Arawak Indians barely survived. The island became populated mainly with slaves from Western and Central Africa and slave owners and prospectors from Great Britain. East Indians were also on the island as indentured servants.

Further, Jews from Europe came, seeking refuge from persecution as well as opportunities. After slavery was abolished, with the help of brave slave rebellions, people from other European countries as well as Chinese, Syrians, and Lebanese continued to settle on the island.

Even with the island's history of slavery, corruption, and colonialism, there persisted a perseverance and hard work among Jamaicans. History and different cultures influenced everything, and they intersected and blended, creating a society and a system.

I never grew tired of hearing that story. The story of how the whole world came to a small island. It was why I believed Naan knew so much and had an eye to this world and beyond. I thought her background gave her an innate knowledge and wisdom that passed through generations and time.

I was now going into unknown territory to discover what my abilities were and how the school—particularly Headmaster Duff, Dr. Braithwaite, Ms. Belzeebar, and the seven students—and I were connected.

Treating my voyage like an experiment, I needed to gather evidence from multiple sources. There would be the library and the internet. Then, there was plain old snooping. If things weren't going to be obvious, I had to find my own ways of sneakily getting information.

But after a couple of failed attempts at snooping, I soon realized it wasn't my thing. In fact, I was *terrible* at it, maybe because I felt like I was intruding, so I hesitated to reach for that photograph or piece of paper on Zoe's desk or sneak an unknown bottle out of Dr. Braithwaite's class. And soon, the perfect moment would slip by as Zoe returned or Dr. Braithwaite's scanning, hawkish eyes landed on me.

When you're snooping, timing is key. But I really shouldn't give you advice on that, should I? It's a matter of ethics, you see.

On the other hand, asking questions and obtaining information from people and sources—I was much better at that.

So I created a plan. **The first step** to gathering information from a person is to pique their interest. Find something they like or are good at and begin to talk or ask questions about it. **Second step,** while they're answering, include your opinion and listen to their responses. **Third step,** during their response, gradually move the conversation into a direction to include the questions you really want to ask.

And, as with any experiment, there are rules:

Rule #1: Remember which information is most important so you don't become confused or sidetracked.

Rule #2: Do not, under *any* circumstances, be fake or say something you cannot support or prove; people can sense falseness. And when seeking the truth, you have to approach the process with truth. Mom had taught me that.

Rule #3: Naan told me never to underestimate the intuition of others. Even if they're not that intuitive, assume they are.

Rule #4: From my own experiences with my brother and his stubbornness, I included the rule of choosing people wisely. Not everyone is available or welcomes questions. That was why I knew neither Atwila nor Dr. Braithwaite would share anything—Atwila was silent and suspicious and Dr. Braithwaite was strict and shrewd.

This was my plan. You could call it **"The Phoebe Douse Plan."**

The library was disappointing; there were basically books for "regular" classes. So, I went there mainly to use the computer. I did, however, manage to find a book about the moon and solar eclipses.

"What are you reading?"

I quickly pushed the book under my hand. "Nothing," I said, looking up at Colin.

"Looking guilty," he teased. "C'mon, I won't tell."

"*Shh!*" an annoyed whisper came from a nearby table.

He slid into the seat next to me and reached for the book from underneath my fingers. Turning it over, he skimmed the back. "Moon cycles, huh?"

"Just a new interest."

"I heard about what happened to you. You know—" Colin's eyes rolled to the back of his head, and he threw himself out of his chair, collapsing on the floor. A few students spun around in surprise but then went back to reading when they saw him jumping back up on his feet.

"Haha, thanks for the reenactment," I said sarcastically.

"Is that why you're reading this?" He suddenly sounded serious.

"You could say that. But all is better now, see?" I held up my finger to my face and made my eyes follow it from left to right.

He laughed. "I like your humor."

Colin was sitting so close to me that I noticed the patterns his faint freckles made on his cheeks. His blue-green eyes moved across my face, as if he were noticing details on it.

"Do you have any special interests in …" I stalled. My brain froze.

Colin looked confused, and soon after, his phone blared a rock music medley in his pocket. He jumped and dug for it. "Forgot to turn this thing off."

"*Shhhhhhhhhhh!*" another student hissed at us. This one's head snapped up and gave us a look of extreme annoyance.

"Somebody needs an exorcist," Colin whispered to me with an amused smile. I welcomed the distraction as he read his message. He eventually glanced at me. "I've got to go, but I'd like to hear more about *special* interests." He winked and left the library in a haste.

I opened my computer, book, and journal again. **Note to self: Figure out useful questions to ask students and Ms. Belzeebar…. And <u>make sure</u> to come up with believable excuses.**

I chose to also test my plan on Ms. Belzeebar after her class that week. Since she loved to talk, I thought, *How hard could it be?*

As she sat at her desk and the others filed out of the classroom, I approached her. "Ms. Belzeebar, I just wanted to share that the solar eclipse last week was absolutely phenomenal. Thank you for telling us about it. Do you have a special interest in moon cycles?"

My question opened a floodgate of enthusiasm.

"Oh, how *wonderful* you have an interest!" She sang the word *wonderful* off-key.

"I couldn't find anything in the library," I went on.

"Anything on what?... Oh! The moon cycles and solar eclipse?"

"Yes."

"Hmm, I see ... well the library can be limited on such a subject, but I would suggest you read this." She began writing something down on a piece of paper. "I also have some materials in my office that I think you'll find *very* fascinating! But first, look into what I wrote."

Then, I tested the third step of my plan.

"You're always so informative. How do you know so much? I would love to understand how." And it wasn't flattery; I actually meant it.

Her hand went to her chest, and she blushed. "Oh, you could say it's a special gift." She made a soft snorting sound as she giggled.

Interesting use of words ... a special gift.

She looked up at the wall clock behind me. "I have to go into town. But let's continue our conversation. Shall we agree on next week during my office hours?"

"Sure, Ms. Belzeebar. That would be great," I said with a tight smile, disappointed I would have to wait.

After classes, I went to the library to look up the website Ms. Belzeebar provided. Her source didn't look like any website I'd used before. It seemed more like an extensive database of folders with codes and files that were password protected. I could only access the folder she shared with me. It had a never-ending password, which matched Ms. Belzeebar's personality: /0veh!$tory@@marve/ou$!h!st0ry@123.

Through her source, I found information that talked about frequencies that emanate from the moon and how it can awaken a part of our mind that houses psychic abilities.

I concluded that the moon had a force that affected me and that the solar eclipse must've reawakened my awareness and heightened my abilities.

Also, through typing in phrases like *knowing the future* and *knowing a lot about a person you just met or never met*, I found: **Clairvoyance. Precognition. Claircognition.**

I'd never heard of these words before. Writing and looking at them made it more real to me … and more acceptable.

By the end of the week, I was drained. I shuffled into my room, threw my bag on the floor, and was about to fall onto my bed for a nap.

"*Ha! Haw! Hawha!*" Ingrid burst into the room with Zoe.

Perfect time to ask, I thought, straightening my back and turning around.

"Tonight," Zoe announced. Zoe must've seen how surprised I was. "You've been trying to get information," she said with a blank stare. "There's a meeting tonight, and you should come."

"I thought you said we shouldn't," Ingrid urged Zoe.

I approached them. "Shouldn't what? What are you talking about?"

"It's what I was trying to tell you that night," Zoe said.

Ingrid shook her head. "I'm not sure she's ready."

"Well, if she's not, that'll be on me. But I think it's time we tell her."

"*Hello*," I said, waving my hand at them, "I'm *still* here, and yes, I want to come. What'll it be about?"

Zoe thought for a moment and then said, "You'll have to come, hear what we say, and see for yourself."

So I barely used **The Phoebe Douse Plan**, and it needed some fine-tuning. But all in all, I did get some answers, and that night, hopefully, I would discover more about the seven students and how I was connected to them.

I stood, waiting with Zoe in our room. We wore sweats as dark as the night to blend into the surroundings we were about to venture into. Zoe was looking out the window when her phone dinged. She read the message.

"That's Ingrid," she explained. "She goes out first and makes sure everything's good. She's waiting for us at the end of the main quad."

We tiptoed down the stairs through the sleepy silence. Zoe seemed to know exactly where to place her feet to avoid making the floorboards creak, so I followed her.

Passing Ms. Daniels's room on the ground floor wasn't a challenge at all. Although she slept with her door ajar, Ms. Daniels would've never suspected any of her amazing Clairmount girls of sneaking out, and we passed her room with ease.

At the back exit, Zoe used one hand to turn the knob and the other to hold the door frame, making sure the latch didn't click too loudly. We stepped out onto the patio, and I was about to keep walking, but suddenly, Zoe slung her hand out in front of me.

"*Ouch!*" I yelped in a loud whisper when her hand collided with my stomach, and she roughly pulled me behind the bushes. Zoe pointed just ahead. There was Mr. MacLeod making his nocturnal rounds.

"He's like clockwork," she whispered. "He should pass soon."

And sure enough, Mr. MacLeod did when the beam of his flashlight turned toward the opposite side at the boys' end of the quad.

"We'll have to run over there." Zoe pointed, then dashed off.

I took off too. "I didn't know you meant *now*," I said in a stunned whisper.

We ran along areas that were densely packed with trees and shrubs, being careful that nothing scratched our faces and hands. Zoe was a pro. I, on the other hand, felt the sting of branches scratching my hands. We ran the entire length of the quad, until we approached a small figure crouched in the bushes. It was Ingrid.

"If you see *any* light or movement, *get* to the ground," she said to me.

Walking and crouching a few times, we then passed the pond and eventually stopped. I recognized the spot. It was where I ran from the owl, and there was a small clearing inside the wooded area. Two bodies in black already sat on a blanket in the open space, one thick and short, the other tall and thin—Atwila and Renaud.

They turned around. I wasn't sure if they were expecting me.

"Yes." Zoe answered my thought in the darkness.

We sat with them, creating a circle.

"Let's see if they'll show up," Ingrid suggested.

Maybe we waited for a minute … or even five … I couldn't tell you for sure, but Zoe broke the silence. "We have to start now," she said.

"It can be difficult with Mr. MacLeod out there. Maybe they need more time," Ingrid begged.

"They're not coming," Zoe said bluntly.

They must've agreed because at that moment Renaud reached behind him and started pulling something out of his bag.

I thought there was going to be some huge revelation at that moment, like a chant or a bizarre initiation ceremony where he'd take out a chalice, which I would have to drink from or swear a blood oath.

But, Renaud only pulled out an electric heat lamp, put it in the center, and clicked it on. Our faces were now dimly illuminated: Renaud's serious and thoughtful, Zoe's determined, Ingrid's disappointed, and Atwila's swollen with his usual huffiness. Mine probably looked intrigued or at least curious.

Ingrid began, "We invited Phoebe because she wants to know more about us. And we want to share who we are with her."

"Before we begin," Zoe said to me, "you should know that we're just a group of friends. We're not a club, and we don't have assigned leadership. We meet like this about once a month to share and learn about our abilities."

Renaud explained, "We meet privately because other students don't know about us. We were first invited by a small group of Murray students who also took our special classes, and they started here before us. We don't know when these meetings actually began, but each year the tradition has continued."

I wondered how much The Murray School knew about us, and then I thought about Mr. Franklin's connection to the school.

They looked at me. It was my turn to speak. "Okay ... but before I start ...," I started, "I first want to hear from one or two of you. I think it's best so I can know who you are before I share about ..." My voice trailed off as I tried to think of the best way to explain myself.

I wanted to know I could trust them. I had just replayed in my mind the time when I told Ava my secret.

Ingrid understood. "You want to know if you can trust us. Or if we are who we say we are."

"Basically."

"Hold my hand," she said.

"What?"

"Hold ... my ... hand."

So I did. There was no weird feeling or sensation, and I just sat there.

Then she began to speak, "Excitement, nervousness … and now surprised with a mix of extreme interest." She let go of my hand and smiled.

I was intrigued—perhaps she *was* an enchanting fairy.

"Not exactly," Zoe remarked.

My eyebrow raised.

"Not a fairy," she said.

"An empath," Ingrid explained.

"Like the word empathy. Meaning you understand feelings, right?" I asked.

"I don't only understand feelings. I also *feel* them." Ingrid's eyes brightened. "And, maybe, one day I'll even be able to impact emotions."

"We're all working on our abilities," Zoe said. "Some of us are more advanced than others, but we're all in training, with the help of Dr. Braithwaite's and Ms. Belzeebar's lessons."

It was all falling into place. And somehow I wasn't surprised as I said, "And Zoe, you must be able to read minds. I've noticed you finish my thoughts or answer questions I don't even say aloud."

"Sorry about that," Zoe said. "Sometimes I can't help it. Other times, I'm trying to practice, but it can be a bit much. Formally, what I have is called telepathy."

All these weeks, I was with students who had such extraordinary abilities. And now, it was my turn. I knew I was surrounded by individuals who were open and accepting. I finally decided to admit the truth—a truth I didn't even totally share with Ava.

"Since I was young," I began, "I've been able to see and know things about the future and facts about people, including their pasts. It's when my thoughts speak. I used to deny it and push it away. I even forced myself to forget, but I can't and won't anymore."

I paused, and they leaned in closer as I said, "When my thoughts speak, I'm not rambling or thinking regular things. It's not even my opinion. When my thoughts speak, it feels different…. I think it's called precognition and maybe also claircognition. It can be a very overpowering experience."

Ingrid squeezed my arm. "That's *incredible!*"

"I always wanted to share with you," Zoe said. "But I had to hold back. Bite my fat tongue. All I can say is, it took you long enough."

"Yeah, fourteen long years," I said, and chuckled.

"It sounds like you could have claircognition or precognition," Renaud explained. "And you could be both. But also the fact that you have some idea of the pasts of others, I think it means something more or different."

Ingrid added, "And just like us, you need practice to improve."

To tell you the feeling I had—all I can say was that I was relieved and happy, being with people who were understanding.

"And you, Renaud, what's your ability?" I asked excitedly.

He looked away into the darkness. "I don't have one," he whispered.

"*What?*" My jaw dropped. "I just thought you did. That we *all* did."

Renaud shook his head in disappointment and looked at me again. It was like he'd just flunked a grade. "I can't be counted as one."

"Renaud is an expert in researching information, gathering facts, and understanding data," Ingrid encouraged. "He understands the value of our abilities and is *very* knowledgeable."

I nodded and smiled. He smiled back at me, and his dimple appeared.

"What about the others? Colin, William, and Wallace?" I asked.

"*We* can't tell you. It's *their* business," a squeaky, animal-like voice piped into the air.

I jumped at the sound and turned in its direction. "Wait a minute. *You're* speaking now?" I'd totally forgotten Atwila was there.

"Of *course*! I can speak whenever *I want*." His squeak transformed into a croak and then gradually went away as his vocal chords became more relaxed. Atwila tilted his head in impatience. "*Anyway*, as I was saying. *They're* not here, and we all speak for *ourselves*."

"Atwila, don't be rude," Ingrid advised.

"I'm just telling her the way it is." He shrugged dismissively.

"I know, but your delivery," Ingrid said, shaking her head like a mother, "is too abrupt."

"And you, *Sir* Atwila? Please do grace me with your words and share," I said sarcastically.

But Atwila didn't even notice and puffed out his chest. "Well, I'm *sure* you couldn't imagine that I'm a medium, which, for your information, means that I can channel spirits."

He had a pesky, frightening grin that was so large that his thick lips spread, exposing what looked like rows of baby teeth with tiny gaps between each of them.

Although I was interested in his ability, I was good at hiding it.

At first, Atwila looked disappointed as his grin dropped, but then he sat up straighter. "It looks like you need *more* explanation. What I'll share is that sometimes I can channel them through an object, but I'm *confident* I'll also achieve it through just silent meditation *very* soon."

That's a shame for the spirits, I thought, rolling my eyes, and Zoe laughed.

Atwila spun toward her. "What's so funny?" he demanded.

"No-nothing," she said, trying to get the word out as she choked back laughter.

Then I did the math in my head. *So there are eight of us. Seven with abilities. Four, including me, that I know about. Three I don't know.*

"Actually, there used to be eight of us before you," Zoe said.

Surprised, I looked over at her. She had a quiet, pensive expression. "Who was the eighth?" I asked.

"There was Cara. She had—I mean, *has* precognition."

Cara? And then I slowly remembered Cara was the name Zoe had mentioned when I was moving in. I even remembered seeing a picture of Ingrid, Zoe, and a girl with curly auburn hair on Zoe's desk. The girl must've been Cara.

What are the chances Zoe's two roommates would have similar abilities?

It also explained the empty stool in Dr. Braithwaite's class, which oddly stuck out as a source of imbalance in his balanced space.

"What happened to her?" I asked at last.

They looked at each other in questionable silence, then Zoe answered, "We don't know. One day she was here, and then before we knew it, Ms. Daniels told us she had left. Something about failing her classes. But I didn't believe her."

"We've been trying find out what really happened. But with no luck," Ingrid explained.

"Even my inquiries have found nothing," Renaud said.

The wind suddenly swirled through the trees and into the clearing. We hugged ourselves for more warmth.

"So all of you have been trying to find her?" I asked.

"Mostly the four of us," Zoe answered. "Colin, William, and Wal-

133

lace, as I'm sure you can see, don't take any of this seriously. They told us we should give it up. Stop making more out of it than what it is. They say Cara really wasn't a bright student, so it made sense that she got expelled."

Suddenly, the rude voice of Atwila reentered the conversation, and it was filled with accusation. "*You* seem *very* interested about Cara. *Why?* What are you trying to figure out? Or maybe you know something. Maybe *you* can tell us," he snapped, pointing his thick, short finger at me.

"What's *that* supposed to mean?" I said as I glared at him.

He glared back at me. "I'm just saying, Cara leaves suddenly and then you appear. You didn't know what your abilities are. You've never seemed to care about Dr. Braithwaite's class. And all of a sudden, you're now so interested, and you *think* you have precognition *just* like Cara. You also think you have *so* many other abilities." He crossed his arms. "As if we should be amazed."

"*Excuse me?*" I snapped back. "Listen to the mess that's rambling out of your mouth. Is it *really* making sense to you? I think it was better when your mouth was *shut*!"

Atwila's round nostrils flared as a gasp escaped from Ingrid's mouth and Zoe chuckled.

"I had no idea about Cara before I came here," I continued. "I didn't even know about this school until they wrote me." And then something rushed to the forefront of my mind. "Wait a minute ... you had a crush on Cara, didn't you? Sent her lots of sappy letters, and you didn't even put your name on them."

Atwila's eyes bulged even larger and darted around like someone had caught him scratching his butt.

"Hate to break it to ya," I added to rub it in, "but I don't think she would've liked you *anyway*."

The dim light couldn't hide how red his face got.

"It was *you*, Atwila?" Zoe remarked. "We were always wondering. Cara suspected but she just couldn't believe."

"*No, no! Not* true, *not* true," he blubbered and repeated as his belly shook like an earthquake.

Atwila's hopeless, never-ending crush was found out and exposed. Ingrid stretched over and rubbed his back. He whimpered pathetically and sunk into her hand. Now, all he needed was a pacifier with a tiny stuffed animal dangling from it.

"Let's calm down," she said to Zoe and me. "And be *kind*."

Zoe and I looked at each other, smirked, and rolled our eyes.

"I saw that," Ingrid admonished.

"We should finish soon," Renaud added, glancing down at his watch.

After wiping his reddened face with his sleeve, Atwila's glare returned with a force, and it was directed straight at me. "I don't trust you," he grumbled.

Zoe and I shot him a look as Ingrid shook her head.

His mouth clamped shut as he pressed his flat palms heavily on the ground and lowered his head in stubborn defeat.

"Zoe and Ingrid can help you with your abilities and tell you more about Cara," Renaud said to me. "Hopefully, with you, we can have a higher probability of finding something out. If something bad has happened to her, it could have consequences for us too. That is, *if* you want to help."

"*Of course* I want to," I said right away. "And I see the importance of needing to find out."

Renaud added, "If you need any information from me, I'm here."

"You *can't* tell *anyone* about our meetings," Atwila piped in.

"I know, A-*twila*," I said, narrowing my eyes at him. "It goes without saying. I *know* how to keep a secret."

"We believe you," Zoe said.

We made it back to Clairmount House without getting caught. Ingrid and Zoe were worried about what happened to Cara, but then again, maybe the reason was as simple and as straightforward as expulsion. But their concern seemed so real that it couldn't be ignored.

Much like my first night alone in Scotland, I replayed the events of the past week in my mind. When I did, things became clearer and I remembered details that weren't obvious before.

My senses had put them in a back filing cabinet of some sorts. These back files would come forward into my mind and then become clearer.

That night, after my meeting in the woods, I could almost be one hundred percent certain there had been someone out there. Not the five of us huddled around a small heat lamp, but a tall shadow hidden in the dark shrubs.... I was *almost* one hundred percent certain.

Chapter Ten

THE FADRIX

Zoe, Ingrid, and I sat on Ingrid's plush rug in her upper-level room. Having slept in from our very early morning meeting in the woods, we were having our first meal at midday.

"Hopefully, Colin, William, and Wallace will come to our next meeting," Ingrid remarked, nibbling on an apple.

"We can't count on them," Zoe said bluntly. "Besides, you know Colin has his reasons."

"What reasons are those?" I asked right away.

They looked at each other, confused.

"Well … uhm …," Ingrid stalled while Zoe scratched her cheek, avoiding my stare.

"I'm a ripe idiot for letting that slip out of my mouth," Zoe grumbled.

"Colin is dealing with some personal … matters," Ingrid said, looking very concerned. "We hope you can understand why we can't say."

"I do," I said, knowing that Colin deserved his privacy.

Ingrid let out a sigh of relief.

After our awkward moment had passed, Zoe moved on to talking about Cara. They shared basic stuff about her, like that her mother was a librarian and her father was an accountant, and that Cara struggled with her abilities and couldn't seem to improve. But when Zoe and Ingrid began to discuss Cara's behavior before she left and how the school staff responded, the situation sounded peculiar.

"Cara kept more to herself. Avoided us," Ingrid explained. "After she was gone, we asked Ms. Daniels and Mrs. Vyda about her. But Mrs. Vyda stared at us and didn't answer. It was as if she didn't hear us."

"And Ms. Daniels lied," Zoe declared. "Her thoughts weren't matching what she told us. Her thoughts were saying that she didn't even know herself."

"What about Duff? He'd *surely* know," I said.

Ingrid scrunched her face. "He's so standoffish. I don't get any vibes from him. Like he's empty. It's a very strange sensory experience."

"I tried with him," Zoe said.

Ingrid spun toward her in surprise. "You *did*? That was bold!"

Zoe shrugged. "It was pointless. He said, 'I cannot disclose any private information,' blah, blah, blah.'" Zoe's pitch had changed, trying to mimic Headmaster Duff's deep, cold voice.

"And when Headmaster Duff spoke," Zoe continued, "my abilities wouldn't work." Her lip curled up, and she growled in frustration. Zoe began knocking on her head. "*Aargh!* I wish I was better at all of this."

Ingrid calmly pulled Zoe's fist away before she could thump on her head for the third or fourth time. "Things are just not adding up," Ingrid said. "It feels slippery."

"*Slippery?*" Zoe and I said at the same time.

"Yeah, slippery," Ingrid said confidently. "You know, eerie, uncomfortable—slippery."

"I see what you mean now," I said, and Zoe nodded slowly.

Ingrid smiled.

Seeing Zoe's frustration, I asked, "How do you both practice?"

"Figure out how it works," Zoe said. "That's the first thing I did."

"Ask yourself," Ingrid added, "does it work through your senses like touching, hearing …"

Then Zoe chimed in. "Something you've smelled? A reaction?"

"An object?"

"A memory?"

"Something somebody says?"

"A place?"

They were going back and forth, like a ping-pong match.

"Wait, wait *stop*," I said, pressing my temples. "I'm trying to take all this in."

"*Oops!*" Ingrid blushed. "We got too excited."

"It's okay, I just need to think a bit."

We were silent as I tried to remember. Then I answered, "It happens in different ways. Sometimes a memory triggers it. Or something I touch or see…. Or sometimes it's a reaction."

"A reaction—how so?" Ingrid asked, and her eyes began to deepen.

"I can become really calm or also … defensive or frustrated." I wasn't proud to say the last part.

"That's natural," Zoe said.

"You can't be unrealistic about your emotions," Ingrid agreed.

I shook my head. "I don't think you understand. It's a frustration that takes over. And it can become really intense and overpowering."

They looked at each other with their mouths slightly open, until Zoe eventually spoke in a low tone. "I think she's talking about the other side to our abilities."

Ingrid nodded.

I put down my plate beside me. "What's this creepy, doomsday voice and nodding about? What do you mean by 'the other side'?"

Ingrid's eyes got a little misty. "Phoebe, our abilities can be controlled by our negative impulses or moods." She sighed. "We have to be careful about this, because it can take over. That's what we mean."

I shuddered. "And how much can it take over?"

"We don't know," Zoe answered, nervously playing with her ponytail, which cascaded over her shoulder. "Sometimes my abilities are strongest when I'm feeling lonely. And when that happens, things can go into overdrive." Zoe paused for such a long time that I thought she had stopped talking. But she finally spoke again, this time with a quivery voice. "One time, I had to keep to myself for *days* until I ... dealt with it ..." She took a deep breath and looked away.

Ingrid rubbed Zoe's shoulder. "All we can say, Phoebe, is that we don't know. And we have to be very careful."

Ingrid's words were an advice and a warning.

I tried to recover from what they had told me. Pushing it aside wouldn't have helped. Actually, it was impossible. Because when something like that is told, it can never go away.

So it lingered in my mind.

I swallowed a bite of my sandwich and cleared my throat. "We need to find answers about Cara," I said.

Zoe leaned into the circle. "We break in and get Cara's files. And we could even plant a listening device. We'll start easy first, which is the admin office. And then we'll try Duff's office." She nodded and smiled in anticipation.

A chip got stuck in the back of my throat. I pounded my chest as I gasped for air. "Let's see—stealing and snooping. I say, no." I said after I swallowed some water and could breathe again.

"Think of it as borrowing and … and …" Zoe stumbled over her words to find a better way of describing plain old snooping. She gave up, and her face began to drop when she noticed that Ingrid and I didn't leap for joy at her idea. "Look," she insisted, "right now we're out of options. Renaud has hit a roadblock. And our questions haven't been answered."

"We should consider other options," Ingrid suggested to Zoe.

Zoe eventually gave in (just a little). "Fine, but it's still my first choice," she grumbled.

My first class with the students since our meeting in the woods was like a do-over of the first day. I was seeing things from a different perspective, and everything was making so much more sense.

I hummed the names of the chemicals as I retrieved them, and my hand did extra twirls as I mixed the compound. Atwila was thoroughly annoyed—in silence. And Renaud was amused by my interest and by Atwila's reaction.

I was even trying to guess what the experiment would yield at the end of the week, and I participated and asked more thoughtful questions. Dr. Braithwaite seemed pleased by my new approach to his class.

In true Dr. Braithwaite fashion, my bubble of excitement burst during the last six minutes and six seconds of class. That was when he announced, "Students, please pay attention. Regarding your final exam in December …"

Immediately, my body tensed as Dr. Braithwaite put his glistening watch back into his pocket.

"This term, your exam will be a practicum." He took one of his dramatic pauses before continuing. "This means you will each be given a topic we have discussed or a compound you will have to recreate. This could be something I lectured about or an experiment we conducted. Thus, you should be *fully* prepared."

William raised his hand and spoke after Dr. Braithwaite acknowledged him with a short nod. "Didn't our experiments take an entire week? How can we do them in one exam period?"

A glint of approval appeared on Dr. Braithwaite's face. "A sagacious inference, Mr. William."

This made William smile despite his nervous eyes.

"Remember, timing is always key," Dr. Braithwaite began. "Those very experiments have a catalyst that can speed up the reaction. A part of your test is to determine how that can be done. And if you think that predetermining the catalyst together while studying will be useful, it will not. There will be a twist, as one might call it. Something not anticipated. Any more questions?"

We sat in worried silence—no further questions. It seemed like some trick, as if Dr. Braithwaite wanted to fail us.

"Announcing this today," Dr. Braithwaite added, "is giving you an ample amount of time to prepare. Rely on your abilities, your intuition, *and* your knowledge. You will also need to recall what I have taught. *All* is important."

Dr. Braithwaite was as thorough as he was going to be.

The next day, I was a mix of worry and excitement. Worry because of Dr. Braithwaite's exam announcement and excitement because I was finally meeting with Ms. Belzeebar.

Ms. Belzeebar's cluttered office was an eyesore and a headache. It was filled with papers, books, teacups, desk lamps, pictures of family members and many animals, and random knickknacks, and I was convinced that she didn't throw anything away. In fact, I didn't see a garbage can anywhere.

The pale yellow wallpaper in her office had large mythical creatures painted on it. They swarmed around us on all four walls. A large, green three-headed eagle was sneering at me from the wall behind her desk as I sat there. And there was an odd smell in the room too—like roses and roasted pork sausage.

But, among all the chaos, I couldn't help but zero in on an object, sitting on her desk and boldly in view. At first, I thought it was a large paperweight. But as I examined it, I saw it was perfectly round and glossy—too unique to be manufactured.

It glistened a translucent white. Then, when I moved my eyes to look at it from another angle, it appeared a deep blue. A bold energy filled up inside my chest. It was an empowering sensation.

"It's called the Fadrix." Ms. Belzeebar's voice drifted into my ears. "It's from the Early Dynastic Period of Egypt and was originally housed in the sarcophagus of a high priest. But it didn't remain there."

As Ms. Belzeebar sat in front of me, she pulled out a book from the untidy pile on her desk. Her thin lips wrinkled as she grabbed her tongue with her thumb and forefinger. She used her wet fingers to rapidly flip through the pages and suddenly stopped and lifted the open book to show me a print of an Egyptian coffin in a deep, dark pit with what must've been the Fadrix brightly spinning above it.

Ms. Belzeebar placed the book on her desk and proceeded to tell the Fadrix's epic journey. "With knowledge of its power, it has been highly coveted by rulers, thieves, and mystics. As a result, records have chronicled its presence during the Persian Empire, where King Darius the First acquired the Fadrix at an *extremely* high price—in jewels as well as slaughtered bodies. Men were willing to kill and die for it. Can you believe? *Kill* and *die!*"

My eyebrows rose, and I shifted in the chair. The threadbare, velvet cushion pulled on my tights.

"Later, the Fadrix was stolen and smuggled into China during the Tang dynasty, where it was used by mystics. It was also used to strategize influential plans that helped to grow the empire to great heights. Oh, Ms. Phoebe!" Ms. Belzeebar placed her hand to her chest as she became flushed in excitement. "I could say *so* much more. However, let's move along into the twentieth century, shall we?

"Nothing was heard of the Fadrix for several decades, until after World War II, when it was found by a monk at Le Mont-Saint-Michel in France. He stumbled upon it while he was fasting and praying for weeks, seeking guidance in the dark recesses of the abbey.

"I would've *loved* to have been there, wouldn't you? To experience, firsthand, the *precise* moment the monk rediscovered the orb. Absolutely *thrilling!*"

"So how did *you* get it?"

"The Murray School has its ways of acquiring important artifacts.

The orb supports our research and learning goals. Go ahead," she said, pushing the Fadrix closer to me. "It's waiting for you to hold it."

She spoke of the orb as if it had feelings. *What an outstandingly odd woman.*

I picked up the Fadrix. It was cool in my palms. And surprisingly, it felt almost weightless. The more my eyes and thoughts fixated on the orb, the more the undulating blue and green patterns on its surface seemed to move.

I didn't want to admit to myself what I was seeing, but the orb was like a miniature earth, resting in my palms … out of orbit.

Hypnotized, I stared intensely, and the Fadrix didn't disappoint. Colors began to swirl and move dramatically, like a storm brewed inside causing oceans to dangerously swell and clouds to fold and billow. It was erratic and forceful, but the orb remained calm in my hands. In fact, its weight lessened as it began to rise slowly into the air!

Instantaneously, my thoughts began to speak and spin, mirroring the movements within the orb. *You are willing to see and understand the Fadrix. Keep this in mind. There's a burden and responsibility in knowing more. And you welcome this power of knowledge. In fact, you relish it. It will show you this.*

The patterns created shapes. The tiny shapes clustered into a collection of characters to create a series of pictures. A message was forming! But it wasn't English; it looked like the ancient Egyptian writing Ms. Belzeebar had taught us—hieroglyphics. Gasping, my hands flew to my mouth. The orb continued to hover, but the hieroglyphics vanished.

"Don't stop! This is *precisely* what should be happening!" Ms. Belzeebar squealed gleefully and clapped.

"W-what is this? What does it mean?!"

Her eyes quickly read the words. "This is fantastic! We thought you were the key, and *now* I'm sure. Absolutely sure!"

"The key to *what*? You're not making sense. What's it *saying*?" My patience dropped to zero as my voice got louder.

The orb seemed to respond, because it began to fall. Ms. Belzeebar lunged her spindly frame forward to catch the Fadrix before it hit the ground. Her desperate and daring acrobatic dive was almost as if *she* would be willing to die for it. A flash of annoyance or maybe even anger appeared on her narrow face as she placed the orb delicately on the desk.

"Phoebe," Ms. Belzeebar said in a serious tone.

I was too caught up in what just happened to answer.

"*Phoebe*," her voice demanded, and I finally looked at her. "D-do *you realize*? Yo-you c-can …?" Ms. Belzeebar's words were incomplete and incoherent. But, she was able to finish. "You have the ability to see what's in the orb. For *so* long, it hasn't awakened … not since …"

"Not since *when*?" I demanded.

"N-n-not since many decades ago," she stuttered, then added, "I don't know why."

It felt like she'd told only half the truth.

"So why did you think I could awaken this sort of crystal ball? What is it about me?"

She pursed her lips and scrunched her face like she smelled something foul. "No. *No!* … It's *not* a sort of crystal ball. I *cannot* allow you to say that." Standing over me, Ms. Belzeebar wrung her limbs and bobbed her head like one of those paper skeletons you see dangling on doorways during Halloween.

She calmed down just enough to continue, but her face reddened. "*This* is an ancient orb. *This* was created from otherworldly inspiration and for a purpose. You *must* see and understand that it's *not* some phony sideshow carnival object used to steal a few pounds or pence from unsuspecting dupes. This is *the* Fadrix."

Suddenly, a shrill nervous laugh escaped from her mouth, and she sat down. "I get so passionate at times," she said. "You *must* forgive me. I was a bit out of order. A mistake on my part. Ehm … what was your question again?… Oh *yes*, it seems you have a psychic ability. Please, tell me more about why you wanted to meet me. I want to help you."

I excused Ms. Belzeebar's behavior as being wacky and overly excited, and my interest urged me to share what I'd experienced and what I knew about my abilities.

I shared that it was all new to me, so I was trying to understand what I could do and how to train myself. She listened intently and nibbled on her lips. I anticipated her response so much that I felt my palms sweating and wiped them in my skirt.

Ms. Belzeebar leaned forward in her chair in amazement. "It sounds like you may have *more than one* psychic ability."

"Is *that* why the Fadrix responded to me?"

"Yes and more. It senses you can summon it. You have a connection to it."

"I wonder why," I said, thinking aloud.

"Could be a number of reasons," she said, sitting back and stroking the tattered fabric of her armrest, as if she were petting her favorite cat. "Maybe your history is linked to it. Or simply because of the potency of your abilities, you have the power to awaken it. One can never truly know, unless you thoroughly learn and research your lineage, your past experiences, and the orb's past." Her fingers stopped moving. "Tell me, if you don't mind ... is there any person or persons in your family who have abilities?"

I hesitated at first but decided that the more she knew, the more I could learn. So I answered, "Yes, my grandmother did."

"I see. And do you have her *exact* abilities?"

"I think so." As I answered, I thought of Naan's special gifts.

"Did your grandmother have other abilities?" The puzzled look on my face caused her to add, "I mean, I can only help if I understand your background and the possible spectrum of your abilities."

I became uncomfortable talking about Naan. She was personal to me, and Ms. Belzeebar didn't know the special person she was. "That's all I know," I said.

"Oh, okay." Ms. Belzeebar looked down at her lap.

Then I turned the questioning onto her. "And *you*, Ms. Belzeebar? Do you have abilities?"

Her head popped up, and she smiled and leaned forward. "Yes, I'm an aligist, which means I am fluent in *all* languages. I also have enhanced memory, particularly on historical facts and subjects."

This made perfect sense. Ms. Belzeebar was a whiz at historical facts and subjects. The irony was that she was completely scatter-brained when it came to day-to-day interactions and conversations.

"I didn't even know there was such a person—an aligist." And then I asked, "Ms. Belzeebar, how do I understand? What can I do to learn?"

"*That* is the question." Her voice lowered. "Are you ready to learn?"

"Yes." My eyes glanced again at the Fadrix. I wanted to know.

"Are you entirely sure?"

"Of course, I'm ready," I answered, getting a bit impatient.

I must be ready … I mean, there's no other reason why all these events have been happening to me, and I'm now accepting them.

Carefully pushing the Fadrix in my direction again, she whispered her instruction. "Try reading it again."

"But I wasn't trying before. It just happened."

"You've realized an important factor to having abilities without even a lesson. That is, it's innate."

"Does that mean it happens just because?"

Ms. Belzeebar sniffed and rubbed a broach on her sweater. "It's not that easy. There's still effort you have to make." Pointing at the orb, sitting on the table, she instructed. "Place the Fadrix in your palms like you did before."

I held the orb again. It felt as if it had just come out of a fridge.

"Now, look into it as you did before."

I did. The translucent white color was dormant inside.

"What were you thinking or feeling when the Fadrix began to respond?"

"Uhm … I was thinking I was ready to know more. And I was feeling curious and filled with anticipation, I guess."

"Try to recapture those feelings. Maybe that's your key to awakening this precious sphere."

I did everything in my core to summon those feelings and thoughts again. I even used a trick Ava told me that she said actors did to get into a role. I started creating a story in my head of a situation where I would've been curious and anticipatory. But the feelings didn't resurface.

So I tried another pointer from Ava, which wasn't to make up something but place myself in a real situation of the past where those feelings were experienced. I shut my eyes and my mind traveled back in time and space to Crockett around our Christmas tree.

It was one of my first memories of Christmas, and we were opening presents. I saw the multicolored lights blinking, heard carols on the radio and my parents' voices in the kitchen as they cut more rum fruitcake. I could smell the sweet and savory aromas wafting throughout the house.

Everything felt so real, and I loved the surprise of opening presents—one of the most incredible moments of anticipation and surprise.

As I was opening the presents in my memory, those past feelings began to grow in Ms. Belzeebar's office.

The orb became weightless, and I smiled.

It was working again as I was split between two realities. In one reality, I could feel Ms. Belzeebar leaning forward to decipher the orb. She was reciting the language aloud. While in the other reality, Naan appeared in my Christmas memory. She was helping Graham and me clear away our torn gift wrapping.

It was time for her present to me to be opened, and Naan placed the shiny silver package in my right hand. Before I could rip the paper off, she stopped me with her hand folded over mine. I looked up and thought she was going to say something cheerful.

Instead, she had a warning. "Don't let your left hand know what your right hand knows."

I wrinkled my forehead. That *wasn't* what she'd told me that Christmas morning. Then, my memory suddenly vanished, as if Naan's words had shut it down. In Ms. Belzeebar's office, the orb immediately dropped into my hands.

"What happened? *Don't* stop!" she demanded. She caught herself. "Sorry, I *really* get *too* carried away."

"I wish I could make it work longer. What did it say?"

"The Fadrix was retelling a historical event from its past, but that's not the important part. What's important is that you can control how to awaken it! What did you think of?" she asked with wide eyes.

"I thought of a past experience," I said, deciding not to tell her the details of my Christmas memory. My memories were personal.

And Naan's message was a warning of some sort.

What she said about my right hand and left hand was an old saying from her upbringing. It meant I should be careful about what I share. I needed to be careful about whom I trusted.

"Well, it's magnificent. Absolutely *magnificent* that it worked again! I have a feeling you'll advance much faster than—" Ms. Belzeebar's face dropped and her eyes quickly scanned the ugly green birds on her walls.

"Much faster than *who*?"

"Than the other students," she finished.

"Oh," I said quietly. The comparison made me feel kind of uneasy. The other students, I felt, were gifted in their own way.

She focused on me again with a serious expression. "So, you think you're ready?" she repeated.

"I know I am."

Ms. Belzeebar started petting her chair and chewing on her bottom lip again. Then, she gnawed on her upper lip. This time, more incessantly, causing her skin to become red and irritated. But Ms. Belzeebar didn't seem to notice or care. She stopped abruptly and placed the orb in a safe underneath her desk.

"Then, I'm not the only person suited for the task," she said at last. "We have to meet with the primary person who is *most* definitely needed. Follow me."

She got up with such speed that her chair let out an earsplitting screech on the tiled floor.

I followed Ms. Belzeebar through the corridors, trying to keep up with her hasty gait as we went upstairs and passed more quiet corridors.

When we eventually stopped, we were standing directly in front of Headmaster Duff's third-floor office door.

Secret Society for Special Abilities and Artefacts

Chapter Eleven

SECRET SOCIETY FOR SPECIAL ABILITIES AND ARTEFACTS

Ms. Belzeebar rapped on the door with her bony knuckles. No answer. She tried again with more urgency. Still no answer. Trying yet another time, we waited. And eventually the excitement on her face faded. Her body slumped, and her ruffled dress looked like wilted leaves barely holding on to a stem.

"It seems like he's not in," she said as she turned to me.

Also disappointed, I wanted to tell her to try knocking harder.

"I'll let the headmaster know we need to meet with him as soon as he's available," she informed me then scuttled away. Reaching halfway down the corridor, she announced, "*Ah!* Almost forgot!" She scuttled back to me. "Ehm?…" Ms. Belzeebar bit the insides of her gaunt cheeks.

I waited, holding the strap of my backpack over one of my shoulders. I shifted my weight to my other foot.

"I'm sure it's not that important," she said at last, and spewed out giggles and some spit at my face. And when she finished, she hurried toward the stairs in the opposite direction.

Already missing Spanish class, I went to Studio Art in one of the detached, modern-looking buildings on campus. And on my way there, I texted Zoe and Ingrid: Have exciting news to share!

We'd been painting a still life for the past week. Standing to paint a bowl filled with assorted fruits and some pine cones was one of the dullest things to do. Bored out of my wits, I sloppily brushed strokes onto the canvas, just waiting for class to end.

Jeans and white high-tops, splattered with paint, walked up to me out of the corner of my eye—Mr. Thomson. I guess like many other art teachers, Mr. Thomson liked bright colors. Today he was wearing a large canary yellow beanie and a matching yellow T-shirt with faded words that said *Groove Along*.

With a rolled-up piece of paper in front of his mouth, he blew, "*Doodoodadoo!*" His waist-length locs jumped behind his back. "You have been summoned by the Fifteenth Earl of Murrayshire," he said so loudly that everyone stared.

I ducked my head behind my easel, hoping he would stop.

Ms. Thomson lowered his voice but was still oblivious to my embarrassment. "Get it? The headmaster is … *aah*, never mind."

My heart thudded as I walked up to Headmaster Duff's office. Before I could even knock, the door opened to reveal him leaning on his cane as he stood over his desk. His silvery hair shimmered against the setting sun.

As I stepped inside, Ms. Belzeebar was already sitting. I looked around to see who might've opened the door, but no one else was there.

Her excitement resurfaced. "Hello *again!*" Then she said to Headmaster Duff, "I'm so happy it works. *She's* a source."

He slowly turned around, revealing a slight smile. "I was already certain she would be."

Ms. Belzeebar's head moved up and down vigorously. "I think she's ready. What say you?"

Headmaster Duff rubbed the top of his cane, which was a golden knob (probably real gold). "Before we commence our conversation, Phoebe, I must ask, Have you shared your experience with the orb? Have you told anyone?"

"I *knew* it!" Ms. Belzeebar exclaimed. "I was supposed to tell her not to tell anyone." She lowered her head and continued mumbling to herself. "That's what I forgot."

"No, I haven't," I said, and she let out a sigh of relief.

"Then this is perfect timing," Duff said to Ms. Belzeebar.

"Yes, *indeed,*" she said.

"Your friends must not know, at least not yet," he said.

"Why not?" I asked.

His fingers immediately gripped the knob until his knuckles turned white. Taking his time to respond, Headmaster Duff sat and propped up his cane against his desk. "For you to fully understand, you have to first trust us and the process."

There's that word again—trust.

He motioned for me to sit, opened his desk drawer, and pulled out a metal frame. He looked at it before handing it to me. And what I saw in the frame was an old photograph of five people around a table.

It was in black and white and not the greatest quality. The people in the picture looked to be in a dining hall or meeting area. Seated in the middle was a tall, serious-looking man.

Although the picture was black and white, his neatly cut hair must've been blond, the way it looked shiny and white in the picture. And although the man's face was turned toward a woman next to him, I could still see his piercing stare. A stare undeniably from the face of a younger Headmaster Duff.

I didn't pay attention to the other three people in the photograph, because the moment I looked at the woman next to the young Headmaster Duff, I froze.

There she was … my grandmother smiling with soulful eyes and looking straight ahead. Her smile revealed beautiful high cheekbones, and her iridescent dark hair flowed in thick waves around her face and down to her shoulders.

Why is my Naan in this picture?!… So this is the reason Headmaster Duff was staring at me during the assembly and during my first meeting with him.

With a shaky arm, I leaned forward to return the picture.

Headmaster Duff began to answer the questions he saw in my eyes. "I met Ericka whilst working in Parliament. I volunteered to be sent as an envoy for the Crown to Jamaica. She worked with the government office as a secretary and was assigned to travel throughout the island with me in order to facilitate the documentation of political matters, record the establishments of institutions, and so on."

Headmaster Duff's voice trailed off until he ceased talking. The ticking of the grandfather clock and Ms. Belzeebar's rapid breathing filled the silence.

He focused on me again. "The more we spent time together, the more we saw in each other that we had innate abilities that were extraordinary. Are you following me?"

My throat felt dry when I swallowed. "Yes, Headmaster Duff," I almost croaked.

"Good," he said. "Your grandmother was open about her abilities. And for the first time in my life, I felt comfortable sharing who I am. We soon recognized how important abilities like ours were and knew they were being exploited and used by others.

"Eventually, your grandmother and I devised an ambitious but necessary plan. A plan to form a society that would preserve as many of the world's artifacts associated with the paranormal and the unknown as we could. To acquire the artifacts, we would seek out individuals and organizations who had knowledge about them."

"Like the artifacts that Ms. Belzeebar has been teaching us about and the orb," I said.

"Precisely," Ms. Belzeebar agreed.

"And regarding extraordinary individuals," Headmaster Duff said, "our aim was to find the cream of the crop, learn more from one another, and protect younger and more inexperienced individuals from the abuse, ignorance, and even the exploitation of others. We *could not* allow special artifacts and extraordinary individuals to be misused and at the mercy of incompetent or vile people."

And then a moment (I've replayed in my mind even to this day) happened next. With an unwavering stare, Headmaster Duff said something that made me shudder.

"I have personally witnessed what happens when power is abused and not responsibly controlled." He leaned forward and pushed aside some papers. When he did, the polished table was bare, and I caught a glimpse of his blurred, distorted reflection in it. I looked up again into his clear eyes with hollow black pupils. "There are principalities of powers and rulers of dark forces in high places, Phoebe Douse. One *must not* be naive to that."

I gulped, unable to answer.

Ms. Belzeebar turned and patted my hand. "You see, there is a duality that exists in these abilities. When practiced, it should be done wisely and with control. *And* they must be guarded from others with ill intentions."

"We named our society the Secret Society for Special Abilities and Artefacts," Headmaster Duff explained.

"Repeat that please? Society for the *what what?*" I was confused, and it sounded like a mouthful.

Ms. Belzeebar chimed in, "Secret Society for Special Abilities and Artefacts. Also called S3A2."

This was *a lot* to take in. I'd *never* heard Naan mention *any* of this. She *never* spoke about Duff, Scotland, and secret societies. I didn't even know she liked collecting items, let alone ancient and powerful artifacts. I stopped myself when I remembered Naan *did* try to tell me about her "grandest adventure."

"How can I believe what you're saying?" I asked boldly.

He thought, with his elbows resting on his desk and fingers pressed together. "You might have seen a photograph of your grandmother wearing a bracelet? In fact," he said, "I remember there is a *particular* photograph of her, when she was younger."

Not only did Headmaster Duff mention the very picture in my journal, but he also described it to a tee—what she was wearing and even how she posed.

I was amazed by his knowledge of such a personal item of mine.

"I know that picture. I have it," I managed to whisper.

"*I* took that photograph of her."

My eyes got even wider, and he opened his drawer again to take out a delicate, shimmery object and handed it to me—a bracelet.

"You will find that she is wearing it in your photograph."

The cool delicate bracelet rested between my fingers. On it was a small engraving. I squinted to see that it was the very same shield for the school with the wolf and unicorn. But underneath this shield was not our school motto. Rather, it was a combination of letters and numbers that looked like part of a math equation or chemistry compound— *S3A2*. And there was also the title underneath in fancy cursive:

Secret Society for Special Abilities and Artefacts

As I whispered the title to myself, I saw that *Artefacts* was spelled with an *e* instead of an *i*. *Must be British spelling*, I concluded. I'd noticed while in Scotland, some words were spelled a little differently than in America. Turning the bracelet over revealed *E. F.* neatly engraved on the inside. They were my grandmother's initials. *F* stood for her maiden name, Fahey.

"It is the insignia of the Society. Each leader wears some form of it," Headmaster Duff said as he stretched over to show me his, which was a large gold and sapphire ring worn on his index finger. It also had the insignia, but the name wasn't in cursive like Naan's bracelet. Headmaster Duff's initials, *T. D.*, were on the back.

I turned to Ms. Belzeebar, and sure enough she pointed to the small copper broach on her sweater.

"And Dr. Braithwaite? Is he S3A2 also?"

"Yes," they said in unison.

Ms. Belzeebar finished, "It's his pocket watch."

I could've guessed that. Dr. Braithwaite and his watch were inseparable.

There was one more person I needed to ask about.

"Mr. Franklin?" I whispered.

"No," said Headmaster Duff. "He is an associate, but not a member of the Society."

"Oh." I paused and then more questions came forth. "If the bracelet was my grandmother's, why do you have it?" Before he could answer, I asked another question. "Why can I read the orb and not you?" And another. "How did you find me?"

"I realize you have more questions that I cannot answer in one night," he said. He was studying me. *Maybe, he's trying to read my thoughts. Maybe … he's telepathic!*

"Can you trust the process?" he eventually asked.

"What?"

"The process," he repeated. "If you truly want to know, you have to trust."

Trust was something I'd been struggling with. Trust was something I was building. Headmaster Duff knew my grandmother. He knew about her abilities. They had worked closely together and developed a secret society. That *must've* been enough to prove he was someone I could trust or least be open to trusting.

I said at last, "I believe I can."

My words gave him the assurance he needed, and he handed me a leather-bound book from one of the neat stacks on his desk. I turned it over in my hands. It was flimsy, and on the cover it read: *1953-4.*

"In this you will learn more about S3A2. Read it and keep it safe. I expect you to return it the day after tomorrow. Only then can I perhaps answer more of your questions. You will also find there are already some answers inside." Headmaster Duff's tone became intense. "You *must not* tell anyone of our meeting or of this journal. *No one.*"

Even so, I was still curious why Ingrid, Zoe, and the others couldn't know about S3A2. They would've been thrilled.

"It is *imperative* that we keep this conversation amongst ourselves, because there are forces …" Headmaster Duff saw the confusion on my face, so he changed his words to say, "There are other organizations and influential people with the means and aim to destroy us, take what we have, and they *will not* stop until they do. We have to discover an important piece of information from the Fadrix. If we do not … Well, I do not want to consider the consequences if we fail."

Ms. Belzeebar added softly, "It's a matter of survival for S3A2. *And* a matter of life and death for special children like you, Zoe, Colin, Ingrid, Atwila, William, and Wallace."

Goosebumps rose on my skin, and my head pounded. *What did Naan get herself into? Better yet, what did I get myself into?*

"You understand the importance?" Headmaster Duff asked.

This was all so real but at the same time so unreal. Words didn't come out of my mouth fast enough.

He commanded that I reply. "*Do* you?"

"Y-yes," I stuttered quietly.

Ms. Belzeebar patted my hand again. "Now, there is no need to be too concerned. If we're able to retrieve information from the orb and soon, we'll all be safe."

"Your roommate Zoe has telepathy," Headmaster Duff went on. "Wear Ericka's bracelet." He pointed to it, reminding me that it was still dangling from my fingers. "It will prevent Zoe from listening to your thoughts. In fact, it will help to prevent the others' abilities from having an effect on you as well. Bear in mind, it is not foolproof, just an extra, potential barrier from those whose abilities are not strong."

I looked down at it in amazement as I slipped it over my wrist. "They're very smart *and* persistent. I'm not so sure it's possible to keep S3A2 and the orb from them," I said doubtfully.

"You *must*," Ms. Belzeebar insisted.

"You are bright as well as clever. I can see that in you. You will know what to say and how to say it," Headmaster Duff said.

I swallowed and gathered the courage to convince myself. Then I became intrigued. "What *else* can this bracelet do?"

There was a glint in his eyes. "I may tell you another time. For now, we should finish for the evening."

Evening? Yes, it was evening, 6:30 in fact. I placed the journal in my bag, and we stood together, as if in a ceremony.

"Remember, *no one* must know about S3A2 and the orb," Headmaster Duff pressed while Ms. Belzeebar smiled to reassure me.

As I began to leave, the door opened, and I assumed it was automatic. I turned one last time. "Thank you, both. I—"

The door shut behind me, and Headmaster Duff's steady eyes were focused on it, even though his body faced another direction.

"How did you …?" I said to him, pointing at the door.

He grinned, and when he did, I saw the young man in the picture.

"I have telekinesis," he said. I wrinkled my brow, so he explained further. "I can move objects with my mind."

"Oh," I barely whispered. When I was able to get over my surprise, I left the office.

Walking across the courtyard, I could feel two pairs of eyes peering down at me from above and knew they belonged to Headmaster Duff and Ms. Belzeebar. What I learned invigorated me. All those years of feeling strange and being an outcast at school. *They* were wrong.

I decided I needed some time to myself, and the library was a great place to avoid, for just a little while longer, the probing questions of Zoe and Ingrid. Luckily, Renaud wasn't there, and I was alone to clear my mind and reflect on my phenomenal day.

Resting my head on the table over my folded arms, I shut my eyes … just for a moment.

Creak! My head popped up, and I groaned, rubbing the slight crick in my neck as I looked around a bit dazed. The moment was longer than I'd planned, and the sound was a cart a library assistant was pushing. She had just reshelved books behind me.

I pulled the journal out of my bag and opened it. The sheets of paper were yellowing and a bit crinkled, and the text was faded. First page read:

15 August 1953:

Today marks the first meeting of S3A2. We have formed a clandestine, global network and aim to meet in undisclosed locations.

Our chosen insignia is an emblem of the wolf and

unicorn, signifying the delicate balance that exists between supernatural, metaphysical forces and the natural realm.

The unicorn symbolises the grace, majesty and otherworldly forces that need to be protected and amplified. The wolf is the strength of the explicable, natural world. The combination of animals also illustrates the universal and inescapable dichotomy that exists within and around us.

That is, the relationship between positive and negative, good and evil, prey and predator.

We must remain vigilant to...

The library lights flickered on and off, signaling to us leftover students around tables and standing in aisles that it was time to leave.

I exited and walked briskly outside to warm myself.

"Look at what you've *destroyed*!"

I jolted to a stop as I turned the corner. Looking down at my feet, my loafers were covered in fresh soil and crushed flowers.

Like a gravedigger, Mr. MacLeod hunched over the bushes with his shovel. Then he menacingly waved his gardening tool at me, as if he wanted to bury me with it. "Why are you just out and about traipsing in my garden?!" he yelled. "You think this place takes care of itself, don't you?"

"No, Mr. MacLeod. Sorry," I called out, backing up. "I just got lost in thought."

"If thinking makes you this bumbly and absentminded, then do less of it, and keep your wits about you!" he snapped and then disappeared into the darkness.

If it were any other night, I would've been upset by his bad attitude.

I mean, the flower bed was messed up but not *destroyed*. And why was he gardening at night, anyway?

But this night was special and profound. This night was a once-in-a-lifetime kind of experience. As I ran my fingers over the cool bracelet around my wrist, I wondered if I should trust Headmaster Duff or tell my new friends.

After all, so much of what he said added up—he knew my Naan, he was the photographer of such a personal picture of her, he shared his abilities with me, and he gave me a journal filled with proof.

Remembering my Christmas memory, I concluded that Naan's words were telling me that I needed to keep each secret separate.

Zoe wasn't in our room when I entered, and I pushed my book bag deep underneath my bed, knowing it housed an important item.

"Where were you last night? Ingrid and I were looking for you," Zoe asked me when I woke up the next morning.

"Studying" was all I said. "You know how that goes."

Zoe examined me. "You look tired or worried about something."

I traced my fingers along the bracelet. *If this works, it better work now.* My thoughts were racing with yesterday's revelations. I daringly looked straight into her eyes. "You're right. I just need to skip classes today, that's all."

She gave me the once-over, and her eyebrows eventually softened. Then her face perked up. "So what's the news?"

I'd rehearsed what I would say when Zoe or Ingrid asked. So I didn't hesitate. "I've thought it over, and I think you're right. We should break in and get Cara's files."

Her face brightened. "Fantastic! But … is there more?"

My text message had raised her expectations.

I gave a goofy grin and touched my new bracelet again. "Nope."

"Well, I'm glad you're in. When we meet, we can plan the details." Then, Zoe rushed out of the room.

"Ten … nine … eight … seven …," I counted. When I got to three, I figured Zoe must've at least exited the house. For safe measure, I scooted out of my chair to look out the window. And when I saw her running across the quad, I reached under my bed to retrieve the thin, leather-bound journal.

Placing Naan's picture beside me, I looked at it and noticed for the first time a long shadow in the foreground—Headmaster Duff. I opened the journal and started where I'd left off the night before:

...preserve, protect and promote our ideals and defeat those who want to destroy and alter what is good. S3A2 has support from world leaders and prominent members within society whom we shall not name in order to protect their identities and positions. They understand the value and importance of S3A2 and are committed to its cause.

The world is ever changing, with power shifts, conflicts, and countries choosing alliances. Many global events are being fuelled and propagated for the purposes of creating instability. Now, more than ever, we need S3A2 to expand and support just causes.

This entry is hereby signed by:

Taggart Duff

Taggart Duff, 15th Earl of Murrayshire, Co-Founder

[signature: Ericka Fahey]

Ms. Ericka Fahey, Co-Founder

[signature: Hortensia Gillies]

Lady Hortensia Gillies, Log Keeper and Secretary

[signature: R Malcolm]

Dr. Rory Malcolm, Development of Substances and
Verification Specialist

[signature: Douglas Thelwell]

Mr. Douglas Thelwell, Outreach, Recruitment and
Communications

The other names must've been the other people in the photograph. I traced my finger over Naan's signature. Then, I looked up Dr. Malcolm. Reports said he died in a car accident during the 1980s. And according to my search, Lady Hortensia Gillies and Douglas Thelwell were missing, since 1957. *Is this what Naan meant about finding them both?*

12 September 1953:
  We continue to establish S3A2 codes. And on purpose, many of them are unwritten. This ensures utmost secrecy and nondisclosure.
  On another note, we are encouraged as to the development of S3A2 and the growth of its satellite locations.

17 October 1953:
  Description of members are as follows: Taggart Duff has telekinesis. And each month we meet, he grows

stronger. Taggart has the benefit of learning directly from the artefacts and books we have obtained.

Ericka Fahey...

I couldn't help but pause when I saw my Naan's name. I felt honored to read about her.

...is a clairvoyant with other abilities that she rightfully chooses not to fully disclose. Ericka has shared that her abilities have been both a blessing and a burden. Nevertheless, she is happy to be part of S3A2.

I, Lady Hortensia Gillies, am a medium. I am quite advanced and enthusiastic to share what I know as I continue to improve. My connections have enabled me to gain access to important individuals and organizations.

Dr. Rory Malcolm's role is vital for confirming the artefacts we find and for developing new substances and materials that are important for our protection and for the enhancement of our abilities. Thus, his ability to alter scientific properties of matter and transform objects is paramount.

Mr. Douglas Thelwell has no abilities. However, through his experiences, he is well connected to people who can acquire or locate artefacts or know the whereabouts of significant people. Let us just say, he has eyes everywhere, and his ears are to the ground.

14 November 1953:

We increasingly realise there is a very negative, potent side to having abilities. Great care must be taken when using them and exercising our influence. The harmful and detrimental consequences can have unimaginable ramifications.

Gifts must be used wisely.

Naan had told me to use my abilities for good. When I held the orb, my thoughts spoke about the burden of knowledge. And my discussion with Ingrid and Zoe confirmed this fact when we spoke about the dark side of our abilities. I turned the page, still thinking about this message.

12 December 1953:
    We have settled on a place of learning, protection
and advancement for youth who have special abilities.
It is an ancestral castle from Taggart's lineage. It
will be a perfect place with appropriate facilities
and...

The more I read, the more it made sense why I was chosen. As crazy and grandiose as it might've sounded, the bottom line was that we were selected by some kind of covert operation and protection program that had global importance. And sure enough, the rest of the entry explained just what I'd concluded:

    ...we will recruit students with extraordinary
abilities in order to train their powers and
provide direction. Ozmantahs are the highest level
of S3A2 association. Further, teachers will provide
instructions that will be held under the guise of a
normal school programme.
    For those who excel, we will consider, whether in
the future, he/she will become a member of S3A2 when
we see it is necessary. The existence of S3A2 will not
be made known to the pupils unless they are deemed
worthy and talented enough to join. This will be done
on a case-by-case basis.

The next two months (January and February) looked like a log of some sort that recorded obtained artifacts and special substances. I saw some objects that Ms. Belzeebar had spoken about during classes as well as some of the solutions in Dr. Braithwaite's tower. Others were completely unknown to me.

```
13 March 1954:
    We have recruited our first class of nine students
with special abilities...
```

The doorknob jostled. Jumping under the covers, I shut the journal and put it and my laptop under my pillow and blanket.

"Why'd you lock the door?" Zoe asked upon entering. It was lunchtime, and she had decided to come home.

"I was hoping Ms. Daniels didn't walk in and wake me up."

She handed me a brown paper bag "Brought you soup." When I took it from her, she made a face. "It's not the best. Actually, it's terrible."

"I'm sure my starving stomach will like anything right now."

"Oh, guess what?" Zoe said as she changed books in her bag. "We've decided to meet Friday night. Different location, though. We try to switch it up to avoid suspicion."

Feeling guilty inside, I actually felt sick to my stomach. I took a sip of the soup, hoping it would calm me; it didn't work.

When Zoe left me to "rest," I continued reading:

```
...and are anticipatory to see how they develop. S3A2
is debating whether the students should be given clear
understanding as to their true purpose and reason
for being at The Murray School. This is a matter we
continue to consider.
```

I turned the page. It was blank.

I turned more pages to make sure, but there was nothing else. *How strange.* I wanted to know about the honor codes, Ozmantahs, the recruited students, and more.

From those few entries, I had learned so much, but there was still other information out there. So many decades of plans, meetings, and activities were unchronicled.

S3A2 was truly shrouded in utmost secrecy and protection.

I closed the journal and decided that a much-needed conversation had to be continued with Mom.

"*Beep. Beep. Beep* ...," the computer rang. "*Beep, Beep* ..."

"You've done more thinking about what we talked about?" Mom said.

"More than you can imagine," I said, looking down at the journal.

"That must be why you're calling me so early and on a school day."

I'd forgotten what time it was for her.

"Did you know I have abilities?" I asked.

"Yes," she said, without hesitating.

I was floored. "And I'm guessing Dad knew too and probably even Graham?"

"Graham doesn't have a clue, and your father ... well ... let's just say he doesn't believe in these sorts of things." She chuckled. "He thinks it's all foolishness."

"Do you?"

"Think it's foolishness? Not at all!"

"No, that's not what I meant. Do you have abilities?"

"I don't. What you have comes directly from your Naan."

"And you didn't think it was important to tell me this?" I demanded.

"Phoebe, keep your voice down," she said calmly.

I tried, but probably not good enough as I kept on, "When I would tell you what was happening to me or when Naan used to share her stories, you didn't say anything."

"I have no excuses," she said, sounding unfazed. "I did what I thought was best."

"And come to think of it," I continued, getting frustrated that she didn't explain herself, "it seemed like you didn't want to hear it."

Mom sighed. "When people don't understand something they can fear it, treat people unfairly, or even worse. I didn't want you to be burdened by it, Phoebe. Forgive me for wanting to protect you."

Taking a deep breath and letting it out, I calmed myself. I couldn't be too mad at her. How could I? In the past, I didn't want to speak about my abilities and had forced myself to ignore them. Trying to forget them.

And now, I had recently promised to keep secrets all in the name of protecting others.

"I understand," I said finally.

"I'm glad you do. And I'm happy you're realizing important things about yourself there.... Tell me, are you comfortable with knowing?"

"I actually feel vindicated. You know what I mean?"

"Absolutely, like who you are was never a lie or made up."

"Exactly."

"That makes my heart smile."

We said our goodbyes, and I felt guilty again.

Chapter Twelve

UNDERGROUND VAULT OF TROVES

$\mathcal{T}$he next day after classes, Mrs. Vyda instructed me to see Headmaster Duff. When I reached his office, the knob turned and the door opened. Headmaster Duff didn't even have to hear my knock. At the doorway, I stood between his stark dominion and the everyday hallway with students passing by.

Headmaster Duff backed away from his window and then turned in my direction.

I felt incapable of taking a step forward. His eyes would never seem normal to me.

"Care for any tea or water," he asked, and sat in his chair.

His invitation allowed me to enter, and my nervousness faded as soon as I sat.

"No, thanks," I answered as I dug in my bag for the journal and handed it to him. I was thirsty for more answers and went straight to business. "Headmaster Duff ... who are the Ozmantahs? Are you one? It was only mentioned once in the journal but definitely seems important."

"Indeed," he said. "And yes, I *am* an Ozmantah. However, I *will not* disclose who the others are. Their identities are concealed." He looked away. "Your grandmother could have risen to the status of an Ozmantah but—" He then observed me with his usual stare, but this time, his silence was commanding me to look him in the eye.

So I tried my best not to focus on a tiny black stain on my skirt. And I dared to look at him with an unwavering stare.

He nodded. "An Ozmantah is more than a title," he explained. "And it is *not* for all S3A2 members. It is for the elite few. To be an Ozmantah, you must be born with an inexplicable degree of power, and your purpose is to acquire a level of knowledge and consciousness that seeks to interpret and control your power as well as the power of others.

"An Ozmantah is eternally a teacher *and* a student. He or she strives for an ideal, a *perfection*. To acquire this title is *highly* honored."

Something inside me was drawn to his words. So much so I needed to ask, "Is it possible that if I tried hard enough and practiced, that I could ...? I mean, since you said my grandmother could've been one ... could I one day be ..." I gulped. "... an Ozmantah?"

It was like he was peeling back the layers of my mind as his stare bore into me. But somehow it didn't feel strange. It was like I invited him to, and when I did, I felt empowered.

Headmaster Duff tilted his head as his praying hands parted and rested on the desk. "My, my, Phoebe Douse," he said at last, "you *are* indeed one with incredible ambition—I see that."

But he didn't answer my question. Feeling confused and uneasy, I tried to change the subject, swallowing and asking, "Why did the entries stop?"

"They were no longer necessary. We established and organized what we needed at the time and found it too precarious to keep writing."

"So that's why my Naan never told me about S3A2," I thought aloud. "Because it was too risky to talk about. I understand she couldn't tell me the details. But she could've told me *something*, right?"

"That, I cannot answer. Perhaps she wanted to protect you. Or wait until you were older."

I absorbed that point and had to honestly admit to myself that I had taken Naan for granted, assuming she would always be around.

"And there were five members," I said. "But I read that two—Mr. Thelwell and Lady Gillies—have been missing for around fifty years. I think they're the ones who need to be found."

A spark of interest flashed on Headmaster Duff's face as he leaned forward. "*Very* revealing that you would bring that up. How did you know?"

"My Naan told me."

"Ah," he said, nodding. Then he explained, "Decades ago, they broke the code of the Society. Ericka, Rory, and I uncovered that Douglas was stealing information, with the aid of Lady Hortensia, and selling it to powerful underground organizations that were and *still* are using the information to advance their own dangerous agendas.

"We sequestered Lady Hortensia and Douglas in order to extract their motives and what information they had shared and with whom. However, they managed to escape before we began the inquisition."

"When you say dangerous agendas, do you mean like …"

"I mean influencing important social and political matters in nefarious ways," he said pointedly. "Things that are too serious for you to understand fully at your age."

I folded my arms across my chest. *Try me.*

Headmaster Duff saw my reaction. "I am talking about military coups, assassinations, the destruction of S3A2 members, and the like."

I sat up straighter. "*What?!*"

"As long as Douglas and Lady Hortensia are not found, S3A2 and others continue to be compromised. The orb houses the information of their locations. Also, it houses important information about other traitors we want to identify."

Naan also talked about a marriage. What did that have to do with anything?

"I can see you are thinking. Did I say something?"

"I was remembering something else my grandmother told me."

"Please do share."

"She also said something about a marriage. What *marriage?*"

He paused and thought, sitting back in his chair. Hopeful, I waited for more information that would've developed her story.

Instead, Headmaster Duff said, "Regrettably, I cannot answer that."

Disappointment seeped in. *If Headmaster Duff doesn't even know, how would I ever find out?*

"Perhaps if you recall anything else she told you, I could help you piece together what she meant," he advised.

"I can't. I've tried to remember it over and over again. *Believe me.*" I felt defeated and sad that I couldn't honor my grandmother's memory by remembering her story.

"If you help find Thelwell and Lady Hortensia," he suggested, "you may also solve your own story. It may very well be connected."

My motivation reemerged. "So, you think my abilities can help?"

"Precisely." His face suddenly hardened and his eyes flashed to the door. It was so abrupt and unexpected that my body stiffened. The door opened, and on the other side, Ms. Belzeebar stood and waved. "You are late," he said bluntly.

She dipped her head and hurried in. "So sorry. So sorry," she said, and sat. Then she turned to me. "We have something *phenomenal* to share with you."

"And we have no time to waste," Headmaster Duff said. "You need to learn and practice as much as you can to hone your abilities and successfully read the orb."

"How do you mean?" I asked.

"Remember when I asked you if you can trust the process?"

"Yes."

"Well the process has already begun, and it continues now."

His head turned sharply toward the bookshelf. A panel began to push open toward us, scratching the floor. I drew back and gripped the arms of my chair. Cooler air filled the room.

"There's no need to be alarmed or afraid," Ms. Belzeebar said. "This is the exciting, *wonderful* part. You shall see!"

The panel stopped moving. Still gripping the chair, I pushed my head forward to see only a dark hollow space. "Wh-what's in *there?*"

"More like, what is *down* there. It is a vault," Duff answered.

"A *vault?!*"

"It is where we house many of S3A2's valuable and precious artifacts."

"Would you like to see?" Ms. Belzeebar asked.

They waited, staring at me.

I absolutely wanted to see. "*Yes*," I said, nodding eagerly.

We walked down narrow flights of metal stairs, behind the secret door. The space was lit with simple bulbs in the ceiling. The stairs were taking us behind the inner walls of the school, and there were closed doors along the way.

At the time, I thought it was weird for stairs to be in between walls. But years later I learned that hidden stairs existed in castles and estates of aristocracy and nobility throughout Scotland. They were constructed so that servants would use the obscured passageways to go about their daily functions of cleaning and accessing rooms. It was a method the ruling class used so servants wouldn't be seen.

When I saw another door at the bottom of the hidden stairwell, I knew we were now entering a subterranean level. Headmaster Duff opened it and handed us lanterns, which were mounted at the entrance of what seemed to be the walls of a cave.

With quick snaps of his fingers, the lanterns' flames rose. I held mine with a tight grip, and as we descended deeper, it became colder and colder. Sliding my hand along the wall for extra balance and support, I felt the damp and grainy stone. We walked in silent procession with Headmaster Duff in the front and Ms. Belzeebar behind me.

Our lanterns illuminated the thick darkness, revealing bugs, overgrown spiderwebs, and floating dirt. Three sets of footsteps, the rhythmic creaking of the lanterns, and Headmaster Duff's cane tapping the stone stairs were the only sounds we made. He used his cane with surprising adroitness and speed, despite the uneven steps. And then, after a while, there were no more steps, and we walked onward on a flat surface. We weren't descending anymore.

I was driven to learn what they would show me in the dark recesses of this space—amid the grays, blacks, and the whites of the lantern light.

Then, I was suddenly face-to-face with a disfigured door of the most vivid blue. The brass locks began to creak and moan, undoing themselves with no assistance of human hands. Levers lifted as a series of gears turned and clanked. The sounds rang out until, eventually, there was silence again.

The door opened smoothly, and a gush of air deep within the vault blew in our faces. Headmaster Duff took the lanterns from our hands and hung them on brass hooks, and with each deliberate step he took, torches that were affixed to the walls lit one by one.

The air inside was fresh as the firelight flickered against the surfaces, revealing shelves of books and objects in glass cases. My eyes darted as I turned around, dazzled by the displays, objects, and jars.

"Here, you will find everything needed," Headmaster Duff said.

"We are now deep within the depths of the school property!" Ms. Belzeebar exclaimed, spinning around. "This vault is an astounding space for ancient relics, books, solutions, articles, personal accounts, objects acquired—"

"She understands your point," Headmaster Duff asserted. The fire in the lanterns crackled and shot up several inches with each syllable he punctuated.

Ms. Belzeebar's gaze darted around at the flames. "Oh right, yes, *yes* of course!"

They watched me discover the new realm. In one case there was a white stone tablet. I walked up to it and almost pressed my nose to the squeaky-clean glass.

Ms. Belzeebar leaned in beside me. "Isn't it grand?" she said. Her stale coffee breath burned my nose. "The Seeing Tablet from Ireland. Created and etched by a medieval soothsayer, whose name is unknown."

I examined the marks on the stone, which looked like a cat had used it for a scratching post.

"The soothsayer was able to predict and document catastrophic and fortuitous events, which she wrote on her tablets. This tablet was discovered near the Cliffs of Moher by Peter Byrne, a nineteenth-century archaeologist," she explained. "There are said to be, in total, five. Unfortunately, we've only been able to recover one at this time."

"Interesting," was all I could say, still thinking it looked like scratches.

Behind her, at the far corner on a golden pedestal, was a brilliant gem sparkling and glistening with deep, bright tones of red. It radiated, practically begging for my attention.

So I approached it with long, determined strides.

The jewel rotated and hovered in space over the pedestal. Yes, just *floated*! It sparkled and brightened even more as if it knew I was watching it. Each side of the jewel had a different shade of red. One side was a rich mahogany color, while another was bright crimson. The third side was—

"Look away!" Headmaster Duff commanded. I jumped back. "The Magna harnesses and feeds off of human energy. It is potentially life-altering for novices like yourself. It can disorient and cripple you."

My mouth opened in astonishment. "Why would you keep such a thing? Why not destroy it?"

He grinned just a little. "Why not see how we can benefit from it?"

After I thought for a moment, I saw his point. "Better S3A2 have it than anybody else," I concluded.

This time, the firelight in the lanterns danced and twirled. "You catch on quite well," he said.

Taking some steps backward away from the stone, I accidentally bumped into something that dug into my back like a dull knife blade. I winced and shut my eyes, hoping nothing would fall and crash to the floor. Nothing happened. Breathing out a sigh of relief, I turned around. It was only the edge of a wooden table that had some shelves on top that were filled with books.

"These books are categorized under different abilities, subjects, and topics," Ms. Belzeebar said.

I scanned a few titles: *The Mastery of Alchemy*; *Substances, Fumes, and Solids for Controlling Emotion*; and *The Process of Mixing Timeless Substances*. Some of the titles seemed too unbelievable, like: *Time Travel and Manipulation*.

On the end of the bookshelf, I saw a large, crooked bone in a glass case. It was so big I thought it belonged to a large animal, but then I saw long bent fingers. "An *arm*," I whispered.

"His name was Etumba. One of the greatest to have the power of telekinesis, and he hailed from Central Africa. Many believed he was deformed. But this arm," Headmaster Duff said, pointing to it, "was no deformity. And those who knew better, knew this to be so. This arm was his power.

"S3A2 was fortunate to have acquired it and housed it in *this* vault."

When Headmaster Duff said "this vault," I realized there must've been other vaults out there operated by other S3A2 members. Vaults probably like this, hidden underground.

Or maybe they were hiding in plain sight, like in a quiet, unassuming home found in a suburban neighborhood where no one would imagine it housed more than parents, children, and pets.

"We believe Etumba's power, or some remnants thereof, may very well have remained in his skeletal remains," Headmaster Duff said. "However, I have not been successful in awakening it. It has been one of my greatest challenges."

In an instant, Headmaster Duff spun to the left, pivoting on his cane. And with his outstretched hand, he made a swiping motion at a bookshelf and then swiftly pointed to me. When he did, a book ejected itself from the shelf and darted toward me. Just in time, my outstretched hands caught it.

He spun again, this time to his right, and narrowed his eyes into fierce slits. A tiny red book at the other side of the vault was stubbornly lodged between two thick books. It began to wiggle out of its position. When it was free, his hand directed it toward my body, and the book landed in my hands. Before I could look up, a thick green book dropped heavily over the red one with a loud thud.

Headmaster Duff rubbed the top of his cane. "These are most suitable."

Ms. Belzeebar stood with her lanky arms dangling at her sides and a broad smile stretched across her face. "In*deed*."

Stepping to a small table, I put them down and thumbed through the pages. "At least they're not in some ancient language," I mumbled sarcastically. I wasn't thrilled to do all this reading.

"They are translated texts," Ms. Belzeebar informed.

My attention wandered as I surveyed the space again. Numerous bottles were lined up along different shelves. Some of the jars contained blobs and shrunken animals suspended in thick, discolored matter.

"You are free to be curious, and it is natural. However, right now, our *utmost* priority is reading the orb," Headmaster Duff advised.

Then, I became overwhelmed. "But what if I can't learn or find out what I need in time? And what about my classes?"

I could've kicked myself for probably sounding like a whining child.

Ms. Belzeebar began to chew on her lip. "You'll have to try," she insisted.

"Like your grandmother, I believe you will learn expeditiously," Headmaster Duff added. "As for your schoolwork, if at any time you think you need extra support with your subjects, let Mrs. Vyda know. Through her, arrangements will be made with your instructors."

"Sure," I said with a tight smile. I was hoping it didn't have to come to me asking Mrs. Vyda for help.

"I would like you to progress in your classes. But this mission with us is *as* important, if not more."

I tried to replace my doubts with some confidence. Naan did say to use my abilities for good and that definitely meant for an important mission like this.

"This will be the arrangement until we can obtain what we need from the orb," Headmaster Duff concluded. "You are *only* allowed to study these books and the orb here or in my office. You understand?"

"Yes, sir."

"When we escort you down here, you will have nothing on your person and you will leave with nothing on your person. You will touch and read nothing else, unless otherwise instructed. These artifacts are only safe down here or when handled and protected by S3A2 leadership."

"Understood."

"We should return now." The vault door unlocked and pushed open the moment Headmaster Duff said those words. "Bring the reading materials with you," he instructed.

Ms. Belzeebar took a book from my hands, and I thanked her.

We exited the vault. The door closed and the gears and shifts of the locks reengaged, sealing it shut.

With lit lanterns in hand, we marched again, forward and then upward.

"One, two, one, two … left, right, left, right," I said quietly to myself as I put one foot in front of the other. At times, I paused to make sure my balance and footing were steady and secure. When I did, Headmaster Duff and Ms. Belzeebar were patient enough to wait.

After we climbed the metal staircase and reached the other side of the office, Headmaster Duff once again directed his eyes, opening the door, and for good measure, pushed it farther open with his cane.

The office was completely dark. He turned on the desk lamp with a swift glance toward the light switch.

Ms. Belzeebar turned to me. "You *must* tell me your impressions!"

"It was …" I searched my mind for the best word to describe the experience of traveling through the hidden staircase and discovering an elaborate vault of S3A2 troves.

Then I remembered a word Mr. Franklin had taught our class when we were learning *Macbeth*, and I thought it was perfect. "It was phantasmogorical."

She belted out a short laugh that ended with a snort.

Did she just laugh at me?

"Before you go …" Duff commanded as I put the books on his desk.

I looked up. He was by the windows—his eyes cloaked by the shadows.

"Remember this." His visible lips moved deliberately to form the words. "Your abilities are innate. Do not rely entirely on these pages." The ring glistened as he pointed to the books. "Your power, conviction, and self-control enables the mastery of all."

Chapter Thirteen

THE PRICE OF KEEPING SECRETS

$\mathcal{B}$y day I was working on schoolwork, and every other night, I was studying books of a different kind in Headmaster Duff's office.

I explained my absences to Zoe and Ingrid by telling them I'd found a solitary place to study on campus. It wasn't completely a lie, except it wasn't schoolwork I was focusing on.

I should've said, "Oh, by the way, I found out about a secret society established over fifty years ago. I'm studying from books retrieved from a vault hidden deep underneath the grounds we walk on. The vault houses astounding objects you've *never* seen before in your life."

My meetings in Headmaster Duff's office had already become a routine. I would enter through a door opened by Duff's powers, sit in the wooden chair, open a book, and quietly study its contents for about an hour and a half. The green book provided details about the ability of clairvoyance. I would ask questions, and Ms. Belzeebar, to the best of her ability, would explain.

Clairvoyance wasn't their gift, so a large part of my research was self-study. However, they were helpful in that they shared insight about how their own abilities had developed.

The red book, called simply *The Fadrix*, told about the orb's history and gave some instructions. The primary way, the book said, was to focus your energy and thoughts on what you wanted it to tell you. Sounds easy enough, right? Well, it wasn't.

The few times I practiced with the Fadrix, there were some intriguing things that occurred. For instance, on the first night, the Fadrix showed a series of numbers. Ms. Belzeebar was, at first, interested. But, the second time I met with them, Headmaster Duff shook his head and said, "It is not their location."

"It's natural you would receive other signals from the Fadrix," Ms. Belzeebar explained. "Since the orb holds so much information and especially because you don't know how to entirely focus your energy."

On the second night, the Fadrix unfolded a scene. Behind the cloudy portal of white were men in dented armor and on horseback in the midst of a battle. The men charged at each other, throwing spears and wheeling their swords above their heads.

Their battle cries were drowned out by the hooves of galloping horses, which were pounding the ground, kicking up chunks of mud into the air, and trampling slain bodies. Curious to see what would happen next, I peered closer. But Ms. Belzeebar's explanation distracted me, and the scene disappeared.

"The orb is showing you a recorded event. It's something it has witnessed or one of its previous owners has experienced. What you just saw was, of course, from the past. But the Fadrix can also reveal an event that is happening now or even in the future."

"Are you *serious?*"

"I wouldn't jest about something this important," she said, shaking her head and twisting the broach on her sweater so forcefully it snagged the fabric.

Then, Ms. Belzeebar's eyes scanned me up and down, and she had a strange expression on her face. It reminded me of when Becca looked at me that afternoon at Wilma's Diner.

"Now you must keep trying," she insisted when she finished scrutinizing me.

On the third night, I was late, distracted by the upcoming meeting in the woods. Running up the stairs and through the corridor, I slid on the sleek tile right up to Headmaster Duff's door and almost stumbled into his office.

"Tardy on the third night, *humph,*" Ms. Belzeebar said with a wrinkled brow.

Her tone was surprisingly pushy and rude. And this time, instead of apologizing, she became silent and looked off into space.

Catching my breath, I waited for Headmaster Duff's reaction, but he said nothing about it. "Let us began, shall we?" he directed.

But I couldn't focus this night, and Headmaster Duff had to cut the session short. "As much as this task is important, this is not something one should force," he counseled me while Ms. Belzeebar sucked in her breath and chewed her lip.

As soon as I left the office and the door closed behind me, a lively conversation began on the other inside. I wanted to hear what they were saying. So, I pressed my ear to the cold wood, but the speaking ceased. Then I heard Ms. Belzeebar's hurried steps approaching the door. Jumping back, I ran down the hallway on my tiptoes.

We met in the wild woods near Dr. Braithwaite's tower, thinking it was the best location to avoid watchful eyes. This time William and Wallace were there. I could make them out in the darkness by their statuesque, identical silhouettes. Renaud and Atwila were also present. But, there was still no Colin.

The overgrown shrubs, vines, and moss were damp and cold with frost. We were reluctant to sit even though we had a thick wool blanket. But we made up our minds and braced ourselves as we began to bend our knees.

That was until we heard "Got it open!" and saw William close by, standing with a broad grin next to the wide-open tower door.

The reality sank in for all of us: We'd just broken into Dr. Braithwaite's *sanctuary*.

"We *shouldn't* be doing this," Atwila pestered.

I actually agreed with him.

William's grin only got larger. "When ye can still use your backsides for sittin' and fartin'—"

"*William*," Ingrid said with a gasp.

"You'll be thanking me that they didn't freeze off," he joked, and walked in.

"What are ye waiting for?!" Wallace called out.

"Both of you are *too* loud," Zoe chided.

Atwila, Ingrid, Zoe, Renaud, and I glanced at each other and silently agreed before we entered the tower together. We walked inside as if we were entering sacred ground. The white moonlight shined brightly through the domed glass ceiling. Its beams radiated between the plants in the balcony above, casting warped and crooked shadows onto the floor, the tables, and our faces. It was all the light we needed.

"*Don't* touch or move *anything*," Zoe instructed as we sat on the stools. "He will know." She eyeballed the brothers.

We were convinced Dr. Braithwaite would notice the slightest object out of place. And maybe his concoctions or strange plants could even hear sounds or record our movements. At this point I knew anything was possible.

"Decided to finally join us," Renaud said, studying the brothers. "What changed your minds?"

William and Wallace looked at each other. And finally William answered, "Can't really tell you a good reason. We were just curious, I guess."

"Fair enough," Renaud answered.

"We told Phoebe about Cara," Ingrid said. "And also about who we are."

Wallace was eager to share. Putting his elbows on the table, he turned toward me with his broad shoulders. "Ask me a question about something you've told me or I saw on you … or what we've learned in class. C'mon, anything."

"Okay … uhm … what town am I from?"

"Easy, Crockett. Something else."

"What was Ms. Belzeebar teaching us three weeks ago?"

"Easy again," Wallace answered, and then he confidently began to explain in detail and even included what she was wearing and who said what during class. And as my questions became more detailed, he fired out more detailed and precise answers.

"Awesome!" I exclaimed after his response to my fifth question.

No wonder he doesn't have to take classes too seriously.

"He's showing off," William said.

"I've got enhanced memory," Wallace explained. Then he laughed. "But I still have to pay attention for it to actually work."

"Like Ms. Belzeebar," I replied.

Zoe turned to me. "I didn't know you knew Ms. Belzeebar's ability."

A mistake. "I figured it out, you know, the way she can talk about anything," I answered quickly.

"Like Dr. Braithwaite," William butted in. "*I* can alter and create substances, and the like."

"You need to practice more and take it seriously," Ingrid encouraged. "If you did, I believe you would become so much better at it."

He shrugged. "Eh, maybe one day. Right now, it's not primary."

"You can't ignore it. It's a part of you," she insisted.

"And what about you?" Wallace asked me.

Without hesitation, I explained what I'd told the others the first time I met them in the woods and added I had retrocognition—the ability to see people's pasts, even through objects.

"You've got multiple abilities!" Wallace exclaimed.

I nodded. "Maybe you have more and just don't know," I advised. "They could be dormant, or, since you're not challenging your abilities, you haven't awakened others."

They looked stunned.

Another mistake. I sounded like I knew too much, especially for someone they thought was just learning.

"*Dormant?* That's a big word," Atwila said, looking me up and down. How would *you* know that? *How* are you so *sure* about things all of a sudden?"

191

Silence.

"I've been reading up on this," I finally answered. "The internet can be useful. You just have to avoid those bogus websites." I grasped my bracelet under the table.

"She's right," Renaud jumped in. "Phoebe has been researching. I've been seeing her at the library. She's obviously telling the truth." Renaud gave me the much-needed stamp of approval.

I was relieved and silently mouthed "thank you" to him and received his slanted smile in reply.

"Atwila, we can't get anywhere if we're suspicious of each other," Ingrid commanded.

"But—"

"It's *final*."

I'd never seen Ingrid so firm and authoritative. Sulking, Atwila's face twisted up. And I felt guilty. Here were actual, real, certified friends vouching for me while I was keeping a huge secret from them.

"Now that we all have an understanding of each other," Zoe started, "can we continue on the matter of Cara's disappearance?"

"Simple explanation," William said. "She left because she got expelled. Mystery solved."

Wallace agreed. "Her grades were slipping. We all knew that."

"She wasn't doing that poorly," the lovelorn Atwila exclaimed.

"Y'all have considered many possibilities … except one," I inserted, feeling pleased that my abilities were improving.

"Aah!" Ingrid gasped hopefully.

"What are you thinking, Phoebe?" Zoe asked.

"You could be right that Cara didn't leave because of grades. But y'all seem so sure she didn't want to leave. Maybe it was her choice."

"Is this your abilities or your logic speaking?" Renaud asked.

Something inside me knew what I had shared was a very important piece to the puzzle. "My abilities," I answered.

Atwila huffed, still scrutinizing me. "You can't —!"

"*Ah*, haud yer wheesht, man!" Wallace exclaimed. Atwila's mouth clamped shut, and his body jolted. "Don't you see she's trying to help? And maybe she's onto something."

They waited with hopeful eyes, especially Ingrid and Zoe. I tried to focus, but, unfortunately, nothing else surfaced. "I'm sorry. I can't come up with anything more."

"It isn't much help if you can't even finish your own thoughts," Atwila muttered with a smirk.

Ingrid jumped in before I had a chance to give Atwila a tongue-lashing and probably expose another embarrassing truth about him. "I think what you shared is important. We just need to understand how to interpret it."

"It's even more important we figure this out," Renaud said. "Consider this, Why would Cara suddenly choose to leave without telling us? Or who's to say one of us couldn't be next?"

"Why do you always have to be so right?" Wallace said, stroking his square chin.

We became somber, silently thinking about Renaud's straightforward remark.

Zoe piped up, "And that's why it's important to tell you this before we go."

"Oh yeah, what's that?" Wallace asked.

"Ingrid, Phoebe, and I've been talking about a way to get some information about Cara. To get some facts, and maybe even see how

Phoebe's input fits into all of this." Zoe paused as the boys curiously waited. "It's about breaking into the admin office to get Cara's files," she finished.

"The plot thickens," Wallace said, and leaned in, very interested.

"No," Renaud said, shaking his head. "Zoe, I've told you already, I don't think it's feasible. And what if her files don't prove anything?"

"It's a start. *Please* let us explain," she insisted, looking around at Ingrid and me for help. Zoe hoped we could patch something credible together on the spot.

"Well, uhm … yes …" Ingrid cleared her throat. "It's the best way to get the facts. Nothing else has worked."

I jumped in, "There may be a chance during one of the holiday events."

"Phoebe's right!" Zoe added energetically. "The end of term party would be *perfect*."

"And someone could distract the teachers while a couple of us slip out and break in," I concluded.

"I don't know," Atwila said. "What if we get caught? What excuse are we going to have. Nothing believable, I'm *sure*."

"Don't be so negative," William said, patting Atwila's head. "You meditate, not tell the future. It can work, you'll see."

Atwila squirmed away from his touch. "Let me remind you that I don't only meditate. And meditation should *not* be taken lightly. It's a *highly* advanced practice that requires skill and *deep* concentration."

"Mm-hmm, we know," William said flatly, examining a scratch on his forearm.

"And I *can't*," Atwila insisted to all of us. "If we get caught, that'll be it for me." He grabbed at the air and made a fist. "My future would be snuffed out!"

"*So* dramatic," Zoe said, shaking her head and looking up at the sky. "Listen," she said to him, "we're not going to force you. But don't stop us, and *don't* say a word about this," she warned.

Atwila nodded. "I won't, Zoe. Promise."

"What about you?" Zoe asked, looking at Renaud.

"It's not without risk, and there's a high probability for errors … *and* the plan needs more details." His eyes shifted from side to side, like he was doing mental calculations. "I would say that William is good at breaking in." We laughed quietly. "And with his abilities, he can create something that could open the door without being detected."

"I'd definitely be seen," William said with his elbows on the table, much like his brother.

"You could make something and give it to us," Ingrid suggested.

"As long as you follow my instructions," William advised.

Ingrid rolled her eyes. "Don't worry about that."

"Just give us what we need, and we'll do the rest," Zoe said assuredly.

"Ehm …" William paused to think and scratched his cheek. "Why not?" he said, and then he smiled with Ingrid and put his arm around her.

And after a long pause, Renaud said, "Then you can count me in. Also, I think as far as breaking in, Zoe and Ingrid should do it."

"Why?" Ingrid asked.

"Because Phoebe's new," Zoe said, revealing Renaud's thoughts, "and they may be watching her. Ingrid is used to being a lookout. And I know the campus and the office layout."

Renaud nodded.

She went on, "William, Wallace, and Phoebe can then help to create the distraction."

"Exactly," Renaud added.

Wallace whistled, leaning back in his stool with his arms folded over his chest. "Seems easy enough," he said. "It's pure barry! It could *definitely* work." William slapped him on his back and smiled broadly.

"So we promise to keep this quiet?" Zoe asked, looking at Atwila.

"Yes," we all answered, got up, and positioned our stools *exactly* where they were.

Peeking out of the door, Renaud decided that the coast was clear. And we filed out and walked together until it was time to part ways.

As Ingrid, Zoe, and I ran and ducked through our usual path, only the sounds of snapping twigs and rustling leaves echoed into the frosty night. Until …

"Did you see that?" I asked.

"See what?" Zoe asked.

"A shadow," I pointed to an area that was barely visible. "Behind those trees. You didn't see it?"

"Nope," Ingrid answered, "But maybe it was one of the guys."

"It wasn't in that direction."

"Or a student breaking curfew," Zoe said as we jogged.

When we saw Clairmount House, we dashed through the grass until we reached the back door. Steadying our breaths, we entered to hear Ms. Daniels snoring. We were just about to call our mission a success when a bedroom door swung open and out stepped Joy.

"Where were you?" she hissed, eyeballing us.

"Go back to bed, Joy," Zoe said. "You're missing your precious beauty sleep." Zoe stepped closer to her. "It's already showing."

Joy rolled her eyes. "I know it's literally impossible for you, but try not to be so rude and classless. It's unbecoming." Joy still demanded for one of us to break. "So where were you?"

"In the kitchen," Ingrid said with a small voice.

Poor Ingrid. She was as bad at lying as I was at snooping.

Joy scoffed. "Dressed like *that*." She pointed at our guilty attire of dark sweats and sneakers. "There's *something* about the three of you. And Cara too when she was here. Some of the other girls think so too." She continued to study us.

"Joy," I whispered steadily.

She focused on me with an "I got you" look on her face, convinced the new girl would be the one to get scared and snitch.

"If anyone knew what secret you're hiding," I continued, "I'm *sure* you wouldn't be able to attend any school within a thirty-mile radius."

Her eyes narrowed at me, and she stared. But the more she stared, the more I stared ... *and* stared. Until Joy broke the standoff.

She nervously played with her hair and backed up. "W-what are you talking about? I ... I'm not keeping any secrets," she stammered as her eyes darted around and her voice trailed off.

"You know *exactly* what I'm talking about."

Stunned and shaken, Joy shrank back into her room. "Never mind," she mumbled and shut her door.

"*Whew*," Zoe whispered with relief as we continued to our rooms. "So tell us the big secret. Because I wasn't getting anything on my end."

"I dunno."

"What?" They asked as their mouths dropped open.

"I dunno," I repeated with a shrug. "I made it up." Their eyes demanded an explanation. So I told them, "People like Joy are the same no matter where you go. And more often than not, they're always up to no good and hiding it. I just thought she wasn't any different."

Ingrid covered her mouth to stifle one of her loud giggles. "You're clever," she managed to say through her fingers. She yawned when she was able to stop her fit of giggles. "See you tomorrow *afternoon*. I'll be sleeping in."

"Good night," Zoe and I whispered, and Ingrid left to go up to her suite.

In the darkness, Zoe turned in her bed. "You awake?" she asked.

"A lil' bit," I answered sleepily.

"Are you sure about the shadow?"

"I think so … but maybe it's like you said. That it was another student."

"I could be right. But then again, you also have good instincts and abilities. What do *you* think?"

"The first time I went with you to the meeting in the woods," I confessed. "I also thought I saw a shadow—maybe even the same one too."

"Not good." She sighed and shifted in her bed, staring at the ceiling. "We should pause our meetings until we can figure this out."

I sighed as well. "Agreed."

Minutes of silence passed between us. I even thought Zoe had already fallen asleep. Until …

"Phoebe?" she whispered.

"Huh?"

"I'm glad we met. We're glad to know you."

· "Glad I met y'all too."

Within that happy moment, my guilt seeped in again. It was like the looming shadow I wanted to forget. I wished I could tell them about the vault with the special artifacts and books, S3A2, the Fadrix, Headmaster Duff, and my grandmother. I wished Atwila's mistrust wasn't warranted. But he was right. I *was* keeping something from them *and* my family.

I felt ripped in two.

Was I untrustworthy, deceptive, driven by my own selfish motives? Or a committed friend, daughter, and student, upholding promises and dutifully keeping secrets that were asked of me?

I was risking the trust of newfound friends while putting our safety in the balance. I was also trying to take advantage of possibly becoming part of S3A2 and learning about my grandmother and her story.

In reality, this wasn't a game. But it still felt like I was gambling with my friendships, their trust, my ambitions, and *so much more* in a high-stakes game of Texas Hold 'em. The cards I held could be a winning hand, but if played incorrectly, I could lose everything.

This was the price of keeping secrets.

Chapter Fourteen

THREE STEPS FORWARD, ONE STEP BACK

*O*utside, thick powdery snow blanketed the ground. I enjoyed feeling it underneath my shoes and having snowball fights.

The season was festive and welcoming, and an enormous Christmas tree was in the center of the main quad. At night, white and red lights flickered from its branches and needle-shaped leaves. Snowmen of all sizes dotted the landscape, which Mr. MacLeod surprisingly didn't smash to bits and clear away with his shovel.

The staff adorned the buildings with festive white lights along the eaves. And wreaths with large red bows, glittered with gold, were hung on the doorways and windows. Inside, garlands and hollies lined the banisters, and scented candles, which were spiced with cinnamon, vanilla, and gingerbread, burned in ceramic holiday trays in the offices.

Our Edwards Hall December assembly was held on the first week because of the upcoming holidays. We shuffled in from the cold and were greeted at the doorway with sweet aromas. Tables on either side of us offered a choice between a mug of warm Scottish Hot Toddy (minus the alcohol) and hot chocolate.

I chose the Hot Toddy, curious to taste the newfound drink. And it was marvelous! The spicy, sweet, and tart combination danced in my mouth. It was so soothing as I swallowed. I closed my eyes and took another wonderful taste.

We sat sipping our delicious drinks while Mrs. Vyda, as usual, stood at the podium. But today, she wore a red headband and matching earrings.

Hmm. Was this fashion choice a spark of holiday spirit within Mrs. Vyda? Or, was it because it coincided with Duff being present? Yes, he had decided to attend. Sitting, in a crisp navy blue suit, he gripped his cane. I looked at him, but if he saw me, he didn't give it away.

"As you know, in December," Mrs. Vyda addressed us, "We at The Murray School enjoy celebrating the festive season. And so the tree-lighting ceremony will be held this Friday evening after classes. Our choir will also be in attendance. We hope everyone will take part in this event." Mrs. Vyda paused and looked at us with her usual rigid expression, but today she had something extra—a glimmer in her eyes.

She turned to look over her shoulder at Headmaster Duff, and he responded with a regal nod. Turning back to us, Mrs. Vyda's stony face actually swelled with pride and there was a slight glow in her cheeks. Mrs. Vyda continued, "We'll be serving holiday meals throughout the month. And don't forget our party with a Ceilidh …"

A Kaylee?

Zoe leaned over to whisper, "It's traditional music and dance. I'll explain more later."

"Get out of my head," I whispered lightheartedly.

She laughed under her breath.

I'd decided not to wear Naan's bracelet all the time. I figured it would seem odd to Zoe if she was never able to read my mind. At that moment, it was snug inside my journal.

"For lower schoolers, their holiday party will be held …"

"I think I'm getting better," Zoe beamed.

"… later this month …"

"Speaking of the party, Renaud and I discussed a good distraction plan," I said.

"… forget to turn in your …"

Then I added, "It's basic, but we think it'll work."

"… last reminder …"

"We can't wait to hear." Her excitement came through, even in a whisper.

"He would like to …"

"It will be——" Something jabbed my ribs, and I spun toward the source of my sudden pain. Ingrid's blackened eyes directed my attention up at the stage. To my surprise, Mrs. Vyda had finished speaking and Headmaster Duff was already standing at the podium.

His deep voice filled the room. "I will be brief in sharing that we hope you have an enjoyable season. And know that, here, at The Murray School, we always strive for excellence. Have a productive end of term and remain steadfast to your goals."

With only those few sentences, Headmaster Duff elicited a hearty applaud from us.

I wondered if he was thinking about us with special abilities or if he was speaking in general. One could never know for sure with Headmaster Duff.

Along with holiday excitement, there was also tension and anxiety about exams. Students were deep in their books, laptops, bags of food—anything to have successful study sessions.

I had a study night with Renaud, and it was vital. Since Renaud worked at the library, we had the benefit of using the back office while other students were jockeying for space in the main area or study rooms. The table was so small that Renaud and I almost sat with our shoulders touching. Several worksheets were scattered on the desk.

"Don't be nervous," he advised, after we had just finished studying for Dr. Braithwaite's exam. "You've prepared. Just remember—take nothing for granted and be thorough."

"It's like *you're* the one with the abilities," I remarked. "You're so knowledgeable and confident."

He sat back in his chair and shrugged. "I just work hard. Read up on many subjects. I'm sure you've seen."

"It's more than that, Renaud. You put effort in everything you do, and you have a strong will. The fact that you work hard says so much more than someone who has an ability but doesn't care." I stopped myself, realizing I was talking too much, and Renaud was watching me closely.

But he seemed interested even though his face became somber. "What I learn makes sense. It keeps me grounded and focused," he said after a long pause.

Seeing Renaud's faraway expression made me hesitant about what I was going to say next, but I wanted to because I cared. "Renaud … I don't want to sound pushy or anything …," I began. "School means a lot to you. I see that. But I notice you don't talk much about your family. And when you have, it's with little interest....Why?" Then I quickly added, "If you don't want to tell me, I understand."

I was taking a big chance asking Renaud about his personal life. He would either shut me out or explain. Either way, it would've been a fair reaction on his part.

Renaud decided to answer after thinking for a bit. "I'm an only child. You know that, right?"

"Yes."

"My parents …" He looked away. "My parents have so much. Do so much. But it has never included me. They don't have the time, and they've never even tried to hide that fact …" His voice trailed off as he stared over my head at an Einstein poster on the wall. "So school," he said at last with a sigh, "and my studies give me purpose."

Without thinking, I placed my hand on his shoulder. He seemed surprised but didn't pull away. "I have no idea what that's like. It must be very confusing. But I do know a little bit about what it feels like to be lonely and need to escape."

Renaud's eyes suddenly clouded over. But it was brief because they soon cleared, and his jaw set firmly.

Trying to change the heaviness around us, I smiled and asked, "And with all your studying and knowledge, what are you going to do with it?" I shook my finger at him and with the shaky voice of an old grandma, said, "What do you want to be when you grow up, young man?"

It worked. The tension in Renaud's shoulders eased and he smiled. "A professor of Biochemistry and Physics. Or maybe … and I know it might sound crazy. But I'd like to train to do the science that Dr. Braithwaite does. *If* that's even possible."

I sat up in interest and admired Renaud's ambition. "It's not crazy at all. In fact, what I've learned from Dr. Braithwaite *himself* is that it's possible to defy the odds."

"That sounds just like him," he said, nodding. "And what about you?"

It wasn't like I hadn't been asked before. And if I'd been asked this question just three months ago, my answer would've been bold and definite—a painter. But now …

"I'm not so sure," I whispered. I was perplexed because even though I was learning more about myself and what was going on around me, other things were becoming so uncertain.

"It's perfectly reasonable that you don't know. Don't lie to yourself. Otherwise, you'll be unhappy."

I didn't realize my hand had lingered on his shoulder until his gaze slowly traveled to it. Suddenly, his pleasant expression became curious and focused as his hazel eyes narrowed.

I followed his stare, wondering what made him suddenly so serious. When my eyes rested on his target, I realized that Renaud was examining the intricacies of my … *bracelet!*

Stunned, I caught my breath, feeling exposed. I moved my hand to scratch my earlobe, trying to act casual.

I wouldn't know how to explain such a unique bracelet to intelligent Renaud. My swift movement was a success, as it made Renaud focus on my eyes again.

"Are you looking forward to your first holiday party here?" he asked.

"Yep," I said, sitting on my hands. "Ingrid and Zoe were telling me what it's like. Do you enjoy the parties?"

"Sure, why not." He shrugged. "I know what to expect … although this year will be different."

We acknowledged our secret plan to break in with a silent nod.

"So are you going with anyone?" Renaud asked in a lowered voice.

I answered matter-of-factly, "With Zoe and Ingrid. But you know because of the plan, they'll have to leave early."

He laughed, and the dimple deepened and stretched on his face. "Yes, I know *that*."

When Renaud's laugh subsided, he quickly turned away, looking around the small room, on the floor, at the papers—everywhere but at my face. His breathing became rapid, and he hesitated but eventually looked at me with a flushed face. "What I *meant* was if ..."

"If what?"

"If you would ..." He stalled.

"If I would what?" I tilted my head at Renaud's strange behavior. "Are you okay?" Then, I sat forward in protest. "Don't tell me you're having second thoughts about the plan?"

Renaud shook his head vigorously. "No, not at all. It's not that." He cleared his throat, ran his hand through his wavy hair, and glanced at me with nervous eyes.

At that moment, I wished I could've read minds like Zoe.

"I'm fine with the plan," Renaud assured. "I was just—"

"Attention, students, the library will be closing in five minutes. Please check out...."

Renaud jumped up from his seat as the intercom's message continued. He bumped his knee on the table but didn't seem to notice. "I have to close the library tonight," he announced as if he'd just remembered.

I started packing up to help him.

"It's okay. You don't need to." He looked me over. "You seem tired."

My hand went to my cheek to hide my face. I knew I'd been working a lot but didn't know I looked so scraggly that anyone would notice.

Renaud shook his head. "I just meant tired. You still look good." He smiled and then started walking out of the tiny room.

"Are you sure you don't need help?" I asked as I followed him out to the front desk to see a line of sleepy, cranky-faced students waiting to check out books.

"I'm sure," he said, taking a book from an upper schooler to scan it into the computer.

"I really appreciate our study session and conversation. In fact, I think I'll be okay tomorrow."

"De rien. C'était un plaisir."

"Huh?" I could barely make out the different words he'd said.

"De … rien. C'é … tait … un … plai … sir," he emphasized, looking over at me. "In French, it means you're welcome, and it was a pleasure."

The scanner beeped again, and a book thudded onto the counter.

I'd never heard Renaud speak French before. It sounded really nice and smooth—*not* like a robot.

"How do I say, 'thank you, good night, and see you tomorrow'?" I asked, excited to hear more.

"Merci. Bonne nuit. À demain."

Trying to do the French language some justice, I carefully repeated the words.

"That was *really* good," he complimented.

But I knew it sounded terrible. "You're too nice!" I said and turned to leave.

While walking to Clairmount House, I practiced saying the words

Renaud had taught me. And before going to bed, I sat at my desk and took out a piece of paper and colored pencils to draw the perfect scene.

Are you the type of person who can't take a test on a full stomach? Well that was me on the morning of Dr. Braithwaite's exam. I know it's said you should have a decent breakfast before exercising your brain, but I couldn't that morning. The only thing I managed to have was pineapple juice.

Yes, pineapple juice. Perhaps an odd choice, but I appreciate its unique taste—the flavor and pulpy consistency of pineapple juice is soothing enough to calm me, sweet enough to feed my brain, and tangy enough to wake me up. I drank two large glasses.

When I opened the door of the tower, Dr. Braithwaite's commanding voice gave his first instructions of the day. "Leave your phones, bags—*everything*—at the front of the room."

As we obeyed, Dr. Braithwaite inched closer to me. "Please take off your jewelry."

My body stiffened, and I looked up in shock. Dr. Braithwaite's steady expression was calmer than the gray tones of his suit. As I slipped off the bracelet and put it in my bag, I wondered what else the bracelet could do since Dr. Braithwaite didn't want me to wear it.

With lab coats, goggles, and gloves on, we sat in our places. Dr. Braithwaite had mounted a special divider between us; it was made of sturdy metal and fastened with screws. There was no opportunity for tricks or cheating—most likely the metal compound was formulated to block our abilities from one another.

Before sitting, I surveyed the room. Zoe gave me a thumbs-up and a weak smile. Ingrid playfully crossed her eyes. William and Wallace were oddly serious and focused in their spaces, and Colin drummed his pencils on the table, looking up at the gallery. Atwila had his eyes closed as he massaged his temples. And there was Renaud. When I looked at him, he said softly, "You'll be fine."

"It is time." Dr. Braithwaite's voice cut through the tension. He swept by us and placed a blank sheet of paper under our noses. "Oh, and before you begin," he added, "it was an adequate attempt. However, you must use a material that doesn't leave a trace within the keyhole."

We gasped. *He knows we broke in!* Wallace cussed under his breath. Meanwhile, Dr. Braithwaite's face didn't give anything away. Except, I could've sworn that the skin at the corner of his left eye twitched, as if he were holding back a smile. He tortured us in silence for a few more seconds before he instructed, "You may turn over your papers now, and all the best."

Immediately, I flipped mine over: $Re_1Gen_{14}So_4$.

My heart skipped a beat. My very first experiment. I was new, doubtful, and not even paying attention. My mind continued to race. I had studied this experiment, but maybe I missed something. And with the curveball he added to our exam, I felt lost.

Plop! Atwila had hopped off his stool. With his stocky legs, he went straight to the back of the room. Next to me, Renaud's pencil scratched the surface of his paper. *How does he already know what to write?!* Toward the back of the room, William and Zoe were at the counter pouring substances into flasks and beakers.

Phoebe, focus! Focus and listen! I stopped looking at everyone. *Breathe, listen, and focus.* I looked at my paper again as I repeated those three words.

Shutting my eyes, I listened to my abilities and let my thoughts speak. They didn't fail me as they resurfaced and what happened next was incredible and unexplainable.

It was like my body was just a shell, sitting in the tower, while my mind went somewhere else. Somewhere I can't picture or describe. So the best I can come up with is to compare what happened with two "real-life" scenarios.

Here goes: Imagine a driver whizzing over eighty miles per hour on a freeway, and all the while he is worried about the upcoming presentation he has to give at work that morning. Twenty minutes later, he ends up in the parking lot of his office without remembering what exit he took or how he chose his parking space. However, this man has completely memorized his presentation.

Or think about a woman who has sleepwalked and wakes up to realize that she is standing in a twenty-four-hour convenience store several blocks from her home. She is fully dressed with a basket of groceries in one hand and her wallet in the other. I don't even think these examples could come close to what I experienced, but they are the best I can use.

There are some fragments of the test I can recall. Like the curveball was that I had to make a living plant die—a sort of retro-experiment, you could call it. Also, the solution I made didn't stink. Instead, it was sweet.

My full memory of the exam only reemerged when Dr. Braithwaite called out, "Three minutes and three seconds," as he flipped his watch closed and returned it to his pocket.

Looking up through my goggles, I saw that only Atwila, Wallace, and I were left. Without stalling, I recorded the last of my observations on the piece of paper that I noticed was already filled with my handwriting, turned the paper over, and left my table. Feeling confused and invigorated, I pushed the heavy wooden door open.

The cold air refreshed my face and released some tension in my muscles. I put on my bracelet, walked away from the tower, and looked around to make sure I was alone.

"*Yes!*" I belted out to the sky.

We would still have a couple more classes before the term ended, but for the most part, Dr. Braithwaite's class, at least for this year, was over.

Now, I just had to wait for my results and wrap my head around what had just happened during the test.

I didn't get used to going down to the vault. I believed it would eternally creep me out, especially the dark, damp stairs, cold draft, and boundless darkness beyond our lanterns.

Ms. Belzeebar led me down alone this time. "Let's hope you'll get some inspiration being down here," she said.

When we reached the vivid blue door, it creaked and groaned as the latches obeyed. And I wasn't surprised to find Headmaster Duff already inside. The Fadrix was waiting for me on the table.

Crack! Crack! I popped my knuckles, knowing it wouldn't help, but it still felt good.

Before I started, Headmaster Duff asked, "What have you learned thus far about controlling your abilities?"

"That I should be comfortable and more relaxed. Or else I sort of panic. Also," I added, "I've learned if I'm not prepared or skilled enough, I can accidentally confuse my abilities and mix them up, like having crossed wires. And then they can become weakened."

He looked pleased. "And someone with one ability, who has greater focus, can be more powerful than someone with multiple who cannot manage or control them."

"Yes, sir," I said, remembering that important part.

"So, tell me, how was your exam?" I hesitated. "Go on," he urged.

"Actually," I said, popping my knuckles again nervously. "I think something strange happened."

"Strange as in you don't have a full memory of doing the experiment but somehow completed it?" Ms. Belzeebar asked.

I was stunned. "*Yeah*, how did you know?"

"Phoebe, it happens," she answered. "It means you're advancing."

I looked at them. "So it happens to you?"

They nodded.

"Is this the first time for you?" Ms. Belzeebar asked.

"There have been other times that I would say things aloud when my abilities speak, and I can't control it. Or, when I'm trying to summon the Fadrix, my thoughts speak in my mind. But when these things happen, I'm totally aware of what's going on. My exam experience was something new."

"You do have control—in *all* instances—complete control," Headmaster Duff advised. "You need to be confident in that fact."

"Will this just start happening to me randomly?" I asked.

Ms. Belzeebar laughed. "No, it can happen only when you're testing yourself at a greater level than what's normal for you or what you're used to."

Relieved, I relaxed. "Although it was strange, I guess it didn't bother me."

"And it should not," Headmaster Duff said. "You should be encouraged by what has happened to you. It is not something that occurs for all who have abilities. This incident shows, even more so, that one day you may very well become a member of S3A2."

I grinned, thrilled for the compliment. Out of the corner of my eye, Ms. Belzeebar shifted from side to side and twisted her broach in between her fingers. She didn't seem pleased to hear any of this.

I confidently focused and peered into the Fadrix again, staring into the dormant white cloud. It began to swirl as it had done several times before. But then, the formation dissipated, and the white cloud reemerged. I blinked, looking up for an answer.

"Just keep at it," Ms. Belzeebar said bluntly.

So I stared at the Fadrix again, but nothing happened. Maybe I wasn't focusing enough, thinking the wrong questions. Or maybe the problem was that I was focusing too much, and my mind was overworked. Frustrated, I pushed the orb aside. My head literally hurt.

"You shouldn't just give up," Ms. Belzeebar insisted, tapping her long, narrow foot. "If I had your—"

"*Do not* interfere," Headmaster Duff cut her off. "That is *not* how this works."

Ms. Belzeebar recoiled, hunching her back.

A tension between them grew.

"Something is blocking me. I don't know what or why," I said.

Headmaster Duff's stern brow softened a little. "I admire your will. Let us recommence next week."

Ms. Belzeebar stifled a sigh.

A break was most welcomed. The end of the week would be the Ceilidh and our plan would be put to the test that night.

Chapter Fifteen

A SIMPLE PLAN

*E*xamining my reflection in Ingrid's full-length mirror, I admired the finished creations of my artistic collaboration with her. There was no doubt that she was a great designer.

The black two-piece dress I wore for the Ceilidh had a long, full skirt that shimmered with iridescent fabric. Ingrid honored my love of dark colors and silver. I had on dewy, natural-looking makeup—all thanks to her as well. As I lingered for a bit at the mirror, I couldn't help but notice I looked more like Naan than ever.

For Zoe, Ingrid had created a long, fitted wintry white mermaid dress. The dress had long sleeves and a deep neckline. It was bold, just like Zoe's personality. Her eyeshadow was a smoky gray, making her green eyes sparkle dramatically.

"Your talent is one of a kind," I told Ingrid.

"I second that," Zoe said, gliding her hands on the delicate fabric of her dress. "I don't think I've ever worn anything so grand."

Ingrid blushed and held her warming cheeks.

For herself, Ingrid had created a short, red satin dress with a wide ruffled skirt and off-the-shoulder cap sleeves. Her heels gave her three extra inches. I didn't know how she managed, but she balanced without effort. The rich red color complemented her glistening short black hair, and she popped the color with a bold red lipstick and cat-eyed winged eyeliner.

We took so many pictures. Some to prove to Ingrid's parents that she was talented. Some to celebrate the end of term. And others for our friendship. Ingrid couldn't help herself—she had to send some to William, even though she would be seeing him soon. He responded soon after.

"Speaking of William, where's the key?" I asked.

Ingrid patted her dress pocket and then pulled it out. It was supposed to be the key of all keys to execute our plan. I held it in my palm to examine the specialness of it, but it looked and felt normal—lightweight, silver, shiny, and with regular grooves.

Although it looked like any other key, it was specially formulated with chemical properties that allowed it to shape-shift and mold to fit into any groove of a lock.

"And you're sure it's going to work?" Zoe asked.

Her doubtfulness couldn't be faulted; William didn't have the best record for being reliable.

"*Of course!*" Ingrid answered as I returned the key to her. "If William says so, I believe him. Plus, he told me he tested it."

Zoe took it from Ingrid, flipped it up in the air, and caught it in her hand. She left the room and locked the door behind her. After some minutes had passed, we could hear the lock clicking and Zoe reentered.

"It just worked on both of our rooms," she announced.

"*See*, don't worry," Ingrid insisted.

It seemed too perfect, so I asked, "And William did this *all* by himself?"

"Well ... he might've had some help from Renaud." Ingrid smiled sheepishly.

"*Aha!*" Zoe said. "Then I have *more* faith in seeing this actually work." She tossed the key up in the air one more time before handing it back to Ingrid.

Everything was set. Ingrid and Zoe's change of clothes were hidden in a restroom stall at Edwards Hall. And William, Wallace, Renaud, and I set our watches and phones for when I was supposed to pull the fire alarm while they distracted the administrators. The plan was elementary—oftentimes keeping it simple is best.

The hall had a Christmas tree and oversized ornaments and gift boxes on the floor. There were also decorations that looked like fallen snow.

The moment I heard the music, with the fiddles and accordions, and saw students dancing in a line and swinging their partners around, it reminded me of when my schools in Crockett would have field day that would include a hoedown.

A major difference was that the Ceilidh had bagpipe players. The unique sound wailed, shrilled, and rung out among the talking, laughing, lively clapping, stomping, and twirling of the students and some of the teachers.

"There they are!" Ingrid pointed excitedly when she saw William and Wallace. Her dress bounced around her knees as she spun away to get them.

The brothers wore blazers and ties, and a great surprise was that they also wore kilts, which represented the blue-and-red tartan of their clan. I also noticed that other guys had on kilts, and it was a great addition to the usual suits most wore.

Holding hands, Ingrid returned with William.

"I guess they've lasted the term together," Zoe remarked to me.

We danced as a small group together. After a few more songs, the band packed up, and the sound system played a modern mix of American and British music. Scanning the crowd further, I saw Mrs. Vyda near the entrance. There weren't many administrators, thankfully. And, as I expected, Headmaster Duff, Ms. Belzeebar, and Dr. Braithwaite weren't there; they had more important things to do—operating S3A2.

"Zoe! Phoebe! Very pretty," Wallace said as he walked up.

Zoe smirked and tilted her head when he tried to ease in close beside her.

"You're really talented," William said, putting his arm around the waist of a giggling and pleased Ingrid.

I turned to showcase her creation. I liked how the fabric swayed. The iridescent layer of organza shimmered with silver studs that reflected on the dance floor like a starry night, and I became the revolving moon.

I was even liking the bare midriff, created by the separate bodice, because it was hot inside. As a matter of fact, my hair was even starting to frizz, but I didn't care. Zoe also turned to showcase Ingrid's creation.

"Ingrid definitely knew who she was designing for," a guy said, walking up to us.

Renaud?

He was in a well-tailored black suit with his hair stylishly moussed.

Without his books or glasses, Renaud looked so grown up. I stared at him, trying to come up with the word that best described him.... *Sophisticated? Yes, sophisticated.*

Momentarily frozen, I must've looked like a complete fool. I caught myself, wiped the stupid look off my face, and shifted my eyes away to a vague spot in the distance as Zoe, Wallace, Ingrid, and William walked off. Then my gaze landed on Joy's powder blue dress. And of course, Colin was with her. I sighed.

"Did you hear what I said, Phoebe?" Renaud said.

"Uh-uh, no, sorry. Could you say it again?"

"I was saying you look.... They've been together for a while," he finished flatly.

"What?" My head snapped up in surprise as I finally looked up at him.

"Colin and Joy. They've been together for a while."

"Oh, I didn't know. I thought Colin was ... single."

Renaud smirked. "Many people think that. It's because Colin's not really serious about anyone. Joy just doesn't know." He paused. "You like him?" Renaud's question sounded more like a statement.

Acting like I was shocked, I put my hand to my chest and my eyes widened. "*Me?! Nooo.* I *barely* know Colin. I mean he's really nice and in our classes, but we don't really talk to each other that much, you know. I mean, you don't know *that*, but maybe you do because you're in our classes. But you're not in *all* of my classes, and it's not like you've been watching *every* person I speak to so ..." My voice trailed off. I was sounding like a babbling idiot, and Renaud's smile slowly grew as he became more and more amused.

"I'll shut up now," I muttered, and shook my head nervously.

Renaud looked down at his feet with his hands in his pockets. "You wanna dance?"

His eyes shot up as his eyebrow arched. "Huh?"

Now, it was Renaud's turn to be put on the spot. He started tugging at his shirt collar and then at his sleeves.

"I said … do you want to dance?"

Renaud's expression had transformed from stunned to utterly petrified. "I … I don't really dance," he said.

"I've never even seen you this nervous during one of our complicated experiments. And those are *much harder* than dancing," I smiled and teased. "Plus, you're not the type to back down from a challenge—especially one this easy, right?"

His scared expression was replaced with a daring smile. "When you put it that way, how can I refuse?" he said, and reached for my hand.

Renaud wasn't bad after he loosened up. A few fast songs had played, and then his feet slowed to a stop. "Okay, okay, I've proven myself now, right?" he said with a laugh with his hands up.

"Pretty good, pretty good," I said, stroking my chin.

"That bad, huh?" he said with a smile.

"Some people would be happy with being pretty good." I playfully pushed his arm. "But I get it. You're an A-plus kind of guy."

When I said that, Renaud's face became serious, and he inched closer to me. The space between us suddenly felt warm as it got smaller and smaller.

"You got Renaud to dance. Impressive!" Zoe said, holding cups in her hands and walking up with Wallace.

Renaud quickly stepped back as I took the cup that Zoe handed me. I took several gulps of water, partially because I was thirsty and mainly because I wanted to drink down my uneasiness and embarrassment.

"Phoebe can be persuasive," Renaud said before taking a drink.

"So we *see*," Wallace said, wiggling his eyebrows and elbowing Renaud.

I took another gulp of water and looked at them, but my eyes didn't focus.

"You both make a good pair—*dancing* that is," Zoe said, smiling slyly. "Don't you think, Wallace?"

"Absolutely, a great couple. *Sorry*, I meant to say *pair*."

Zoe looked at Renaud and me with her mischievous eyes. I avoided Renaud's face. Relief spread over me when Colin approached, *without* Joy, and the attention shifted to him.

"I'm ready for the end of term!" he declared as he entered our circle. "I thought I failed Dr. B.'s test." Colin reached up to pat Renaud on the shoulder. "I'm sure you got the highest mark."

Renaud stepped out of his reach. "We'll have to see," he said. His computer voice had returned.

If Colin felt the chill, he seemed to ignore it as he turned to me and smiled. "You really caught on this term. No one would've guessed you're new."

"Phoebe's not new anymore," Renaud said. "Plus, she's been working hard. It's no surprise that she's improved."

Colin's smile slowly disappeared as he raised his hands. "Yeah, I believe, man. I believe."

Wallace spoke up, thankfully with perfect timing. "So, ehm … Ingrid, my brother told me you're going to Thailand."

Ingrid beamed and nodded. "I can't wait to ride an elephant!"

"You'll have to share what it's like," I said.

"You're happy to go home?" Zoe asked me.

I nodded. "Mostly because of my family."

"I'll be with family too," she said dully. "But not because I want to."

"We can definitely keep in touch. Share pictures!" Ingrid said with a cheerful smile, trying to keep the mood lively.

"We'll be in Edinburgh," Wallace started, pointing to his brother. "And Colin's going to join us for Hogmanay."

"Hogmanay, what's that?" I asked.

The brothers' eyes widened. "You don't know?!" William asked.

My face was blank. "Nope, not a clue … I don't even think I could guess."

"It's our New Year's. *Very crazy* and lots of fun," Wallace said.

"Next time, you should come to Edinburgh. And we'll show you a good time," William offered.

Before I could answer, Colin interjected. "Being there also means I won't have to be at home for too long with my old man." His face hardened, and the others exchanged knowing glances.

"What about you?" I turned to ask Renaud.

Standing close beside me, he still dipped his head to make sure I heard. It was as if he was only speaking to me. "Geneva. My grandparents are there. I'll also see my mother afterwards in Monaco."

"I see," I said softly, seeing the slight pain in his eyes.

He added, looking relieved, "I won't be gone for the entire time. I'm returning to school before our break ends."

"*Oh!*" Ingrid said, "and Atwila's spending his holiday with his family. *Seven* brothers and sisters! Can you imagine?"

"*Seven!*" I exclaimed.

"Yep, and he's the middle child."

Zoe smirked. "That's why he's so moody."

Just at that moment, Ingrid squealed. "I *love* this song. William, you *must* dance with me! We'll be back," she said as she pulled a reluctant William onto the dance floor.

"And Phoebe and I need something to drink," Zoe said.

"But we *just* had water," I insisted, but still followed her.

Zoe stopped when we were next to a wall and out of earshot. "So, you have to tell me more about what's going on," she asked with her hands on her narrow hips. Zoe's curiosity was in overdrive, and when it was, it was almost impossible to stop.

"With what?" I asked, even though I knew. I eventually gave in. "There's nothing going on. Renaud is kind. He's a good friend."

"That's obvious. But it's also obvious how much you two get along."

"What are you cooking up in your head? You know that Renaud gets along with *everyone*. He's a nice guy."

Zoe shook her head. "Phoebe, you're not getting it. Renaud doesn't open up to people, not even to us."

My eyebrows rose. I had no idea. "Well … maybe it's because he's been my lab partner."

Zoe couldn't accept that. "Deny and avoid all you want, but I see the attention he gives you. *More* than a regular tutor. I should've noticed before. The way he talks only to you and defends you." Her eyes glimmered. "What spell have you cast on him?" she teased.

I looked over at the guys chatting with each other. Beyond them, I could hear Ingrid's trademark laugh traveling through the room and even above the music.

Watching my friends was a nice feeling, and I felt happy being a part of it. And then I focused only on Renaud—tall, super smart, easy to talk to, and sophisticated.

Renaud's head slowly turned in our direction.

I caught my breath and quickly looked at Zoe, hoping he didn't catch me staring. "He's a friend" was all I could manage to say again.

The glimmer in Zoe's eyes faded. "It's time," she said bluntly.

"What?"

"It's *time*."

Milliseconds later, a quiet but persistent sound emanated between us. My watch. Across the room, William, Wallace, Renaud, Ingrid, Zoe, and I shared a quick glance.

"Hope you've enjoyed the party tonight!" a teacher announced on the stage. Everyone cheered and hollered. "Our band will be returning to close the night. So get ready for a few more dances before we say goodbye and until next year!"

Action. It was just like we had expected, except I wondered how we'd pull it off with Colin around us. Luckily, at that moment, Joy and her friends reappeared, and Joy pulled Colin away from the group.

I squeezed Zoe's hand. "Ready?"

Her face was steadfast. "Always," she said. And like a lightning bolt in her fitted white dress, Zoe took long, quick strides through the crowd. Ingrid joined her at the door to the hallway. Then I took a last look at the boys as the band prepared on the stage, pepping up the crowd with some raucous notes before they started.

My heart was pounding as I slowly made my way to the fire alarm at the back, left side of the hall. Our plan was that I'd pull it immediately after the last song ended, ensuring that everyone would have to exit and gather in the main quad. This would allow Zoe and Ingrid more than enough time to go unnoticed, as they took an obscure path to the castle and got what they needed in the office.

I timed my pace—not wanting to reach the panel too soon but definitely not too late. My eyes scanned the room. Wallace, William, and Renaud were already doing a great job of distracting most of the teachers. The brothers were being wonderfully obnoxious around the table, acting like they were having a drinking contest.

As expected, this made administrators, including Mrs. Vyda, eyeball them, hoping William and Wallace wouldn't go too far and become completely out of order. Renaud was engaging several teachers who gathered around him. He was probably in the middle of some impressive college-level conversation.

I counted my steps. *One-two-one-two*, much like I did when going to and from the vault. The band started to play another song. When I was just about to reach the panel, my phone dinged. I hastily pulled it out of my hidden dress pocket. It almost fell out of my sweaty palm, but I managed to hold on to it.

A text had popped up and brightened the screen. It was from Ingrid to the boys and me: STOP. We think we've been found out.

My heart dropped to my stomach, and I quickly turned back to where I came from.

The temperature rose inside of me and around me as I elbowed my way through clusters of dancing bodies and eventually bumped into William. I held his arm and then noticed we were surrounded by his friends, including Colin and some girls. When Wallace joined the group, the brothers played it real cool while my nerves were bouncing and firing, as lively as the music.

Minutes went by. All the while I bit my lip and wrung my sweaty hands, wondering where Ingrid and Zoe were. I joined in the dancing circle, acting like I was having a good time. But I felt even more uneasy when I realized that Renaud hadn't joined us. *Where are they?* Colin was beside me saying something, but I didn't hear him as my eyes scanned the hall, hoping for them to return.

After what seemed like my hundredth glance at the doorway, I finally exhaled and wiped my wet forehead. There they were, in wrinkled dresses and behind them was Renaud. The last song ended as the students cheered and the lights brightened the hall.

When Zoe, Ingrid, and Renaud reached the group, I was so happy I hugged them. Renaud seemed surprised, but he slowly returned my embrace.

"What happened?" I whispered.

But they didn't answer.

Among the hyper, adrenaline-filled students, we left Edwards Hall not saying a word. We were confused and disappointed, and I was sure we were thinking the same thing: *Who could've known? It was airtight.*

Ingrid, Zoe, and I parted ways with William, Wallace, and Renaud. Colin was behind us, walking with Joy. Whatever civility she might've had for the night had expired. But whatever Joy was complaining about didn't matter.

Feeling defeated, we entered our house and lumbered up the stairs—without any care or grace. In fact, we had unbuckled and dragged those torturous contraptions (also known as high heels) off our feet the moment we entered the doorway.

In our room, Zoe and I were still stunned and exhausted. "Tomorrow" was all she had said when I looked at her. I ran my hand over Naan's bracelet. The action was becoming a habit. It seemed like two major things had become one big failed attempt—the stubborn orb and now the Ceilidh. It was supposed to be a simple plan that should've worked.

"*Ugh*," I said under my breath with frustration. It was only after my frustration subsided that I realized there was a suspect who could've been the reason for our failed night—the tall shadow.

Chapter Sixteen

THE PEOPLE WE TRUST

*A*twila. It might've been him," Ingrid suspected. "He was afraid to get in trouble, and he didn't want to help."

"Could be," Zoe responded, "but he promised not to tell anyone. And he wasn't lying."

"Now that you say that," Ingrid said, "I did feel his fear. But people can change their minds."

"*But*," I added, raising a finger, "he would want to find out about what happened to Cara just as much as we do."

It was the day after the Ceilidh, and our speculations were swirling. Zoe and Ingrid had explained that during the Ceilidh, after they went to the restroom and changed, the window they were supposed to sneak out of was unusually and unexpectedly sealed with a wooden bar on the outside. They also saw teachers through the glass, walking the area they would've run through to get to the office. It seemed as if the teachers had suspected something was going to happen.

And then Ingrid and Zoe sent the text to the boys and me. While they were changing back into their dresses, Renaud knocked on the restroom door, asking if they were okay. He had also helped them stash their clothes in a hidden bin to be picked up later.

"Maybe it's one of the brothers. Many times they can't shut their mouths about things," Zoe said.

"That's *unfair!*" Ingrid exclaimed. "They were a part of the plan the *entire* time."

"I'm *not* saying they would've done it on purpose," Zoe insisted.

"Ingrid's right," I said. "They were committed ... then again, Zoe's making sense too. Who's to say they didn't tell Colin just for fun, and then Colin told someone else?"

Ingrid shut her mouth stubbornly. Then she finally responded, "Well, if they're suspects, then Renaud has to be one too."

"*How* could you say that?" I jumped in. "Renaud was the one who distracted the teachers *and* helped you out." My voice was high-pitched. Although I was being logical, I was also defensive.

"Okay, okay, we get it," Ingrid said, and then a small grin appeared. "Am I hearing some interest there?"

I sat back. Not even my bracelet could help to hide how intense I sounded.

"Let's just agree it wasn't any of the guys, okay?" Zoe said. Ingrid and I nodded. "So if it's not them, then it could've been someone who overheard us."

The possibilities now expanded. We sat in silence, overwhelmed.

"Also," I said quietly, "there's the shadow."

They stared at me, each remembering the time I had told them about seeing a shadow.

I added, "But whoever it was, it's strange we weren't reported."

"That means this lurking shadow chose not to tell," Zoe concluded.

I didn't know if I should've felt comforted or disturbed by the mysterious entity.

"I think, unfortunately," Ingrid said with a sigh, "we have to shelve our plan for finding Cara. And hope this sneaky shadow doesn't do anything else."

"And we can't meet anymore until this is figured out," Zoe added, looking sullen.

"I'm sorry it didn't work out. Cara seemed like a good friend to you," I said.

"She was," Zoe replied. "But like you said, maybe she left for her own reasons and didn't want to tell us. We all have our secrets, and Cara was allowed to have hers."

Gulping down a knot in my throat, I thought about how I was keeping secrets too.

"And," Ingrid added with a smile, "we can think of it this way—if Cara hadn't left, maybe we wouldn't have met you, Phoebe."

She always knew how to see the bright side.

"You have made progress. I see how you can be a benefit to S3A2. Unfortunately, it has not been timely enough."

I was sitting in Headmaster Duff's office, and I felt like I was getting scolded. Sucking in my breath, I waited for what he would say next.

"We received news that S3A2 in another region has been compromised, and the artifacts they were housing have been stolen." I stifled a frustrated sigh as Headmaster Duff continued, "They had to disband and go into hiding, with the hope their identities would not be exposed."

This time, I let out a soft, frustrated groan.

Headmaster Duff then restated something he had stressed to me before. "We *need* to find Douglas Thelwell and Lady Hortensia."

Trying to be helpful, I said, "Maybe … if we focus on finding Thelwell's and Lady Hortensia's connections, it would then be easier for me to locate Thelwell and Hortensia in the orb. Like working backward to follow the trail."

He shook his head. "No, we need to find Thelwell and Lady Hortensia *first*. Or if they are deceased we need to discover what they have been doing these past decades."

"But why?" I insisted.

His blank expression hardened. "When there is an incessant problem, you *must* go to its source. Or else the problem will fester." Headmaster Duff's voice softened, but only a little. "I believe you have been trying." He stood, walked over to the windows, and looked down at the scene below. "I need to think of a way to speed up your progress," he thought aloud.

It almost sounded like he was making me one of Dr. Braithwaite's experiments that needed to be catalyzed.

I'd come to know Headmaster Duff a little more; he respected learning and was committed to his cause. But he was driven for reasons and by something I couldn't fully understand.

"I know it's important, sir, but so are the moments during the journey. You know what I mean?" I said.

He suddenly turned from the window and stared at me.

My eyes widened as I shrunk back in the chair. I was mortified I had blurted that out. I'd said something Naan used to say. She would tell Dad that whenever he got impatient or Mom when she became anxious. I said it forgetting I was sitting in front of the headmaster *and* an Ozmantah.

"Sir, I'm really sor—"

A grin?

"You're not mad?" I whispered.

"Your grandmother used to say the same thing."

I sat up. "She said it to you *too*?"

"Yes, quite often. She was determined and led by strong ideals." His eyes even thawed. "She would also say that we have a duty and responsibility that goes beyond ourselves. We did not always agree, but Ericka had strong convictions, which I respected and admired."

His mind wandered to someplace in the past as he looked out into space. Maybe he was in 1953 when he met my Naan. It sure seemed that way when he said, "She was more than just compelling. She was dynamic and …" Headmaster Duff looked down. In our silence, we could hear sounds from the students outside. "Well, enough about the past," he said eventually. "The point is we must be expeditious."

"I understand," I said, disappointed and wanting to hear more.

Whenever Headmaster Duff spoke about the past, especially about Naan, he seemed unlike himself—almost caring.

My abilities allowed me to anticipate the action before it happened. So I readied myself when the urgent grasp gripped my sleeve and pulled me behind some trees.

I also knew it was Renaud before looking up.

"*What* was *that* for?!"

"*Shh,*" he silenced me, looking around.

It was the first time we'd spoken since the Ceilidh. And the seriousness in his face was alarming.

When Renaud was sure we were alone, he turned to face me. "There's something I have to ask you. That bracelet …" He pointed to my wrist. "Where did you get it?"

I thrust my hand behind my back as if I could pretend it didn't exist. "What bracelet?"

He tilted his head. "C'mon, you *know* what I'm talking about."

My voice failed me. I couldn't lie to him. *Or could I?* If it was to protect him and all of us, I absolutely would. But I didn't lie. I settled on being evasive. "It was a gift," I finally answered.

He grinned just a little. I think he was impressed by my tactic but was also impatient. "There's no time for this, Phoebe."

A smattering of sounds invaded our space. Our heads darted around. We'd been a bit jumpy since the Ceilidh. When we looked, we saw it was only students talking as they passed.

Renaud pulled me further behind some tall shrubs around the trees. "When I saw it on your wrist the night before our exam, I *knew* I recognized that symbol. But I couldn't remember from where. I just couldn't place it."

My heart thudded as I listened.

"It bothered me that I couldn't remember, and I *had* to figure it out. Why was it *so* familiar? I asked myself."

Thu-thump. Thump. Thump. Thump.

"And then I remembered. It was Cara who drew it only days before she vanished."

Thump. Thump. Thump.

I swallowed a thick knot in my throat. *How would Cara know about this symbol?* I assumed that Renaud was mistaken.

But as he spoke, I realized he wasn't. "She was sitting in an area of the library where I was shelving books. She must've been mindlessly drawing it. It caught my attention because the shield looked *just like* our school emblem. But instead of our motto, it had S3A2 underneath it, *just* like your bracelet. At the time I didn't think much of it. I assumed it was something else about our school."

I tried swallowing again, but this time it felt as if I were eating shards of glass. Renaud went on, staring into my wide eyes, "I thought and asked myself, why would you and Cara be connected to the *same* symbol? Two students who never met and—"

"I don't know *anything* about Cara's disappearance," I declared with my hands up.

"Wait, hold on. I wasn't finished."

I shut my mouth, fearing I looked guilty as he continued, "Two students who *never* met, with similar abilities who know the *same symbol*. But the rest of us have *no idea* about it."

Renaud's stare was steady. I could even see my reflection through his glasses and into his eyes. I felt like I was being interrogated. "Where did you get the bracelet?" he asked again. His expression softened.

I sighed. "It was my grandmother's."

Although still evasive, my answer gave a little more information than before. I didn't tell Renaud right away that Headmaster Duff gave it to me.

And thinking back, it was for a number of reasons. I felt like I was still protecting the students by saying less. I was defensive because I knew my grandmother didn't do anything wrong by having it. And as much as I didn't want to admit it to myself at the time, I also didn't tell Renaud right away because deep down, there was a part of me that relished the privilege of being the only student who knew about S3A2 and the possibility of being part of a powerful, secret organization.

"Okay," he said, but looked confused at the same time. "I researched S3A2."

"Oh, I see," I whispered, looking down and around—anywhere *but* into his inquisitive eyes.

"You don't seem surprised, as if you've known about this." Without waiting for my response, he said, "It wasn't easy to find. *Believe* me. *Very* top secret. *Very* covert. But with the help of a friend back home and my own access to database systems, I decrypted some data and found something."

My eyes widened. "Wait ... hold on ... you *hacked* into a system. That's impressive *but* illegal."

He shook his head but couldn't hide a slight smile. "Don't try to change the subject. It's not going to work."

Thu-Thump. Thump. Thu-Thu-Thump.

Renaud continued, "I found names associated with our school—Duff, Gillies, Malcolm, Thelwell, and Ericka Fahey." In that moment, Renaud actually sounded excited, because he was able to uncover deeply hidden information. "We both know one of the names—Duff. I found that Malcolm died and Gillies and Thelwell are missing. And I remembered you've called your grandmother Naan Ericka. So, I'm concluding that Ericka Fahey was your grandmother?"

"Yes."

"Phoebe," he said. I looked into his eyes again. "You told me it was your grandmother's, but did she *give* it to you? I didn't see you wearing this bracelet until months *after* you arrived."

Avoiding his stare again, I looked down at the grass, shuffling my feet. "I ... I ... could've been wearing it before. You just never saw."

Renaud became stern and pleaded with me. "Stop. *Stop* this. And just tell me. Did *she* give it to *you*?"

There was no point in hiding information from Renaud. I looked into his expectant eyes. "No … no, she didn't," I whispered.

"If it wasn't your grandmother, then something is off." Renaud's jaw clenched. After a long pause, he said, "Whoever gave you this bracelet may have had something to do with Cara's disappearance."

"Why would you say that?"

"Aren't the coincidences between you and Cara obvious? And Cara avoided us and acted odd around the time I saw her drawing the S3A2 symbol, and now she's gone."

"Well, putting it that way …," I said as I also remembered that I'd thought the coincidences between Cara and me were interesting. I began to think aloud. "He never told me why he had the bracelet and not my grandmother. And it *is* strange Naan wouldn't have been the one to give me something so important to her … *isn't it*?"

A strange feeling oozed inside of me.

"Who do you mean by 'he'? Who is *he*?" Renaud insisted. "Is it Duff?"

I shivered and replied, "Yes … and Ms. Belzeebar was there too. But it was Headmaster Duff who gave me the bracelet."

Renaud drew back, obviously stunned.

I rushed to add, "He's been helping me. *He knew* my grandmother when they were young. *He invited* me to this school. It was Lady Hortensia and Mr. Thelwell who broke the code. My grandmother even said they broke the code."

I hadn't realized Renaud was holding my shoulders until he released his grasp. "I don't think you're lying. But there must be *something* wrong in what you interpreted."

"It just doesn't add up. *I'm* not missing, and I've never felt in danger when I was with Headmaster Duff. I mean … I won't deny that Ms. Belzeebar is weird and can be rude sometimes, and he's very intense. But does that make them *horrible* people? Why would they be helping me? Why would my grandmother be a part of something wrong? S3A2 is something I want to be a part of, just like she was. And she wasn't a bad person. She was a *good* person," I insisted. I was now pacing in the small, hidden space.

"I believe what you're saying about your grandmother. But there's still *something* off."

I closed my eyes and pressed on my temples, trying to be logical as I looked at all sides of the situation. "Okay, let's say your theory is true and Headmaster Duff and Ms. Belzeebar are in on this in some major way. Then Dr. Braithwaite could be too? I mean he's a S3A2 member."

"He's S3A2?" Renaud arched an eyebrow. "I figured after what I read but wasn't sure."

"Yes, he is. So what can we do to find out?" I asked, still not convinced.

"The only people in this equation who would have information and not be on this campus are Lady Hortensia and Mr. Thelwell."

"But they're missing or maybe even *dead*!" I protested. "Plus, we still don't know if they can be trusted. That would be too risky."

"You're right." Renaud's eyes moved from side to side. When they stopped, I knew he'd just gotten an idea, and he finally spoke. "But, there *is* someone who might know where they are. Someone you trust *and* who can provide more answers."

"*Who?*"

He looked at my bracelet, and I suddenly realized who he was talking about.

"*Naan?!*... But she's not here anymore. She's pas—" Before I could say "passed away," I knew exactly the person who might be able to help.

If he wanted to help.

Atwila Hogg.

Renaud and I decided we would have to play it cool and not let on about what we knew. We would get Atwila's help after class. I thought it wouldn't be difficult since Atwila practically idolized Renaud.

I was still skeptical about Headmaster Duff and Ms. Belzeebar being conspirators in the disappearance of Cara and other sinister activities. I couldn't imagine that two people I had spent so much time with and who were helping me accomplish what I wanted would've been *dangerous* and *evil*.

The next day, when Ms. Belzeebar's class came around, I walked there with Ingrid and Zoe.

"You're quiet today. More than usual," Zoe observed.

"Just thinking about upcoming exams," I lied.

We were the first to arrive, then Atwila entered the room. It felt awkward examining Ms. Belzeebar as she hastily arranged papers on her desk and set up the projector to prepare for our lesson. Looking at her, I tried to imagine her being villainous.

Could she be? Headmaster Duff and Ms. Belzeebar had been very persistent. And if I was honestly remembering, at times, Ms. Belzeebar became too impatient and annoyed, which I did think was strange.

Then Colin, William, and Wallace followed ... but no Renaud. Two minutes until class started, I looked at the door.

It was unusual for Renaud to be late.

When it was time for Ms. Belzeebar to take roll, Renaud still wasn't there. Ms. Belzeebar marked Renaud as "absent." I pictured he would rush in after just a couple of minutes, slinging his book bag off his shoulder while sitting down. But he didn't. Renaud had been absent before, maybe twice, but it seemed too timely on this particular day he would be. My stomach churned with worry.

Ms. Belzeebar began her lecture, and I tried to stay focused. But each time someone passed in the hallway, I stretched my neck to sneak a peek through the glass panel of the door, hoping it would be Renaud.

Our last conversation began to eat at me and replayed in my mind. *I think whoever gave you this bracelet may have had something to do with Cara's disappearance,* Renaud had said.

Headmaster Duff seemed so encouraging, but maybe I misread his seriousness. And maybe he told me those stories of my grandmother to use me. But it didn't add up because he seemed genuine when he spoke about her.

I couldn't be sure what was real anymore. I was wrestling with the duality and behaviors of Headmaster Duff and Ms. Belzeebar and how I'd interpreted their responses, silences, and actions.

I had emphatically told Renaud that Lady Hortensia and Mr. Thelwell had broken the code. *I know because that's what my Naan sai—*

I couldn't finish my thought. I couldn't finish it, because I never *did* hear Naan say who broke the code, only that it had been broken. I'd just conveniently inserted Lady Hortensia's and Mr. Thelwell's names, and I was quick to believe what Headmaster Duff and Ms. Belzeebar had told me. Stunned, I felt like a thin, frail sheet of paper as the blood drained from my face.

I'd been too eager to help, to advance my abilities, and to do things on my own that I'd pushed aside obvious signs. I trusted the wrong people—yet again.

But this time it wasn't like Ava, my attention-seeking, childhood friend who had spread hurtful rumors about me. This time they were powerful people, and there were *serious* consequences.

Renaud was in trouble.

I wanted to panic, scream, and even cry. *What have I done?! How could I be so stupid and gullible and not pay attention to what was right in front of me? Not pay attention to the signs!*

No wonder Headmaster Duff had Naan's bracelet and not Naan! No wonder Naan told me in my vision that I shouldn't tell people everything I know!

Maybe Duff was even the tall shadow watching us. What did they do to Renaud?

My eyes flashed angrily at Ms. Belzeebar. She looked like a common grackle in that long black dress that draped over her bony back and spindly arms. I had underestimated Ms. Belzeebar and mistook her behavior as just eccentric, but, wow, she was so much more.

"Stop squawking," I began to mutter under my breath, glaring down at my desk. "Stop droning on and on about some dumb slide as if you care. You evil, selfish, conniving—"

"Phoebe, is there something you would like to share with the class?"

My head popped up; Ms. Belzeebar had turned around and was examining me. Dripping from her face was a fake, syrupy smile.

Trying my hardest to hide my anger and fear, I forced my mouth open. "No, Ms. Belzeebar, I was just thinking aloud.... Sorry." It was *extremely* difficult to say that last word. She didn't deserve such a feeling.

"I always like a student who is enthusiastic. But you *must* remember to keep listening during class, okay?" she admonished.

"Yes, Ms. Belzeebar," I answered.

Another sickeningly sweet smiled appeared, and then she turned to face the board to continue her lesson.

Needing to make things right, I listened to Renaud's instructions and my own instincts. I decided it was time to tell the group. But I *needed* to be patient. I would have to wait to tell them the next morning during Chemistry class. We would all be together and not around Ms. Belzeebar's and Headmaster Duff's watchful eyes. That would be the best time. Although I still wasn't sure Dr. Braithwaite could be trusted, it was a chance I had to take. The hours that followed would be crucial.

On a mission the next morning, I put Naan's picture safely in my pocket, knowing Atwila would need something to connect with her.

When Dr. Braithwaite took roll, it felt extremely odd not to hear Renaud say "Present" when his last name was called right before mine. And my table felt so empty and hollow. I sighed.

"Where's Renaud?" I heard Zoe whisper to Colin. "It's not like him to miss *two* days in a row."

Colin shrugged and shook his head. "I didn't see him this morning at the house either," he answered quietly.

I knew Dr. Braithwaite had heard Colin and Zoe, because he looked at them and narrowed his eyes but didn't say anything.

And my lab experiment was lackluster. I drudged through it not caring about what I was mixing and for how long. To get my attention, Atwila poked my hand with his pencil (the end with the *eraser*, not the lead tip).

Eventually, I mustered the courage to surreptitiously write on a piece of paper. I wrote: **Important! About Renaud. Need to meet after class in the woods nearby.**

After I slid it over to Atwila's side of the table, he read it. A look of fear appeared on his face, then it transformed to suspicion. But, thankfully, Atwila nodded and slid the piece of paper back to me, hidden under his chubby palm.

During the end of class, while I was returning supplies, I walked to the back of the room. Luckily, Ingrid and Zoe were there together.

I whispered to them, "We have to meet after class in the woods nearby. It's about Renaud. Tell your table without Dr. Braithwaite hearing. Act normal."

Zoe and Ingrid looked stunned, and then silently agreed.

The news had quietly spread; I knew because the tension was thick. At 10:03:03, when Dr. Braithwaite ended class, I went straight to the nearby woods as the other students filled the space beside me. I had replayed it over and over—the moment I would tell them what had been going on.

I gathered the courage to look into their worried faces. I had to be ready to receive whatever backlash could be hurled at me. They impatiently waited for me to speak.

So I began, "There's a society ... it's called S3A2 ..."

I told them what I could in the limited time we had—a little about the bracelet, a lot about Headmaster Duff and Ms. Belzeebar and what they told me about the danger we were in and how I could help, nothing about the orb, and most of my conversation with Renaud the last time we saw each other.

While I spoke, I studied them. What I saw was confusion and fear on all their faces, accusation on two, disappointment on one, and understanding from most. Afterward, I couldn't bare to look at them and examined the gnarled trunk of a nearby tree.

The silence seemed to last forever until Zoe spoke, and what she said caused me to stare at her in disbelief. "*How* could you keep this from us?!" she accused harshly. "*All* this time when you said you were studying for classes, you were *lying*?! If something happens to Renaud, it'll be *your* fault."

"Phoebe said she was trying to help. You *must* see that," Ingrid urged. "I'm disappointed too. But she was in a difficult position."

Zoe stubbornly stepped away from Ingrid.

"I'm sorry," I pleaded, "but you can't totally blame me for this. I thought I was doing what was best. I'm *so* sorry for being wrong."

"I told you we shouldn't have trusted her," Atwila said, looking around at the others and angrily pointing at me.

I had made a mistake, but I wouldn't accept his accusation.

"Surprise, surprise," I said dryly, glaring at him. "You never liked me and wouldn't have trusted me anyway."

Atwila drew back with a short growl, shaking his head.

"Look, we don't have time for this. Renaud's in trouble. That's what we need to focus on," Colin said.

"Colin's right," William replied. "We have to be levelheaded about all of it."

Atwila leered sideways at me. "Well, *she's* messed things up. I say we do this without her."

"I think maybe that's best," Zoe said quietly, looking down.

I gasped, surprised she had sided with Atwila over me. Looking at my feet, I tried to push back the tears.

"She doesn't mean that, Phoebe. She's hurt and—"

"*Don't* speak for me, Ingrid," Zoe demanded.

"Atwila, what you're saying is senseless. Phoebe has more information than any of us. She's needed," Colin said.

I rolled my eyes when Atwila raised his hand as if he were in class, waiting to be called on. "If I may have another word. I thi—"

"There's nothing more to be said. *Done*," William ordered as he towered over him. Atwila dropped his hand and pouted.

When I had no more tears welling up in my eyes, I looked at Zoe. She stared back at me, still angry—her mouth set in a thin, firm line. "I'm Renaud's friend too," I said. Then I looked at Atwila, who avoided my stare. "*Nobody's* going to keep me out of the plan. I *will* be a part of it *and* make it right."

Zoe's hair tumbled and flashed around her face as she shook her head, and her eyes switched between hurt and anger.

"Please, get a grip," Wallace said to Zoe, trying to calm her down. "Phoebe was in a tough situation."

"Oh, so now *everyone's* against me?" she yelled, glaring at all of us.

We watched Zoe silently fume. Finally, she threw up her hands and started backing up. "I'm not staying here for this. I'm *not* going to be around people who let me down. *Always* having excuses!"

"No, it's not like that," Ingrid pleaded, looking extremely sad.

My voice softened. "Zoe, how you're acting is not just about me. I know I made a mistake, but—"

Zoe spun away and stormed off. I tried to follow her, but a strong tug on my elbow stopped me. It was Colin.

"I'll go after her," he said. "You need to stay and help fix this."

I nodded regretfully, and we watched him run off with smooth, quick strides.

"We have to think," William advised after we turned to face each other again. "We have to rely on each other to figure out this mess we're in. There's no other option we've got."

"What is it we need to do?" Wallace asked me.

Trying to refocus and with a shaky hand, I pulled out Naan's picture and handed it to Atwila. He reluctantly took it. In this moment he knew there was no time to say "I told you so" to everyone again.

"This is my Naan," I said to him. "She may know the answers that we need. Can you reach her?"

Atwila held the picture and studied it.

"Can you?" William insisted.

Then he looked up at each of us. "I … I'm not sure. I'm still practicing. You *know* that," he said nervously.

Wallace tried to calm him. "We understand. All we're asking is for you to give it a try. Can you do that?"

"Okay," Atwila said finally. His round cheeks swelled as he filled them with air, and he straightened his back. "*Nobody* talk, please." He began waving the picture in front of him, like some odd ritual.

The silence among us was strained as Atwila shut his eyes and moved the picture again in an erratic formation. We were nervous but hopeful as we waited for several minutes. I could feel William and Wallace growing impatient beside me.

Then Atwila's eyelids popped opened, and he smiled triumphantly. "She says you need to go see her."

"Who?" I asked.

"*Lady Hortensia*," he stressed. "You need to go see Lady Hortensia." *She's alive!*

"Why? We need to find Renaud," Wallace objected.

Ingrid leaned closer to Atwila and asked gently, "Where is she, Atwila?"

"Is there anything else?" William insisted.

"*Hold on*," Atwila answered in a strained voice.

As we waited again, I looked around to make sure we were still alone. By now our next classes were well in session. I wondered if Headmaster Duff would know we weren't in them. My attention returned to our small gathering when I heard Atwila's voice again.

"She's on a small island ... poisonous fumes.... You need Popolycide." Atwila paused and then looked straight at me. "She says you've seen where it is. When you arrived."

My mind went blank as they looked at me anxiously. Their anticipation only heightened my senses. And so I dug into my memories. *Arrived.... Arrived ... in a plane ... landing ... looking out the window. I saw a—*

"I know where!" I announced. How amazing that for so many weeks I was trying to search for someone, and I already knew where she was! Lady Hortensia was hopefully not far from the school.

Ingrid held my arm with trembling fingers. "*Where*, Phoebe?" she whispered.

"When I came here. I mean, while I was on the plane and it was landing, I remembered seeing a small island. Even then, I had a feeling about that place. She's *there*. Lady Hortensia is there!"

William and Wallace let out loud sighs of relief.

"I can't hear anything else. That's all," Atwila said flatly.

I was so thrilled I almost hugged him. He didn't notice, because I stopped myself just in time; I wasn't going to hug brooding Atwila. *No way.*

"By now teachers will know we're not in class. I don't know how long it'll take for Headmaster Duff and Ms. Belzeebar to find out. We should act fast," William said.

"There must be a way to get off campus without being seen," Ingrid said.

William looked over in the direction of the tower. "The only person who could help at this point is Dr. B."

"But he's also S3A2, like Duff and Belzeebar," I said.

"Have you ever met with him when you were with the headmaster and Belzeebar?" William asked.

I shook my head.

"Then I think we can take a chance on him," William concluded.

We marched to the tower, hoping Dr. Braithwaite was still there, and William opened the door. We rushed to the back of the classroom, toward the solitary door that Dr. Braithwaite always entered from. Before William could open it, Dr. Braithwaite pulled it from the other side and appeared as if on cue.

"What is it? Something is wrong," he said knowingly.

I only told him what was necessary, making sure to leave out Lady Hortensia's name. Dr. Braithwaite listened with such a stillness that neither his face nor his body seemed fazed or surprised.

When I finished, he said, "We had our suspicions about those two, for quite some time, especially when Cara left. But we needed more proof."

We were stunned by his brief revelation, but Dr. Braithwaite didn't elaborate. Instead, he continued, "From your description, it sounds like Glenn Miller Loch."

Wallace's face brightened. "I remember that loch and island from when I was little. We even shared stories about it being haunted."

Dr. Braithwaite went straight into action. "There is no time for further discussion." He looked at the brothers. "You must go to class like everything is normal."

"*What?!* But, *no!*" Wallace declared.

"We should be *here*," William insisted.

"It's imperative that Duff and Belzeebar don't realize you are *all* not in class," Dr. Braithwaite commanded.

There was no further arguing that could be done as Dr. Braithwaite wrote a late excuse note for them. William and Wallace grumbled something in disappointment and shook their heads. Ingrid hugged William as he walked out, and we told them to be careful.

Then Dr. Braithwaite turned to Atwila, Ingrid, and me. "Mr. Atwila, you are needed. And Ms. Ingrid, I believe Ms. Phoebe will need your support."

Ingrid nodded and smiled while looking at him and then at me.

"I will contact Mrs. Vyda to inform her that you are with me for extra tutoring to prepare for next term. That will give us some time to leave." He paused, as if he just noticed a detail. "Where are Ms. Zoe and Mr. Colin?"

"They ran off," I answered sadly, looking at the floor.

"Good."

I quickly lifted my head and stared at Dr. Braithwaite in surprise.

"It won't seem as if you're all together. Hopefully they will be fine," he explained. Dr. Braithwaite went to his office. His voice was low while he spoke on the phone. We tried to peek into his private room, but he shut the door on our curious eyes. Then he reemerged. "You said you need Popolycide, yes?"

"Yes, Dr. Braithwaite," we answered.

As he went up the metal stairs, the soles of his shoes clanked on each step. There were times he wasn't visible on the balcony as we tried to catch glimpses of him. But when we could, Dr. Braithwaite was pulling leaves from a short, stocky plant as well as a prickly, purple flower on the other side of the balcony.

He descended with a tray in hand, which he placed on the counter before us. Dr. Braithwaite selected four bottles of solutions from different shelves and three empty vials and beakers from a drawer of supplies.

He crushed, mixed, heated, and stirred with such efficiency and precision, it took him only a few minutes to complete his creation. With his back to us and his arms engaged in deliberate movements, he was like a maestro conducting a symphony. We were captivated and entranced. The final creation was a thick, bright purple liquid— Popolycide. Dr. Braithwaite filled each vial and pulled out three surgical masks from a drawer.

"When you get to the island, you must use half of the vial *before* you set foot into the woods. Pour it onto the mask, making sure it is thoroughly saturated. Then place it over your nose and mouth," Dr. Braithwaite explained while demonstrating with succinct hand movements. "The Popolycide will take effect *immediately.* And it will begin to evaporate. You have ten minutes to get to where you need to go. Based on the size of the island, there should be no delays. You may need to run."

That meant *no* mistakes and *perfect* timing. The task seemed impossible, but we had no choice.

"As the solution evaporates," Dr. Braithwaite continued, "the color will fade until the mask eventually becomes white again. If the mask is white before you are at your destination, then it will be too late for you."

We didn't dare ask what the consequences of being "too late" were as he gave us the masks. And after the vials were placed in protective pouches with a leather cord like a necklace, he gave them to us as well.

"Use the other half of the vial *before* you exit the building to leave the island. Do not, I repeat, *do not* take your masks off when you're amongst the plants outside. Even if you feel like you need fresh air and want to take it off, I promise you, that will be the last breath you will ever take. You understand?"

We took big gulps to swallow our fear. "Y-yes," we stammered. We hastily but carefully put the vials around our necks and the masks into our bags.

"Follow me." Dr. Braithwaite motioned for us to exit from the back.

It would be the *first time* we would see his office. However, the big reveal was an impossible blur as we were quickly led to a van that was parked outside. We sat in the back.

"You need to get down, onto the floorboard," Dr. Braithwaite said before slamming the van door shut.

We looked at each other with scared expressions as we crouched onto the vinyl flooring. We heard the front door open and shut and the ignition start. Dr. Braithwaite slowly pulled out of the driveway. Huddling so close together, our warm breath could be felt on each other's faces.

Dr. Braithwaite drove as if nothing was out of the ordinary. The wheels crunched and popped the loose gravel on the partially asphalted driveway, and the hum of the engine filled our silence.

And when we heard a groaning sound of iron, I knew we'd reached the gates of the school. *Would anyone stop us?* I wondered. *No, because we have a good alibi.* As the van picked up speed, it jerked and jostled us around.

I coughed from the exhaust fumes rising through the floorboard while Ingrid held Atwila's hand, trying to calm him as his chest heaved—up and down, up and down. *Poor Atwila.* In that moment I felt sorry for him. We stared at the leather seats in front of us as time ticked on.

Then, the van eventually rolled to a stop, and the door slid open with a forceful push from Dr. Braithwaite. We jumped out of our crouching positions, and my knees popped as they straightened. Ahead of us was a small single-platform station, but it wasn't the one I'd arrived at months ago.

"Take the express train," Dr. Braithwaite instructed as he walked with us to the platform stairs. "It will be the fastest way to the island. The next one should be arriving in five minutes. You *must* get off at the *third* stop."

"Okay, Dr. Braithwaite," I answered.

"The train stops here every two hours on the half hour. Return here by half past five this afternoon. That is the *only* time I can return. Do not tell *anyone* where you are going," he urged. "S3A2 has its networks. And we don't know all the traitors."

As the train approached the station and slowed to a stop, we turned and ran up the stairs to the platform.

"And students," his commanding voice yelled out behind us. We turned to see Dr. Braithwaite farther away as he was getting into the van. "Think *only* of possibilities! Believe you will succeed, and you *will!*"

Chapter Seventeen

A BRIDE AND GROOM NOT MEANT TO BE

Twenty minutes. Twenty minutes. Twenty minutes. Three more stops. Three more stops, I repeated to myself.

Since leaving Dr. Braithwaite, Atwila, Ingrid, and I hadn't said a word. Atwila eyeballed me skeptically, as usual, while Ingrid gazed out the window with her chin resting on her arm. For a few minutes, I was able to settle my nerves and rest.

Just then, the cabin door slid open; it was the conductor. "Tickets, please," he said to three passengers in front of us and punched their paper stubs.

Before he was in earshot, I leaned in and whispered, "Let's buy a longer journey ticket so he won't know where we'll be getting off."

Atwila and Ingrid nodded as we took out our money.

The moment the conductor came up to us, he surveyed the empty seats nearby. His bushy eyebrow began to rise. "Not in class? Where's your teacher?" he probed, and his critical eyes assessed us in our uniforms.

"We're going on a field trip," Ingrid said while Atwila and I nodded. "And we're late, *oops*," I added with a smile and a shrug.

He clucked his tongue. "None of my business," he mumbled, and thankfully took our money.

We bought a ticket for the last stop on the train—a small village in the Highlands. Obviously, the conductor didn't believe that we were going on a educational trek through the mountains. But when he gave us our tickets and went on his way, we were relieved.

I rested, feeling the relaxing motions of the train as I stared blankly at my lap. The train slowed to a stop. The doors parted again and then eventually slid shut. We looked up to survey our surroundings. No one came into our cabin, and there was now only one person sitting in front of us.

Twelve minutes. Twelve minutes. Twelve minutes. Two more stops. Two more stops. I stared into my lap again. This pattern repeated.

Until finally, it was time. We got off the train before the doors slammed shut behind us. Having been in the warm cabin, we were stunned by the wintry air.

"What should we do now?" Ingrid asked hoarsely. She looked around and hugged herself for warmth.

"*There* it is!" Atwila squealed, pointing at the small island in the distance. He began to run to the taxi stand.

"Wait, *stop!*" Ingrid gripped his backpack, and he stumbled backward and jerked to a halt. "We shouldn't," she instructed. "Dr. Braithwaite said we can't tell *anyone* where we're going."

"We'll have to go on foot," I said.

Before Atwila could respond, Ingrid and I bolted in the direction of the island.

We ran down a grassy moor toward the sandy shore where the island was on the other side of the lake. Balancing our bags on our backs, we tried to manage the wind. Beads of sweat formed on my face, but they evaporated the moment any dared to fall. My veins pulsed with blood, warming my body as my lungs filled with sharp, cold air.

Suddenly, my left foot caught on something hard and stubborn. "*Aaaahh!*" I screamed. Instead of falling forward, I shifted my weight and my bottom hit the hard, slick surface. Rapidly sliding down the hill, I tried to stop myself, but that just caused mud to cake onto my hands and fill up underneath my fingernails. Finally, at the bottom of the hill, where the grass transformed into pebbles and sand, I skidded and slowed to a bumpy stop.

"Are you okay?!" I could hear Ingrid calling out behind me.

I checked my legs and ankles. They still moved and nothing hurt. Surprisingly, those tights I could never stand came in handy. They were as sturdy as Teflon and protected my skin. "Y-yes," I yelled shakily over my shoulder.

Atwila eventually stood over me with a smirk on his face, but he stuck his hand out to help me up.

"Thanks," I muttered, reluctantly taking his hand and standing.

"Are you sure you're okay?" Ingrid asked while I was still trying to pick off clumps of mud and grass from my clothes.

"Who's there?!" a voice hollered.

We spun around and noticed a tiny, run-down boathouse and a heavyset man lumbering over to us. A thick brown sweater, wool cap, water boots, and olive green fishing waders prepared him for his work and the weather. His full white beard covered half of his face while a cigarette wobbled from his lips.

Spitting out the cigarette and crushing it with his boot, the man teetered over to us. "Why ye here?!" he demanded, looking at us warily.

Although he looked intimidating, I believed in some way he was connected to Lady Hortensia. So I told him who I was and that we needed to see her. The moment he heard the names Lady Hortensia Gillies and Ericka Fahey, his eyes brightened.

"Aye," he said, tugging at his beard, "that's a name I've heard from the Lady." He smiled, revealing several rotting or missing teeth. I tried not to stare. "Mah name's Lazarus," he said as he stretched his thick, large hand out and shook mine so vigorously I thought my shoulder would dislocate.

"Nice to meet you, Mr. Lazarus. This is Ingrid and Atwila," I said, pointing to them.

Lazarus shook their hands with equal vigor. Abruptly, he turned away and started preparing his small motorboat at the water's edge. "Get in if ye want to see the Lady," he declared.

"Is this man okay?" Atwila whispered hesitantly.

Atwila was concerned about the way Lazarus stumbled around and about his glassy, bloodshot eyes, visible underneath the brim of his cap—obvious signs that Lazarus loved the boozy bottle a little too much.

"*Eh?* What was that?!" Lazarus yelled.

"N-nothing," Atwila stammered.

"Are ye comin' or no'?" he demanded, already sitting in the boat with his thick arms folded and resting on his ample belly. He tapped his boot with impatience.

We had to commit to this. We were almost to our destination. Sharing a look of reassurance, we climbed into the boat. With Lazarus's harsh yank of the cord, the motor rumbled and our bodies jerked back and then forward as we launched out into the cold Scottish lake.

Lazarus expertly steered while singing at the top of his lungs. It was a tune about a bonnie lass or something of the sort. Meanwhile, Ingrid, Atwila, and I huddled together for warmth in the bouncing motorboat.

It was then, while whizzing through spraying water and harsh wind, that I noticed my embarrassing slide down the hill had made my tights and skirt soggy. My teeth chattered uncontrollably.

The woods that surrounded Lady Hortensia Gillies's red- and brown-bricked home, with its gabled roofing and spiraling towers, were unassuming. Nobody would know just by looking at the beautiful green vegetation that it was entirely filled with Popole plants.

Popole plants emit a toxic, odorless, and invisible gas that when in close proximity, disrupts and scrambles the body's cellular composition, causing organs—skin and all—to disintegrate in less than five minutes.

Although Lady Hortensia lived in seclusion, and to the rest of the world she was considered missing, she took the precaution of surrounding her home with these plants—an extra protection from those who sought to harm her. It had of course served her well for many decades, as those who thought they'd found her location perished before even taking ten steps into the woods.

The only antidote known to counteract the gas is called Popolycide, and the formula was known by only three trusted and masterful S3A2 members, Dr. Braithwaite being one of them.

If by some unfortunate reason, a dangerous person had gotten hold of the antidote, which had thankfully never happened, he or she would still have to know the shortest path to take, which was following the round black stones.

This was another added protection for Lady Hortensia.

Atwila, Ingrid, and I didn't know these details when Lazarus shut off his motor and coasted quietly to the dock of her island. We just knew we had ten minutes. *Ten minutes!*

Throwing a heavy rope over a wooden stump, Lazarus fastened it to secure the boat. His horn blew with an awkward tune that sounded like quacking ducks. "*This* is where Ah go no further," he bellowed. I noticed Lazarus only spoke in one pitch—deafeningly loud. "Do ye ha'e pockets?" he asked.

We nodded.

"Best to lea'e yer bags. Easier to ge' around. Ten minutes is doable, but it's tight. Ye ha'e no time for mistakes."

We pulled out the masks and dropped our bags into the belly of his boat. I felt for the vial around my neck and Naan's picture in my shirt pocket. She was safe and secure. We climbed out.

"Follow the wee roun' black stones on the ground. No other ones. They will lead ye to 'er. Ten minutes. There's no playin' around wi' that. And make sure yer masks are on tight. The times folks ha'e entered wi' nothin' …" He rolled back with a guttural laugh, his face turning deep red underneath his snowy beard. "Hee*heeee!*"

Lazarus's motions were so forceful I thought the boat would capsize. But it was like a second pair of legs to him, and his body effortlessly balanced inside as it rocked from side to side. Dragging the tears of laughter off his face with a calloused palm, Lazarus said, "Let's jist say, aw was found was piles ay mangy clothes. They meant no good anyway." And then he belted out another laugh so boisterous that his round body jolted back again.

We looked at each other and blinked. Lazarus had an interesting sense of humor.

"How does she know we're here?" Ingrid asked.

"Oh, *believe me*, she knows." He pointed up at the house through the woods. "Sight isn't the best, but 'er hearin' is sharp." He continued more seriously, "She knows from the sound of mah horn. Now go! *Go!* Ah don't ha'e time to sit around. Come back to this spot. I'll see ye."

"Thank you so much, Mr. Lazarus!" Ingrid said.

"T-t-thank you," I said, and waved as Atwila smiled sheepishly.

Lazarus's motor rumbled and roared to life, and he departed straightaway. Ingrid suddenly looked worried.

"W-w-we c-c-can do this…. We *h-h-have* to. I b-b-believe in us," I said as my teeth chattered, and I shivered in my damp tights. I looked straight into Atwila's and Ingrid's eyes while saying that. They were doing this for Renaud, Cara, and the others. And I was doing this for them and more. "I'll k-k-keep t-track of time," I volunteered as I set my watch.

We then prepared our masks with the solution and secured them over our faces. Without hesitation, we entered the thick, wild shrubs and trees in search of those wee, round black stones.

Almost immediately, Atwila yelled, "Here's one!" with a muffled voice through his purple-stained mask.

We ran to it and rushed forward to find the next stone. Walking briskly, our shoes snapped twigs and crushed the grass as we pushed back branches and stared at the ground.

We were desperately looking for the next life-saving stone.

"E-e-eight more m-m-minutes!" I yelled through my fading purple mask. I had decided to call out an alert every two minutes.

Ingrid jogged ahead of us, her head moving left and right. "*Look!*" she yelled, and pointed. Atwila and I ran to her.

There was no time for nervous energy, and it was raw will and instinct that drove us deeper and farther into the woods.

Just before I called out "Two minutes left!" we saw the wooden gate of Lady Hortensia's hideaway.

Beyond the gate and along the path that led to her door was completely bare—no trees or shrubs, only slabs of paved stone. *Are we safe?* We didn't dare take off our masks to find out as we ran through the stark terrain.

Bam! Bam! Bam! Ingrid pounded on the arched wooden door with her small fist. It creaked open, and we surged inside without thinking. The door slammed shut like a hungry beast devouring us.

Jumping, we spun around to see—

Well ... I didn't know what we saw, because the person wasn't visible in the dim foyer. He was like a silhouette. Even to this day, if someone were to ask me what the man looked like, I couldn't say. Only that he was abnormally tall and rail-thin with an oblong head.

The figure wore a long, dark brown robe, and when he moved, the fabric swept the floor, covering his feet (if he had any feet). It was like he was airborne—maybe he even defied the law of gravity.

Barely a whisper, his baritone voice still traveled to our ears. "Take your masks off now, and follow me."

We obeyed and cautiously walked behind the floating form through the small, darkened corridors with bare walls and scratched wooden floors. His garment fluttered silently in front of us while our steps thudded and then echoed throughout the hallway. He stopped us with his long skeletal-looking hand, lifting it straight up at attention beside his shoulder. Curling his hand, his knobby index finger stood alone and then pointed to the door on our left. The door was ajar so he opened it wider with a smooth but forceful push of his finger.

Inside, a woman sat with her back to us—Lady Hortensia Gillies. She wore a white lace dress and had matching white hair styled neatly in a bun, adorned with an ornate diamond hair accessory. She sat at the head of a long dining table, with her only table guests being polished silver candelabras standing on an array of cream-colored doilies. The room was warmed by freshly stoked burning logs in the fireplace.

Atwila, Ingrid, and I just stood, frozen.

"Who did you bring for me?" Lady Hortensia asked.

However, Lady Hortensia only spoke to us, because the person who'd led us to the room was already gone.

When she turned to face us, I noticed how pale and delicate her skin was, how it glowed like a pearl. Deep brown eyes contrasted perfectly with her paleness. And just as Lazarus had told us, her eyes didn't focus too well. Another contrast was that a surprisingly robust and commanding voice had come from her thin, small body. It filled the lonely room.

"Don't tarry over there. Join me," she said cheerfully, with a large, toothy smile. It was welcoming and revealed many layers of pleats on her face that reminded me of an accordion when it's squeezed.

We struggled to pull out the large, heavy wooden chairs.

"Tea? Biscuits?" Lady Hortensia was about to ring a small, silver handbell she'd picked up.

"No thank you, Lady Hortensia," I declined politely.

She set the bell down, hearing the seriousness in my voice. Observing us with a tilted head, she eventually spoke, "I don't receive many visitors. The last one was two years ago. So if you're here, it's something serious. And if you're *here* sitting with *me*, it means you're good people. Or else it would be nothing but a pile of your uniforms out there."

She pointed out the window that faced her, and I looked out between the heavy, plaid curtains and noticed I had a partial view of the woods and lake. I shuddered at the thought of what we'd just escaped and what could've happened if there was one tiny mistake.

I cleared my throat. Instinctively, Lady Hortensia's face turned toward the sound, and I spoke with purpose and conviction, "Lady Hortensia, my name is Phoebe Douse. I'm here with Ingrid Lee and Atwila Hogg. We're students at The Murray School. I was sent here by my grandmother, Ericka Fahey. She told me I needed to find you."

"Ericka Fahey's granddaughter!" she declared. "Come closer."

I leaned toward her, thinking she needed to see me better. But Lady Hortensia shocked me when her hands lifted toward my face. Before I could pull away, her cold fingers studied my cheeks, nose, forehead, and mouth—poking and rubbing. It was swift and hurt a little. Then her probing fingers traveled to my hair as she examined some loose strands, twisting it in her fingers.

"Your face is wonderful proof!" she exclaimed. She squinted as the corners of her mouth turned upward, and her skin pleated once more. Then her smile disappeared. "But I still need more proof."

I slipped the bracelet off my hand and placed it in her palm. Her expert fingers read it, moving nimbly over the metal surface.

"The bracelet," she said as her eyes went wide. "I can feel her energy." She tilted her head again. "So why are you here?" she pressed, after returning the bracelet to me. Before any of us could answer, she said, "I presume the only reason you're here is because of that blasted Taggart Duff. He's been seeking revenge. Did you know that?"

"I'm realizing that now," I said. "Headmaster Duff told me he would help to improve my abilities and save S3A2 and the other students."

"*Save* S3A2!" she declared. "Is that what he told you? How noble! *Ha!* The reality is that Duff has been poisoned by his own power and has been for a long time."

I shook my head in disappointment. "Now my friend Renaud is missing, and I failed my grandmother. We need your help to connect with Naan and find our friend. I need help finding answers."

When I finished, I slumped breathlessly in the chair. Ingrid's eyes softened in understanding and Atwila's widened as if he was finally beginning to understand my predicament.

Lady Hortensia squeezed my hand. Although her hands were like ice, there was only warmth in her deep, dark eyes. "You mustn't be too hard on yourself," she said. "With someone as cunning and charming as Taggart Duff, the Fifteenth Earl of Murrayshire, it's difficult not to fall victim to him, especially someone as young as you."

Lady Hortensia turned in Atwila's direction. "Atwila, is it?" He perked up in his seat. "Go to the cabinet behind me, open the drawer, retrieve what you see, and bring it to me, please."

"Yes, ma'am," Atwila whispered. Filled with wonder, he went to the antique cabinet and opened it timidly.

"You see it?"

"Yes, Lady Hortensia."

"Good. Very good. Now bring it to me."

Closing the cabinet door, Atwila returned to the table with a jewel box in the palms of his carefully cupped hands. The delicate box was covered with intricate latticework of sapphires, emeralds, and diamonds that glistened and sparkled in the room. There was no doubt it was for royalty.

"Now, don't any of you think of nabbing it!" Lady Hortensia warned, and narrowed her eyes. "I may not see well, but my other senses are just fine."

Before we could tell her that we wouldn't dare, she chuckled, and we relaxed in our chairs. Much like Lazarus, Lady Hortensia's humor and informality was something we'd have to get used to.

"Open it," she instructed after Atwila placed the box before her on the table.

Atwila's nervous fingers fumbled with the small latch at first, but then he managed to lift the jeweled lid. Ingrid and I leaned forward to look inside. Lying on deep purple velvet was a gold chain with an elaborate pendant that had the S3A2 insignia. The insignia was embedded with tiny diamonds.

"It's like what's on your bracelet!" Ingrid exclaimed. Her eyes sparkled like the jewels as she admired the necklace.

"All top-level S3A2 members have one. It's an amulet," Lady Hortensia explained. "If used properly *and* with experience, it can sometimes block others' abilities. And even amplify one's own abilities—but *that* needs extra practice."

"Wow!" Ingrid and Atwila said at the same time.

She turned to Ingrid. "Would you be a dear and help me, please?"

"Would love to!" Ingrid jumped from her seat, retrieved the necklace, and carefully placed it around Lady Hortensia's neck to fasten it.

"*Mmm*, feels wonderful. I haven't worn it in years. Never needed to—until now, that is." Lady Hortensia was preparing to channel her ability.

"Phoebe, I need something that is personal to you … of your grandmother. Not the bracelet. Something more sentimental. Hopefully you have something?"

I nodded and then realized again she couldn't see me clearly. So I said "yes" as I pulled out Naan's picture from an inner pocket and handed it to her. She examined it with her fingers.

"A photograph! Sometimes they're excellent objects. But other times …" She scrunched her mouth. "Mixed signals. There's so much that can be going on in a photograph. Not just the person in it, but the person taking the photo, people in the photo, and so on."

"It's just of her, Lady Hortensia. But Headmaster Duff's shadow is in it because he took the picture."

I could feel Atwila's and Ingrid's eyes grow as more was being revealed.

"I think it should work. But we shall see," she said. "And please, just Ms. Hortensia. Lady doesn't mean a blasted thing in my situation." She waved her hand around.

Ingrid and I stifled a giggle as we looked at each other.

"I'm so excited that you're a medium!" Atwila exclaimed.

"Let's hope I'm still good at it," she answered, smiling at his enthusiasm.

"*I'm* a medium *too!*"

"Well, take note, then," she said to him. "Hold my hands, Phoebe and Atwila."

I figured she needed Atwila because he was a source of energy for connecting to the other side, and she obviously needed me because I was related to Naan.

"Now you must remain silent. I only channel what the spirit wants to say. If you ask questions, it breaks the spirit flow. Your Naan will tell you what she wants to tell you and also what she can share. It's a difficult process, and the energy can be disrupted on the other side as well. You understand?"

"Yes, Lad—I mean, Ms. Hortensia," I answered as Ingrid and Atwila nodded eagerly.

She placed the picture on her pallid chest where the pendant rested. And just as soon as she did, a large owl swooped past the window, causing an enormous shadow to move across the room. Ingrid, Atwila, and I gasped.

"She's coming," Lady Hortensia said in a deepened voice. "Now close your eyes."

I looked at Naan one last time before closing my eyes. I felt Ingrid's small, warm hand in my left hand and Lady Hortensia's slender, cold hand in my right. Atwila and Ingrid had to lean over the table to clasp hands. My heart pounded with anticipation, and there seemed to be silence on top of silence—never-ending silence.

"Aaa-*choo!*"

I jumped.

"*Shhh,*" Atwila and Lady Hortensia said.

"Sorry," Ingrid said, wiggling bashfully.

We prepared ourselves again and waited, and it felt longer than an eternity, but I kept believing something would happen. *C'mon, Naan. Please come. I need your help.... I miss you. Where are you? Please come.*

Suddenly, the fire began to hiss and pop behind me. An eruption of sweat burst out of my pores and flowed down my neck and back. The heat was so intense, as if the flames had jumped out of the hearth. When my hand began to tremble, Lady Hortensia tightened her grasp. It felt so firm and familiar—like a *vise.*

Just then, the room became bone-chillingly cold. Rapid shivers rippled in my body, causing my limbs to twitch and jolt. Lady Hortensia squeezed even harder, and her nails dug into my skin.

The smoke from the extinguished fire drifted throughout the room and stung my nostrils. Another shiver jolted through my back and stomach, this time in anticipation.

And then, everything was still.

"Mm-hmm, yes, I know. It's been years.... Not too bad.... Haven't been seeing too well these days.... *Yes,* I see! Looks just like you.... They can be stubborn at that age, I agree." Lady Hortensia chuckled, and her fingers shook in mine.

Is that ...? Yes, it is!

Lady Hortensia was talking with Naan!

I opened one of my eyes and found that Ingrid's were already wide open, looking confused and then amused. But Atwila was still deep in meditation. His practice was paying off. Lady Hortensia cleared her throat and grew serious. She was silent, and her eyes were still closed.

Ingrid and I shared a look that meant: what now?

Then we closed our eyes again.

"Phoebe darling, you've been misled."

I caught my breath. It was my grandmother. The husky voice

265

was Lady Hortensia's, but it was *certainly* Naan speaking through her.

I wanted to speak but stopped myself as Naan continued, "You didn't listen to me that day I told you to make it right. You need to believe. Believe not only in others but first in yourself. *That's* how you will improve your abilities. *That's* how you will know who to trust."

She stopped. My chest constricted, hoping Naan hadn't already left. But she spoke again. "Remember to be good. Don't be controlled by your weaknesses, including your own ambitions. You're learning." There were pauses between her words, like a bad phone connection. "You will get things … mixed up … or even wrong.… But don't doubt who you … are and what you're capable of."

"Naan, I've found Lady Hortensia. Why did you want me to find her?" I broke the rule. I shouldn't have spoken. But I couldn't help myself.

It seemed to be okay because Naan answered, "To show you that you're capable. Before I crossed over, I had a vision of you here in Scotland.… You would've *never* learned who you are if you never came here.… You have learned so much about yourself, your will, your determination, and the importance of trusting the right people." And she repeated, "Before I left you, I saw you in Scotland."

The pace quickened. "You're where you need to be for yourself *and* for me. I also needed you here to find them to get information that can help S3A2. Make things right. Expose Taggart. Make it right."

Then the words came out in an endless flow of sounds that sometimes slurred together. "I turned away from S3A2 I couldn't stay and fight him I regretted that I had no choice the Fadrix doesn't reveal arbitrarily the summoner is not the only person who controls it I had no choice but to leave."

I silently gasped when I realized she knew about the Fadrix.

"Make it right. Find them both …" Naan's message was fading.

"What about Renaud? Can you help us?" I begged.

"Hortensia can.…," she said. The voice sounded weak. "He helped when she escaped.…" The words faded again, and then there was silence.

"*Wait*, don't go! I have more questions. So many more things I should've said to you," I begged, not realizing tears were streaming down my face until I tasted salt. Naan was a lifeline. I needed her now more than ever. I sobbed and couldn't stop myself. "Naan, I'm trying to be good. I'm sorry I didn't listen to you. I miss you! Why did you leave the Society? Why didn't you have the bracelet? What about Mr. Thelwell? How do I find him? What about when you said a marriage? Why should I find him? Tell me more about the orb. What do you mean that the summoner is not the only person who controls it? I miss you!"

"We have no time for this, Phoebe," Atwila warned harshly.

My eyes popped open as I tried to catch my breath in between quiet sobs. That was when I also realized the room had warmed and illuminated, as the fire burned again.

Naan had left. I'd lost her again. She had so much more to teach me, but time had been too short with her. Hiding my face and shaking my head, I cried into my hands. My pride had been stripped away as I was exposed in front of Lady Hortensia, Ingrid, and, unfortunately, Atwila. Ingrid rubbed my back as Atwila sat watching.

Get it together, I told myself. *She wouldn't want you to cry for this. She would say to be grateful for the moment we just shared.* Taking deep breaths, I calmed myself. I'd just experienced a connection some people would only dream of having.

With her sweet chocolate eyes now open and looking at my face, Lady Hortensia cleared her throat. "I always hate when this happens," she said, shaking her head. "It usually makes people *so* sad when I do this for them.... Others sometimes become annoyed or even angry. But it's always the worst for me when people are saddened."

She leaned over to Atwila and poked his waist with a swift finger.

He jolted in the chair and turned to stare at her in shock.

"To be a good medium," she admonished, "you *must* be caring. Do away with false pride. Otherwise, you will *never* be able to progress."

Atwila lowered his head, stunned and humbled. It was a much-deserved chastisement and lesson for him.

She turned to me while returning Naan's photo. "You can never have all your questions answered at once. Hopefully, you'll have them answered when the time is right."

"Hopefully," I whispered, and looked at Naan again before tucking her inside my pocket.

"There was a young village lad," Lady Hortensia explained. "He was about ten or eleven years old at the time. He, along with Ericka, helped Douglas and me to escape that night. He knew The Murray School and the area inside out. His father's side of the family were caretakers of the estate for generations. He'll know where to find your friend. If your friend is ali—" She stopped herself.

"That was so many years ago. He's no longer little. And how could he still be there?" Ingrid pleaded, standing over me while I wiped the last of my tears with my shirtsleeve.

"True, indeed. His name was Russell. Very sweet and kind. Loved all the toffees Ericka and I would give him. Maybe a bit too much. And he loved to read. That young one could read the leaves off of a tree!" Lady Hortensia chuckled at the memory. But then her face dropped when she said, "His father always hit him over the head with the books. Told him to put them away, and that he didn't need to know so much. Poor thing!" She looked at us with large blinking eyes, expecting that we would catch on.

It was as if she thought she provided us with useful clues we could use to easily figure out who she was talking about. But nothing about the description was familiar.

She was describing a boy so many decades ago! We became antsy when we realized so much time had passed. Atwila's stomach grumbled violently. Mine responded just as noisily.

"No, we're sorry, Lady Hortensia. We're not recognizing any of it. Do you have a last name by chance?" I asked.

Her brows furrowed in thought. "Well, we just called him Russell. But ... if I remember correctly ..." Then a huge smile spread across her face. "*Yeeessss*, he used to call his father by his last name. The kind laddie was so afraid of that wretched man. Mr. Macky was what Russell called his father. Does this help?"

Atwila, Ingrid, and I looked at one another as our jaws dropped and minds settled on the same person. It was the same old miserable, elusive man who yelled at students and took care of our school grounds.

Together we exclaimed, "*Mr. MacLeod?!*," absolutely stunned.

"Yes, yes! *That's* it! Russell MacLeod was his name!"

"Are you *serious*?!" Atwila insisted in disbelief.

"Of *course* I'm serious." Lady Hortensia bristled at her memory and authority being challenged.

"Sorry," Atwila whispered.

We still had a shot. A good chance to find and help Renaud. I wished I could've stayed to learn more about Lady Hortensia, Naan, and S3A2. But, we had to leave.

"Thank you so much, Ms. Hortensia. We don't mean to seem rude, but we must go," Ingrid said.

"Please, please," she insisted, waving her hands and giving us permission to leave. "I understand. Take care and do be careful." Her face turned to Atwila. "And remember what I told you about being humble."

"Yes, ma'am," he said quietly.

Atwila left the room and then Ingrid. I turned to follow.

"Phoebe," her throaty voice whispered.

It stopped me in midstep.

Naan? I was hopeful as I walked over to Lady Hortensia. It wasn't. I knew better, because Lady Hortensia didn't have my picture, and she didn't call me, "darling."

"Yes, Lady Hortensia?"

"We're alone, right?"

"Yes, Lady Hortensia."

"Close the door."

The moment Lady Hortensia heard the latch click, she began, "*I* was the one your grandmother was talking about. Douglas Thelwell and I were to be married."

I froze.

"He was the son of a fisherman and a maid. Unfortunately, as a Lady it was unheard of for me to love someone like him." She sounded like she was experiencing the same emotions of falling in love all over again. She even chuckled a little.

"I wasn't much of a beauty. Actually, I wasn't one *at all*. 'Hortensia's the ugly one, but she's sweet. Make sure people notice how sweet she is' is what they used to say when talking about my sister and me. It used to bother me.

"But when I met my Douglas, he made me feel like I was the only person for him. We were special for each other."

Her back straightened. "We were going to risk it all. And Ericka told us we shouldn't ignore who we're meant to share our lives with. I really adored your grandmother. We were both very spirited.... You're spirited much like her, Phoebe."

I smiled. "Thank you, Lady Hortensia."

"Douglas and I were willing to take on whatever challenges we might have to together. We knew life would only be better together— more complete."

Lady Hortensia shrank back in her chair as her face dropped. "But in the end, we *still* couldn't marry, because we discovered the truth about Duff and his activities. Douglas had proof—evidence and important files that would expose Duff and other subversive members of S3A2. Douglas told me he even had more proof. Somehow, Duff found out."

Her dark, glazed eyes looked longingly out the window. "I was also suspected. And Duff captured us. If it wasn't for your grandmother and Russell, I'm certain Douglas and I would've been tortured and killed." She sighed. "Unfortunately, Douglas and I could never be together. And we had to live in hiding. It was for our own safety, you see. We tried to correspond. Your grandmother even helped us. But it became too dangerous, and we had to stop."

She shook her head, still staring out the window at the woods. "Time is a funny thing," she whispered. "It seems to tick by so slowly, and then when you look back, you realize decades have passed right before your eyes, even eyes that have become blinded."

Clearing her throat, Lady Hortensia spoke again after a long silence. "Phoebe, I think your grandmother wants you to find the information Douglas took. She believes you'll know what to do with it. I've always imagined Douglas to be alive, but if he's not, I hope he had a good life. I've *always* hoped for that."

When Lady Hortensia looked up at me, her face was so sad that my chest tightened and hurt. She retrieved a lace handkerchief from her sleeve and dabbed some fallen tears from her cheeks. "If you do find my Douglas," she managed to whisper, "if he's still alive and okay … please tell him I *never* stopped loving him."

That afternoon in Lady Hortensia's solitary room, adorned with expensive furniture but no warmth of love from others, I learned that the loss of a loved one wasn't only experienced in death. Loss is also experienced when you don't have the opportunity to see or speak to your loved one ever again. I also saw undying hope through Lady Hortensia and Naan. Hope is being assured that, in time, the truth would be revealed and things would be made right. Hope is also believing that a long-awaited message could still be sent to a loved one, even after so many years had passed.

I placed my hand gently on Lady Hortensia's small shoulder. "I hope to find him. And when I do, I promise I'll tell him."

She patted my hand and smiled.

I walked out of the room and carefully closed the door behind me.

When I saw Ingrid and Atwila in the hallway, with their shifting eyes and jittering bodies, I was reminded of our urgency. Neither Ingrid nor Atwila asked me what was said in the room. They seemed to know it wasn't secrets I was keeping. Rather, it was my own discovery and promises I was trying to fulfill.

The dark figure waited in the background as we braced ourselves for the journey. Setting my watch, we prepared our masks.

"Let's see if we can make it back to the boat in *six* minutes instead of eight," Ingrid said with a playful smile.

It was fun to make light of a pressing situation. It helped to steady our nerves again. We laughed as we put on our masks.

Chapter Eighteen

UNLIKELY ALLY

I would be exaggerating if I told you that our journey through the woods was more dangerous than the first time, and that we almost perished but heroically triumphed. I would also be outright lying if I told you we were faster and managed to get back in half the time. In reality, we were adequately able to find the stones, and there wasn't a near death experience along the way.

We returned to the lakeside in seven minutes and forty-eight seconds—not the six minutes we'd dared ourselves but still an improvement, nonetheless.

"Got the information ye needed from the Lady?" Lazarus asked after he saw us on the dock and sped over to us.

"Yes, Mr. Lazarus," Atwila said as we climbed into the boat. Atwila seemed less leery of the boisterous man.

"Good to hear! Sometimes she can be a bit testy," he said as he started the motor.

While we sped back to the other side of Glenn Miller Loch, I turned to see the island becoming smaller as we gained more distance. The sandy, pebbled shore and lake was now cast in a blanket of vivid orange and deep red hues of the setting sun.

The boat eventually slowed to a stop on the other side, and we stumbled out.

"Where do ye need to go?" Lazarus asked, observing our tired legs.

"The train station," Ingrid replied.

"The one up the hill?"

"Yes, sir," Atwila answered.

"I'll take ye. You'll get there faster."

We wondered how that was possible. But then Lazarus pointed behind the boathouse. There, parked on top of the ragged, makeshift pavement, was a small delivery truck. "It's how Ah get supplies for the Lady." He winked, knowing we could keep the secret.

Very relieved we didn't have to go *up* a hill on empty stomachs and tired legs, we accepted. As soon as we climbed into the bed of the truck, Lazarus fired up the engine and pressed on the gas.

During our journey to the station, Lazarus drove his truck much like he steered his boat—with uninhibited speed. With a wool blanket that smelled like raw fish as our only hope of keeping warm, we held onto the railing, trying not to slide and bounce around. The loud motor and biting wind burned my ears.

"Okay back there?" Lazarus belted out through his open window.

I stuck my thumb up to show him we were fine.

When we made it to the train station with time to spare, Lazarus helped us out of his truck and shook our hands vigorously again. "Good luck," he bellowed. The truck creaked and groaned and almost sunk to the ground when Lazarus jumped heavily into his seat. Then it sprung back into position as he slammed the door. "Min', I'm here if ye ever need me!" And with a rowdy laugh, he lit a cigarette and sped off, leaving a cloud of wild dust in his path.

As the sun disappeared in the sky, nerves overtook us while we sat in the train. The bounciness we felt inside was like being in Lazarus's motorboat or in his truck. Then, when the train arrived at our destination, our jitters ceased and were replaced with a heaviness as we exited the station.

Shamelessly holding hands, we walked into the grassy field where we last saw Dr. Braithwaite.

Two headlights popped on. "You've managed to return in time. Well done."

We stunk of raw fish and sweat. We were cold, hungry, and tired. My clothes were stained with mud and dirt. Our limbs ached and heads hurt. And yet, we were recharged by Dr. Braithwaite's words in the darkness as we stepped into the van.

"What should we do when we get back?" Atwila asked as we rode in the van, surrounded by thick darkness.

"Return to our dorms, rest, and then meet," I said. "Do you know where Mr. MacLeod stays?" I asked, hoping it was somewhere convenient and on campus.

"He has a small house near a shed by the pond. And after he makes the rounds at night, he returns around two a.m.," Ingrid said.

"Then we meet there at two," I replied.

"Atwila," Ingrid said, "you'll get the boys together."

"Okay."

"And we'll get Zoe …" My voice trailed off.

"She's probably calmed down by now," Ingrid consoled.

"Yeah," Atwila said.

I raised an eyebrow. He was *actually* being supportive.

"Do you think we should tell Dr. Braithwaite?" Atwila whispered.

But before we could answer, Dr. Braithwaite finally spoke, as if he knew we had just mentioned his name. "Did you get the needed answers?"

"Yes, Dr. Braithwaite," I answered. I wasn't sure how much he'd heard—probably everything. Protecting Lady Hortensia's identity, I said, "We were told that Mr. MacLeod might know where Renaud is. And as we figured, Headmaster Duff can't be trusted."

Dr. Braithwaite's head moved up and down as I spoke. Then he glanced at us through the rearview mirror as the van slowed to a stop. "Get down."

There were smaller iron gates ahead—another entrance into the school grounds I'd never noticed before. We obeyed his command, and he drove onward.

"Take care," Dr. Braithwaite said, slowing the van. "If I'm not there, I have confidence you can proceed without me. You are capable and talented students. And I promise I'll be present when you need me again."

He cut the headlights, with the engine still running. We tried to arrange our clothes and comb our hair with our fingers and stepped out. The darkened van reversed and drove in the opposite direction.

"See you at two?" I said to Atwila.

He bit his lip, nodded, and then walked away with quick, sturdy strides.

I hoped nothing would happen to him.

"He's stubbornly tough," Ingrid said as we walked together to Clairmount House.

When Ingrid and I entered Clairmount House, we grabbed a quick snack in the kitchen. The girls were studying in the living room or in their bedrooms. Books and other study materials were splayed out on the couches and floor around some housemates. And of course, it would have to be Joy among them to see us in our ragged state.

"What a *disgusting*, rank smell!" she said, making sure to say it so loud that everyone heard.

"What happened to you two?" Alexa asked.

Joy turned to her, squeezing her nose. "Does it matter? If we want to eat our meal tonight, it's best we don't know."

"We fell in the pond. Get over it," I said dryly over my shoulder as Ingrid and I dragged ourselves up the stairs.

I didn't care if Joy thought we were smelly, clumsy, and stupid. I only cared that our plans remained a secret.

"See you later?" Ingrid whispered.

"Yeah, see you," I whispered back.

Opening my door and scanning the room, I noticed that Zoe's side was its usual mess, but something felt different, like she hadn't been in there all day.

She's probably trying to avoid me, I told myself.

But after I took a shower and reentered the room, a sinking feeling emerged when Zoe still wasn't there.

I dashed up to Ingrid's room. The last hope would be that Zoe was in there. "Ingrid, it's me—Phoebe," I said in an urgent whisper and knocked.

"What's the matter?" she asked after she opened her door.

I walked in, hoping to see Zoe but knew I wouldn't.

"Tell *me*!" she insisted, wringing her hands.

"Zoe didn't come back."

"Oh *no*. *Noooo*." Ingrid began to panic. Her eyes rapidly switched between amber and black as her small mouth trembled. "First Cara, then Renaud, and *now* Zoe." A look of absolute terror enveloped her face. "Phoebe, do you think they're—"

"*Don't* even say it. We have to believe they're fine, and we'll find them, okay?"

Looking around in complete helplessness, Ingrid trembled. I forced her to look at me when I held her shoulders and squeezed them.

"*Okay?*" I insisted.

"O-okay," she whispered.

"I didn't know Cara, but Renaud is one of the smartest people we know, and Zoe is a fighter. Wherever they are, we have to imagine they're figuring something out."

Ingrid's eyes focused and slowly blackened. "You're right." Just then, her phone beeped, and her timid hand picked it up. "You read it," she said, pushing the screen at my face.

I braced myself for the worst and read the message.

"What does it *say*?" Ingrid pleaded.

"Atwila says they'll be there."

"Should we tell them about Zoe?"

"Best not to. Not yet."

She nodded. "You're right, we shouldn't worry them."

"What we should do is get some rest."

She nodded again, gazing listlessly at the wall.

"Get some rest," I insisted.

Ingrid finally looked at me. "Yes," she said with a faint smile.

After leaving Ingrid's room, I set my alarm and collapsed on my bed. The moment my body hit the mattress, I passed out in exhaustion.

Tap. Tap. Tap. Tap.

I jumped up, half-awake. "Zo-weee?" I slurred.

Tap. Tap. Tap. Tap.

The noise was coming from the door.

"You don't have to knock," I said as I tiredly got up and dragged my bare feet to the door. When I cracked it open, Ms. Daniels stood on the other side. My shoulders slumped in disappointment.

"Zoe didn't check in," she whispered, and stretched her neck over my shoulder to examine Zoe's side of the room. "Hmm …"

I shrugged. "I don't know where she is, Ms. Daniels. Ingrid and I came home after studying, and I haven't seen her."

Ms. Daniels fidgeted—scratching her forehead, tugging at her sleeves, pulling her thin brunette hair. And eventually, she just stood there, completely still. "If you hear anything," she pleaded, "*please* let me know, no matter what time it is and no matter the issue."

After Ms. Daniels left, I couldn't sleep anymore.

Lying in bed, I tried to clear my mind—to prepare myself.

Despite what Lady Hortensia had said about Russell being a sweet young boy, we believed old Mr. MacLeod was still the snarly, miserable man we knew him to be. But it would be silly not to think that, like everyone else, Mr. MacLeod had a better side to him.

When Atwila, William, Wallace, Colin, Ingrid, and I converged in the woods, Dr. Braithwaite wasn't there.

There was a light on in Mr. MacLeod's cottage, so I knocked and peeped through a small window to see if he was in. All that was visible was a small desk with a lamp and several books.

"Where's Zoe?" Colin asked. "I talked her out of her mood, so why isn't she here?"

I turned around. "She didn't come back."

Wallace clutched the back of his neck. "What do you mean, 'didn't come back'?"

"You lot," Mr. MacLeod cut him off as he rounded a corner. He exposed us in the darkness with his flashlight.

"Mr. MacLeod ...," I started.

The beam pointed squarely on my face, stinging my eyes as I squinted.

"Well, out with it!" he ordered.

"My name's Phoebe Douse and these are my fri—"

"There's no need for all of that. Don't come to me in the wee hours of the morning for introductions." He turned his back, switched on a porch light, and started arranging something in his shed.

"There's always something with you students." His voice went up in a whiny, pinched tone as he said, "Mr. MacLeod, I can't find where. Mr. MacLeod, we need that cleaned. Mr. MacLeod, you must come over here now. *Mr. MacLeod, Mr. MacLeod.*" Then it dipped to a low rumble. "So what is it that *you* want?" he demanded over his shoulder.

"I'm Ericka Fahey's granddaughter."

He turned around and looked me once over. "Are ye now?"

I wasn't sure if he was surprised or being sarcastic.

"I am and … and we recently learned from Lady Hortensia that, with my grandmother, you helped her and Douglas Thelwell escape."

"*Again* I say, what is it you want? What's your *point*? Don't bumble, wasting your breath to tell me what I *already* know," he snapped as he rummaged through the bushes.

I hesitated. "Go on," I could hear Ingrid urging softly.

After clearing my throat, I continued, "Uhm … Lady Hortensia told us you could help. You see … our friends are missing, in danger, much like Lady Hortensia and Mr. Thelwell. And we believe Headmaster Duff has them."

His body became as stiff as a plank of wood. "All the best to them," he said, deadly serious. "The headmaster isn't one to fool with."

I was about to give up, but then Mr. MacLeod turned around and faced me. "Your grandmother was a smart one. Smarter than you. Ms. Ericka knew danger. You don't. Always having those secret meetings with the headmaster and Ms. Belzeebar."

My jaw dropped.

"You thought no one knew, eh? Well you're grossly mistaken *and* careless." He shook his head. "And you don't even know how to be discreet." Mr. MacLeod walked over to a metal garden chair and plopped down in it. "*Aaah!* Feels good to finally sit. Always up on my feet, you know?" A taunting smile formed on his lips as he examined each of us.

"Finding this funny, old man?" William said just loud enough to be heard. "You're really something."

"As a matter of fact I do, *boy*," Mr. MacLeod challenged as he daringly stared out at him.

William gritted his teeth. Ingrid had to reach for his arm to calm him.

Mr. MacLeod shrugged dismissively. "You never know when to let things alone. Always meeting in these woods, making foolhardy plans, and meddling in things out of your depth. You needed to be stopped."

Ingrid's eyes widened as she stepped forward. "Are you *saying* what I *think* you're saying?"

"*You* stopped us at the Ceilidh!" Wallace exclaimed.

"*You* were the tall shadow," I whispered.

"Tall shadow?" the boys asked.

"*Ooh*, tall shadow," Mr. MacLeod jeered. "Hmm …" He sat back and scratched the stubble on his chin, acting like he was pondering a deep philosophical question. "I like that one. Well done, whoever came up with that." Then he answered flatly, "Aye, it was me."

"It wouldn't have worked," he explained, sitting back and crossing his legs. "You wouldn't have pulled it off in time and avoided people. Besides, it's *my* grounds. You don't run this place. *I* boarded that window shut. *I* told the administrators to keep an eye on that area."

The brothers' blood boiled. William clenched his fists and Wallace's mouth transformed into a tight, thin line. Colin zeroed in on Mr. MacLeod's neck. I couldn't see Atwila, but I was sure he had one of his bulgy-eyed glares.

"Anyway," Mr. MacLeod said, letting out a loud "I could care less" sigh and reaching for a nearby cloth, "as I said, the headmaster isn't one to fool with. I wish you luck and good night." He wiped dirt off his fingers and tossed the cloth in a bin.

As he began to get up, Ingrid stepped directly in front of him. "Sit back down, Mr. MacLeod," she demanded, wagging her finger at him.

Frozen in a squat, he wrinkled his forehead into an ugly pattern as his eyes went wild. Mr. MacLeod looked like a hideous forest creature dragged out of its cave. His broad mouth dropped open, forming a crooked, gaping hole.

"Go on, take a seat," she directed.

"Are you sure this is the right way to go about it?" Atwila whispered.

But surprisingly, Mr. MacLeod obeyed.

"You're a rude, miserable man. We get it," Ingrid said. Her voice softened to ease his shock. "But there's a reason why you helped so many years ago. And although you knew our plan, you didn't turn us in. That means something." Mr. MacLeod licked his dry lips and his mouth closed. "Whatever you think about us, that's not the point. We have friends, and they're in trouble."

I chimed in, "We're not asking much. Just for you to tell us where they could be."

"You're helpful," Ingrid added. "We see how you take care of our school, and you do a wonderful job. What you do should never be taken for granted."

"No need to coddle him," William grumbled.

This time Mr. MacLeod didn't hear William as he seemed enchanted by Ingrid's sweet and sincere words.

She continued to cast her spell, "And you did a heroic thing many years ago, helping Phoebe's grandmother, Lady Hortensia, and Mr. Thelwell. This is for the same cause."

Ingrid's imploring must've touched a place in Mr. MacLeod's rusty, slow-beating heart, because he finally looked at us—*really* looked at us, and the deep furrowed lines in his face gradually loosened.

When his craggy voice spoke again, it was with some thoughtfulness. "I haven't seen Headmaster Duff or any sign of him or Ms. Belzeebar leaving the school grounds for a few days now."

He rose from the chair and told us of all the movements and goings on at The Murray School in such detail it was equally impressive *and* bizarre.

Going unnoticed and unappreciated, as Mr. MacLeod had always lived, allowed him to notice everything without anyone having a clue.

"If Headmaster Duff is part of this scheme you're thinking about," Mr. MacLeod said, "then he has moved them someplace during a time I was sleeping. But it's unlikely, since I only sleep four hours a night."

"You think he has them somewhere on campus, then?" Ingrid asked as we felt hopeful.

"Aye, and if that's the case, he's taken them someplace I or others wouldn't be able to see. So *if* they're still on campus, I can only think of two places." We waited nervously as he continued, "They're either in the vault or in an old, unused cellar behind the dining hall. Both can be accessed through an underground network from the main building."

I didn't have time to wonder how Mr. MacLeod knew about the vault, because my thoughts began to speak as I weighed the two possibilities in my head. Looking down at a random patch of moss, I teetered back and forth on my feet.

Ingrid noticed. "Let's be quiet. Phoebe's onto something."

If they were in the vault, then Headmaster Duff knew I had knowledge of that location. That could mean he probably was expecting me, knowing I would suspect there first.

But, if they were in the cellar, then it most likely meant he wanted them to disappear.

Suddenly, an image surfaced in my mind. Zoe's head was bent down as she was sitting on a dusty floor in a dark space. Her hands and feet were tightly bound with rope. I also saw brown pants and black leather shoes standing in front of her. I recognized those pants and shoes.... And then I saw dark red spots on the floor. I gasped.

"What is it?"

I wasn't sure who asked, and I couldn't answer, because just like what had happened during Dr. Braithwaite's exam or similar to when I summoned the Fadrix for the first time, I was in another space. This space felt unfamiliar. The air was damp. It wasn't as cold as the vault and it smelled musty.

When I noticed the woods around me again, I looked up but didn't see faces. Instead I saw shrubs and trees. Confused, I turned in a complete circle. "Oh my—," I whispered.

"What just happened, Phoebe? You just started walking off," Ingrid said behind me.

"It's my abilities. It can happen," I answered as I walked over to join them again. "I'm told it's a good thing, nothing to be concerned about."

"Oh," she said quietly, but I still saw concern on her face. The others seemed surprised or thoughtful.

"Did you see anything that could help us?" William asked.

"Tell us," Atwila insisted.

"They're in the cellar," I said. "I saw Zoe and Headmaster Duff's legs and feet. Zoe was tied up with rope. I also saw ... blood."

They looked around at each other, worry painted on all their faces.

"Are you sure it's the cellar? Because we can't make a mistake," Wallace asked.

"If Phoebe saw it, then it's so."

I stared at Atwila. He surprised me once again.

Ingrid hoped to hear more. "Anything else? Renaud? Ms. Belzeebar?"

I shook my head.

"Even if you didn't see Renaud, did you see anything about him? His glasses? Or a piece of his clothing?" Wallace asked.

"No, but I think he's okay too," I said. I didn't know how much I believed in my own words. But they seemed comforted, which was good.

Mr. MacLeod pointed, and our heads followed his finger. "I know a secret passage that's faster than going through the hidden walls of the main building and then underground. Nobody else knows about it but me. You have to enter an old mining tunnel about half a kilometer away. The tunnel has become narrowed over the years. I used to crawl in it when I was a wee one."

His eyes surveyed us and landed on the brothers. Mr. MacLeod shook his head. "You two lads definitely can't do it."

William and Wallace looked utterly disappointed. They had been rearing and ready for the challenge and wanted to help. But for a second time they had been stopped.

Atwila's thick lips began to quiver. "I … I ca-can't go either," he managed to say.

"Why not?" Wallace asked.

"He's afraid," Ingrid confirmed.

"O-of of s-s-small spaces," Atwila said.

"It's okay, Atwila. You've helped us more than enough today," I said, and even lightly patted his shoulder.

Atwila was so pleased by my words that a kind, small grin appeared on his face.

"There's no need to stress yourself and do something you fear," Ingrid seconded, placing her hand on his other shoulder.

"And you've already done and been through a lot, too," I said to Ingrid.

Ingrid shook her head. "Uh-uh, *nope*. You're not going to stop me."

Everyone now focused on Colin. It was then I noticed he'd barely spoken the entire time. He looked at the ground, kicked his foot in the grass, and ran his hand through his bangs.

"What about you, mate? You in?" William asked him.

"They'll need ye," Wallace added.

Confident, charming Colin looked surprisingly uncomfortable and nervous. "Yeah, I know. Just give me a moment," he said.

"You'll be the best person to deal with the headmaster," William insisted.

"I know you're uneasy about using your ability," Wallace said. "But we have no choice right now."

"What does he have?" I whispered to Ingrid as the boys were going back and forth.

"Telekinesis," she whispered back, then added quickly, "He's had a bad history with it, though."

Telekinesis! My eyes widened.

That was all Ingrid could share, because just then Colin looked straight at us. "I'm coming with you," he declared.

"*Aww*, so touching!" Mr. MacLeod mocked, back to his old self. "Can you get on with it?" He pointed. "The door is behind that tree."

"*Which* tree?" Colin said, obviously annoyed.

Mr. MacLeod smirked. "Walk up ahead, and it's beside that tree at the flower bed. The one where the purple heathers grow. Got it?"

"Yes," Colin, Ingrid, and I said, and began to walk in that direction.

"Hold on," William stopped us. He then handed me a narrow, rectangular plastic container. It was about six inches long.

"What's this?"

"It's from Dr. Braithwaite. I ma—"

Wallace butted in, "Does he know you have this?

"As I was *going* to say," William said, "I made it with Dr. Braithwaite in his lab earlier this afternoon." He pointed at the container. "It's a paralysis dart, formulated to temporarily stun Duff. Usually it can work as long as twenty or thirty minutes, but we didn't have time to make the best version of it."

With his brow set firmly, Colin turned to me with his hand out. "It's best I have it. I'll be the one to take care of Duff and Belzeebar, if she's there. You and Ingrid help Renaud and Zoe."

I'd never seen Colin look so focused.

"Okay," I said, handing him the container. Colin zipped it in the front pocket of his fleece jacket.

We said "good luck" to William, Wallace, and Atwila as they walked away, leaving us with Mr. MacLeod.

"When you're down there," Mr. MacLeod explained, "you'll see several branches of tunnels. Just keep straight and onward. It'll take you to a trap door that used to be sealed, but I loosened it from the inside of the mine. Open it, and the hidden room is right there."

He gave us each a flashlight, slapping them into our hands. It stung our palms, but he didn't care. "I'm doing this out of respect for Lady Hortensia and Ms. Ericka. But if you get caught, it won't matter one iota to me that you're connected to them. I won't know you, and you'll leave my name *out of it*!"

Mr. MacLeod started walking off, but then stopped and turned toward us again. He stepped closer. "What are your names again?" he asked quickly.

"Mr. MacLeod," Ingrid said, "Phoebe introduced herself. But maybe you didn't hear our names. I'm Ingrid and this—"

"I asked—what … are … your … names," he demanded. His eyes narrowed, which revealed yet another one of his wrinkles. This one was long, vertical, and smack in the middle of his tall forehead. It traveled from his missing hairline down to the top of his nose.

Ingrid shook her head in confusion at Colin and me.

I looked up at Mr. MacLeod's sour face and into his angry eyes. "You don't know our names and don't need to know them," I said.

He smirked. "Correct answer."

We nodded, knowing he had a fair demand.

Then Mr. MacLeod stomped away, grumbling something about being tired.

"Let's crack on," Colin said, stepping onward.

Chapter Nineteen

YOU MUST FIND THEM BOTH

$\mathcal{C}$olin pointed his flashlight on the partially visible, dingy wooden door of the old mine shaft. We pulled the vines and weeds aside, unlatched the door, and tugged forcefully at the metal handle. But the door was stubborn.

"Step back," he directed after a few more useless tries.

When we let go, he waved his hand over the door. And with two fluid swipes in the air, it popped open with a soft groan.

That was the *first time* I'd seen Colin use his ability, and I stared completely stunned as we coughed from the dust that rose in our faces. The dust particles dispersed the beams of our flashlights, revealing a ladder.

When Colin stepped on the first rung, a clang rang out throughout the hollow shaft. He tested the first rungs' durability by pounding his foot on the ones he could reach. Then he climbed down as we lit the way for him from above. I knew he'd reached the bottom when we could no longer hear his footsteps and the beam of his light scanned the surroundings.

"Everything good? good? good? goo … goo …?" my voice echoed as I called down.

"Yeah … yeah … yea …," Colin responded.

So I decided to climb down next, and then Ingrid followed and shut the door above us.

"There's really nothing much down here, just some piles of rocks, old barrels … and the path is flat," Colin observed after he had a little more time to survey the space. Colin was right; it was just a series of tunnels.

We began to jog, remembering to keep straight. Our feet pounded the ground, and we advanced deeper into the tunnel. At first, we could stand upright, but soon the path narrowed just like Mr. MacLeod had explained. We were forced to crawl, scooting our flashlights forward on the ground. The gravel dug into our knees, the air was dank, and water dripped from above, wetting our hair and faces.

And then the space narrowed so much we had to crawl one behind the other. Stony, sharp edges of the walls tugged at my shoulders and ripped my sleeves. In those moments, I worried for Colin. He led the way and had to adjust his shoulders to make way for his larger frame.

"Not much farther," he said. "I can see the space getting bigger ahead."

We crawled until the space opened up into a rocky, hollow area where we could sit as we made our flashlights follow our eyes—up, down, and around—looking for the trapdoor.

"Here," Colin said. He bent down and inched it open. Ingrid and I poked our heads around his shoulder.

With the trapdoor low to the floor, we could only see the lower half of the cellar. Inside, Ms. Belzeebar frantically paced and rambled.

Her skirt tossed around her gangly legs. "We need to think of something to do with them. Get rid of them somehow." Her pacing stopped, then started up again. "Ooh! I know! *I know!* I finally have someone in mind," she excitedly proclaimed and bounced. "Dr. Orville. He's *the* best. And very willing. No one comes better than him in my opinion." Her laughs and snorts filled the room. "And he owes me a favor."

And there Zoe was, sitting on the floor with her head slumped forward. Her feet were bound together while her hands were tied behind her back. I recognized those long, thin legs in starched brown pants with black leather shoes. They belonged to Headmaster Duff, who was standing over her.

My eyes widened. I couldn't believe that moments before in the woods, I envisioned this very moment. I'd seen the *future!*

Headmaster Duff moved, and I put my hand to my chest with relief when Renaud was revealed. His back was to Zoe, and they were tied together. They looked terrible and exhausted, but they were alive!

"One is a nuisance, but *two* at once! *That's* a problem." Her feet created an invisible zigzag pattern on the ground, over and over again. "I don't know why they pried. They're far too overbearing. *Always* have been." Ms. Belzeebar spat out her words. "Unbearable most of the time. *So* annoying! *So* impetuous! They don't even deserve what they have! I had to work hard to gain my position in S3A2.

"And here comes this ignorant girl. I don't know why you always praise her. She's been too slow if you ask me. It's a shame we haven't found anyone useful. I—"

Whack! We jumped as Headmaster Duff slammed his cane violently on a small tabletop. "Jealousy Imogen Belzeebar," he said in a seething voice, "is a nasty look, and you are evidence of that."

293

She gasped but still fidgeted.

Instead of yelling, Duff's voice dropped to a deep, hollow pitch. "Phoebe has more ability than what you could piece together in that scrambled head of yours. Now, *shut it*. Or I will quiet you *myself*."

Ms. Belzeebar let out a strange-sounding whimper, and her feet froze. Colin and Ingrid were shocked, but I wasn't surprised. For me, Ms. Belzeebar's vileness was already explained by the odd looks, mocking laughs, and sighs she would make during my sessions.

Colin eased the trapdoor closed. We sat back against the stone walls and closed our eyes, taking a few deep breaths to steady ourselves. When we were ready, Colin unzipped his pocket, pulled out the container, and opened it. Inside revealed a thin, silver dart with a long, razor-sharp point.

"You *can't* miss," I warned him. "He's very powerful."

"The moment I get this dart into Duff and he's paralyzed, we jump out, okay?" As Colin spoke, he took an unexpected shiny object from his pocket. It was a medium-sized set of garden shears, and it looked mighty sharp and dangerous.

"Colin!" Ingrid exclaimed in a loud whisper. "Where'd you get *that*? You could've fallen on them."

He smiled mischievously, which made the right corner of his mouth raise much higher than the left. "I nicked it from Mr. MacLeod's shed. He'll probably miss them, but, eh, who cares? He'd deserve it, wouldn't he?" Colin handed the shears to me. "You said you saw rope."

I nodded and smiled as I took them.

When Ingrid and I opened the door, I still didn't know how Colin planned to take care of Ms. Belzeebar, but I had a feeling he wasn't the kind of guy to plan much ahead of time.

Laser-focused, Colin's eyes narrowed on Headmaster Duff's legs. If he was even an inch off, he would hit Ms. Belzeebar—*or worse*, Zoe or Renaud. He said silent words to himself, closed his eyes, and held the dart up.

But he didn't throw it. His fingers let go of the needle-shaped object, and it stayed hovering in space right in front of his nose. Then, he swiftly guided the dart with his mind as it lanced in a straight path. It was *perfect* precision. Colin's eyes popped open just as the sharp metal pierced Headmaster Duff's calf.

"Wh—?" Headmaster Duff said. The effect was immediate as the cane clattered onto the concrete. He stumbled to the ground in a stiff heap. When Headmaster Duff's head turned awkwardly in our direction, his eyes were rolled back, and we jumped out.

Confused, Zoe and Renaud popped their heads up in our direction. I gasped. Half of Renaud's face was caked with dry blood. His eye and cheek were swollen and purple like a plum. I shook off my surprise and got right into action as I ripped the duct tape off his mouth. He winced.

"How did you find us?!" Zoe asked as soon as Ingrid freed her mouth from the tape.

"Long story. Later," Ingrid responded hastily.

I began cutting and sawing into the stiff nylon rope that bound Renaud's and Zoe's hands, and they helped by wiggling their wrists.

"*Ee-ee! Eeeek!*" a heinous screech from Ms. Belzeebar bounced off the walls and stabbed my ears.

My hands continued to cut and saw, and my skin became tender from the never-ending action. Ingrid grumbled in frustration beside me. Just then, a deafening bang burst throughout the room. We jumped as our heads turned toward the sound. It was Colin. He was thrown against the shelving as cans and bottles tumbled around him in a cluttered pile.

The dart must've already worn off! I wasn't sure if Colin was momentarily knocked out or unconscious, as his head drooped and his arms and legs went limp. But then he shook himself awake and lifted his head. With just a glare, Colin hurled Headmaster Duff against the opposite wall. Headmaster Duff hit the stone surface with a solid thud.

The single bulb above us swung wildly, bouncing dazzling light against the walls and illuminating and darkening objects, corners, and our faces all at the same time. Out of the corner of my eye, I saw Ms. Belzeebar's skirt move toward the door like a swarm of startled bats.

A thin piece of the rope snapped apart and then another as I continued to watch the gravity-defying duel between Duff and Colin. On the ground, Headmaster Duff outstretched his arm toward Colin. The S3A2 ring glistened when he pointed his finger.

Colin shot up into the air in a spread eagle position as his limbs were forced straight out. He hovered in place for only seconds until he slammed to the ground. It was a horrible noise that burned my ears and thundered in my head.

I thought it was over for Colin. The only hope was that he had landed on a pile of cans and not the concrete floor.

And where's Ms. Belzeebar?

"My wrist!" Renaud yelped.

His cry forced me to look down. The garden shears were dangerously close to his skin. "Sorry," I said through the banging and crashing.

Again, the room thundered with an awful noise, and I was dizzy but feverishly persistent. When the final strands of the stubborn rope tore loose, Renaud and I hastily bent over to undo the rope around his ankles, and as we did, Ingrid's and Zoe's legs and feet elevated above our heads. They were weightlessly launched out of the room.

"Renaud! Ph—!" Colin yelled. But, he was ejected from the room before he could finish. The door slammed shut, and the remaining bottles on the shelves shook and rattled.

Suddenly, an uncomfortable, thick silence filled the room. It was like the creepy feeling you get when you're alone but you think an invisible presence is watching you. Only I wasn't alone, and the presence watching me was obvious—Headmaster Duff.

After only two attempts to balance on his cane, he was back on his feet. In full power, he yanked the dart out of his leg, flicked it away, and smoothed his silvery hair with a bloody-knuckled hand.

The once thrashing bulb slowed to a tired, motionless halt, allowing me to see the room and Headmaster Duff towering above us. Ms. Belzeebar was gone, the place was ransacked, and I was left with my friend and the man I thought was my mentor and a respected Ozmantah. The entire day rushed through my mind. It was exhausting and enraging, and worry burned my stomach.

"It's okay," Renaud whispered, trying to reassure me and himself.

Sounding rabid and furious, Ingrid, Zoe, and Colin yelled and banged on the other side. But with just his ringed finger pointed at the door, Headmaster Duff kept it firmly shut.

"Let us refocus, shall we?" he said calmly. And with a flick of his wrist in the direction of a tiny table, he summoned a box. It flew into his open hand, and he clasped it. "I brought this. Certain you would come," he said, looking at the box and then at me.

"What are you talking about?" I asked, wanting to grab his cane and splinter it over his head.

"You have been one of the brightest pupils I have known. I knew you would be. You are your grand—"

"Oh, shut it!" I snapped.

A smile slowly formed on his lips, and I fumed even more. "I like your spirit," he said. Then he sighed, picked up the chair, and sat. "You are definitely Ericka's kin." Headmaster Duff's voice became softer. "I cared for her."

"You don't know what that word means," I seethed.

His face hardened again. "But my past is not the issue right now. There is a higher cause worth fighting for."

"Were there even members in danger? Information stolen? *Tell* me!" I demanded.

He shook his head. "You must quiet yourself. Noise does not lead one to answers."

Although I hated it, Headmaster Duff's words still had an influence over me. And I was immediately silenced.

"S3A2 has been compromised," he went on, "because of certain members' failure to understand how it can evolve. They *do not* have vision and fail to understand what is required to progress. They needed to be dealt with."

"In other words," Renaud said dryly under his breath. "He's a maniac and has been lying to you."

Before I could scream something horrid at Headmaster Duff, he opened the box with a piercing glance. When it popped open, the dark Fadrix peeked out.

"I'm *not* going to do it," I scowled, folding my arms across my chest. "Find someone else," I added sarcastically.

"I have tried, but to no avail," he said.

What?

"I see what you are asking in your eyes, but, *that*, I cannot answer."

"That's not what I was thinking," I denied. "Anyway, I already know that Douglas Thelwell and Lady Hortensia have been innocent."

"Why do you say that?" Sitting, he moved closer to me. "Unless you know something more. And *who* would tell you more?"

"*I* did," Renaud lied.

Headmaster Duff's cold, clear eyes widened, and then he nodded. "I am not surprised. However, your information was froth." He then looked at me. "Douglas Thelwell and Lady Hortensia did steal S3A2 information. *That* is *not* disputable. Contrary to what you may believe or have heard, they were involved in subversive activities to destroy S3A2."

"Even if that's so, what could they possibly do at this point? It's been decades," Renaud argued.

Headmaster Duff let out a short breath in annoyance. "It is about principle, Renaud. Moreover, finding them, knowing their where-abouts over these decades and what they have been—" He stopped short and looked down at Renaud. "No further explanation is war-ranted."

"'Track down'?" I asked. "And what did you mean before when you said that S3A2 members needed to be dealt with?"

"It means what you already know it means," Headmaster Duff answered in an eerie tone.

"You're a murderer," Renaud pressed in a whisper.

I swallowed. "The orb wasn't useless when I summoned it, was it?"

"The Fadrix is meant for you," Headmaster Duff said. "What it revealed to you was always for a purpose. I knew what that purpose was."

"No, you abused it for your own benefit," Renaud insisted.

"How can you ever understand?" Headmaster Duff said. "You cannot fathom what these abilities and artifacts can do." Resting his hands on his knees, he had a slight smile. "Do not fool yourself into thinking you are something more than you are, Renaud Bertrand. I appeased Dr. Braithwaite's request for you to be in those classes."

Renaud's jaw clenched, and his eyes widened.

"You deserve to be in them just as much as the rest of us," I insisted.

Headmaster Duff sat back, glanced at the orb, and then stared at me. "You are intrigued by what you can do. I have seen it when you practice—the motivation behind your eyes. You *cannot* deny that." He knew I couldn't as he continued confidently, "Your drive and ambition is quite reminiscent of my younger self, actually.

"*Don't* listen to him," Renaud urged.

"I will train you and continue to help you. Think of all you can learn and accomplish. You have progressed, but there is so much more." Headmaster Duff became increasingly persistent as he spoke each word. "You will come to see what I know and understand—it has *all* been for S3A2."

"He caught Zoe and me in his office," Renaud insisted. "Why would he need to tie us up and plan to get rid of us if he wasn't—"

Suddenly, shards of glass flew through the air and darted dangerously close to Renaud. They hovered in front of his shocked face as he scooted backward on the floor. Then the shards shattered when they hit the ground, only inches from his feet.

"I missed because I meant to," Headmaster Duff warned. "Next time, perhaps I will not.

"Phoebe, in this world, nothing is simply wrong or right. I believe you know this already."

His words seeped into my thoughts. If I kept improving, I could secretly find Douglas Thelwell and learn all Naan knew, maybe even more.

Releasing Renaud's grasp around my arm, I went to the Fadrix. Headmaster Duff put it in my open hands. The energy of the orb sought out familiar bends and turns inside my body. We were connected.

Maybe Headmaster Duff didn't harm anyone, he was just misunderstood. Or, maybe he didn't plan on harming people but it happened by ... accident. I shook my head, wanting to kick myself for thinking those things. I swallowed and felt light-headed, realizing that there was something inside of me, a force that was drawn to what he promised. And I was afraid to look at him.

"This isn't who you are," Renaud warned.

"Oh, but it *is* who she is," Headmaster Duff said. "The Fadrix and S3A2 are her past, present, and, if she chooses, her future. This has *nothing* to do with you. She just met you."

I flinched, remembering I'd said those same biting words to Zoe when she was trying to help me.

The orb began to swirl and levitate.

"You see how it listens to you?" Headmaster Duff said.

Make it right. Trust yourself.

"You and the Fadrix can do great things together—for yourself, for S3A2, and for the world." Headmaster Duff's voice was hypnotizing.

"I am here to support you throughout the process. Just as I invited you to this school and began your training."

Find them both. Don't doubt who you are and your abilities. Trust yourself. I saw you here in Scotland. Make it right.

Naan's words kept swirling around in my head. My months at The Murray School were also unfolding as the orb ascended higher into the air. I slowly turned away from the Fadrix and looked straight at Duff. I studied his stoic demeanor and wondered what had gone wrong within the serious young man who was once filled with ideals and admirable goals.

He studied me, peeling back the layers of my mind. He had a way of reaching inside my thoughts. Why did he have this unexplainable power over me? I gulped.

"I want to be a part of S3A2 ..." I thought aloud, looking at the orb.

"And you can be," he continued.

"Do you *realize* what he's saying?" Renaud pleaded.

Headmaster Duff continued, "Phoebe, you only become great when you free yourself from hindrances and distractions. This includes people you may think are closest to you. Too many times, they disappoint and are counterproductive to the overall aim. And then you realize you were never close to them at all."

He said that like he cared, like he sincerely hoped I could learn a valuable lesson from him.

Whoosh! The door flew open, and I spun around to see the dining hall on the other side. The Fadrix immediately dropped into my hands. It felt cold and heavy.

Colin was with William *and* Dr. Braithwaite. They ran toward us, and Colin held up his hand. Headmaster Duff summoned his powers in his right hand to try to pull the Fadrix from me while his left hand stopped Colin, Dr. Braithwaite, and William. But the Fadrix's connection to me was too strong. It didn't budge.

I began to realize that as long as the Fadrix existed, evil and dangerous people and organizations would seek to use its power for nefarious reasons—much like it had been throughout history. I would be hunted by rogue S3A2 members or even other people with the aim to use me to access its power. If there were others out there who could read it, I had no clue. And I had to conclude that if there were people out there who could read it, they couldn't all be good.

And maybe one day, I would unfortunately be drawn by the allure of power. I didn't want to be controlled by what Ingrid had called the "other side" of our abilities and what Naan had warned me about. So I did what I had to do—at least what I thought was right at the time.

"I want to be a part of S3A2," I declared again. "But *not* like this! *Not* your vision of it!"

When Headmaster Duff saw me lift the Fadrix above my head, his face twisted in surprise as he tried to reach for it. Renaud hurled himself at Duff. With as much force as my body and mind willed, I threw the smooth orb. The blackened sphere spun and arched gracefully in the air.

The Fadrix hit the unforgiving stone. It didn't make a noise as it instantaneously pulverized into an unrecognizable bluish-gray dust. The moment all the dust settled to the ground, I slumped against the wall, and my vision momentarily blurred.

"*Noooo!*" Headmaster Duff's desperate cry rang out as Renaud fell on top of him. But his cry was stopped short as he suddenly became rigid like stone again.

Confused, Renaud and I looked up. There, Dr. Braithwaite stood over Headmaster Duff, holding the contorted arm of Etumba.

My mouth hung open in surprise. "Dr. Braithwaite … how…?"

With an assured stance, his sharp gray eyes looked at me. "Duff thought it was he who could awaken it. Little did he know, the arm is, in fact, awakened by alchemy."

"*Ha!*" a guttural laugh boomed. "Look at his face!" William laughed again as he stood over Headmaster Duff.

"Didn't even see it coming!" Wallace naturally joined in.

"Is he dead?" Colin asked dryly.

"No, he's very much alive," Dr. Braithwaite answered. "You could say he's frozen in a sort of cryogenic state."

"He should've died," Colin mumbled, and turned away.

Colin's face was spotted with cuts. When he pushed his bangs back with his bruised hand, I saw a large welt forming on his forehead just in time before his hair flopped back into place. Colin looked tired. In fact, we all looked worn, some of us more than others.

But with Colin there was something different. It was an extreme tiredness caused by more than what had happened to us this night. And there was something else that was more potent that seemed to simmer inside of him, underneath the tiredness—a silent rage.

Colin must've felt my stare, because he looked over at me. As our eyes remained locked, the rage in his face slowly disappeared and a shaky smile replaced it. I returned his smile but then looked away, feeling uneasy.

"Young men, focus," Dr. Braithwaite commanded at the brothers, who were taking turns poking Headmaster Duff with his own cane.

Dropping the cane, they straightened up, at attention.

"Mr. Renaud, I'm glad to see you're okay," Dr. Braithwaite added.

"Thank you, sir," Renaud said, leaning tiredly against the wall.

Dr. Braithwaite walked out of the cellar and into the dining hall, and we followed. "Get the tablecloth over there to cover the headmaster," he instructed Colin and the brothers as he pointed to the nearest table. "Help me take him to the vault."

The boys pulled off the tablecloth, rolled Headmaster Duff's stiff body like a mummy, and hoisted him over their shoulders. Headmaster Duff now looked like a piece of furniture wrapped in cloth—that's how it would've looked to anyone who didn't know.

"This is the best I can do with him for now. I'll need to find a way to extract from him more of what and who he knows," Dr. Braithwaite thought aloud as he walked out with the boys who were maneuvering Headmaster Duff out of the dining hall.

I watched them, especially Colin, who was holding Duff's wrapped feet over his shoulder and limping.

Just then, Zoe and Ingrid ran in, blocking my view. Their clothes and faces were streaked with mud.

"Where were you?" I managed to ask.

"She ran," Ingrid said with big eyes, "to escape."

Ingrid choked on her words and nothing else came out, but I didn't have to ask who she meant.

The blood in Zoe's face seemed to vanish. "We followed Ms. Belzeebar through the woods, and she fell into the marsh." Zoe's mouth clamped shut. The fireworks in her eyes snuffed out as she quickly looked around our heads.

"Go on," Renaud prompted.

Zoe looked confused, even disoriented.

"It's okay," Renaud said to her in a reassuring manner.

"Er … We searched for a vine, a branch, *anything* to get her out. But when we returned to the spot, there was no sign of her—just bubbles."

"Do you think Ms. Belzeebar is … gone?" Ingrid whispered.

"That's the only reasonable explanation, *right?*" Zoe begged.

Reasonable was a word I'd accepted couldn't be limited to what our eyes could see, ears could hear, or hands could touch. As much as concluding that Ms. Belzeebar was gone would've brought some sort of closure, cloaking it with the word reasonable wouldn't help. Reasonable, as I'd learned at The Murray School and through my abilities, wasn't only what we thought was possible; it could also include what most thought was impossible.

"That's the most plausible conclusion," Renaud responded.

All I could say was "I don't know."

The holiday lights on the Christmas tree and buildings were still on when we walked outside. The cheerful, made-up setting was odd to see after we'd just experienced mayhem. I rubbed my forehead, trying to soothe my dull headache.

"It's one of the better outcomes," Renaud thought aloud. "We're all walking out of the dining hall alive, and Headmaster Duff is neutralized, at least for now."

"You're still able to have a genius thought at this moment, despite it all," I kidded and marveled, figuring that his head probably felt like it was exploding over and over again. Then disappointment and regret overcame me. "Renaud … I…"

We stopped walking.

"Yes?" he asked, waiting.

"I'm sorry I put you in danger," I whispered.

"Don't be."

I looked up to see Renaud staring down at me with an expression that made him look years older. "You were betrayed by someone you trusted," he said. "And I decided to investigate further, because I wanted to. I wanted to help our friends … to help you."

Out of the corner of my eye, I saw Zoe and Ingrid circling back. Renaud and I had lagged behind.

"Keep up the pace," Zoe joked, hooking her arm around my neck.

Renaud's face became boyish again when his brow softened. "Get some rest."

"You too. Remember to ice it," Ingrid said, pointing at the ugly cut on his face.

"The pain won't make me forget," Renaud said, trying to smile. He turned to me. "I'll see you before you leave?"

"Absolutely."

As he headed to his house, Zoe and Ingrid looked at me funnily.

"Don't go there," I insisted.

"Okay, okay," Zoe smirked with her hands up.

Walking to Clairmount House—dirty and tired—we not only looked like we'd experienced a nightmare but also like we *were* the nightmare.

Zoe was still in her uniform, but it was torn and streaked with mud and dirt. Her usually vibrant chestnut hair was dull and partially matted onto her head. Ingrid's sweats were equally streaked with mud, crinkled, and torn at the sleeves and knees. And I looked like I had rolled in ash, covered in tunnel dirt. Most of my hair had escaped its bun in a crazy halo.

"I used the key," Zoe broke the silence as we walked.

"And it worked." Ingrid seemed pleased.

"Yeah, but unfortunately, I was a ripe idiot." Zoe laughed at herself under her breath. "In my anger, I didn't even consider that the headmaster could be in his office in the middle of the day." Zoe stopped walking, causing us to stop alongside her. "Phoebe, Duff kept saying he knew you'd figure it out and find him."

I shuddered. Even with his twisted ambitions, he still appreciated my abilities.

"I judged you," she said. "I jumped to conclusions and should've been more understanding. You were right that I was taking out all my past hurt on you." She stomped on a broken piece of a snowman's belly. "My aunt and uncle took me in."

"You don't have to explain," I said right away.

"But I want to. You're my friend," she insisted.

When she looked at me, her expression told me that I couldn't stop her from sharing.

"My aunt and uncle raised me after my mother couldn't take care of me. I always felt like they were scared or ashamed of me." She kicked the rocks along the path as we approached the back entrance of Clairmount. "Telling me that I was overreacting and that my frustration was because of something else, just made me more upset, because you were right. And I didn't want to face the truth."

"It's already been forgiven," I said, looking at her tired profile and kicking a few rocks myself.

Ingrid shamelessly wiped tears from her cheeks, giving us a heart-felt hug. "I'm so happy when my friends make up. Actually, I'm happy when *anybody* makes up."

Silent and exhausted, we let ourselves in through the back door, hoping Ms. Daniels would be deep asleep, snoring. And she was.

While in bed, I pulled out Naan's picture. I was forever changed by what I'd learned and experienced. And although I hadn't found Douglas Thelwell, I was confident I would continue trying, even without the Fadrix. I was refusing to fill my head with dread and the sinking feeling that this night I had come face-to-face with the other side of my abilities. I had been attracted to Headmaster Duff's promises. *That* scared me.

Instead, I chose to focus on Naan. Thinking about her words—"finding them both" and "make it right"—I realized her message actually meant something more than Lady Hortensia and Douglas Thelwell. With Naan's clairvoyant abilities, maybe she foresaw what I would face in Scotland, because her words also seemed to include my pursuit to find both Headmaster Duff and Ms. Belzeebar and also Renaud and Zoe.

I made it right by choosing friendship and trust over power and ambition.

Chapter Twenty

DOUSE, SAID LIKE *ZEUS* BUT WITH A *D*

*F*or more than twenty-four hours, Ingrid, Zoe, and I slept. We missed our exams. We missed our meals. We missed all phone calls and messages. And somehow, Ms. Daniels got the memo not to disturb us because *no one* knocked on our doors.

When I finally woke up, our room was dim, and my eyes focused on our muddy, torn clothes partially hanging out of the hamper. My mixed feelings of triumph and emptiness resurfaced, as I knew my experience had been real.

It was the afternoon. I knew this because when I looked at my clock, it was around 4:38 p.m. However, what I didn't know was that it was 4:38 p.m. the *next day*. It was only after dressing in the bathroom and opening my laptop to read messages that I realized this fact.

The first message was from my parents. They asked me how my exams were going. Leaning back in my chair, I thought for a moment, pressed my temples, and then typed my response:

I'm good. As far as exams … We'll just have to wait and see :-)

After clicking the "Send" button, I laughed to myself. I'd just summarized the past whirlwind days in two short sentences. The next message was from Mrs. Vyda:

It has come to my attention that you weren't able to take your exams yesterday. And, due to your credible, unforeseen circumstances, we are allowing you to postpone and sit for your remaining exams at the beginning of next term. Or, through special arrangements, you may take your exams before you leave for the holidays. Please let me know your decision.

This is unexpected! Another message from Mrs. Vyda directly followed:

Please note Ms. Belzeebar is absent. Her exam has been cancelled. Your grades will be an average determined by your class performance throughout the term. Thank you for your understanding and patience.

Most likely, it was Dr. Braithwaite who had made those arrangements. I couldn't even imagine how that conversation went between him and Mrs. Vyda. Oddly, there was no message or announcement about Headmaster Duff.

And speaking of Dr. Braithwaite, I received a message from him as well. My stomach somersaulted. I slowly clicked to open the message, closed my eyes, and then opened them:

B: Ms. Phoebe Douse has shown great improvement during my class this term. She has and continues to learn what is essential and important to successfully advance. Ms. Douse's exam was methodically thought out, explained, and sufficiently executed.

I pumped my fists in the air with excitement.

Ms. Douse needs to improve on her timing and techniques. With more practice, she will be able to do these experiments with even more efficiency and confidence. I look forward to seeing what Ms. Douse can accomplish next term.

My mouth hurt. I couldn't stop smiling. *Dr. Braithwaite, I'm up for the challenge.*

"I slept that long? Fantastic!"

I spun around in my chair to see Zoe sitting up in bed.

"I guess you didn't plan to," I said.

She nodded. "I just wanted to sleep in." Zoe stretched her arms, twisted her back, and then pulled back her hair in a ponytail.

"You should check your messages. *Lots* of unexpected updates."

Her eyes widened, and she rubbed her hands together. "Let's have a look."

Zoe, Ingrid, and I went downstairs to eat our first meal of the day around dinnertime. The girls were surprised, and a barrage of questions were fired at us as we took our plates and silverware out of the cupboards and drawers.

"What happened?"

"Where were you, Zoe?"

"Yeah, Ms. Daniels has been looking for you."

"She thought you had disappeared!"

"Are you okay?"

"What are you going to do about your missed exams?"

We weren't prepared to answer them. So what did we do instead? We acted like we didn't know what they were talking about.

"Yeah, I'm great. Just tired from exams. Can't wait to go on vacation," Ingrid answered as we pulled some items out of the fridge.

"We missed exams, really? No way! Actually, we've taken some and will take the others later," I replied.

"Oh, she was looking for me? It was probably the night I fell asleep in the library," Zoe said in between bites of her salad.

They were even more confused than before while we smiled secretively at each other over our plates.

I decided to take my exams before the holiday break. Why prolong the inevitable, right? I used the next couple days to study and arrange special times. While taking my Algebra exam, I thought about how grateful I was for Renaud's help. I'd specially scheduled it and sat alone while a teacher's assistant proctored it. With everything that had happened, I felt like I could at least conquer math equations.

So in a way, the past events helped to build my confidence. During my English exam, I looked to see if Colin would be there since I took that class with him. But he wasn't there.

As a matter of fact, I hadn't seen any of the boys since the events in the cellar. It was strange not to see them out and about on campus, but maybe they were laying low—resting, studying, or processing what had happened.

At Clairmount House, the day before I was going home for the holidays, Ingrid, Zoe, and I exchanged gifts. We were cheerful, as we chose to set aside the big questions looming over our heads. Questions like if Cara was truly missing or simply expelled. Or, with the absence of Headmaster Duff, who would assume leadership of The Murray School?

I also set aside that night in the cellar when my thoughts tried to justify Headmaster Duff's actions.

Instead, we tried to enjoy the holiday spirit. We gave each other silly handmade things, except Ingrid. Her gifts were the dresses she had made.

"Ingrid, this is fantastic. I don't deserve this!" Zoe exclaimed.

"You *must've* known I couldn't make them and keep them," Ingrid insisted while hugging us.

"It's still a surprise!" I said.

We enjoyed the rest of our morning together—listening to music, eating *lots* of candy and chocolate, and packing. My goal was to finish packing before the afternoon because I had one more important gift I needed to give.

Are you free later this afternoon? I texted while folding some clothes.

I received a reply about two hours later: Yes, what time?

In 30 minutes.

See u then.

Smiling, I inserted my gift into an envelope. After getting ready, I examined myself in the mirror, wanting to be sure I looked my best.

"You're going to bore a hole through that mirror if you stand in front of it any longer," Zoe joked, sitting on her bed among piles and piles of clothes, papers, and books. "You look great. Anyway, we've all seen you look your worst, and we weren't frightened off."

I threw my pillow at her, but she ducked in time as it collided with some clothes, and they all fell off the bed. "Focus on *finally* getting this mess cleaned up," I said.

"Take your time," she teased.

It was like traveling to unknown territory going over to one of the boys' boarding houses. I hadn't been over there before. I said "hello" to the house master as I walked in; he was in the foyer, taping up some boxes. Holding the envelope in my hand, I looked at myself in the hallway mirror.

"Here to see Evan?"

Backing away from the mirror and embarrassed for getting caught, I looked at the guy with ginger-colored hair who had come around the corner. "No," I answered him.

"Or Gerard?" a second guy asked, sauntering up with a permanent scowl on his face.

He wasn't welcoming like the other guy. Instead, he looked menacing and bitter.

"Why do you want to know?" I challenged.

"Well, if you're not here to see anyone, then you must've wandered over here." He stepped closer. "You're the transfer student, right? Are you lost?"

Now, he was annoying me.

"You seem like the lost one," I said.

Stunned, his face turned white. It seemed like I'd just exposed a deep, hidden truth about him. And I probably did.

The redhead threw his head back and laughed. "She got you with that one, Finn!"

Finn's face burned. Just then, we noticed Renaud. He was standing at the bottom of the stairs. With his hands in his pockets, Renaud was wearing a black T-shirt and light gray sweatpants. His hair was tousled, and it fell a little onto his forehead. Seeing Renaud outside of his uniform or a suit, my eyes widened when I realized he wasn't lanky at all. Instead, he was athletically lean.

Renaud's expression was daring Finn to try something dumb. Finn thought twice and then a third time. Then he muttered something and walked off with the other guy.

"Ignore them," Renaud said to me. "They're, how do you say? All hat and no cattle?"

I laughed. "Yeah, that's it. How do you know that?"

"I must've heard it from some TV show. I used to watch old westerns with my dad when I was little."

Speaking of an old western, the black-and-blue skin around Renaud's eye looked as if he'd been in a saloon fight. He now had a line of stitches over his eyebrow.

"It's not too bad anymore," Renaud said, feeling my stare. "Follow me." He tilted his head toward the stairs.

"So, this is your habitat?" I joked as we passed suitcases strewn around, boys in their rooms and hallways loudly laughing and talking, and music blaring.

"It's a wild territory," he answered as I followed him.

When we reached his door, he opened it. Inside, Renaud's room was serene and pleasant, much like him. I ran my hand over his many books—leather-bound, paperback, worn, and new.

"Your room is nice. Very you," I said, still admiring the space.

He seemed pleased.

When my eyes scanned his walls, I was surprised to see posters of artwork by Magritte, Dali, de Chirico, and Picasso. Renaud liked art!

"They are some of my favorites," I said.

"Oh, yeah?" Renaud was equally excited.

"The fact they broke from the norm of what was expected. It was——"

"Bold," Renaud said, practically finishing my thought.

"Exactly!" I kept looking around, and Renaud allowed me to. There were photographs on his neatly organized desk. One was of young Renaud in the lap of his mother. I could see where he got his height from, because his parents were tall. His father looked friendly, while his mother was gorgeous, but her smile looked forced. Her big, white teeth glistened through thin lips covered in beige lipstick. Renaud had his mother's hazel eyes and wavy hair. Her hair was glamorously styled in shoulder-length layers, and she had a classic and expensive taste in clothing.

I also saw some swim team photos. Examining one closely, I recognized Renaud smiling among the group. I pointed. "That's you!"

"I used to swim.... But I don't have time for it during my last years here."

"All I can say is, *wow*. I didn't know you were into sports."

"Just thought I lived in books?" he asked.

"Something like that." I looked away, embarrassed.

"It's no problem." He shrugged casually. "Not a bad reputation to have, is it?"

We shared a smile, and he seemed to wince a little.

"It *is* looking much better," I said softly while pointing. I moved closer to him, wanting to touch his face, but I held back.

He touched it instead. "Yeah, it hurts less now.... I got it after I broke into Headmaster Duff's office the night I spoke with you. When he caught me, he hurled a desk lamp into my face. There's nowhere to hide in his office!"

"But it was pretty cool you successfully broke in."

Renaud looked pleased with his accomplishment. "The next thing I knew, I was tied up and locked in that musty cellar with blood dripping down my face."

We became quiet again as I thought about Renaud, unconscious, effortlessly floating down the stairs by Duff's silent command. And I gulped, thinking about the headmaster again.

Renaud broke the silence. "You may sit if you want," he said, motioning to his desk chair. I did while he sat on the edge of his bed, facing me.

"It's strange Duff won't be our headmaster and that we're the only ones who know the truth," I said.

"Dr. Braithwaite told me they're looking for a replacement." The new information fed my interest. Renaud saw and provided more. "They, meaning S3A2."

"What about in the meantime?"

"They want the position to be filled soon—during the break."

"I hope they choose wisely."

Renaud nodded. "Dr. Braithwaite is one of the best. He'll be careful."

The envelope felt heavy in my hand. "I came by to give you this," I said, awkwardly leaning over and shoving the envelope in his direction. "I'm glad you like art." I continued as he took it and opened it. "Because it's a drawing."

I drew it the night Renaud helped me study for my exams. It was a scene of him reading on a bench with the castle in the background. I'd seen him sitting there one day and thought it was a perfect scene to re-create. Renaud's eyes studied it with amazement; he even traced his finger over some of my pencil marks. My face grew warm from feeling self-conscious about someone looking at my art for the first time.

"I knew you could draw. But this is amazing!" he said, looking up.

"I'm glad you like it."

His appreciation made me feel a little more relaxed. I'd never seen Renaud this excited. Well, actually, that would be a lie. He was also equally excited when we were learning a challenging topic in class.

"I wanted to say thanks for your help and for believing me. You're a really good person."

"I understand why you destroyed it," he said quietly.

To be honest, I was still wrestling with my decision about the Fadrix.

"You did what you felt was right," he continued. "And did the best you could given the circumstances."

"I'm still trying to make sense of everything that's happened."

"Me too," Renaud said. "I have something for you too." He stood up and pulled out his desk drawer. When he returned to the edge of his bed, he handed me a box wrapped in black shiny paper with a silver bow.

"Thanks!" I said, holding the box. "*And* my favorite colors too."

"I concluded they were … especially from your dress." Renaud's voice trailed off as he looked down at his feet and his neck reddened. I was happy that he had remembered. He lifted his head when his skin faded back to normal. "I think you'll appreciate it."

Still admiring the sleek, shiny present in my hand, I said, "I'll be old-fashioned and open it later. To keep the surprise."

Renaud stood and did a dramatic bow. "As you wish, Mademoiselle."

I laughed as he sat. *I like seeing this side of him. Actually ... I like all sides of Renaud*, I thought as I realized that his wavy hair sometimes had a life of its own and the golden flecks in his hazel eyes brightened whenever he got an important idea. And I couldn't leave out how much I admired Renaud's smile, which I'd noticed for the first time in Crails. It wasn't only attractive but also meaningful and had perfect timing—not overdone or rare. It revealed itself at the best moments.

I was staring. The moment I knew, I turned my head away, trying to hide my face. Something about Renaud made me feel awkward and excited at the same time.

A guy yelling out in the hallway snapped me out of my daze.

"I should go. I need to finish packing," I said as I got up and went straight to the door.

Renaud slowly rose and followed me. "You must have an early flight."

"Too early," I commented over my shoulder and reached for the knob. As I turned it, Renaud pulled the door open.

I caught myself and slowed my pace in order to face him again. Folding his arms across his chest, Renaud leaned against the door jam, and looked down at me with a thoughtful expression.

"I wish you a good holiday," I said.

His lopsided smile, though smaller to avoid the pain, still revealed his dimple. "You too, Phoebe. Have a good holiday. We'll see each other next year."

"Yes, next year."

I woke up in the predawn darkness and stillness of morning. I'd spoken with my parents only a few hours before. Assuring them I knew exactly what to do and in what sequence, I listened to Mom giving me pointers. "Don't feel like you're too grown to ask for help from the airport staff," she had said. "And remember to watch your luggage. Even though people have spent money to buy tickets and went through security, there are still many strange ones in the crowd. Don't forget."

"Yes, *yes*, I *know*," I insisted. I felt okay about my journey.

"Am I bothering you? Because what I'm saying is very important. Unless you already think you know," Mom challenged, and put me in line.

"No, sorry, Mom. I understand. I'm listening."

"Good," she said. "I'm glad you're trying to pay more attention."

Zoe, of course, woke up without an alarm. She walked with me to the taxi in her pajamas, worn-out red Converse shoes, and a black overcoat. "I'm hoping you won't get yourself into any trouble while you're away."

"Nothing goes on in Crockett," I answered. Then in a serious tone I said, "I'm always available if you need to talk. I hope you know that."

"Oh, you'll hear from me." She smiled, glancing sideways at me. "I *always* have something to say. Plus, I need my friends."

The taxi driver helped with my bags. Then Zoe waved and quickly turned away. But not fast enough. I saw her stubbornly wipe a tear from her cheek. And up high, there was another person who gave me a warm, heartfelt send-off. The light turned on in Ingrid's top-floor room, and she stuck her head out the window and blew kisses. "Bye-bye! Enjoy your holidays, clever Phoebe Douse!" she yelled happily, and I laughed and waved back.

While in the taxi, I looked behind me to see the colossal silhouette of the castle. Turning to face forward, I caught a glimpse of Mr. MacLeod cutting bramble. The iron gates cranked open. Once I exited the school, I couldn't see much in the dim morning. But I had an idea of what I was passing. I was familiar with some of it—the hills, the trees, and the sea.

Sometime soon in the future, maybe not next term, but the term after that one, I believed if I closed my eyes, I would be able to know *exactly* what bend of the road I was taking and what turn would lead me where.

I thought about "The Murray School Eight"—Renaud, Ingrid, Zoe, Colin, William, Wallace, me, and even Atwila. It felt awkward to return to the entirely different world of Crockett, but Naan would be my connection to Crockett and to Scotland. She would continue to guide me. The unanswered questions perplexed me, and I was also driven to solve them. Then I shook my head at the treachery of Headmaster Duff and Ms. Belzeebar, and the orb I chose to destroy.

Eventually, the taxi slowed at the train station—the very same one where I'd arrived with Mom. The sun was just about to rise over the horizon as the driver helped me with my suitcase up the stairs to the platform. I made sure to give him a tip for his help.

"Much appreciated," he said. "Safe travels."

When he was out of sight, I was the only person at the station, but I welcomed the silence. Sitting on a bench, I thought of Renaud and his gift. I excitedly pulled it out. The black paper and silver bow glowed in my hands, and a small note dangled from the top. It read:

I know how much the Fadrix meant to you. Although it's destroyed, I hope having what's left of it makes you feel a little better and reminds you that you made the right choice. – Joyeuses fêtes, R.

Renaud must've returned to the secret room that very day and carefully collected the powdery remains of the orb. My insides began to fill with regret because of what I'd done to it. With the box in my lap, I unwrapped the bow and lifted the cardboard flaps, spreading them open like a four-pointed star. The moment I looked inside, the air in my lungs rose and stuck in my throat.

"*What?!*" I exclaimed when my breath could finally escape. My eyes shot up and scanned the platform—I was still alone. Quickly inhaling some fresh oxygen as the veins in my temples pulsed, I felt my heart pounding so hard that my chest hurt.

There *wasn't* any bluish-gray powder.

Instead, the growing sunrays beamed on the brilliant surface of the Fadrix in its *full form*. Rotating the orb in my hand, I examined it—up, down, around, and up again. It was perfectly smooth and round, as if *nothing* had happened to it.

I hadn't heard of or studied anything like this about the Fadrix. Even Headmaster Duff's reaction when I threw it against the wall showed he believed it had been destroyed.

Slowly, I began to realize that the Fadrix's ability to regenerate may have been a well-kept secret throughout time. A secret probably only a few knew and didn't reveal.

Maybe, I began to wonder, *I underestimated how much this orb is connected to me. Maybe, the Fadrix allowed me to hurl it against that wall. Naan did say the summoner isn't the only person who controls it. Does that mean … it can control itself?*

Suddenly, the Fadrix began to react with swirling colors and vivid flashing patterns. And as fast as they appeared, they were sucked into the darkness of its core. Then a white cloud appeared, and it started to mold and form a shape.

A letter?

Yes, the letter—*D*. With the *D* solidly in place, the white cloud created another pattern to form an *o* and then *u* appeared.

My palm tightened under the orb, hungry for the next letter. Just then, a roaring sound blared throughout the air and rumbled in my ears, forcing me to look up. The sleek silver-and-white train was approaching the platform. Reluctantly, I placed the Fadrix back into its box and then into my duffel bag.

"D-o-u," I spelled aloud as I slung my bag over my shoulder and lifted the handle of my suitcase. *D-o-u*, I thought as I stood and walked to the slowing train. *Is it a place? A name? A sentence?*

I knew the answer.

They were part of a name, and there were only three names I knew of in my *entire* life with that *exact* combination of letters—Ava Dougherty, Douglas Thelwell … and Douse.

The Phoebe Douse Trilogy

Book Two

With S3A2 leadership and loyalties in question,

Phoebe must escape from rogue members and find answers in a new city.

There will be surprising arrivals, and

in order to preserve S3A2, unexpected alliances will have to be formed.

in...

PHOEBE DOUSE: THE RETURN